Praise for *High Vaultage*

'Comic fantasy, grounded and shot through with the sharpest wit . . . Chris and Jen Sugden have created their own wild world, and it echoes to laughter'

— James Naughtie, broadcaster

'A joyous, delightful romp . . . filled to the brim with clever jokes – perfect for anyone looking for a Pratchett fix'

— Caitlin Schneiderhan, screenwriter, *Stranger Things*

'More please'

— SFX

'Hilarious'

— Matt Young, co-creator of *Hello from the Magic Tavern*

'Exactly what I've come to expect from the Sugdens – inventive, imaginative, and *hilarious*'

— Lauren Shippen, creator of *The Bright Sessions*

'This charming, funny, meticulously plotted book is unputdownable'

— Miles Cameron, author of *The Red Knight and Artifact Space*

'Best in class world-building with heart, soul, power and love'

— Adam Simcox, author of *The Dying Squad*

HIGH VAULTAGE

Chris and Jen Sugden

First published in Great Britain in 2024 by Gollancz
an imprint of The Orion Publishing Group Ltd
Carmelite House, 50 Victoria Embankment
London EC4Y 0DZ

This edition first published in Great Britain in 2025.

An Hachette UK Company

The authorised representative in the EEA is Hachette Ireland,
8 Castlecourt Centre, Dublin 15, D15 XTP3, Ireland (email: info@hbgi.ie)

1 3 5 7 9 10 8 6 4 2

A CIP catalogue record for this book is
available from the British Library.

ISBN (MMP) 978 1 399 60417 8
ISBN (eBook) 978 1 399 60418 5
ISBN (Audio) 978 1 399 60419 2

Typeset by Born Group
Printed and bound in Great Britain by Clays Ltd, Elcograf S.p.A.

www.gollancz.co.uk

For Bill

Dusk was falling over Even Greater London, and the night wind stirred under the purple pools of crackling sky where lightning skipped like stones.

Somewhere nearby, it whirled up and around the Tower, watching it cast its boundless energy into the heavens and outwards across the capital.

But here, by the Thames Glacier, the wind swept low, chilling its belly on the ice and launching up the snowbanks, pummelling the rickety houses that had the bad luck to be close by.

Inside, sensible folk kept their curtains shut and their bodies close to a toasty fireplace or radiator lamp. They curled up with a nice book or, far more often, an utterly gruesome book. Or they listened to a mandatory radio address on whatever topic of the day had piqued the Royal Interest of Queen Victoria. Or, at least, of the increasingly mechanical monarch that still insisted it was Queen Victoria. And it was best, and indeed legally quite important, not to argue about such things.

Kathleen Price, however, was doing none of these activities. Her lights were off, her best coat and mittens were on, and she was pressing herself against her draughty window, bracing it against the gale, watching the man waiting on the empty Blackfriars Bridge for the love who never came.

He was standing where he always stood: the fourth lamppost along on the up-floe side. He was dressed as he always dressed: the same smart suit, the same shoes buffed until they shone like lamps themselves. And he wore the same firm expression, the same upper-lip rigidity, the same barely concealed abject desperation.

1

Every night he came, and every night Kathleen watched, fascinated by his obsession and failure.

'He's there again, Tommie,' she said. 'Think she'll come this time?'

Tommie did not reply. Tommie could not reply. Kathleen had run a spear through some of his favourite and most critical systems when they both had spied a gold sovereign before them, not too deep down in the glacier. And then she had left his eight-foot-tall metal body to sink into the snowbanks, but not before taking the head to mount on her wall next to all the others.

Their own fault, Kathleen thought. *Tommie Tons shouldn't dig for shinies in the ice. That's human work.*

She turned to her nearest automaton trophy head and checked the clock she had installed in its astonished, terrified mouth.

Ten past eight.

She knew the man would wait until nine before giving up and leaving. She would only watch for a bit most nights, just in case. Even though it had been weeks like this, in her romantic heart she always felt that tonight might be the night.

The man pulled up his collar against the flecks of ice the merciless wind was launching from the glacier towards him. He shivered, but remained fixed to the spot.

I wonder what he did . . .

She recalled the message she had seen in the classifieds:

Alexandrina, do not forsake me! I will wait for you on Blackfriars Bridge every evening at eight.

Kathleen took one last look up and down the bridge, empty but for the poor man and the whirlwind of ice, and humphed.

You're pretty forsaken, mister.

2

She closed the curtains and walked to her table to get on with polishing the trinkets she had unearthed from the glacier banks earlier that day.

She stopped.

Or is it 'forsook'?

Before she could decide, she heard a sound through the howling wind. A distant rumble and clattering.

She walked back and opened the curtains to see a two-horse carriage speeding along the bridge. The man turned slowly towards it, as if reluctant to let his hopes be raised.

Kathleen's pulse quickened.

Could it be her at last? Why tonight, of all terrible nights?

She watched as the carriage raced towards the man, the horses puffing clouds of breath into the cold air like the old steam engines she remembered from the days before the Tower.

The man waited, straightening his tie and tidying his hair. Soon enough, the carriage neared him, and slowed down to stop.

'It's her!' Kathleen cried. She tried to peer through the carriage windows to see this fabled Alexandrina, but it was too far off, and the inside was unlit.

The driver jumped down from his perch. Curiously, he did not head back to open the carriage door, but instead walked to the man and said something.

Confirming who he is, perhaps.

The man nodded and replied. The driver nodded back. Then, suddenly, he lunged at the man.

Kathleen shrieked and dropped below the window frame, terrified that she might have been heard.

'Get help!' she whispered at her Tommie heads, before remembering they could no longer do anything at all.

She dashed onto the landing and down the staircase, grabbed her trusty ice-spear from the umbrella stand and

3

turned the door latch. The wind burst inside, flinging her onto her back and compressing her lungs into an involuntary '*Gnng!*', as ice blew through the space as though it were a shaken snowglobe.

She gritted her teeth, pushed herself up, said some understandable-but-unrepeatable things at the wind, and charged out of the door, leaving her home to the elements.

She darted across the narrow road, onto the bridge and towards the carriage. The man's legs were kicking as he was dragged into the vehicle, and she could see now the windows were blacked out. There was the sound of shouted protests muffled by cloth, and the driver hurried out and climbed up onto his perch.

'*Stop!*' she cried, knowing he would not.

The driver flicked the reins and the carriage turned around and began to hurry back the way it had come, far too quickly to be caught.

Nothing else for it, thought Kathleen, lifting her ice-spear. With luck she would hit the driver, or at least a wheel. Hopefully not impale the man inside. That would take some explaining.

She sprinted, came to a sudden halt, and launched her weapon into the sky so that it arced towards the escaping carriage. Her aim was true, and her strength just enough. But the wind was having none of it, and whipped the spear around and around the frozen vortex and down over the side of the bridge, where it crunched into something digging away in the ice on a night shift, something metal and innocent.

Kathleen listened to the familiar sound of the impaled automaton first apologising for failing to finish its work, and then collapsing.

For once, it brought her no joy.

Hmm, she thought. *Wasn't even trying that time.*

She looked out, far along the bridge, and watched, helpless, as the carriage raced on and vanished into the endless city and the cold, darkening, electric night.

Chapter 1

Inspector Archibald Fleet arrived at the bus mooring on the main road near his home at exactly the same time as the No. 61: it, eight minutes behind its posted schedule as always, and he, exactly on time for its delayed departure, as he was well acquainted with the actual schedule and how it related to the works of timetable fiction they displayed at the stops.

The voltaic omnibus glided to its best approximation of a halt, bobbing and listing slightly as it floated six inches above its copper tracks. Fleet hopped on through the open door at the back and found the rearmost seat, which gave him a view of the rest of the cabin, including – crucially – all of the newspapers on board.

'This is the Number Sixty-one to Clay Lane,' shouted the driver as the omnibus silently resumed its journey. 'Calling at Willenbrook High Street, Old Road, Ratherbile's, New Road, Swinford Bridge, The Thrikes, Friar's Turn, Friar's Leap, Friar's End . . .'

The driver continued to list the three hundred or so stops he would be calling at between here and Clay Lane, but, like everyone else, Fleet had already stopped listening.

Fleet didn't usually catch the bus to work. Detectives, if they fail to spend considerable amounts of time walking the streets, up close to the sights, sounds and smells of the city, tend to lose their appetite and fall ill, the way sailors come to find that they cannot sleep without the rocking of the waves, and grimly resent the land for being so still. Fleet was, technically, no longer a detective, thanks to an administrative problem he didn't like to talk about. But regardless, he was a detective in his blood, and only taking the bus to work today to gather critical information.

Eleven other passengers were on board, distributed evenly through the cabin in the London fashion, which is to say: avoiding physical contact, avoiding eye contact, and, at all costs, avoiding emotional contact – although, to be honest, there was very little danger of the last one if proper precautions were taken about the first two.

On the strips of wall above the windows, squat advertisements blared their wares. Boarding houses. Greengrocers. Apothecaries that wouldn't be beaten on the price of laudanum. Tickets to events at parks and other public spaces across the capital in celebration of Victoria's golden jubilee. 'Fifty years our Queen – 50 per cent off a hot towel shave,' offered a Soho barber, presumably to the passengers rather than the monarch.

Fleet spotted a discarded newspaper on the seat in front of him: today's *Morning Chronicler*. The visible part of the headline read 'EVES STRIKE A'. At a speed born of reflex he uncoiled his wiry frame over the seat-back and grabbed the paper. An old woman reading *The Graphic* on the seat opposite noticed nothing, but the ageing Dandie Dinmont on her lap was severely startled and spent the remainder of the journey eyeing Fleet suspiciously as a possible threat to its entire universe.

A few months ago, Fleet would never have imagined that he would be reduced to gathering information on the latest criminal cases from abandoned newspapers on omnibuses. But that was a few months ago, and things had been much simpler back then. Fleet's position at Scotland Yard had provided him with access to intelligence on matters felonious that was now beyond his grasp, and so, just like any ordinary member of the public, he was forced to rely on the press.

Still leaning over the seat in front, Fleet unfolded the paper to read its full headline: 'BANK THIEVES STRIKE AGAIN'. A quick flick through the pages revealed eight sides of coverage. This came as no surprise to him. It had been this way after every bank so far, and for good reason, as the city had never seen such an audacious series of crimes. Nor any quite so exquisitely done, with the culprits leaving no trace of how they got into – or indeed out of – the impenetrable – and indeed inescapable – vaults. Yet, despite the extensive press coverage, police activity and public interest, no suspects had been found, which, given the lack of clues, Fleet could understand. But neither had there been a call from his former Detective Chief Inspector to draft him in to help figure it all out – which, to be honest, Fleet could also understand, never exactly having been in his good books, nor known him even to have any good books for someone to be in.

Fleet buried himself in the articles as the vehicle drifted through the streets like a low, metal cloud. Ahead, twenty minutes as the bus floats, a brick, steel and glass tower speared a mile upwards into the sky.

This was London in 1887. *Even Greater London*, to use its proper title, which nobody ever did. An uninterrupted urban plane encompassing the entire lower half of England, and, for complex reasons, only the upper third of the Isle of Wight.

It was a ravenous, sense-numbingly vast expanse of city: an ocean of homes, shops, offices and public houses, all stitched together with roads and criss-crossed by an untidy lattice of rail tracks, stretching off to what you had to assume would be the horizon if you could see past all the buildings in the way.

And at the centre of all of this growth, this commerce, this constant change and urban vitality, was the Tower. For over a quarter of a century it had been the symbol of London's industrial mastery, beaming electricity outwards through the sky, across hundreds of miles of unbroken city, and allowing its citizens to let their imaginations run free and to charge forth into the future far more quickly than might really be sensible.

To live in Even Greater London was to be in a state of perpetual bewilderment, a bee in a tornado of innovation and progress happening at a speed and scale beyond human, or indeed bee, comprehension. It was best just to keep your head down and not really think about it all that much.

In the south-east of the city, Clara Entwhistle was doing just that, arriving for an early-morning appointment in a grand tearoom unforgivably named the Greenwich Observatea.

The Observatea had once been the site of the most powerful telescope in the city, and traded on this history without shame. The immense, domed ceiling had been painted in the deep blue-black of the heavens and decorated with the constellations of the night sky. A functioning orrery was rooted in the centre of the room, its metal arms of varying lengths slowly rotating above the patrons, carrying on their orbits all the planets of the solar system, with each planet spinning around itself however many moons it was believed to have. And there were functioning telescopes, elegantly but quite impregnably bolted onto every table, through which, if you were lucky enough, you might be able to witness the rather thrilling Transit of the Chef de Cuisine Across the Little Round Windows in the Door to the Kitchen.

It was a ghastly place. You paid for the pizazz; the tea was average.

Clara – having recently moved to London from Yorkshire – had never been in an astronomy-themed tearoom before, and found it quite interesting and exciting. Keen not to miss any of the details, she took her time traversing the room, delighting in the decor – not least an intriguing cluster of stars painted on the far side of the dome that she was certain she had never seen before, because they were the shape of an iced bun, and she would have remembered something like an iced bun in the heavens.

Eventually, Clara made it to the back of the tearoom, ducking carefully under Saturn as she came near to it, and approached a table where a sixteen-year-old girl was enjoying her tea along with one or two of the Observatea's famed caramel Tycho Brahzilnuts. The girl was wearing an extremely fashionable dress of brilliant wine-red satin and floral silk brocade, topped off with a large feather-trimmed hat. Clara, ten years the girl's senior, was by contrast in a plain grey-blue poplin day dress – and drew some raised eyebrows from the more couture-minded lady patrons of the tearoom with her unadorned and decidedly out-of-fashion straw bonnet, underneath which her dark hair was neatly tied up.

At the sound of Clara's approach, the broad brim of the girl's hat lifted to reveal a hopeful face.

'Miss Entwhistle, so glad you could join me. Please, sit.'

'I hope I find you well, Lady Arabella?' asked Clara, as she lowered herself into a chair.

'Tolerably well, Miss Entwhistle, thank you. Although I trust the news you bring will leave me feeling a little more than well.'

'Of course. Your suspicions regarding your governess.'

'Miss Louisa Smith, yes.'

'No,' Clara said gravely, keeping in check her own excitement regarding the information she was about to reveal.

Arabella rustled forward in her seat. 'No?'

'It seems your family has been duped, Lady Arabella.'

'No!'

Arabella contorted her face in horrified delight. She held her teacup close, protecting it from this exquisitely shocking news.

'She is very likely not named Smith,' Clara continued, 'and she is almost certainly not a governess. At least, not one with any record of having existed prior to her reply to your father's advertisement in *The Times*.'

Arabella sat in silence for a few moments, cradling her teacup pensively. Clara sensed she was being weighed up, but could only guess at the details of Arabella's doubts.

The difficulty was that Clara had been efficient. Could it be possible, Arabella wondered, that a stranger had been able to discover her wretched governess's secret in a mere matter of days? How far could she really trust this peculiar Miss Entwhistle, whose services she'd engaged through a *servant*, who'd seen an *advertisement* in a *newspaper*? Arabella knew that one always had to be on guard against fraudsters, hood-winkers and flimflammers, that she must take note of inconsistencies and contradictions. Indeed, she thought, the very service itself was an incongruity with the world: a sort of spy for everyone? A personal policeman? She could see that Clara was a gentlewoman, that much was clear: the way she held herself, the care in her movements – besides which, she enunciated too well not to have been taught. But her clothes, *that bonnet*. Her eyes, wide with excitement at such a humdrum old place. And serving as a secret snoop for a girl ten years her junior? She must have fallen on very hard times indeed, in which case, Arabella reasoned, she might say anything to gain favour from someone still in good standing.

Clara waited for Arabella to conclude that further scrutiny was required. Better to wait for the question than anticipate it: she would value the answer more. After a moment, Clara noticed a young couple at table three – near the centre of the room and directly under the perihelion of Mercury – who were staring nauseatingly into each other's eyes as they fed one another forkfuls of the tearoom's most chocolatey dessert, the Galileo Ganachilei. A rather severe older woman – their chaperone, no doubt – grimaced at the sight from her table nearby.

'But her character reference, Miss Entwhistle?' Arabella said finally. 'The Luptons of St Neots?'

'A forgery, I'm afraid,' Clara replied, snapping her eyes back to her client. 'The address was for a lodging house, and the proprietor confessed she had been paid to write a glowing recommendation – paid by a woman matching precisely the description of your governess.'

'She just admitted it?' asked Arabella, with the most suspicious eyebrows she could apparently muster.

'Some of the proprietor's correspondence was in view, and the handwriting was a clear match with the false reference. She confessed when presented with that fact.'

'The charlatan!' cried Arabella, appalled, but also – Clara noted happily – convinced. The young woman's outrage suddenly vanished, replaced by the triumphant grin of someone whose long-held suspicions had been proved correct. 'You've found her out, Miss Entwhistle. Very well done!'

Her hat feathers danced in approval.

Clara beamed. 'All in a day's work.'

Arabella's face contorted more rapidly than should be possible from delight to hopelessness.

'But Father will not believe me! He has been taken in. It was all for naught.'

She flicked a porcelain bowl of sugar lumps to punish it for something.

13

'Fortunately,' said Clara, 'I was able to retrieve some other discarded written material from the proprietor. Your father can compare.'

She handed Arabella an envelope, which she had helpfully, and in her finest calligraphy, labelled 'Proof'.

Arabella's face instantly reverted to its previous state of pure joy.

'Well done, Miss Entwhistle. Well done. You have my thanks.'

'It was nothing.'

'Of course, I knew all along,' Arabella continued. 'Competent at arithmetic, but her Latin and French were atrocious. I fear I know less than when she began tutoring me! And her *accent*. She sounded as though she was from Manchester! These things rub off on young people, you know. But now Father will have no choice but to dismiss her, and I will be granted a real governess. A less provincial one, I hope!'

'Fingers crossed,' said Clara with a grimace, before noticing the chaperone – entranced by the majestic conjunction of Mars and Neptune on the far side of the room – being lightly concussed by a passing moon of Jupiter.

A waiter dashed off discreetly for medical aid as the young lovers exchanged a knowing glance, quickly threw some money onto the table, and made their exit.

The bus glided to a halt. Fleet's peripheral vision was good enough to tell him where he was, and he folded his newspaper and got up. He noticed the dog and its owner had alighted some time earlier, leaving her paper – *The Graphic* – on the seat. Further along, someone had abandoned a copy of yesterday's *Evening News*. Fleet hurried down the bus to the front exit, accumulating papers as he went, narrowly besting a vicar in a race to The *Herald* and receiving a scowl of benevolent concern as a reward. He jumped through the open doors onto the street, the papers bundled under his arms whacking the doorframe as he went.

Fleet walked through a small square that was bounded on three sides by past-their-best stone buildings of shopfronts and offices, their eaves overlapping and colliding over ginnels that led to back alleyways that were also quite successful places of business, only for thievier, stabbier types.

A mass of people were criss-crossing the square: clerks in dark suits heading to work; shopkeepers in overalls carrying crates of produce; tradesmen with toolboxes and the occasional ladder; the crossing sweeper furiously brushing dust across the path of well-dressed folk in the hope of a few pennies to get him to stop.

Crammed in among the other buildings was London's thirty-fourth most disreputable pub, the Grouse and Chisel, out of which some people having a bad time of it were staggering, and into which people having an even worse time of it were heading. A police wagon was parked up outside, as always, because the police had learned that when it came to the Chisel, it was just easier to have a unit on hand.

An enormous picture painted on the side of the wagon caught Fleet's eye. Queen Victoria. Or, at least, what passed nowadays for Queen Victoria. Even the most devoted monarchists agreed she had seen better days. Not the days that had featured any of her eleven-and-counting assassinations – those had been very bad days. But they had been followed by the very good days when she had returned, just a tad more made of machinery than before, to the sound of exultant crowds. Not to mention the great relief of her Royal Medical Engineers who, frankly, were astonished that their efforts to revive her kept working, but felt safe in the knowledge that if they ever truly bungled it one day – if they ever failed to devise suitable

15

mechanical replacements for her shot, stabbed, exploded or just good-old-poisoned organs – then their employer would be much too dead to reprimand them.

Truly, Victoria represented the limitless and somewhat frightening technological possibilities of the age, the extremely limited possibilities of who was allowed to benefit, and the ever-popular appeal of trying very hard not to think about things like that and just get on with your day.

And there were very few people as practised at not thinking about things like that and getting on with their day as Fleet, who merely shuddered at the image of the monarch and returned his attention to the front page of his *Courier* as he weaved his way across the square.

'Paper, guvnor?' a young voice asked.

Fleet looked up. The boy was standing next to a pile of newspapers, and didn't seem to have registered that Fleet was well on his way to amassing an equal-sized stack.

'Which one?' asked Fleet.

'What?'

'Which paper are you selling?'

The boy looked puzzled. 'Today's.'

Fleet looked closer at the folded broadsheet the boy was waving above his head. He knew journalists roamed in packs when it came to high-profile cases – encircling any poor witness with notebooks and portable recording cylinders – so usually the papers had only the same information. There was always a chance, though, that one had happened upon an additional detail and managed to keep it from their rivals, so every paper was worth gathering.

'Oh, you've got the *Herald*.'

'Yeah, the *'Erald* all right. International 'appenings, national goings-on and whatnot.'

'I've already got today's *Herald*.'

'Then how 'bout a tip?' asked the boy. 'I've some shocking inside info on the four-fifteen at the electro-velodrome.'

'It's happening at half past twelve?'

'No, no, it's one of the mechanics in the stables.' The boy leaned towards Fleet conspiratorially. 'Got a new gear system, 'asn't 'e? But who stands to benefit? Might be Twilight Sands. Might be Gibbous Moon. Might be Winter Complicity. Penny, I'll tell ya.'

'Tell you what,' replied Fleet. 'I'll give you a penny if you keep an eye out and let me know about any crimes going on around here.'

The boy's eyebrows shot up with excitement, pulling him briefly off the pavement. 'Really?'

'Yes.'

'Penny per?'

'Let's try one and see how that goes.'

The boy considered this. 'Am I allowed to commit the crimes?'

'What? No, of course not.'

'Bit of thieving, maybe I cut loose a carriage horse here and there?'

'No!' exclaimed Fleet. He had never known street lads to be particularly respectful to authority, but now he didn't have any, it was clear they had previously been on their best behaviour.

'All right, just pickpocketing then. Stick with what you know – that's what the man who knifed my dad always said.' The boy winked at Fleet to confirm the plan.

'No! No crime!'

'Seems like that'd be the best way for me to 'elp with what you're after.'

'It's clearly not in the spirit of the idea,' said Fleet.

'It's your fault for establishing perverse incentives, guvnor. Can't fault water for trickling.'

Fleet pointed a disapproving finger at the boy. 'You ought to be careful who you say that kind of thing to. I might be the police.'

A steely voice came from behind Fleet.

'Impersonating a police officer is a criminal offence, sir.'

'I didn't say I *was* police, only that I *might* be,' retorted Fleet as he spun round, immediately regretting this decision as he came face to face with a stocky man dressed almost identically to himself – the same simple shirt and necktie, loose-fitting trousers, brown flat-bottomed waistcoat and equally brown woollen overcoat – who was grinning with delight like he had just won a prize in a contest he didn't know he had entered.

'Archibald Fleet, it is you! As I live and breathe. And as you . . .' The man prodded Fleet in the chest. 'Whatever it is you do now on that front.'

Fleet stepped backwards and began fastening his coat. He had never cared much for Inspector Collier's weaponised joviality, nor the fact that despite both of them having the same dozen years' experience, Collier had a way of making him feel like he was a new recruit.

'Hello, Collier.'

'And you, boy!' Collier barked past Fleet. 'Show this man some damned respect. Acts of heroism, line of duty and all that, you know.'

The paperboy shrugged and turned towards other passers-by who seemed more likely to buy from him.

Collier rolled his eyes and reverted to grinning at Fleet.

'Marvellous to see you, Insp— Well, I suppose it's just plain old "Mr Fleet" now, isn't it? Although better than "dearly departed", I'm sure. Remarkable, what you've been through. Lucky for you Her Maj was in a generous mood *vis-à-vis* her . . . help.'

Fleet shuddered. 'Keeping well, Collier?' he asked, indifferently.

'Me? Oh yes. Busy busy. The bank case is a beast, I'm sure you can imagine.' Collier glanced down at Fleet's bundle of newspapers. 'Or perhaps you don't need to imagine! What are you up to these days?'

Fleet tucked the papers under one arm.

'I'm still detecting. Private cases.'

'Oh, yes!' said Collier, nodding enthusiastically. 'I heard you had spun up a little police station of your own. Interesting idea. Good for you.'

'Good for a number of people, really.'

'I don't doubt it! It's a public service, if you think about it. Keeping all that sort of personal business away frees up the Yard to focus on real cases.'

'They are real cases, Collier.'

'Oh, Collier! Both feet inside the mouth, once again! Up to the ankles!' Collier jabbed his fist halfway into his mouth and popped his eyes wide open in mock panic, before laughing. 'I do apologise. What did I mean?'

'Hard to say.'

'I suppose I meant . . .' Collier paused, smiling benevolently at Fleet. 'Actual crimes.'

A waiter with a trolley orbited the tearoom, attempting to entice the morning customers with a variety of overpriced sweets.

'She meant to rob us, Miss Entwhistle. I am sure of it.' Arabella's youthful face hardened into a scowl.

'It is possible,' said Clara, as a nearby diner selected a rather sad-looking tart the waiter explained was filled with something called Copernicustard. 'Some criminals do jump from identity to identity as suits their needs.'

'How appalling. But, Miss Entwhistle, you were as good as your word. I should discharge my end of the bargain.'

A delicate hand pushed forward an envelope that Clara assumed, but was too polite to check, contained monetary payment. She placed it carefully into her satchel.

'I must say, Lady Arabella, your instinct that there was something amiss with your new governess – it showed remarkable intuition. Perhaps you'll become a private investigator yourself one day.'

A laugh chirruped from Arabella's lips. 'Miss Entwhistle, how very droll you are.'

'Why not?' asked Clara. 'I didn't know I was going to be one. I wanted to be a journalist. In fact, I still am.'

She suddenly remembered the article she had promised her editor would be submitted yesterday, and felt a pang of missed-deadline guilt. Two jobs was a lot. She might have over-committed.

'You are a journalist as well as a private investigator?' asked Arabella.

'At the *Morning Chronicler*, yes. I report on crime.'

'Goodness!'

'They overlap more than you would think.'

'How so?'

'The truth, Lady Arabella!' said Clara, well above proper tearoom conversation volume. 'They both concern digging out the truth from beneath all the knotted roots of intrigue and deception.'

'How thrilling,' said Arabella, studying Clara as though she were some particularly bizarre zoological specimen. 'What an unusual life you must have led to bring you to this sort of grisly work, Miss Entwhistle.'

Clara considered this. As the daughter of an earl, her upbringing had, in truth, been almost identical to the one Lady Arabella appeared to be having. The only difference being that Clara didn't want anything to do with it, and had given it up several months earlier to come to London to be a journalist. Her mother, Lady Lucretia Entwhistle, had responded unsurprisingly with bitter outrage but, with time and a great deal of effort, had managed to translate this into the far healthier abject grief. She could still be seen wearing full mourning dress months later – a significant improvement on the two weeks she managed when her husband, Lord Entwhistle, was lost at sea. Clara's decision had seen her cut off from the family money, as she had fully expected – but this had had the opposite of its intended effect, affording Clara a freedom she had never before known, a freedom she was keen to proselytise about to others.

'What do you want to do when you are older, Lady Arabella?'

Arabella looked puzzled. She did not seem to understand the question.

'There's nothing you want to do?' continued Clara.

'Of course there is. I plan to marry very well. Good land, hopefully some hunting grounds to keep him out of the house. Someone who isn't too much of a gambler. And no industrialists. "Factory money is unsatisfactory money" – that's what Mother says.'

'Don't you have a dream of any sort beyond marriage?'

Arabella thought about this for a moment. 'I hear very good things about Tuscany.'

Clara was stumped. She stood up.

'Well, it was a pleasure doing business with you, Lady Arabella. I must be getting back.'

The feather-trimmed hat nodded gravely. 'And I must expel an imposter from my home. Thank you, Miss Entwhistle.'

As Clara walked out of the tearoom, a server behind the patisserie counter spotted his moment, and successfully convinced her to buy a green, ribboned box, decorated with stars and

21

labelled 'Kepler Kakes', which Clara would discover on the train to her office were just what the Observatea called scones.

Fleet walked into Mrs Pomligan's Coffee House, Beginners Pottery Studio and Museum of Nearby Horrible Murder: once a deteriorating café, now blossoming into its full potential as a deteriorating multipurpose refreshment and education centre.

Small, square tables with mismatched chairs kept their distance from one another around the room. A handful of patrons sipped their drinks, ate pies and cakes, and occasionally yanked their chair legs free of holes in the floorboards. Here and there, paint peeled itself off the walls in shame.

'Morning, Archie,' shrieked a crocodilian voice from behind a counter. 'Usual, is it?'

The proprietor didn't wait for an answer to her question, knowing full well that it was indeed the usual, and began filling a crooked mug with a thick, black liquid that smelled like it either should be, or already had been, used to protect ships' hulls.

'Good morning, Mrs Pomligan,' Fleet replied into the copy of the *Courier* he was reading as he walked.

He dodged past half a dozen people enthusiastically, if clumsily, slapping their hands onto lumps of wet clay spinning on wheels in front of them, as they attempted to create coffee mugs that they did not yet know Mrs Pomligan would charge them extra to keep. Their inevitable refusal to cough up ensured her a constant supply of mugs to replenish her own, which smashed on the floor about once an hour, after slipping from a customer's grasp due to their incompetent construction by the previous day's novice ceramicists.

Fleet continued on, past several of the local-homicide-themed displays that lined the walls: 'The Vengeance Axe of Miss Cordelia Harper', clearly unused; a poster displaying the formula for 'The Lord Batesford Poison', which looked suspiciously like a recipe for béchamel sauce; and some framed strips of suit fabric labelled 'Clothes of Poor Dead Dr Salik', which Fleet knew for certain had absolutely nothing to do with the scientist who had been murdered nearby, and were probably the remnants of a jacket Mrs Pomligan had confiscated from a punter for taking too long to decide what to order.

One might say Mrs Pomligan was a serial entrepreneur. This, however, would be a cowardly lie: she was an unrepentant con artist. But she was a con artist with great affection for Inspector Fleet, who, while his mother had toiled away selling flowers on the street, had spent many a childhood day in her coffee shop, developing a lifelong addiction to caffeine, and associated sleeping problems so severe he didn't really remember what it was like to be well rested.

'You found my dog yet, Archie?' screeched Mrs Pomligan, adjusting her volume not one bit as Fleet arrived at her counter.

'Mm?' replied Fleet.

He continued to read the *Courier* column. It was now hypothesising about why so little appeared to have been stolen from each bank: only two safe-deposit boxes broken into in each vault.

Suddenly, a muscular arm, strengthened by thirty-five years of grinding coffee by hand, swung down through Fleet's armful of papers, sending them flopping onto the floor.

'Hey!' he cried, finally looking at Mrs Pomligan's ruddy and wrinkled face.

'You find clients reading all those newspapers, do you?'

'Just keeping abreast of things,' said Fleet, retrieving his papers. 'Keeps the mind sharp.'

'Sharp enough to find my lost dog like you promised?' asked Mrs Pomligan, plonking the wonky coffee mug onto the counter.

'I've had cases on, you know that.'

23

'And now?' pressed the proprietor, keeping one eye on Fleet and the other on some bacon cooking away on a large stove behind her.

'Now? At this exact moment? No.'

'Well you've got one, haven't you? My dog!'

By now, Mrs Pomligan had raised her voice above both the sizzling and the increasingly long queue of people behind Fleet, who had begun to grumble quietly.

Fleet sighed. 'I think we might not be fully agreed on what a detective actually is, Mrs Pomligan. And besides, you didn't even like that dog.'

'I loved that dog.'

'No, no you didn't. You kept trying to feed him your pastries and getting upset when he refused them.'

'Neither here nor there. If I want rid of him, should be my decision. Can't let him run off without me first casting him out.'

Mrs Pomligan waved her spatula at Fleet, flicking pork fat across her faded floral pinny.

By now the queue behind Fleet was quite considerable, largely city types who were anxiously assessing the length of the line and looking at the clock to determine whether there was time to grab a pre-work coffee, and all concluding that there probably was, but only because Mrs Pomligan always had the clock running ten minutes slow for this exact potential customer time/coffee calculation scenario.

Fleet ran a hand over his face wearily. 'Didn't that dog just appear here one morning, and come and go every few days? Is he even yours?'

'He's spent enough nights kipping under this here counter.'

Some bacon fat hit the ceiling.

'I'm not sure that's how pet ownership works, Mrs Pomligan.'

'And I'm not sure this is how getting me to recommend your detective business to prospective clients works!'

24

Fleet threw up his hands. 'I'll keep looking.'

Mrs Pomligan nodded once to indicate he had made the right decision.

'And I'll keep you posted if I find any *leads*,' said Fleet, with an eyebrow.

'I should bloody hope so!'

'Any *leads*, Mrs Pomligan.'

'Yes! You'd better!'

Fleet stared at Mrs Pomligan, who stared back at him. He was not sure why he had attempted this.

'Right,' he said, shuffling his papers under his arms and picking up his mug of energising tar with a free hand. 'I should be getting on.'

'Archie,' said Mrs Pomligan, softly.

'Yes?'

'I'm glad business is picking up.'

'Thank you, Mrs Pomligan,' said Fleet, warily. 'I appreciate the supp—'

'Picking up enough for you to start paying me some rent.'

There it was, Fleet thought. The world suddenly making sense again.

'You're a small business owner,' he said, walking towards a staircase at the back of the room. 'You understand how important it is for me to keep a close eye on outgoings.'

'Look,' Mrs Pomligan called after him, her voice returning to the volume of a gong falling into a cellar. 'I didn't mind helping you find your feet, for your poor mother's sake, but I'm not a charity! If you're earning, you're paying, or you're out!'

Already halfway up the stairs, Fleet shouted back: 'If you chuck me out, who's going to correct all these "museum" pieces you've got around here?'

'Nothing needs correcting,' Mrs Pomligan screeched defensively towards the room of customers. 'It's all legitimate artefacts of nearby 'orrible murders! Buy a self-guided walking tour pamphlet here at the counter.'

'You've mixed up the order of things in "That Nasty Business With the Scientist Who Got Done In Just Out Front of the Grouse and Chisel".'

Mrs Pomligan looked over at a wall-mounted, earthenware tableau depicting a medley of murder and deception.

'You sure?' she shrieked.

'Reasonably sure, Mrs Pomligan. I died solving it.'

The detective, his mug of coffee, and his armful of crumpled newsprint vanished through a chipped wooden door at the top of the staircase, onto which was bolted a new and incongruously shiny metal plate. It read: 'Fleet-Entwhistle Private Investigations'.

Chapter 2

To say that Even Greater London was a city of crime was rather like saying that the Atlantic was an ocean of wet. True, no doubt. But something you would expect the average man on the street to already be aware of. Unlike, say, the location of his wallet.

This problem had created a number of law enforcement solutions, chief among which was Sir Robert Peel's Metropolitan Police (or 'Bobbies', as they were known, after the familiar form of 'Robert', which Sir Robert hated). The most recent to appear, however, just two months past, was the city's first independent detective agency: Fleet-Entwhistle Private Investigations.

Clara had met Fleet only weeks before. She had just arrived in London and started work as a crime reporter, and pursued a murder case alongside Fleet despite his repeated objections, until he eventually conceded – as Clara had known he would – that they were making a good team, and furthermore proposed – as she hadn't a clue he would – that they go into business together.

Since accepting Fleet's offer, Clara had come to learn that nobody really understood what a private detective agency actually was. But that, to her, was just another intriguing puzzle to solve, and she already had a plan.

First, though, she had to give her partner a comprehensive debrief on the conversations, locations, events and pastries of her morning, and so an hour after leaving the Observatea, Clara skipped up the stairs from Mrs Pomligan's and swept open the door to their office.

Truth be told, it didn't look much like an office. It had the slanted roof of an attic, bare walls and a rough, boarded floor. And if it seemed like it had once been a storage space, that was only because it still was one, with dozens of bags of sugar, flour and other miscellaneous ingredients stacked in piles next to the wall, and a ziggurat of jute sacks whose Cyrillic lettering Clara had once decoded – with the help of several borrowed dictionaries and an Orthodox priest – as 'COFFEE, DOCKER GRADE'.

In fact, the only real clues that this was a functioning detective agency were the two large, battered oak desks facing one another at the centre of the room and, on the back wall, a sparsely-covered pinboard labelled 'CASES' – which featured various documents relating to recent investigations, as well as a photograph of a beagle with the words 'My Dog' added in powerful handwriting. There was also the fairly strong giveaway of an actual detective, in the form of Fleet, who was surrounded by another daily haul of newspapers – possibly the largest Clara had yet seen him collect.

'Good morning, Fleet!' she chirped, shutting the door behind her. 'Wonderful day for it.'

'For what?' replied Fleet from behind a broadsheet.

'Oh, all sorts of things, I imagine.'

'Including your meeting with Lady Arabella?'

'Yes! She was rather pleased with our work. And I must say, wrapping up a case to a client's satisfaction has made for a wonderful start to my day. You should have come – it was a joint effort, after all.'

'Meeting Arabella once was plenty, thank you.'

Clara remembered Lady Arabella repeatedly calling Fleet 'Fleep' and chastising him for being so poorly dressed for a butler.

'I bought you a Kepler Kake, but it's not very good, I'm afraid.'

Fleet peered over the top of his newsprint. 'Aren't they just scones?'

'They're very bad scones,' replied Clara.

'Ah, yes, I remember.'

Clara squeezed herself through the small gap between Fleet's desk and her own, and headed to the far corner of the room, where a small iron safe was tucked away under a table, on top of which were two tins, labelled 'BISCUITS' and 'BISCUITS, CLIENT'. She pulled the payment envelope out of her bag and put it in the safe. She also considered whether a potential client might enjoy a Kepler Kake, but decided that this wouldn't paint their business in the best light and put the bright green box in the bin before turning back to the newspaper-eclipsed Fleet.

'What are you doing?' she asked, knowing full well.

'Reading the morning papers.'

Clara sat at her desk, watching with an amused smile, and waiting for Fleet to realise the conversation could not possibly be over.

A few moments later, he lowered the paper. 'Yes?'

'Cracked it yet?'

'Cracked what yet?'

'The banks! You're working the burglaries through the papers, yes?' Clara's words came out a little more accusatory than she had intended, so she shot her colleague a smile.

'No,' he replied definitively, before glancing down to his desk. 'A little. Yes.'

'Did you ever see anything like it at Scotland Yard?'

'No one's seen anything like it, Clara.'

This was correct, assuming Fleet was excluding the perpetrators of these burglaries, who had, of course, seen something very much like it while in the process of doing it.

'Seven vaults now in two months,' he continued. 'All across London. Two safe-deposit boxes each time, with—'

'Nothing in common in their contents.'

Fleet had not been the only one keeping up with the papers, and the details of the case were so unusual, Clara could understand why he was so drawn to it.

'Right.' Fleet shook his head. 'They don't know what they're doing.'

'The thieves?'

'No, the thieves definitely know what they're doing. It's the police. Although, to be fair, it's not easy when thieves know what they're doing.'

'Maybe they are making progress and they're just not telling the press,' said Clara.

'No, they'll have every detective working on this. Someone would talk.'

'It doesn't seem to be stopping every paper filling up their columns with the break-ins for days after each time.'

Clara recalled the recent redeployment onto the bank case of several of her colleagues at the *Morning Chronicler*, the paper where she was still somehow employed as a journalist, despite spending most of her time solving cases with Fleet. This had even included the fashion illustrator, who had been forced to produce a three-page spread speculating on the sartorial choices of the burglars, and did this with such flair that he was immediately poached by a leading fashion house to design an entire *Felonious Chic* collection.

'True,' replied Fleet. 'It is an interesting case. But it's not our case. So.'

He closed the paper with a quiet sigh, and stuffed it with the rest into a deep desk drawer, before turning his attention to some correspondence.

Clara felt a pang of sympathy. She didn't know that many things about Fleet, despite her numerous failed attempts to get him to reveal crucial points of personal trivia such as his birthday, middle name or top five orchid varieties. But one thing she did know was that even compared to his usual state of mind – less a buoyant joie de vivre, and more a harried why-won't-this-city-just-let-me-vivre-in-peace – his spirits would descend significantly whenever he read about particularly fascinating crimes, such as this bank case, that were not the sort of thing he nowadays got to investigate.

And not without reason, she thought. After all, not long before they set up shop together, his career as a Scotland Yard detective had come to a rather abrupt end. No more abrupt than one would expect, given he had been killed in the line of duty – that sort of thing tends to put the full stop after most careers. But abrupt considering he had shortly thereafter been revived by Her Majesty's Royal Medical Engineers, given a quick dust-off and a nerve-settling chocolate biscuit, and sent on his way.

As a recent arrival in London, Clara found a lot of things about the city new and exciting when to others they were utterly mundane, but she was assured that resurrections were not a typical occurrence.

In fact, Fleet was the only person, other than Queen Victoria herself, to have gone through this process, and it was only thanks to Her Most Majestic Whims that he had, since she felt that a detective plummeting to his death while attempting to apprehend a villain on the roof of the Fortress of Westminster, where Parliament did its business, sent the wrong sort of message about her government's priorities.

31

And there was no visible trace of any of this on Fleet's person, since the revival team had become a lot better at their job over time. Indeed, much of Victoria's machine-like appearance nowadays was because she had come to like it, finding that the dark colours of the metal went with more or less everything.

Overall, Clara couldn't generalise, but she found it nevertheless surprising that Fleet's death had been less of an impediment to his career at Scotland Yard than had the bureaucratic flywheel it had kicked into motion.

It turned out that withdrawing an official document – a death certificate, for example – was not a straightforward matter, partly because Central Administration Chief Records Officer Calligan was an absolute stickler for the required documentation, much of which he had designed himself, but largely because he had been at lunch for almost eighteen years, and no one else understood his forms well enough to have him dismissed.

Sticking with whatever was originally submitted was, therefore, generally the best way forward. Which usually meant little more than an annoyance at having to spell your name 'Thmasmot' instead of 'Thomas' for your entire life, because your father had had one too many before registering your birth. But for others, the consequences could be quite grave: the Marquess of Abergavenny, for instance, mistakenly filed his marriage certificate in triplicate and was subsequently incarcerated for bigamy – the jurors particularly appalled that he had married multiple women with the same name, *on the same day*.

And in the case of Inspector Fleet, officially being dead meant the police could no longer employ him, and he'd been informed by a rather unsympathetic clerk at Central Administration that rectifying this mistake might take up to two years – and, moreover, that Fleet's demands for a speedier resolution had no legal force because, according to these documents here, he was dead.

It would be enough, Clara thought, to take the wind out of anybody's sails, dispiriting except for people like her who knew – both from sheer optimism and actual sailing lessons – that all it takes is a little gust to get going again.

'I know it must be difficult to sit in the wings while your old colleagues investigate,' she said, before adding in a rush of enthusiasm: 'But we're picking up real momentum with cases, and we've only just started! It takes time to build a reputation among a potential client base. That's what Posner says.'

'Who?'

'W. M. Posner,' said Clara. 'Not sure of his actual names. William, perhaps. Or Wilfred. Can't rule out Winston. Nor—'

'Who is Posner, outside of his name?'

'Ah.' Clara pulled a book out of her satchel and held it up at Fleet. 'A Guide to Business for Gentlemen. The librarian at Mudie's said there wasn't one for ladies, and then I think he muttered "Nor should there be", so this will have to do.'

There was a light tapping from outside the room, so faint that Clara took it to be a sound coming from downstairs.

'You're reading about business?' asked Fleet.

'Of course! Detection is our skill, but business is how we shall make a living doing it.'

'Is that more than charging people for what we do?'

'So much more, Fleet! Advertising, strong client relationships, clear organisation, marketing – which Posner claims is different to advertising but he's very unclear on why.'

Fleet eyed the book sceptically. 'And what makes Mr Posner an expert in these things?'

'He was in the soap game.'

'Soap has a game?'

'Everything has a game! Soap has a game. Fish has a game. *Game* has a game – there's a whole chapter on the grouse trade. But, for the detection game—'

Fleet shuddered.

'—the key will be to build a strong reputation for successful outcomes, regardless of the case. Start small, build over time.'

The distant sound returned, slightly louder – perhaps Mrs Pomligan was kicking that skirting board back into place again.

'Which you'd know,' Clara continued, 'if you'd read my sixteen-point plan.' She pointed to the wall, where she had pinned a document entitled 'Success'. 'I got the idea from Posner. He suggests a five-point plan, but I felt we have more potential.'

'I feel we have more potential focusing on what we're good at than on Mr Posner's game of soap.'

''Scuse the interruption,' said a woman's head poking out from behind the door.

'Ah!' cried Fleet. 'Where did you come from?'

'I've been a-knocking, but I don't think you heard me.'

'Apologies,' said Clara. 'Please, come in.'

The woman closed the door behind her. She was short with angular features, her weatherbeaten face full of crags and hollows and as rough as the navy woollen dress she was wearing. Her greying hair sat untidily under a flower-trimmed bonnet that could have done with some deadheading.

Clara walked over to greet her. 'Clara Entwhistle. Welcome to Fleet-Entwhistle Private Investigations. This is our head office, as you can see.'

The woman seemed to accept this.

'Inspector Fleet,' said Fleet, nodding slightly.

'Price,' replied the woman with a bob of the head. 'Kathleen Price.'

Keenly aware this was a potential new case, Clara reached for the 'BISCUITS, CLIENT'.

'How can we help you, Miss Price?' she asked.

'Well, you'll probably think it's nothing.'

'I'm sure that's not true,' said Clara. 'We work on all sorts of things.'

Kathleen silently studied her shoes and fidgeted with her fingers.

Clara looked over to Fleet for assistance, but his eyes were fixed on the woman as if she were covered in runes he was translating one by one.

'I feel quite silly for coming, if I'm honest,' said Kathleen. ''Specially after the bobbies laughed me down the road. Asked me how much I'd had to drink they did!'

'I'm quite positive there's no cause to feel silly,' said Clara, in her most reassuring tone. 'Why not try us?'

Kathleen looked at Clara, and then at the door. 'No, I should go.'

Clara was distressed by the woman's unwillingness to share her burden, but knew she couldn't force her to speak.

'Well, if you're really sure.'

'I'm not sure!' Kathleen cried, suddenly overcome. 'I'm not sure about anything. I don't know who he is, I don't know who *she* is, I don't know who that other person was and I don't know where they've taken him!'

Through the floorboards rose the sound of Mrs Pomligan aggressively upselling some poor soul on some of her 'Fortnight Fresh' chocolate biscuit cake. Fleet straightened up in his chair.

'Why don't you take a seat, Miss Price?'

The private investigators hadn't yet splashed out on seats for clients, so a few minutes later, Kathleen Price was settled at Fleet's desk, holding a Garibaldi biscuit. Clara faced her from behind her own desk. Fleet was in the corner, leaning against the pile of coffee sacks, studying this woman as she took a moment.

He reflected on their clients so far. They had all come with the mundane, personal problems of the wealthy: background checks on offspring's potential suitors; a young lady seeking to get her governess dismissed simply because she didn't like the way they spoke; a witless young lord requesting an investigation into his valet, whom he suspected to be an imposter – having forgotten that his previous valet had simply resigned, largely because of having to put up with exactly this sort of thing.

Upper-class problems. Grievances. Nuisances.

Kathleen was clearly a worker. She didn't enjoy the level of comfort where the only problems are imperfections. She had seen something awful. She was shaken for good reason.

Eventually, and after her restorative Garibaldi, Kathleen composed herself.

'They took him from the bridge. Right off it, while he was waiting for her.'

A bridge, thought Fleet. Even worse. The closer you got to the glacier, the more likely that something that seemed bad was indeed terrible.

He vaguely remembered the newspaper adverts and giant colourful posters from when they first built the Tower, explaining how, in order to cast ever-so-handy electricity out across the capital, it would draw its energy *somehow* from the very earth beneath it. There was usually a small footnote about the concern that this process might end up drawing every last mote of energy from the nearby Thames, leaving it permanently frozen, but also that the risk of this was so low as to be hardly worth mentioning.

'Who is "he"?' asked Clara.

36

'I told you. I don't know. I never spoke to him. I just saw him from a distance. He was waiting for her on the bridge, like he did every evening. I could see from me window. He'd come at eight, stand by the fourth lamppost and wait an hour for her. Then he'd leave. She never came.'

'How do you know he was waiting for a woman?' asked Fleet.

'Ah.' Kathleen smiled for the first time since she'd walked through the door, and her eyebrows made a break for it towards the top of her forehead. 'In the classifieds, wasn't it?'

'Wasn't what?'

Kathleen performed the message as if she was auditioning for a part – although if she had been, she wouldn't have got it, unless the part was Mourning Fishmonger: '"Alexandrina, do not forsake me! I will wait for you on Blackfriars Bridge every evening at eight."'

'A jilted lover!' exclaimed Clara.

'Must be,' agreed Kathleen. 'And normally I wouldn't pay no mind, but me window overlooks the bridge – I live in Mudlark, you see. So named 'cause of all the—'

'Mudlarks,' deduced Fleet.

''Sright. Treasure trove them riverbanks used to be. Except there's no mud to lark no more, just the ice, and unless you've got yourself an engine drill to bore through it, or a Tommie Ton with some sharp hands, you're out of luck.'

'Tommie Ton?' asked Clara.

'Yeah, you know. Machine men. Dustbins walking around doing our jobs.'

'Automatons?'

Kathleen wrinkled her nose at Clara's clarification, and turned her attention to Fleet.

'Shame how things keep shuffling on, isn't it, Inspector?'

Fleet didn't hear this. He was completely absent from the room, listening to the ticking in his chest, which only he could hear. He had a vague sensation of lying on a table, unable to move or speak. Voices in the distance were describing the appalling condition of his body and how many of his organs they would need to replace with mechanical alternatives.

'Policeman pulled off a rooftop by a Tower warder,' said one. 'Made a right mess.'

'Why fix him up?' asked another.

'Favour to Vicky,' the one apparently in charge had replied.

'Lucky,' said the first.

Something metallic began to whirr, and then moved closer.

'No,' Fleet failed to say.

'Sort you right out then, won't we, Inspector?'

The whirring was inches above Fleet's body. His muscles weren't listening to him.

'Inspector? Inspector?'

Someone clapped. Fleet looked up and saw Clara putting her hands down, almost managing to hide her concern with a smile. He wiped some sweat off his neck.

'I know, Inspector,' said Kathleen. 'I get awful nostalgic thinking about them, too.'

Fleet had no idea what she was talking about, so he nodded, prompting her to resume a story she had been telling about the good old days. He didn't find this particularly believable. Not the story itself, just that people tend to forget that the good old days were also, in many if not most ways, absolutely horrible old days.

He steered Kathleen, and himself, back to the matter at hand.

'So, after you saw the advertisement . . .'

'Right, that evening at eight o'clock, I took a peek out me window. And there he was. Mr Lonely Hearts himself. Smartly set, pocket watch. Must've been, ooh, three weeks ago. Been there every evening since. Then a few nights ago, ten minutes after he gets there, a carriage pulls up, driver jumps down,

38

paces up to him, then – quick as you like – hand over the mouth, arm twisted behind the back, frogmarches him to the carriage, chucks him in and shuts the door. Then I saw the windows were blacked out. Couldn't see a thing. Driver jumps back up to his perch, takes the reins and they're off.'

'Did anyone else see this?' asked Fleet.

'No. I dashed out to where he'd been, but there was no one else on the bridge, and it didn't look like anybody else was taking an interest from the houses like me.'

'Anything left behind?'

Kathleen shook her head.

Fleet paused before continuing, 'And you don't know anything about who this man was, who Alexandrina is, or whose carriage it was?'

'No.'

Clara looked over her notes. 'Can you give us a description of the man? Other than "smartly set with a pocket watch", did he have any distinguishing characteristics?'

'If I were a betting woman, I'd say he was about thirty years of age. Red hair, clean shaven, about the same height as you, Inspector. Bit more athletic looking though.'

Fleet straightened up slightly against the sacks.

'And that's all the information you have?'

Kathleen rubbed her temples and gave a firm nod of her head before adding:

'You'll look into it, then? I'm ever so worried for him. He only had love in mind. He didn't deserve to be carted off like that.'

'Well, obviously this is a serious crime,' said Fleet.

'And serious crimes are our speciality,' added Clara.

The two investigators looked at one another, and then met the gaze of the beagle watching them vacantly from the photograph on the pinboard.

'We will take the case,' Clara said cheerily.

'Oh! That's wonderful, thank you. How can I ever repay you?'

'By paying us,' said Fleet.

'Course, of course,' said Kathleen, rummaging through her pockets. 'Um. Course.'

Fleet suddenly remembered he was speaking to a woman of limited means, and caught Clara's eye, hoping she might have an idea. Clara grabbed Posner's *Guide to Business for Gentlemen* and began to leaf through.

'We do have a discounted rate for first-time clients,' she began. 'Bear with me, Miss Price.'

Kathleen pulled a toothy grin – she seemed to have found what she had been looking for – and took out a ball of dirty fabric. She unwrapped it to reveal something tiny and bright, which she flipped into Fleet's hand.

'How'd this do you?' she asked.

Fleet saw he was holding a gold coin, embossed with Latin words and the profile of a man who appeared – as with everyone who makes it onto coins – both important and miserable. He showed it to Clara, whose eyes shot wide open. They looked back at Kathleen for answers.

'Told you them riverbanks were a treasure trove,' she said. 'Couple of those got dropped by some unlucky Tommie Ton that speared itself onto a sort of, well, spear I was holding.'

Fleet briefly felt very ill, which distracted him from this apparent confession of criminal damage.

'Anyway,' Kathleen continued, repocketing her dirty fabric, 'feels right to give a bit back to help someone out after my good fortune.'

'Well,' said Clara, 'I think this will definitely do. Is there anything else we should know about the case?'

'Apart from what we already know about the unknown man, unknown woman and unknown second man, about whom we know nothing,' added Fleet.

'Exactly,' said Clara.

'I don't think there's anything. I've told you all I know.' Kathleen leaned forwards with a curious eye. 'How are you going to find him?'

Downstairs, a customer had just finished telling Mrs Pomligan what he thought of her chocolate biscuit cake, and now there was the terrible sound of Mrs Pomligan telling the customer what she thought of him telling her what he thought of her chocolate biscuit cake.

'Miss Price,' said Clara. 'The classified advertisement. Which newspaper was it in?'

Kathleen opened her mouth as if to speak but, instead, snapped her fingers at the ceiling, reached into her bag, and – with the satisfied expression of a cat offering its owner the mangled corpse of a songbird – pulled out a battered edition of the *Morning Chronicler*.

Chapter 3

As in all societies, except perhaps the happy ones, the news in Even Greater London was everywhere. You couldn't walk down the street without it being waved in front of your face by a paperboy, or plastered on a wall you were forbidden to look at unless you had a subscription to it, or blared out from pre-recorded public address machines that loudly posed questions like 'Which cabinet secretary was today expelled from Parliament for speaking un-cummerbunded?' and offered to tell you the answer if you shoved a ha'penny into them.

There was a lot going on, and far more money to be made out of the people who wanted to stay up to date with current affairs than from the people who viewed this whole idea as a total con, and now and again would pop up from their books just to make sure there wasn't an election or a war or something.

There were countless newspapers, of course, specialising in different types of content: politics; business; society gossip; sightings of the motionless Prussian armada – waiting for something, the right moment perhaps – on a clear day from Scarborough. Some papers had even started to claim that the outcome of twenty-two men scrapping over a leather ball was a type of news, with headlines like WARBURTON FC BATTLE NEMESES BADHAMPTON ATHLETIC TO HEART-RACING 0–0.

London, like every modern civilisation, had fallen prey to what researchers at the Swindon Informatorium's Department for Phenomenistics had termed 'inkflation': the process by which, as a society becomes more complex, so too do the attempts to summarise its events in the form of news, leading the value of individual pieces of news to decrease over time.

The *Morning Chronicler*, the newspaper in which Kathleen Price had seen the missing man's plea to Alexandrina, was not immune to this inkflationary spiral, and was one of many that boosted its appeal by stuffing in instalments of scandalous, serialised fiction: 'The Bigamists of Ballaghmore', 'The Good Doctor's Not So Good Secret', and so on. But it also did a decent job with actual reportage, particularly after Clara became its newest crime reporter a few months back and immediately set about joining Inspector Fleet in solving some major cases and then writing up the scoops.

This success had led to Clara being given her own column, which her editor had insisted on calling 'Tales of a Lady Detective'. But they hadn't recently worked on a case that had provided suitable material, and so Clara's latest column was now overdue.

The two investigators had arrived at the *Morning Chronicler*'s offices that afternoon for another reason, however, so as they walked into its busy entrance hall Clara kept her head down, attempting to use her colleague as human camouflage to avoid being seen by her editor – a manoeuvre Fleet helped with in absolutely no way.

'Ah, Miss Entwhistle,' a clipped voice boomed, its vaguely threatening chipperness amplified by the room's crumbling brick walls and cracked tile flooring. 'Fancy seeing you here.'

Clara looked up to see Augusta Bell, a lean, silver-haired, immaculately presented woman in her late fifties, standing at the top of the foyer staircase, which gave her a perfect vantage point from which to spot errant journalists.

It was terrifically bad luck for Clara, but she knew it was hard to evade a Bell for long. They were, after all, one of London's most influential families. Certainly the one with the most siblings. And because of their influence and sheer numerousness, there was hardly any part of society in which a Bell brother or sister could not be found: Julius Bell was Private Secretary to the Queen; Dr Septimus Bell was up to his elbows in forensic pathology; Director Aurelia Bell headed up the London Museum of Other Nations' Antiquities; Girton College, Cambridge – the only one to survive the Great Fenland Flood – had Heraclea Bell as its principal; floating commandingly somewhere in the North Sea there was Admiral Commodus Bell; Maximus Bell was burrowed deep within the bureaucratic warrens of the Foreign Office; and least but by no means last, there was Tiberius Bell, a poet of no renown.

There were probably more. No one was keeping track. Much like when tunnelling work for an extension of the Gladstone line led to the 1879 collapse of Leamington Spa cathedral's newly-expanded steeple, the Bells were absolutely everywhere.

Including, to Clara's misfortune, right here.

'So,' continued Augusta, her stern expression betraying no emotions, except perhaps an affinity towards deadlines, 'you've finally remembered that you're a journalist, have you, and come to file your next column? I am cock-a-hoop, as you can see.'

'Ah, yes, well, about that . . .'

Clara scampered up the stairs, keen to prevent what was quite clearly going to be an impromptu review meeting from being broadcast in a place with such excellent acoustics. She threw a look of apologetic panic back at Fleet – who replied with thrown-open hands and an expression of betrayed bewilderment – and vanished down a corridor after Augusta.

Clara had to walk quickly to keep up with her employer, who was striding down the newspaper's hallways without checking to see if the person she was speaking to was still there. Every so often, Augusta would dart her head into a room to check on a board of illustrations, or the layout of tomorrow's front page, both assessing the work and providing feedback in the half-second it took to pass the doorway.

'Now don't get me wrong, Miss Entwhistle,' Augusta began. 'You've proved yourself to be an effective journalist, which is why I agreed to your column in the first place. I was sceptical, I'll admit, but your piece on that fabulous Egyptologist murder at the museum was bloody business and sharp copy. Just the thing.'

Clara was wary. She had expected worse given she was behind on her submissions. And positive comments from Augusta tended to presage something more devastating, like an executioner complimenting one's neck.

'That's very kind,' she said.

'It isn't kind, Miss Entwhistle, it is the truth. I don't go in for praise, I find it tends to encourage employees to seek a mentor-mentee relationship, which in turn can lead to the most ghastly displays of sentimentality. Or worse, you end up— *Toole!* No more full-page advertisements from the Huxley Bakery! They still owe us for last July, and despite what Messrs Huxley might claim about the quality of their wares, I do not accept payment *in baguettes*.'

As she followed past the doorway a few steps behind Augusta, Clara peeked through to see a young clerk sheepishly placing a telephone receiver back on its cradle and brushing his shirt clean of crumbs.

45

'Or worse,' Augusta continued, not even having paused for breath, 'you end up with people like my brother Tiberius. Age eleven, his Latin master makes one favourable comment about his understanding of poetic metre and now look where we are: four volumes of metaphysical blather and monthly recitals I never attend and for all I know are just him in a room causing some chairs to lose the will to live. What I mean is, your last piece was very good, and our readers are eager for more.'

Augusta stopped outside her office and turned to face Clara for the first time. There was an uneasy silence, the sort senior managerial types tend to be perfectly fine with because of some defect in their humanity.

'Can you give it to them, Miss Entwhistle?'

Clara was not in the business of letting people down. Particularly people like Augusta, who had given her the very opportunity she had moved to London hoping to find.

'Of course, Miss Bell. I just need to hit upon the right case.'

'Well, hit upon it quickly. The public is a ravenous beast, a slavering animal that cannot be sated. Its jaws drool even now, and all you can do is feed it news every day and hope it doesn't bite your entire arm off as you do.'

Augusta stepped into her office, and turned to face Clara through the door. Her expression softened imperceptibly. 'You have promise, Miss Entwhistle.'

Clara blinked in shock; she had expected the axe to swing differently.

'Thank you, Miss Bell.'

'Do not thank me. The promise is to yourself. And promises are to be kept.'

Meanwhile, Fleet was making his way down a narrow and dusty corridor that led away from the entrance hall, looking around for anything that might point him towards the Classifieds Department, but nothing was to be found. He paused to think, and a few moments later a harried young man came hurtling towards him with reams of printed copy covered in angry red ink.

'Excuse me,' said Fleet, 'I'm looking for Classified Advertising.'

The man gave Fleet a contorted look that communicated both that he didn't have time to answer, and that the very act of having to convey this had cost him valuable seconds and possibly his job. The man dashed past and vanished down the corridor.

'Downstairs.'

The Yorkshire drawl had come from inside one of the offices a few yards away. Fleet hadn't noticed before, but the door had been left ever so slightly open – enough for the person inside to hear any conversations in the corridor, not so much that anyone would easily notice.

Fleet walked up to the door. The brass plate said 'Lester Horrocks' and then, below, 'Senior Crime Reporter'. Inside, Fleet was greeted by the soles of Lester's shoes, facing him from on top of the desk, one crossed over the other and resting on a blanket of newspapers, photographs and official documents Fleet was fairly certain a journalist should not have. Around the desk were notebooks, jottings and other assorted auxiliary thinking, spilling out onto stacks of yet more newspapers and the floor.

Lester was leaning back in his chair. He was a crumpled bloodhound of a man in his late forties. His tie was loosened wildly, and he wore a shabby brown suit. To say Lester was dishevelled was accurate, but it's very possible the man had never been shevelled in the first place.

Fleet had only met Lester a handful of times, but he knew him well enough to be sure of three things:

47

Firstly, the tie was always this way, presumably from the moment Lester put it on in the morning. Lester was in the business of getting people to spill their guts, and was clever enough to know that the best way to do this is to avoid seeming clever at all.

Secondly, Lester had spent the past twenty years at the bottom of a pint glass, on the outside of reputable journalism. This was after he'd followed a hunch about a serial killer – a hunch that was absolutely right, but as Lester had had no way to prove it, his youthful drive had ended up getting him cast out as a crank. He had only recently been proved correct and brought back into the fold, and was acting like he had twenty years of assignments to catch up on.

Thirdly, the horrendous mess of his desk and office was not because Lester was lazy, but rather because he was cursed. Cursed in the way many journalists, detectives, scientists, artists and others are cursed: with obsession. Their brain causes them to notice odd patterns, and then compels them to explore, to understand, and to find out the truth. And Lester, like Fleet, had seen enough of the city to know that the truth, contrary to the poetic notion that it is beauty and beauty it, is generally as ugly as sin (a sentiment captured in the 1819 Romantic odes 'This Doesn't Look Anything Like An Urn, Grecian Or Otherwise', and 'Why Did I Ever Let You Talk Me Into Coming To This Pottery Class').

'Not having much luck, your lot, are they?' asked Lester.

'With what?' asked Fleet, correctly interpreting 'your lot' as 'the police', despite Lester knowing full well Fleet didn't work there any more.

Lester bent forward and grabbed a broadsheet from the newspaper-drift on his desk.

'"With what?"' he mocked.

He licked a fingertip and whipped through the top corners of a couple of pages, folded them over and flung the paper towards Fleet. It flapped wildly through the air like fighting seagulls, landing on the wooden floor and coming to a halt in front of Fleet's feet. It was folded neatly in half, the right way up from Fleet's perspective, and open on the page Lester seemed to have in mind. Fleet recalled a warning someone had once given him never to play cards against anyone who can shuffle a deck in one hand.

The article's title shouted its opinion: POLICE REDOUBLE BANK EFFORTS, REMAIN BAFFLED.

'They ought to get you on it,' said Lester. 'Can't you just get your . . . your . . .'

He gestured at Fleet's body.

'Status as a deceased person corrected?' asked Fleet.

Lester nodded. 'Aye, that's the one.'

'It's going to take some time. It's with Central Administration.'

'Ah.' Lester shook his head. 'Bloody bureaucrats. Well, I'm sorry for you, lad. Looks like the Yard could do with the help.'

He nodded at the paper's message of police hopelessness.

'They'll get to the bottom of it,' said Fleet, unsure if he believed himself.

'No doubt, no doubt. Hopefully before every last bank in the city's been cleared out, eh?'

'There's only been seven.'

'So you are keeping track! 'Course you are. Can't imagine finding lost dogs is making the best use of your noggin.'

'It's just the one dog,' Fleet retorted, before wincing in regret.

'Bloody hell, I was joking! You've actually been finding dogs?'

'Yes. Well, no.' Fleet muttered into his collar: 'Haven't . . . actually found it yet.'

'Give me your card, for Pete's sake. I can hand it out when I run into people who need help with real problems.'

'We *are* working real problems, Lester,' Fleet replied, more quickly than he intended.

'Oh, aye?'

'Aye! I mean, yes.'

'What you got on then?'

'A kidnapping, if you must know.'

Lester whistled in approval. 'That's more like it. Where'd this happen then?'

'On Black—' Fleet stopped. He had, like countless others, temporarily forgotten that this heap of laundry was never really just making conversation and always had a deadline.

Lester leaned forwards dramatically. 'Not . . . Blackbeard's island fortress?'

'Obviously not.'

''Cause there's a scoop right there if you'd found that.' Lester beamed, absolutely delighted with himself.

'Obviously it's nothing to do with pirates, Lester,' sighed Fleet.

Lester relaxed back into his seat. 'Blackfriars Bridge then.'

'No.'

'Aye. It were.'

'Lester—'

'You don't seem too bad at police work, lad, but you need to work on your own fibs as well as sussing out others'.'

'I just need to get to the classifieds,' Fleet weakly implored. 'Is it actually downstairs or were you just luring me in to talk about the bank thefts?'

'The latter.'

'Lester!'

'Four along from me, Inspector.'

Lester bent the fleshy fingers of one hand into the shape of a gun, pointed it at the wall to his right, and mouthed a 'pow!' at Fleet as the gun recoiled.

'Thank you,' said Fleet, before turning to the door.

'Oh, Fleet.'

Fleet continued turning until he completed a circle.

'Chuck that paper back, would you?'

Fleet picked up the paper and flung it towards Lester's desk. The seagulls made it halfway before suffering a stroke mid-flight and crashing in a heap on the floor. Lester flattened his lips in disappointment. Fleet was even more disappointed but, refusing to reveal this, shrugged and walked out.

Clara had been searching the hallways for Fleet since her conversation with Augusta, and found him just as he shut Lester's door, squinting and shaking his head like he'd gone inside for a painkiller and been met by bagpipes.

'There you are, Fleet. Where have you been?'

Fleet paused, made some confused looks between Clara and the room he had just left, and finally pointed at the door. 'Isn't this the waiting room for detectives whose partners have run off? There were a few of us in there. Quite a lot in common.'

Clara suppressed a grin into something more disapproving. 'You're not as funny as you think you are, Inspector.'

'Well, I don't think I'm very funny, so I'm probably close. Lester lured me in on the promise of directions.'

'Did you get them?'

'You lead the way and we'll see. Good meeting with Augusta?'

Clara pondered this. 'Hard to say.'

'Maybe next time.'

'But things are looking up, Fleet! An exciting new case, full of intrigue.'

'Concerning a man who might be in serious danger.'

'Yes . . .' replied Clara, sheepishly. 'Of course.'

'Don't mind her, Fleet,' called Lester, his voice resonating from behind the oak-panelled door that Clara could have sworn she saw Fleet close just moments ago, but which was now slightly ajar. 'It's the journalist's instinct in her. She's a natural.'

'Yes, thank you for that contribution to our private conversation, Lester,' said Fleet, pulling the door to for a second time.

'You're most welcome, lad,' came the muffled reply.

'Right then,' said Clara, starting off down the corridor. 'Let's find our Mr Lonely Hearts.'

The investigators walked into the Classifieds Department, which was either a small office or a large cupboard, and were met by an unholy assemblage of metal, leather and cogs forming the vague shape of the upper half of a woman, bolted onto a desk.

'Aah!' observed Fleet.

The machine-woman had half a face but somehow both eyes, each a small, bright white light casting rays around the room. Her three skeletal arms were grabbing bits of paper, stuffing them into small capsules, and shoving the capsules into a pneumatic tube attached to her side, which noisily sucked its contents upwards into the ceiling. She handled this business speedily, apparently not at all bothered by the ticker tape running from a telegraph at the side of the room to an opening on the side of her head, into which the tape, and presumably the telegraphed advertisement orders printed on it, slowly moved.

Clara generally found automatons to be a charming novelty and admired the ingenuity that went into making them – from the wind-up boats children played with on park lakes, to the tiny figurines that attached to your wax cylinder player and danced along, to the more thorough attempts to replace humans and human enterprise entirely, such as with this uncanny clerk-desk. But she had worked with Fleet long enough to know he saw them – the ones that he had to talk to, at least – primarily as incompetent nuisances that slowed down their investigations.

She glanced over. He was studying the machine and, despite the heat in the small room, had fastened several of his coat buttons.

'Good morning,' said the woman, with a cheerful but horrifyingly off-the-mark attempt at a human voice.

'Now, come on,' Clara replied, amused. 'It's well into the afternoon, isn't it?'

'Good morning,' the woman repeated, in precisely the same tone as before.

'Yes. We were hoping you could help us with—'

'Good morning,' the woman insisted.

'Good morning!' snapped Fleet.

'I am Miss Clack. Welcome to Classifieds. Please state the type of advertisement you wish to purchase. Lonely Hearts, Items Wanted, Items For Sale, Lost and Found, Employment, Announcements, or Accommodation.'

'Actually, we have a question,' said Clara.

'You are selling . . . a kestrel,' said the machine-woman.

'No. I do have some birds, as it happens, but kestrels really aren't suitable for the home.'

Fleet shot Clara a look that seemed to question her trying to educate a piece of furniture.

'Please state the type of advertisement you wish to purchase. Lonely Hearts, Items Wa—'

'We don't want an advertisement,' said Fleet. 'We need your information.'

The woman considered this. 'Diagnostics should be performed with caution.'

'Diagnostics,' Fleet agreed. 'Yes. Perfect.'

'Are you a licensed engineer of Donnington Mechanical?'

Clara and Fleet stared at the slowly spinning mechanisms visible through openings in the woman's metal torso, the bunch of wires running down where her throat should be, and the impossibly intricate web of tiny rods and fulcrums on her wrists and hands that appeared to govern the orientation of the segments of her fingers. It was a fiendishly complex machine, the competent repair of which clearly demanded years of study.

'Yes,' said Fleet.

The woman's eyes began to flash on and off. Clara thought about her complicity in voiding the machine's warranty. Eventually, the flashing slowed, then stopped. The woman's eyes were entirely black.

'Hello?' said Fleet.

There was no reply.

A wave of dread began to slosh somewhere in Clara's mind. 'We've killed her.'

'We haven't killed it. It'll be fine.'

'I'm so sorry, Miss Clack,' Clara said gravely.

'Don't apologise to the machine.'

'What happens if you kill an automaton?'

'They can't be killed,' replied Fleet, with the bemusement of someone asked at what temperature it was best to bake a thought. 'They're machines.'

'What happens if you stop one working?'

'I don't know. What happens if you break someone's kettle?'

'They're without boiling water for days! No tea!'

'Exactly. It's an inconvenience, not a capital crime.'

Clara squinted at Fleet. She realised now that he had meant to lower the stakes, but he had chosen a woeful analogy. It was clear he had not thought through the consequences of tealessness on personal wellbeing, let alone the ripple effects on friendship-building or the functioning of wider society. She was about to spell this out for him when she saw a white, jagged question mark appear in the centre of each of the woman's black eyes.

'Instruction?'

'Oh!' replied Clara, relieved to see these signs of not-quite-life. 'Yes. We'd like to know who sent in a certain advertisement, please.'

The woman contemplated this for a moment. 'Instruction?' she repeated.

Fleet and Clara glanced uncertainly at each other.

'Previous advertisements,' tried Fleet.

The woman was again silent for a processing cycle. 'Instruction?'

'You're right,' said Fleet. 'We've killed it.'

Clara thought for a second, then picked up some of the ticker tape where it exited the woman's head and trickled down her back. She was hoping to find some kind of human–automaton Rosetta Stone to bridge the divide, and noticed a word repeated many times over, seemingly once for each advertisement the woman had handled. Perhaps the clerk would understand this concept.

'Records,' said Clara.

The woman's eyes turned completely white.

'Records of advertisement purchases. By date. By author. By purchase method. By content.'

The question marks returned.

'By content,' Clara cried, excited by the breakthrough.

The eyes once again found the instruction comprehensible. 'Content?'

'Yes,' Clara confirmed.

The woman considered this for a moment.

'One hundred and forty-nine advertisements with content "yes",' she declared. 'Readback begins. Record one.'

'Oh God,' sighed Fleet.

'Purchased October eleventh, 1884. "*Balding? Undesirable? Ashamed? With good reason! And yet everyone, yes, everyone – even you, sir – can have the mane of a stallion . . .*"'

'No, no,' said Clara.

'". . . *with patented Crème de Chevaux, exclusively imported from Marseille. Inquire Charles Pharmacy, SW11.*"' The woman paused briefly. 'Record two.'

'Stop!'

'Purchased October fourteenth, 1884. "*Were you on the No. 97 voltaic omnibus yesterday?*"'

'Off! Off!' pleaded Clara.

'"*Did you steal my mother's bonnet she placed beside her on the seat? Yes? You fiend! But it is not too late for your soul.*"'

'Fleet, do something!'

'What kind of something?'

'Any something!'

Clara scanned the machine frantically for an off switch, as Fleet searched the top drawers of the desk it was bolted to, but as soon as she saw the small red antenna protruding out of the woman's shoulder, she remembered these devices were all powered by the Tower: they didn't have an 'off'.

'"*Do the decent thing, you headwear-rustler, and meet me in plain of day . . .*"'

'Aah!' Clara screamed. 'You stupid machine! Stop talking!'

Driven to what metropathologists would have identified as a minor case of Machine Panic, Clara picked up an empty pneumatic tube capsule and threw it at the machine-woman's head. The capsule struck her, ricocheted off and tore through the ticker tape connecting her head to the telegraph, which furled into piles near each machine. The woman fell silent, and her eyes turned black once again.

Clara and Fleet looked at each other, then the door, then back at the slightly dented head of the woman. After a few seconds, her eyes lit up in their original, brightest white.

'Good morning,' she said.

Clara and Fleet stared at the machine.

'Good morning,' they replied.

Chapter 4

Fleet and Clara's second attempt at speaking to the machine-woman was more successful. Carefully responding to the query 'Content?' with the reply 'Alexandrina', they were rewarded with a single record: the advertisement they had heard in their office earlier that day. The record revealed that this order had been placed by someone with the name Mellanby, using the purchase instruction 'The Iron Bridge Club'.

According to the notes for the abandoned Even Greater London census of 1870–1884, there were at least 543 gentlemen's clubs in the city. Naturally, many of these revolved around having attended a particular elite boarding school, the men viewing themselves as uniquely bonded by trials such as rugger in the cold, and having a piece of chalk thrown at you by the Latin master for penning limericks that were obscene both in the behaviour of their Pompeiian protagonist and in their use of incorrect declension. But many clubs focused more on shared professions or interests.

Club Roland, for example, was open to applications from any scholar or supporter of the poetic arts, while clubs such as Cavendish's had been established to serve the scientific community. And, of course, there was Poseidon's, where members had to be of a nautical persuasion, be they naval officers, sculling enthusiasts, or old, grizzled types who sat alone in front of the fireplace, responding to any new member's polite but ill-advised 'good evening' with a haunted stare and a four-hour monologue telling the story of the worst evening you can possibly imagine.

Mr Mellanby, it seemed, was a member of the Iron Bridge Club, which drew its members from the world of civil engineering. The Iron Bridge Club was a fairly recent addition to the extensive catalogue of gentlemen's clubs in the city, set up in the last forty years alongside numerous other establishments that aimed to cater for the newer breed of middle-class, working gentleman. It was for this reason that it wasn't to be found in the heart of clubland in the exclusive St James's area of London, but rather on the other – or, according to members of the more aristocratic clubs, wrong – side of the Thames.

Handily for Fleet and Clara, the club was just a short underground ride away from the *Morning Chronicler* offices, and the pair soon arrived in front of 97 Belvedere Road, which announced itself as the correct address by being the only building to boast an elegant triangle of black iron girders, emerging from the side of the building twelve feet above the ground and jutting out halfway across the street, causing passing carriage drivers to whistle in admiration at the structure's playfully asymmetric design as they ducked to avoid being decapitated.

'This must be the place,' said Clara, her voice bubbling with excitement. 'Come along, Fleet!'

Fleet watched as Clara sprang towards the large ironwork-decorated entrance.

'Clara, they don't—' he called after her, but it was too late. His colleague had already wrenched open the door to the club and disappeared inside.

Fleet sighed, checked his pocket watch and waited for the inevitable. Out of habit, he turned to scan the street. Ten seconds later, he heard a muffled protest. The door opened and Clara was shoved out of it and into Fleet, who had been expecting her to return but not at this speed.

'*Clarmph!*' he said, into the side of her bonnet.

'Oh, hello again, Fleet,' Clara chimed, extricating herself. 'It would seem that these gentlemen's clubs are very closed-minded. No women allowed, apparently.'

'Yes, that's what I was trying to tell you as you ran head-long into the building.'

'But not even for just a few minutes, just to pop my head in and ask a few questions! And they didn't take at all kindly to my pointing out how dated such a rule is.'

'I'm sure they didn't.'

Clara suddenly turned back and shouted at the building: 'Nor how cowardly it is – how *benighted*, sirs! – to hide behind protocols and regulations, and to refuse to engage in honest debate!'

Fleet suspected Clara knew no one inside could hear her, but a few men he had seen walking along the other side of the road were now speeding up and staring straight ahead. They would think twice in future about the wisdom of gentlemen's clubs, or at least of walking past them.

Clara spun back round, animated and smiling.

'Manhandled me out of the building, Fleet. Did you see?'

'I did.'

'Oh, yes. Sorry.' Clara yanked down on Fleet's lapel to straighten the coat shoulder she had knocked askew. 'There.'

'Thank you.'

'You'll have to go in. You're a man, you might pass for a gentleman if you walk well.'

'If I what?'

59

'Just go in and act the part,' said Clara.

'What are you going to do?'

Clara reached into her satchel and pulled out Posner's *A Gentleman's Guide to Business*, which she waved at Fleet like a trophy, before walking over to a nearby bench and taking a seat.

'See if anybody knows where he lives.'

'Where he lives? Why didn't I think of that? I was going to ask about his favourite colour.'

'Don't make fun, Inspector. I'm barred from the building; at least grant me a little detective work by proxy.'

'Fair enough.'

Clara opened her book. 'Now then. "Business".'

Fleet took a deep breath and strode up the stairs and through the door that Clara had been unceremoniously thrust out of a few moments earlier.

Behind the ornate ironwork, a wood-panelled entrance hall revealed itself. On the walls were sullen portraits of the most famous engineers from the last hundred years, each holding a small model of a bridge or tunnel they had designed, or at least taken credit for. On the ceiling, a staggeringly detailed mural portrayed the history of engineering, from a bearded man in a toga pointing with immense pride at a rock on one side of a seesaw, to an image of the Tower spearing out of a modern cityscape, casting red, rippling waves over its surroundings. The ceiling was bordered by ships progressing through the ages: a mighty Roman trireme; an Elizabethan sail-flying ship of the line; a steam-powered ironclad; and, finally, a sleek, metal battleship with a large red antenna receiving waves of energy from the other side of the mural.

In the centre of the room, a uniformed, well-set man was standing at a desk – no doubt this was who had shoved Clara back out onto the street. An archway to Fleet's left led to a staircase. Next to the archway stood a round, polished wooden table, on which there were some flowers in a vase, a bowl of oranges, and a large, leather-bound book.

Fleet considered the man at the desk. During his time in the detective police, he had encountered many receptionists and knew them, roughly speaking, to fall into eight categories, each requiring a different approach if you were to gain information or access they wouldn't otherwise provide: flattery, trickery, a nice eclair or what have you.

He observed the following about this one: pristine uniform; name badge recently polished; shoes newly shined; and currently using a metal ruler to write out a perfectly aligned address on an envelope. He was a category five, no doubt about it: fiercely loyal, proud of their work, and, most unhelpfully of all, competent.

Fleet knew the only way to be sure of getting past this sort was with a police warrant, but that wasn't an option any more, so his best chance lay in avoiding engaging with him at all. Confidence was the key in situations like this.

He strode past the table, picking up an orange as he went, in his best impression of someone used to casually taking free fruit.

He made it four steps further.

'Excuse me, sir.'

Fleet turned around and found himself face to chest with the receptionist, whose significant muscle mass was stretching his uniform so completely that there was a good chance his top shirt button would fly off and hit Fleet in the eye if at any point he decided to smile.

Fleet looked up to meet his gaze, and realised this wasn't very likely.

'Hello,' he tried.

'Are you a member, sir?'

'A member?'

'Yes, sir.'

'No. But I'm thinking of becoming one. I like what I see so far.' Fleet waved at the far wall, where a colourful mosaic explained first how to create a canal, and then how one could use it to transport tiles to create a colourful mosaic about both canals and mosaics. 'But really I could do with a look at the lounge.'

'Membership is restricted to engineers, sir. Are you an engineer?'

'Yes, of course,' replied Fleet, before adding: 'I'm an engineer.'

'Very good, sir. The catenary equation, if you wouldn't mind.'

'Yes. The what?'

'The catenary equation, sir. You remember: describes a hanging chain or the cable of a suspension bridge. Proves you're an engineer, sir.'

Fleet attempted a chummy frown, which came off as a confused scowl. 'I wouldn't want to bore you with that. You seem very busy.'

'No bother, sir,' the receptionist said. 'The equation, if you wouldn't mind.'

Fleet realised there was no way around this, and tried to remember back to his last schooling in mathematics.

'X . . .'

'I'm afraid you've gone wrong already, sir.'

Fleet's eyes darted for options. 'What? Um, no. I'm starting from the other end.'

'I'll give you a hint,' offered the receptionist.

'I don't need it, but I am interested to hear what other people find a useful hint.'

'Hyperbolic cosine, sir.'

Fleet stared at the man. 'I mean, I'm not sure "hyperbolic" is fair – we all say things we don't mean sometimes.'

'I will also accept any equations describing the deformation of a beam under varying loads, and – tell you what, I'm in a good mood – any formula for torsion.'

Fleet stared harder. Perhaps he could reach the man's soul and beseech him to stop.

'You start and I'll join in.'

The receptionist shifted his weight and sighed. 'Sir, are you an engineer?'

'No.'

'In which case, the exit is behind you.'

A muscular arm gestured towards the door, and Fleet envisioned his own unceremonious exit.

'Wait!' he said, retreating to his only remaining option. He had hoped to avoid the truth, if only because it took longer. 'I'm here to find out what happened to one of your members.'

The receptionist studied Fleet for a moment. 'Why?'

'Because something's happened to him.'

'What's happened to him?'

'Very much the question I have as well,' replied Fleet.

'I mean,' said the man, 'what makes you think something's happened?'

'A concerned citizen saw him being kidnapped.'

The receptionist stared confusedly at Fleet. 'And you're here to find out if that happened?'

'No.' Fleet rubbed the bridge of his nose with his forefinger and thumb. 'I should have been clearer. I know very roughly what happened, and I'm here to find out *more* about what happened.'

'Are you the police?'

Fleet's mind rejected the word 'No,' offering instead, 'I'm a private investigator.'

'Which is . . .'

'Similar.'

'How similar?'

'Crimes, questions, that sort of thing.'

Something approaching alarm flickered across the man's face. 'And you might arrest someone here?'

'No, I can't do that. In that respect it's dissimilar.'

'Sir, if you're not the police, and you're not an engineer, I really must ask you to—'

'He's in a lot of trouble. I'm trying to help him, to find him. Surely you can make an exception for that.' Fleet suddenly remembered the way to win over a category five. 'Surely . . . if one of your members is in need, it is your duty.'

The receptionist twisted his lips, appearing to compute which of his employer's commandments superseded which, before walking over to the leather-bound book on the table and opening it at a bookmarked page.

'Which member?'

'Mellanby.'

The man flicked backwards a few days' worth of pages, then a few weeks more.

'Looks like he comes every Tuesday and Thursday,' he said. 'But he missed this Tuesday.'

'I just need to talk to some of your other members.'

The man walked back to Fleet, screwing his lips together some more and furrowing his brow to size Fleet up. Eventually, he held out his mighty paw of a hand, palm up. Fleet forfeited his orange.

'Fifteen minutes, sir,' said the receptionist.

Fleet nodded his thanks, and darted through the archway and up the staircase towards the members' lounge.

He entered a room full of luxurious green and brown leather sofas and armchairs, and scanned the scene. He counted twelve people scattered about, with room for twenty more. The smell of whisky and tobacco mixed in the air. Through the murmur

64

of muted conversations and rustling newspapers, Fleet heard a well-dressed gentleman at the bar order a 'Boiler Room', at which the bartender nodded, poured some triple-sec and vermouth into a shaker, and started crushing some coal in a garlic press. Three ruddy-faced men in their fifties were having some sort of competition involving building beer-mat bridges between adjacent tables, and they were tipsily debating whether weighing down the foundational mats by soaking them in spilled sherry, as one of them appeared to have done, was an inspired bit of ingenuity or an outrageously underhanded move that should see their membership revoked.

Fleet walked over to a heavily bewhiskered, older gentleman in a battered three-piece tweed suit – which had probably looked exquisite when he bought it in the 1850s – who was sitting alone by a large window, looking out onto the city.

'Good afternoon. Archibald Fleet. I wonder if I could ask you a few—'

'Nothing like it, is there?' croaked the man.

Fleet looked out at whatever the man might be staring at. As with more or less every view in London, there were thousands of buildings, roads and criss-crossing rail bridges stretching off into the distance. It could have been any number of things that had nothing like it.

In fact, he wondered how the man was able to stare out at the view at all, since the sheer scale of the city tended to send most people dizzy, then slightly unwell, then utterly mentally overwhelmed, and finally onto the floor curled up whimpering in a ball until someone drew the blinds and coaxed the patient back to the here and now with comforting words and a wet flannel to the face.

Fleet only managed it because he had learned not to try and take it all in, but rather to keep his eyes fixed on just one building at a time – ideally one that wasn't too big or too far off. He presumed that the man's glasses were for reading, and when he looked out of a window they protected him from seeing much more than an urban blur.

'Heyford's?' guessed Fleet, referring to a well-known department store that loomed a few streets away. He suspected it was the type of thing an engineer might admire – partly because of its impressive stonework, but also because several of its floors rotated, to disorient shoppers and keep them running into great bargains instead of the exits.

The gentleman chuckled, sending his white whiskers dancing like a field of dandelion tufts.

'Heyford's. The Arkwright Building. Bullockgate. Over that way, Seventeen Dials. Nothing like it.'

Fleet waited for a conclusion to the thought, but none was coming.

'Do you happen to know—'

'All majestic in their own way . . .'

Fleet gave up and sat down.

'Each a triumph of engineering, of imagination over nature,' the gentleman continued. 'Since the Egyptians we've been about this. The Romans, very good indeed: can't knock the Pantheon. Plantagenets knew a thing or two. But not like us. Not like these last few decades. What's this city without engineers, eh?'

'Smaller,' said Fleet.

'Nothing, that's what! Nothing at all. Doesn't make sense, a city without engineers. You'd be living under a lean-to, my good man! And not a sturdy one! Not a good one at all.' The man finally turned to look at Fleet. 'Oh. You're new. Trombley, Percival. Viaduct man, man and boy.'

'Fleet,' said Fleet.

'Let me guess,' said Trombley. 'Bazalgette man?'

'No.'

'No shame in it. Vital work. The sewers are the intestines of the city.'

Fleet grimaced.

'Indeed!' continued Trombley. 'Before Bazalgette, you'd have had a good chance of going out the cholera way, my boy. Important work. Disgusting, important work.'

'I'm not a Bazalgette man. If you'd just let me—'

'University chap, I see it now. Pure theory. Ivory tower, and we all know ivory doesn't have the compressive strength for a tower of more than about fifty feet. I know your sort. All numbers, no lumber. All tricks, no bricks. You want to be out where the action is, my boy. Seeing calculations come to life, breathing life into the city. Never too late to earn an honest trade.'

'I'm a detective.'

'What?'

'My name is Inspector Fleet. I'm a private investigator.'

'An investigator? Of collapses? Well, you'll get nothing out of me, my boy. Every engineer tries his best and I won't be giving you anything to let you claim otherwise.'

'No, it's nothing to do with that. I'm here to ask about a member of this club who has been abducted. Someone named Mellanby.'

A flicker of recognition passed across Trombley's face. 'Mellanby? Oliver Mellanby?'

'Possibly.'

'Corps man, isn't he?'

'What?'

Trombley thought for a moment, before turning round to crane over the back of his armchair towards the bar, while his suit remained more or less facing Fleet.

'Stafford! Stafford!'

A dusty gentleman swivelled in his bar seat.

'Oh, hello, Percy. Didn't see you there.'

'Mellanby, Stafford. Corps fellow, no?'

'Mellanby? Yes, yes. In the Fifteenth. He's a Surveyor-Captain, or Supply-Chain-Corporal or something.'

'That's it, yes. Captain or Corporal. One or the other.'

'One or the other, yes,' said Stafford. 'Doing very well for himself.'

'Doesn't sound like it, Stafford. Sounds like he's one truss failure away from a collapse.'

'Dear!'

'Quite,' agreed Trombley.

'Well then.'

'Yes. Obliged, Stafford.'

'Not at all, Percy,' said Stafford, before turning back round and returning his non-drinking arm to the spot on the bar it had been dusting previously.

Trombley rotated within his layers of tweed to face Fleet once more.

'Corps fellow.'

'I still don't know what that is,' said Fleet.

'Isambard's lot. Everywhere, aren't they? Scurrying about, bashing together a viaduct in sixteen hours whether there's a train line either side or not. Absolute madness.'

'A Brunelian?'

'Well, "Brunel Corps", I believe they prefer. "Brunelian" sounds a bit like they're in a cult or something.'

Trombley chuckled to himself. Fleet mirrored with a smile – the man had become informative, and he needed him on side – but the flippant joke about this organisation made him uneasy. The Brunelians were the worker-followers of Chief Engineer of the Empire Isambard Kingdom Brunel: hundreds of thousands of engineers, masons, joiners, navvies, landscape architects and demolition experts, who were responsible for actually carrying out much of the growth of Even Greater London as it absorbed most of southern England. But the improvement works never stopped, and Fleet, like most residents, would still occasionally see them as they roamed across the city in their tightly organised divisions and autonomous companies, setting up encampments and supply lines, flattening entire neighbourhoods and replacing them with ones facing the other direction, building railway bridges five-high across each other, flooding Cambridgeshire for the hell of it, and generally creating whatever immense structures they felt like, according to some undirected swarm intelligence aiming to interpret the will of Brunel himself, who hadn't been seen for years and was last heard of wearing a laurel wreath and referring to himself as *Brunelus Imperator*. A cult was more or less exactly what they were.

'Do you know where Mr Mellanby lives?' asked Fleet.

'I barely know his first name, my boy – it's not as though I'm often over for supper! You could try Bassettpole, he's the club secretary. He'll have it in a book, I'd have thought.'

'That's perfect.'

'Not in today, mind. Probably off seeing his wink-wink.'

'I . . . his what?'

Trombley scrunched every feature of his face towards his nose, before nodding at Fleet meaningfully.

'Never mind,' said Fleet.

'He'll be in tomorrow evening, for certain. It's the anniversary of the club's founding.'

'Right. Thank you.'

'Ah!' continued Trombley, raising a fleshy finger in triumph. 'You know who you should talk to? Redfield. He's a Corps fellow, man and boy. And looks like he's in.'

Trombley pointed across the room to a man sitting alone at a table, holding a small notebook with a pen clipped to it. He was in his late thirties, with short salt-and-pepper hair and a disciplined posture that surpassed his chair in stiffness, and he was currently in conversation with a waitress in mobcap and apron, who looked remarkably like Clara Entwhistle.

Fleet shook off his surprise as he walked over. He should have known Clara would make it in. Her tenacity had been clear to him since she had first leapt the police roping at a crime scene of his. It was one of the things he admired about her, even if she didn't always check whether there was somewhere to land.

Fleet arrived at the table as the pair were laughing in response to something Redfield had said.

'Sorry to interrupt. Mr Redfield?'

Redfield turned to Fleet, still grinning. 'Yes?'

'And . . .' Fleet checked the name badge pinned to Clara's apron. '. . . Deirdre.'

'It's all right, Fleet,' replied Clara. 'I've entrusted Lance-Corporal Redfield with my identity. The disguise just got me past the staff. I don't think the members mind at all.'

'Not at all,' agreed Redfield.

'I thought you were reading about business,' said Fleet.

'I was,' said Clara, 'but then I got to the part about how some businesses have a uniform to make their staff's dress appear more—'

'Uniform?' asked Fleet.

'Exactly. And then I thought, well, a nice club like this will have that, so I just need to find someone through the service entrance at the back, tap them on the shoulder, and—'

'Clara, please tell me this story doesn't end with a poor waitress lying unconscious somewhere.'

'No, she's fine. In fact I gave her the rest of the afternoon off.'

Redfield laughed. 'Good for Deirdre! She deserves a rest, the poor thing.'

'That's nice for Deirdre,' said Fleet. 'So are you going to work her entire shift, Clara?'

'Umm . . .'

Redfield laughed again.

'Well,' said Clara. 'Lance-Corporal Redfield says he knows Mr Mellanby.'

'Shame what's happened,' said Redfield. 'Seemed a nice enough sort.'

'Well, hopefully he still is,' said Fleet.

'Is what?' asked Redfield.

'A nice enough sort.'

Redfield stared at Fleet. 'Why would he stop being nice?'

'No, I mean, you said "seemed",' said Fleet. 'Like he might be dead.'

'He might be *dead*?'

'That's not what I meant.'

'Good God.'

'Fleet!' added Clara.

'I don't think he's dead!' said Fleet. Then, after a pause: 'I mean, he could be, these things happen.'

'A bit blasé, aren't you, man?' snapped Redfield. 'This is a Lieutenant-Supply-Captain we're talking about.'

'In the Fifteenth something?' asked Fleet, trying to steer back on track.

'Fifteenth Division, yes,' Redfield continued, keeping an eye on Fleet while turning his attention back to Clara. 'Some good work up at Nuneaton. Rotated and widened a Norman church to make room for a new rail line to Warwick. Goes right up the aisle now. Fine most of the time as the building's often empty but, my word, weddings have to be timed extremely carefully.'

'Lance-Corporal,' said Clara, 'we would like to speak to anyone who worked closely with Mr Mellanby. Where can we find the Fifteenth?'

'Haven't run into them in a while. I'm in the Eighth, myself.' Redfield tapped his lapel pin, a small brass shield with 'IKB 8' in embossed lettering. 'Trouble with our divisions is we roam where we please. I mean, that's the advantage as well. Means we can really go wherever is the greatest need. New bridge needed this week in Farnborough? Not a problem. But by the time you work out where a division is, it's often gone.'

Fleet shook his head in disbelief at how anything ever got done in this city.

'But if you really need to talk to some other Fifteenthers,' continued Redfield, 'I will make some enquiries at camp tomorrow morning. Give me your card.'

Clara took a small steel case out from somewhere under her apron and handed Redfield a card with the details of Fleet-Entwhistle Private Investigations on it. He placed it carefully into a card container of his own, before nodding at the investigators and returning to his notebook.

Clearly delighted at their progress, Clara told Fleet that she would stay and work Deirdre's shift – partly because she was having a marvellous time, but primarily because to do otherwise might cost Deirdre her job. She went off and began cheerfully taking drinks orders from the various tables, before attempting to convince the bartender – who tried to explain that it wasn't within his power – that they really ought to stock a wider array of newspapers, including, for example, the *Morning Chronicler*.

Fleet was retrieved by the receptionist exactly fifteen minutes after their previous conversation, and stepped out onto the street. He felt the familiar satisfaction that accompanied forward movement in an investigation, together with the unease of now having to wait to progress further.

He pulled his coat shut as a convoy of omnibuses floated past at great speed, carrying with them a localised gale that whipped a young man's hat thirty feet into the air and onto the eaves of the building opposite, where it was immediately set upon by pigeons. Fleet nodded sympathetically at the dumbstruck man, and walked off into the immeasurable city.

The following morning, the London sun decided – as it often did – that it couldn't really be bothered with the whole 'dawn' thing, and instead cast across the city its favourite grey: the one that meant you needed a clock to know whether it was day or night. A vague drizzle hung in the air, a weightless moisture trap which everyone had no choice but to plough through and get slightly damp, but not nearly damp enough to be worth mentioning or doing anything about.

Fleet, like countless others, was walking through this to his place of work, the levitating rain helping to refresh his mind after another night of poor rest.

He was turning over in his head the facts of the case, as he had been since leaving the club. A man puts an advertisement in the paper to win back this Alexandrina. What had he done to her? Did he have no other way to contact her? Was she behind the kidnapping, fed up with his embarrassingly public pleading, hiring someone to throw him in a cab and give him a quite deserved talking-to? And if not, what else could he have got himself mixed up in?

And running through these thoughts, a parallel strand: what if he could not be found? Fleet knew from his years as a detective that most missing persons are missing for good; the city was simply too big to always find people who wish – or whom others wish – never to be found. Alice, he had to assume, was out there somewhere. His first missing person case, just as missing now as when he had been assigned. He calculated. She must be fourteen by now. Or else the same age, now and forever, as when she vanished.

He remembered Sutter, a bull of a detective he had learned the trade from, finding Fleet in the Yard after midnight, staring at some documents he knew led nowhere. Sutter would have had his own Alice. They all did: the job is walking through little hooks, and sometimes they catch hold. Fleet heard Sutter walk over and pause behind his chair. Nobody knows how to remove the hooks, of course; you just remember other people have them too. Sutter didn't say a word – he just clapped a giant, sympathetic hand on Fleet's shoulder.

The impact brought Fleet back to the here and now. He regained his balance and turned to see a man barging past wearing a coat that would have protected him from an avalanche. Fleet realised he had been standing still in the middle of the pavement. He resumed his walk, and cast his attention outwards to the countless details of his surroundings.

After a while, Fleet noticed a carriage following him, matching his speed. This was, in Fleet's experience, never anything good. If people wanted you, they could just call you. A carriage suggested a matter sufficiently criminal that it couldn't be mentioned on the telephone, or, perhaps even more straightforwardly, that you were about to be kidnapped yourself.

Taking a mental note of nearby ginnels into back streets, and shops into which he could dash if the situation turned nasty, Fleet stopped to face the carriage. The carriage stopped as well, and Fleet could see now that it was almost certainly the most exquisite vehicle he had ever encountered. Generally speaking, if they're in any way good at their job, criminals try to blend in. And this carriage – with its wooden panels painted a brilliant red, its ironwork a mixture of polished black and silver, and its driver dressed as if he were receiving a knighthood, or possibly bestowing one – was something close to the opposite of blending in.

Fleet was trying to work out whether this made his situation worse, better, or just more confusing, when he noticed a

74

familiar face grinning at him through the dark window: Clara Entwhistle, looking like the cat that had not only got the cream, but had divided it up into small cartons, sold it on to other, less entrepreneurial cats, and used the profits to buy its own dairy.

Clara waved, beaming, before raising a thumb and beckoning Fleet into the carriage, which he could now see contained two more people. He pulled open the door and hauled himself up.

Next to Clara there was a man in his fifties: slight, with neat, thinning hair, wearing small, round spectacles, and dressed in the finest suit Fleet had ever seen. He could conceivably, Fleet thought, have been the owner of the carriage. Opposite them, a statuesque woman in her thirties was sitting alone, wearing a simple, dark-green dress that did not immediately scream wealth – and a silver necklace, embedded with an emerald the size of a kitten's head, which did. She could, conceivably, have been the owner of every carriage in the city.

'Inspector Fleet?' asked the gentleman.

'Yes,' Fleet replied from the doorway. 'Who are you?'

'Of Honiton Street?'

'Yes. Who are you?'

'Formerly of Scotland Yard?'

'On accidental sabbatical from Scotland Yard, yes. I'm a Sagittarius as well if that helps move this along.'

Clara widened her eyes with interest and quickly jotted something in her notebook.

'Sorry, who are you people?' asked Fleet.

The man seemed satisfied that this was who they had meant to pick up, and turned to his employer. Clearly she had a preference to introduce herself.

'My name is Amandine,' said the woman, with the Paris-by-way-of-Zurich accent of international schooling and unimaginable European wealth. 'This is Cosgrove.'

Cosgrove nodded at Fleet and Clara; he was indeed Cosgrove.

'Then we are all met,' continued Amandine. 'Bon. Let us be underway.'

'Hold on a minute,' Fleet protested.

'Do take a seat, Inspector,' said Cosgrove. 'The matter is rather pressing.'

Fleet looked at Clara, who was still smiling happily. It was not clear whether she knew more about what was going on, or was just excited about the prospect of being involved in a pressing matter.

Fleet sighed, and moved into the carriage. As he did, Cosgrove shuffled towards Clara, leaving on his other side a space theoretically large enough for a third person. Fleet looked over at Amandine, who watched impassively, flanked by several feet of empty seat. He shut the door behind him – which closed with the most pleasingly sonorous 'thunk' he had ever heard a carriage door make – clambered through the cabin, and squeezed in next to Cosgrove.

Cosgrove rapped his knuckles twice on the painted teak ceiling, triggering a 'H'yup!' command from the driver, and the carriage began trundling forwards.

'I understand from Cosgrove that you are investigators,' said Amandine.

'I obtained your business card from a counter at a local eatery,' said Cosgrove. 'I might not have noticed, but someone had written on it the words "Pick me up" – the boldness of which rather piqued my curiosity.'

Fleet glanced at Clara. She grinned back, eyes wild with pride, before tapping her bag and mouthing the word 'Posner'.

'We are investigators, yes,' Fleet replied to Amandine, before adding, slightly pained: 'But you understand that we're not the police?'

Amandine leaned forwards and fixed her eyes on Fleet.

'That, Inspector, is exactly why we are speaking.'

Fleet furrowed his brow. The clatter of carriage wheels on cobbles filled the silence.

'I have been the victim of an unusual crime, you see,' continued Amandine. 'This very night.'

'What kind of crime?' asked Fleet.

'A burglary.'

'A burglary at a bank, Fleet!' fizzed Clara, before explaining: 'Mr Cosgrove has already filled me in on some of the details.'

'The lady was rather unable to wait until we were all gathered,' Cosgrove confirmed.

'We were otherwise sitting in silence, Mr Cosgrove,' replied Clara. 'That's no way to begin a morning.'

Fleet could hear the ticking again, as if a metronome was keeping time in his chest.

'You're a banker?' he asked Amandine.

'I have bankers in my employment, Inspector. I have a bank.'

'Which bank?'

'La Banque Chalon.'

Fleet sat back. Chalon was a private bank for the elite. A place for great families to lock away their secrets without being troubled by any impertinent questions – questions such as where those secrets were acquired, whose blood it was on them, and, in particular, who the person opening the account even was. He glanced at Clara, who nodded excitedly.

'You are a Chalon?' he asked.

'I am Madame Amandine Chalon. The founder, Argentine, was my grandfather.'

'Which is why you're asking us. Unofficial. Low profile.'

Amandine nodded. 'The matter is delicate. The police, generally speaking, are not. And as they have not had any success with the other break-ins, I thought a change of approach might be in order. Unless you are not interested?'

'We are interested,' said Clara. 'Aren't we, Fleet?'

Fleet tended to believe that the only thing fate ever drops in your lap is soup. But his eye was caught by a newspaper blowing past the carriage window, and he was taken to a memory, a firm handshake of approval from Detective Chief Inspector Keller, before realising that that event had never taken place. The metronome was increasing its tempo, the pendulum weight shaking itself lower and lower on the rod.

'Yes,' he said.

'Delightful,' said Amandine. 'Everything is as Cosgrove found it at six o'clock this morning. We will be there before long. You can take a look around.'

'What's been stolen?' asked Fleet.

'It would appear that nothing has been stolen.'

Clara scribbled furiously in her notebook. 'And was there any damage?'

'Not that we can see.'

'I hate to ask this, Madame Chalon,' began Fleet, 'but if nothing is missing, and nothing is damaged, why do you think you've been burgled?'

'Because the thief is still in the vault, Inspector.'

'Ah,' agreed Fleet.

'But there is only so much air in there. It is sealed, you see. And so before long he will not even be a thief; he will just be a thief's body.'

'Good God!' said Clara.

'I think his position will rather help your interrogation,' Amandine added cheerfully. 'He has about an hour.'

Cosgrove checked his pocket watch and nodded solemnly. 'I did say it was rather pressing.'

Chapter 5

Clara spent the journey to the bank looking out of the carriage window, drinking in the features of this city that was still so new to her.

The carriage moved quickly, keeping to wide roads where it could overtake other traffic – perhaps the driver understood the urgency, or perhaps Amandine was never kept waiting.

Clara watched the neighbourhoods flash by. Fulworth, a wealthy commuter area, with its authentic Parisian-style apartment buildings and even more authentic Paris-stolen lampposts. Doghill Market, all fabric-roofed side streets crammed with bric-a-brac stalls and the scent of fried meat, the din of vendors haggling with regulars and making a week's wage letting people wandering over from Fulworth think they'd driven a hard bargain. Broughborough, a small neighbourhood with no residents or businesses, just a single street of facades with no buildings behind them, which locals strongly suspected had been created to root out foreign spies by having a name that was unpronounceable by almost all peoples everywhere.

After Broughborough, they climbed a hill and crossed a bridge, giving Clara a clear view across the city. She tried to orient herself by finding something familiar among the endless blanket of cityscape. She saw a battle airship circling above an enormous, grand building with a perimeter of black defensive towers spearing out of the ground.

Buckingham Palace . . .

Clara shuddered. It wasn't at all like the postcards. The postcards just said 'Image Forbidden'.

She continued scanning for sights she recognised, but the scale of the vista very quickly made her feel nauseous and overwhelmed, and she had to sit back in her seat and look away from the window.

She kept forgetting about that, even though numerous concerned citizens, on numerous occasions, had warned her that looking out of windows with good vantage points should be avoided at all costs. Even if it was very, *very* interesting.

The other passengers all had a hand up to blinker themselves from the view outside. Amandine regarded Clara with concerned curiosity, as if she'd caught a child staring at the sun. Cosgrove kept checking his pocket watch and nodding, presumably having decided that their speed was acceptable. Fleet was pretending to review a notebook – which Clara knew to be empty – and surreptitiously looking over their companions. Perhaps he was deciding how much to trust them. Or perhaps he was deciding what he would do with these people if they arrived to find the thief asphyxiated.

Clara felt a London vista migraine coming on and closed her eyes. She let herself drift away into the motion of the carriage, and listened to the wheels rattling out their four-and-a-half-beat rhythm:

Alexandrina, Alexandrina, Alexandrina . . .

'Not now, wheels,' thought Clara. 'That's the other case.'

The carriage stopped, the driver opened the door and the passengers stepped out onto the pavement.

Clara recognised the neighbourhood. Quiet as a sound-proofed grave. Clean as a whistle that had never been used. No vehicles, save for a line of private carriages waiting for their owners to return. Elegant commercial townhouses running along both sides of the street, with no storefronts or window displays, only painted doors with tiny brass plaques.

It was an utterly desolate place, and it really didn't seem that there was any reason at all for anyone to be there, which was, of course, the point.

Clara saw the polished street sign — Newnes Row — but even she had been in London long enough to know it by its nickname: Little Luxembourg.

The establishments weren't very keen on this. Clara's editor, Augusta, had once told her about a letter she'd received from a legal firm demanding that her paper stop using the nickname — to which Augusta wrote a courteous reply reflecting on their demands, the principle of a free press, and the vibrant culture of Luxembourg, before having her letter boiled into a hot, beany *Bouneschlupp* and poured through the lawyers' letterbox.

Amandine and Cosgrove were already up the steps in front of one of the buildings, and someone from within opened the dark green, handleless door as they approached.

'We could open a business account while we're here, Fleet,' Clara said through a grin. 'We probably only need a hundred thousand pounds. And that we can probably find in the vault.'

She looked at her colleague. He was staring wearily back at her. How could someone have so little humour this early in the morning? Didn't he sleep?

'Let's rescue this thief from certain death,' Fleet muttered, 'and then see how we are for time.'

The atrium of La Banque Chalon welcomed Fleet and Clara as little as a room possibly could, outside, perhaps, of Ealing's well-loved Museum of Exit Signs.

Dark marble columns stood in formation across the hall. Clerks behind desks, having smiled cheerily at Amandine and Cosgrove, let their faces fall into suspicious scowls as they watched these visitors – who clearly were not clients – walk past. On the wall, an immense oil painting of the bank's founder, Argentine Chalon, watched over everything. Beneath it was a gold plaque inscribed with the five words that were Monsieur Chalon's credo, the secret of his success and his bank's guiding philosophy:

We Don't Want To Know.

Cosgrove and Amandine stopped at the end of the room by two doors and turned to the investigators.

'This is where I must leave you,' said Amandine. 'I have other plates to spin.'

'Other than the man in your vault who's robbed you and who'll be dying any minute?' asked Fleet.

'Bien sûr. Many, many plates.'

Amandine opened one of the doors, revealing a small lift and, in it, a man-shaped heap of metal gears, leather flaps and marble, which was dressed like a lift attendant and bolted to the wall. In a masterstroke of ghastliness, its head and limbs seemed to have been harvested from Greek statues, which Clara imagined was intended to seem luxurious, but instead it looked to her like some ancient hero who been cursed by the gods to operate this lift forever – possibly as a punishment for some mortal no-no like cheating death, but more likely just from the bad luck of trying to cook a pheasant or something and discovering it was Zeus on holiday.

There was also a faint groan coming from somewhere nearby, which Clara quickly realised was Fleet. She gave him a slight elbow in the ribs, which prompted him to turn to her with a horrified expression frozen on his face.

'Mon bureau, Simon,' said Amandine as she stepped inside.

'D'accord, Madame,' the thing replied, before extending the marble arrow it seemed to have instead of a hand, and jabbing it into the lift's only button.

Amandine smiled at the investigators as the door began to close.

'A pleasure to meet you both. We never met.'

The second lift came to a halt one floor beneath the atrium, and the lit-up button labelled 'Vault' extinguished itself to confirm that Fleet, Clara and Cosgrove had arrived.

This lift was mercifully empty of automatons, but it was also unmercifully small, so the three had ended up squished together in single file, with Fleet at the centre, wincing at everything.

When the door opened, they burst out into a short hallway. Cosgrove smoothed out his suit jacket and walked on, and Fleet and Clara followed, as small portraits of various members of La Famille Chalon glowered at them from the walls.

At the end of the corridor, the wall was entirely steel, much of it taken up by a round vault door. Cosgrove headed to its side, where there was a control area of some kind.

At the top of this, Fleet saw a square glass panel the size of a bathroom mirror, inside which a metallic liquid slowly glooped, forming a very rough image of a small room.

A locution glass? thought Fleet. *Pricey enough just for calls. God knows how often they would have to repair it if they keep it on all the time.*

He squinted at the vague shapes in the panel. The room was empty but for a figure sitting curled in a corner with his arms around his knees.

Cosgrove shook his head scornfully at the person in the image, before turning to the other parts of the control area.

He tapped a dozen numbered buttons, spun some combination wheels, inserted a card from his pocket into a slot, and finally flicked open a flap to reveal a hole in the metal roughly the size of a man's head, which he immediately filled with something exactly the size of a man's head.

'My word!' said Clara.

'Mmhmhph,' replied Cosgrove, jiggling his shoulders.

'Um, do you need help?'

'Nnnggg.'

She stepped closer. 'Is that a "no"?'

'It's an "nnnggg",' said Fleet. 'I say we leave him to it.'

After a few moments of struggling, the Headless Cosgrove stopped moving. A lightbulb lit up on the control panel, and the door played a tinny recording of the first four bars of the Ode to Joy.

'Oh good,' said Fleet. 'He won.'

Cosgrove pulled himself out of the headhole and flattened his hair.

'Cranial security. The very latest.'

'It only opens to your skull?' asked Clara.

'Mine or Madame Chalon's. Everyone else's it ignores, unless you have a particularly deviant skull shape, in which case you get clamped there.' Cosgrove pushed a button and the heavy door began to swing open. 'Keys can be stolen and combinations can be learned. But you can't take someone's head.'

'You absolutely can,' said Fleet.

'True,' replied Cosgrove, 'but then that person's problems are over.'

The three stepped out of the way of the swinging door. Inside, a scrawny man with the look of a petrified rabbit jumped up from the floor and grabbed the bars of the vault's inner door.

'Oh!' the man cried. 'It *is* someone! Thanks be to God! I thought I was going to die in here!'

'Calm down,' ordered Cosgrove.

'Sorry, sorry.' The man stepped back from the bars. 'It's just so hot in here. But I suppose I would have been all right until I needed water.'

Fleet looked around at the total absence of ventilation in the vault.

'No, the air would have run out in about four minutes,' said Cosgrove, matter-of-factly, eliciting a frightened '*Eep!*' from the man behind the bars.

'We would have been quicker but Inspector Fleet here' – he waved a hand in Fleet's general direction while continuing to glower at the miscreant – 'insisted on asking questions before coming along.'

'In my defence,' said Fleet, 'I didn't know you were about to die.'

'Neither did I!' squeaked the man. 'Can you get me out of here, please?'

Cosgrove shot his head back like a startled hen.

'"Get you out"? Perhaps you will answer our questions, you pond life, and I won't shut you in there for good!'

'Eep!'

'No,' Fleet said firmly. 'He's not going to do that . . .'

'I might!'

'. . . Because that, Mr Cosgrove, would be murder.'

'Not undeserved! You would rob *Madame Chalon*?'

The man looked bemused. 'Who?'

Cosgrove dropped his jaw in astonishment.

'"*Who*"? Only the finest young banking magnate this city has ever known, you snivelling little p—'

'Mr Cosgrove,' Clara swiftly interjected, 'would you like to take a seat and let me and Inspector Fleet handle the

85

questioning? I think you might be a little close to the matter.'

Cosgrove paused, then set himself down from his tiptoes. He was shocked to notice his own balled fists, and seemed to disappear into himself, despairing at his loss of self-control.

'Perhaps you are right,' he said, quietly.

He wandered over to a chair by the wall, and sat down without unbuttoning his suit jacket, causing it to spread out in fat curves around his midriff. He stared at his splaying buttons, apparently settling in for some hard thinking about his momentary Cosgrovelessness.

Fleet had ignored all of this, instead scanning the man and his surroundings.

The vault seemed to be a studied compromise between the functional and the ornate. Steel walls, largely covered in a grid of safe-deposit boxes. A steel floor, with the same dark stone columns as in the atrium upstairs rising from the corners. And a steel ceiling, painted with a Renaissance-style fresco of a man in a white robe and a group of merchants and money-changers in a temple, all enjoying each other's company and generally having a lovely time.

As for the imprisoned man, he was presentably dressed, working class. Far too old to work for a burglary gang, thought Fleet, not that they would be able to get in here anyway. And he clearly couldn't have talked his way in – they would have sent him away with the day's rubbish. But someone must have opened this door and the cage. There was no other way into the room, not even a small hole to crawl through. Nothing for it but to hear his story.

'Who are you?' asked Fleet.

'Tom Hodges, sir.'

'What are you doing in this vault, Tom Hodges?'

'I don't know.'

'Careless to forget the plan halfway through a heist.'

86

'I don't know a plan! I don't even know where I am. A bank, it looks like?'

Fleet looked into the man's eyes. He seemed genuinely confused and afraid.

'What do you do, Mr Hodges?'

'I'm a porter at St Barnaby's.'

A hospital in Doghill, thought Fleet. *Not far.*

He began pacing in front of the bars.

'You know,' Tom continued, 'moving what needs moving, helping people in their wheelchairs get along. Long corridors.'

'How did you get here?' asked Fleet.

Tom's shoulders slumped. 'I don't know. I was in a caff on Long Lane, having my breakfast.'

'When was this?'

'Last night, maybe eight.'

'You work nights?'

'Some nights, some days. Depends. I don't know whether I'm coming or going sometimes, hard to keep track. But Mav's – that's the caff – they'll do me two eggs on toast any hour, bless them. They keep saying I should try them poached, but I don't know. That's a bit new. I've got enough going on.'

Fleet paused and scratched his ear. He was quite sure now this wasn't an act.

Clara, who had been furiously scribbling down notes, suddenly jumped in.

'What's the last thing you remember, Mr Hodges?'

Tom chewed his lower lip as he thought.

'Oh no!' he cried. 'I didn't pay!'

Clara flinched in horror, nearly dropping her notebook.

'That's the last thing you remember?' asked Fleet. 'Something that didn't happen?'

'No, no, it's just . . . I just realised I never book.'

Fleet stepped forward. 'Did you *leave* without paying?'

Tom thought hard again.

'I don't remember. I don't remember paying, but I don't remember leaving either. I remember my coffee. It was awful. Just . . . strong, ashy.' He looked forlornly at Clara. 'That's the last thing I remember.'

There was nothing further that Tom Hodges knew of his situation. Fleet took his address in case they needed to speak again, before appealing to Cosgrove that this was almost certainly an innocent man.

Cosgrove – who by now had regained his composure – was hesitant to let a possible nemesis of his employer go free, even if he did appear to be quite a discombobulated nemesis, so Clara suggested verifying his employment with St Barnaby's. Cosgrove did so, using a telephone speaker on the vault control panel, and the hospital was happy to report that Tom Hodges was not only a porter of theirs, but also a key member of the St Barnaby's Facilities Department Male Voice Choir – a detail that Tom eagerly offered to prove before Fleet demanded that he did not.

With this aspect of his story confirmed, Cosgrove was finally satisfied, and agreed to free Tom from the vault cell, which he did with a key he pulled from his inside pocket.

Using an intercom, he summoned a clerk downstairs to escort Tom back up in the lift and order him a hansom cab to wherever he wanted to go.

He also wrote Tom a cheque, for an amount of money Fleet and Clara could not see, and expressed his sincere hope that his rash words would not leave him with any ill feelings towards La Banque Chalon. Tom glanced at the cheque, coughed like he'd been punched in the gut, and agreed that this would do fine.

After he had gone, Fleet, Clara and Cosgrove stepped into the vault that had nearly been the porter's tomb.

Fleet surveyed the room again and scanned the inside wall around the door that had been hidden from view before.

Nothing.

'Mr Cosgrove,' began Clara, inspecting a row of safe-deposit boxes, 'if you haven't yet been in here, how did you know nothing was taken?'

The question filled Cosgrove with so much pride in his employer's security systems that he appeared to gain an inch of height.

'Each door is part of a circuit. If the door is unlocked, the circuit is broken. If the circuit is broken, there would be a bulb illuminated in a control room upstairs. And no bulbs were lit when I checked this morning. So every box remains locked.'

'They broke into an impenetrable vault,' said Clara, continuing to scan the grid of boxes. 'Don't you think they could circumvent that system?'

'Impossible,' said Cosgrove.

'Could they have just switched it off?' asked Fleet.

A flutter of alarm crossed Cosgrove's face. 'No, because you see . . . because even if they had, the locks, they're Trilling locks. Unpickable. No one could ever—'

'Someone has had a good go at these though,' said Clara, pointing to two safe-deposit boxes close together.

Cosgrove adjusted his glasses and looked over to where Clara was pointing. Two of the tiny doors did indeed bear deep scratches and marks on and around the keyhole.

'Oh my . . .'

He went to take a closer look.

'One-four-one and One-four-nine.'

Cosgrove shrank slightly in trepidation, and took a deep breath. Clearly he felt his life's work was hanging in the balance. He pulled at the handles of boxes 141 and 149 in turn, but the locks held fast. He breathed a sigh of relief.

'Well, thank God for Trilling!'

'That doesn't prove anything,' said Clara. 'They could have relocked them.'

'Not Trilling locks,' said Fleet, walking over and inspecting the boxes. 'They have a fail-safe, so even if they were ever picked, they wouldn't be lockable again.'

'Exactly,' said Cosgrove, whose professional pride had once again reinflated him to his full size.

'Can you at least tell us what's in the boxes?' asked Clara.

'I would never violate our clients' trust in such a way! But also I have no idea.'

'Well,' said Fleet, 'another case wrapped up.'

'But it isn't remotely wrapped up, Fleet!' said Clara.

'No, of course, I was—'

'There's the question of how the thieves got in here, what they were after, and why they drugged poor Tom Hodges!'

Cosgrove nodded. 'This is all very true, but as our clients' property is safe, and I can do a thorough security review with the appropriate professionals, I think it is time for us to leave and I can go to provide Madame Chalon with the update she will be expecting.'

Fleet and Clara took one last look around the vault, and left with Cosgrove. Upstairs in the atrium, he thanked them, wrote them a cheque for their services, and escorted them politely but unavoidably towards the exit. Outside, they once again found themselves in the deserted streets of Little Luxembourg.

The pair stood in silence for a few moments, ruminating on what they'd seen and heard. Fleet turned over in his mind the two safe-deposit boxes, and the scratches around their locks.

The deep, clumsy scratches.

'Clara,' he said.

'Yes?'

'Are you thinking what I'm thinking?'

'Oh!' Clara chirped. 'I don't know. Give me three guesses.'

'No. But listen.'

'All right.'

'What do the numbers one hundred and forty-one and one hundred and forty-nine mean to you?'

Clara thought for a moment.

'They're both odd. A hundred and forty-nine is prime. But otherwise, nothing. Why? What are you thinking?'

Fleet looked back at the row of terraced buildings, the dozens of other businesses surrounding La Banque Chalon, each with their own tiny plaque and their own immense secrets.

'I'm thinking those aren't the only numbers.'

Chapter 6

Detective Chief Inspector Keller was sitting at the large oak desk that was his usual combat vehicle, in the Scotland Yard office that had been – in the many years since his promotion to that most senior investigative rank – both his field of battle and his barbarically stifling prison.

Such men are not meant for desks. Perhaps no men are.

But for men such as Alwyn Keller, the sinews twitch against chair-bound inactivity, the muscles howl in protest at being asked to lift only a pen, and the memories of earlier physical trials colour the present day as a sluggish torment – a punishment for being born in a different time, and surviving long enough to meet a new one.

If it were up to Keller, there would be no desks at all. For what is a desk other than a place to handle documents? And what is a document if not a conversation avoided by a coward?

Not that he was glad to be having his current conversation. He closed his eyes and rubbed his temples with his free hand. It wasn't doing any good. He still regretted answering the telephone. One day, the law of averages would deliver him someone with good news. Surely.

'*How*, Hinton?' he growled. 'Exactly *how* did the suspect evade you?'

The timid voice on the other end of the line managed three words before being cut off.

'No, Hinton. I didn't ask where you are now . . .'

Why are they all like this? Is being a detective really the most danger they've ever experienced?

'Yes, I'm sure it is frightening. You are easily frightened. And for good reason given your likely death at the hands of most foes.'

Don't people learn how to survive any more? Have these men never come face to claw with the wilderness and been forced to discover within themselves their dormant, terrifying, primal power? Not even by the age of twelve?

'Yes, it is fortunate all he did was lock you in his bathroom, and indeed *remarkably* fortunate that he keeps a telephone by the tub . . . Presumably for relaxing scrub-time chats with friends, Hinton, I have no idea . . . Yes your situation *was* avoidable, because you could have handcuffed him *to* something before using the facilities . . . I don't know, Hinton, I wasn't there. A radiator? A doorknob? *Yourself?* . . . No, Hinton, I'd have to say that what would be awkward would be to lose a suspect entirely, become incarcerated by them, and then telephone your Detective Chief Inspector and force him to decipher your pleas for assistance through the sound of barely concealed sobbing.'

The voice sniffed loudly, and composed itself by breathing deeply into a flannel. Keller stared longingly at the blunderbuss mounted above his office door.

No, Alwyn. That's not how we teach laggards.

'Hinton, listen to me. Is there a window?'

The voice sobbed in the affirmative, before starting to protest.

'Have you thought about whether that might be an exit route?'

The voice squealed in despair about the distance to the ground.

'*Improvise*, Hinton! Is there a drainpipe in reach? Is there a soft-topped carriage below? Is there a butcher's wagon with a sufficient display of meat? . . . *I don't know if that's sufficient*, Hinton, I'm not there! Obviously you'll accelerate towards the earth at thirty-two feet per second per second, so for each half-second you'll need at least an extra few dozen hanger steaks or two-thirds sirloin equivalent . . . Yes . . . No . . . I don't know . . . Well, good luck, Hinton. See you back here, perhaps.'

Keller hung up the telephone and sank his face into his powerful fingers.

Just a minute of peace, Lord. Even hiding in the trees in Borneo you could—

Two swift raps on wood shattered the silence, and the door flew open, revealing a young woman wearing a neatly tailored brown check dress. She walked swiftly towards Keller's desk and deposited an armful of folders.

'Case reports, Chief Inspector. Just forty-eight today.'

Keller gripped the edge of his desk and squeezed. The wood had yielded to this over the years and visitors could clearly see two groups of four finger-length indentations on his side of the desk, radiating out towards them like a crudely chiselled diagram of artillery fire.

He surveyed the pile of reports with contempt. Part of him accepted that he was responsible for all detective policing across the sprawling capital, and that the sheer number of his detectives and the volume of their work demanded that matters be summarised into reports, tables, targets and so on.

But another, deeper part of him viewed the entire enterprise as an affront to the natural truth of who we all are as vital, living animals.

We were never meant to *review*, to *sign off*, to *provide useful feedback and a positive, growth-oriented workplace*.

We were meant to survive.

Keller had been forged in a different world, moulded by the type of far-flung horrors that penny-press authors, not knowing the first thing about it, glamorised as *Adventure*. By which the authors meant rope bridges and high jinks, while the people who were there knew it meant death.

Keller had known death, of course. He had seen it. Heard it. Been within a neatly barbered whisker of it.

He knew it was no ominous wraith, keeping to a distance and politely floating into view whenever It Is Time, like a maître d' informing you that your table is ready, or a butler that your bath is drawn.

No. Death was a wolf, starving, staring back and forth between you and your foe as you figure out who will survive and who will be its meal.

Sometimes, yes, as a younger man, he had been forced to summon the wolf himself. Nothing to be proud of, but when the choice is between you and a Frenchman pinning you to the forest floor at the end of a bayonet, there's nothing ungentlemanly about a swift ankle-kick-and-rising-charge, sending him into the ravine to which he really should have been paying more attention. Nothing ungentlemanly at all.

But in time, as people do, he returned to the country of his birth and started a life in Even Greater London, the gaping Leviathan's maw into which the krill of opportunities were increasingly slurped.

By this point, there was a new kind of job that hadn't existed before. A new type of police. *Detective* police.

These were no longer the halcyon days of village life, where suspicion as to who had stolen the prize cockerel would naturally turn to, say, whoever had arrived in the village last, or perhaps the person whose bulging coat seemed to be concealing the most panicked clucking.

No, nowadays things were much more complex. People had come to accept that in a city as vast as London there were things beyond their immediate reckoning, that matters were often confusing and required investigation, and that sometimes an upstanding gentleman of good character might nevertheless be a bigamist, a forger, or, more often than you'd think, a melter-of-a-rival-heir-into-a-bathtub-of-sulphuric-acid.

Character and reputation were no longer accepted guides to guilt, so an entire profession was needed to solve the problem of solving crimes. One which demanded a certain authority and confidence. Working-class men tasked with subjecting lords and ladies to questions as to their criminality – with *accusing* their social betters. It took a certain sort of gumption, and if there was one thing Keller had – along with the memory of the horrified faces of quite a few plummeting Frenchmen – it was gumption.

So, he joined their ranks and eventually became their Detective Chief Inspector. They weren't always forged in fire any more – Hinton was a case in point – but it was nevertheless Keller's duty, his honour, to lead these detectives and serve the people. To be a bulwark against the forces of criminality. To lend, from his paperwork fortress, some sort of order to this rampant knotweed of a city, even if it meant no peace for him.

'Thank you, Miss Waverley. That will be all.'

He closed his eyes and savoured a moment of calm, as if sitting by a still lake. No one asking questions. No one demanding signatures. Just existing.

He felt a weight of unease, as if the quiet had betrayed him, and opened his eyes to see that the young woman had not left.

'*Will* that be all?'

'I'm afraid not, Chief Inspector.'

'I see. And what else is there?'

Miss Waverley shuffled slightly.

'Inspector Fleet is here to see you.'

Keller grimaced in dismay.

How could she do this? How could someone so unfailingly competent fail to respect this one straightforward command?

'*Inspector Fleet?* I don't believe there is anyone by that name and title, Miss Waverley.'

'I can actually hear you, Chief Inspector,' came a voice from just outside the doorway.

'Be quiet, Fleet,' Keller barked. 'This doesn't concern you.'

'It doesn't harm anyone,' said Fleet. 'I don't see the prob—'

'*Quiet!*'

Miss Waverley snapped her fingers in realisation. 'Ah. Yes. *Mr* Fleet is here to see you.'

'Oh, *Mr Fleet!*' Keller gave a single deafening clap, as he imagined a genuinely delighted person might. 'Of course! Our esteemed Scotland Yard alumnus, my good friend and confidant, the redoubtable and dependable Mr Fleet, trained for years at the expense of Her Bionic Majesty's police force and now working as some sort of investigatory mercenary for whoever has the sobs and the cash. I'd love nothing more than a visit from Mr Fleet.'

'So I can come in?' asked Fleet, leaning into the doorway.

'Well, all I have are forty-eight reports to review, a phone call with the Home Secretary in nine minutes, and a detective who might or might not have survived a swan dive into the flesh of one or more cows, so obviously I have time for a cup of tea and a biscuit with Mr Fleet.'

'Would you like me to send in tea and biscuits, Chief Inspector?' asked Miss Waverley.

'Yes, but only one of each.'

Miss Waverley paced out of the office, and Fleet gingerly stepped in and folded himself into one of the excruciatingly

97

acute-angled chairs opposite the desk, which Keller used to ensure visitors knew that outstaying their welcome came with the risk of thrombotic damage.

The Chief Inspector picked up the stack of folders and banged their edges into line in an ear-splitting smash on the desk.

'How's business, Fleet?'

'It's fine, thank you, sir.'

Keller frowned.

'Hair is fine, Fleet. Weather is fine. Circumstances are detailed.'

'Sorry, I thought . . .' replied Fleet, wriggling his body into a less agonising position. 'Business is improving. We have two serious cases open at the moment.'

'Very good. And where is Miss Entwhistle?'

'Outside speaking to Miss Waverley. There's a contact we believe we are likely to need.'

'Well, glad we can be of service to you both,' said Keller, his eyes boring into his former subordinate's head. 'We are, after all, the telephone directory.'

'It's just because we were already here . . .'

'If these crimes are serious, why didn't the people come to the police?'

'One did,' replied Fleet. 'A kidnapping – but it sounds as though the case has stalled.'

'Very possible. You try finding someone in this city.'

'I am doing, sir.'

'Right.'

Fleet took a breath and pressed on. 'And the other was a suspected burglary, but with nothing stolen.'

'A burglary with no losses, Fleet? You weren't joking about those serious cases.'

'This is the case I was hoping you could help with. It's more what the culprits seem to have left behind. And where it was.'

Keller sensed a bush going undisturbed by a nearby beating, and narrowed his eyes in preparation for whatever unpleasantness awaited him.

'*Yes?*'

Fleet squirmed slightly.

'It was a bank, sir.'

Keller paused, and looked down at his diary, which showed, every day, a one-hour meeting with a team of his detectives on their progress, or inevitable lack thereof, on the many, unsolved, national profile, Of Prime Ministerial Interest, utterly confidential cases regarding the ongoing spate of bank break-ins throughout the city.

Perhaps he had misheard.

'A banquet?'

'A bank,' Fleet repeated.

Keller leaned forwards on his elbows, pushing the desk ever so slightly into the floorboards.

'A bank, you say?'

'I do, sir.'

'Blood?' offered Keller. 'River? Piggy?'

'Financial.'

Keller felt a vein twitch.

'You've been investigating a burglary at a bank.'

'Yes, sir.'

Keller pushed himself up onto his feet. He was no taller than the average man, but somehow seemed to tower regardless. Standing gave even more force to his lungs, and his words began to lash his visitor's hair like an approaching gale.

'And you're aware, Fleet, that there have been a series of such burglaries going on through the city . . .'

'I a—'

'. . . the responsibility for the solving of which rests with me . . .'

'Of cou—'

'. . . and those detectives of mine who are continuing to turn up at work and haven't chosen to go off and do other things and generally just have a jolly old time?'

'I didn't choose,' cried Fleet, jumping to his feet, 'but officially speaking I'm dead.'

'And whose fault is that?' Keller roared.

Fleet pulled a face of appalled incomprehension. 'Gravity's!'

'How long have you been working this case?'

'About three hours.'

'Three hours before coming to me?'

'I don't need to come to you! This is a private client who engaged me and Miss Entwhistle!'

'It's a felony, Fleet!'

'Nothing was stolen, Keller!'

'I beg your pardon?'

'Nothing was stolen, Chief Inspector!'

'The drugging, Fleet! The drugging of the man in the vault is a felony!'

Fleet paused and stepped back. Keller sat back down in his chair. There was a silence while the men regained their composure. Eventually, Fleet spoke.

'How did you know there was someone in the vault?'

The Chief Inspector made no immediate reply, instead sitting back and silently studying Fleet for roughly a minute, while weighing up whether to answer this question.

Fleet waited patiently, alternating between avoiding Keller's gaze and avoiding seeming to be avoiding it.

During this time, refreshments were delivered, and soon the terrible silence that had fallen over the office was broken by sips of scalding tea, the occasional powerful munching of Chief-Inspectorial molar upon biscuit, and the hideous scuttling of a corgi-sized metal-and-leather crab-thing as it carried its empty tea tray diagonally across the room, then diagonally into the hallway, and then, from too far away and with one of its upsettingly many legs, reached up and closed the door.

Fleet clapped his hands over his face in horror.

'Ordinarily,' Keller began, biscuit finally vanquished, 'I would insist you sign an agreement ensuring that neither you nor your business partner will reveal to further parties outside Scotland Yard any of what I am about to tell you.'

'We're very happy to do that,' said Fleet.

'No.'

'No?'

'No, because you don't need a contract to understand that, were you to reveal any of this information, you will be immediately sacked.'

'I . . . don't work here.'

'*Sacked*, Fleet. Bound in a sack, your sack thrown into a pile of other sacks, until your eventual release from your sack in a marketplace in Cádiz, where you will begin a new life *at best* making further sacks – but I can't promise anything, those merchants are their own men and who knows what they'll see fit to do with an Englishman with no skills falling out of a sack and blinking helplessly in the burning sun.'

'Perhaps they would help me get home.'

'No, Fleet. I'll make sure of that.'

'I see.'

'Good. And any information you somehow glean about the bank break-ins, through luck or perhaps the good sense of Miss Entwhistle, you will immediately report back to me.'

'Yes.'

'Good.'

Keller unlocked a drawer in his desk, pulled out a slim folder, and began reading from the top sheet.

'David Gilbert, Oliver Wolf, Adam Papinson . . .'

101

'Sorry, who are these?' asked Fleet.

'These are the people found in the other banks that have been burgled. All drugged, none with any memory of arriving there. I assume yours was the same?'

Fleet nodded. 'Tom Hodges, a hospital porter. Drugged at Mav's café on Long Lane.'

'We'll follow up, but I expect it will be the same as all the others. Something presumably slipped in a drink, but nobody saw anything.'

'None of this was in the papers,' said Fleet.

Keller contorted his face into the slack-jawed, taut-browed expression of someone knocked into a stupor by the most shocking news anyone had ever heard. 'It wasn't? Really? The drugging and kidnapping of more than half a dozen people who woke up trapped in bank vaults? The horrifying prospect that any random member of the public might be next?'

'I get your point.'

'Glad to hear it.'

'But,' Fleet continued, 'the druggings aren't actually what I was going to ask you about.'

Keller set down the paper and clasped his hands.

'And what were you going to ask me about?'

'The items stolen from the banks, they had nothing in common, correct?'

'Correct.'

'And sometimes it was unclear exactly why anyone would even want to steal them?'

'Also correct.'

'And were there any vaults from which nothing was stolen? In Chalon, the thief couldn't open the safe-deposit boxes, but there were clear marks left. And it occurred to me, for a criminal who is capable of leaving no trace of how they entered an impenetrable bank vault, the markings were much

102

too clumsily done. Did that happen anywhere else? Anything marked or moved at all?'

Keller picked up the folder and started leafing through pages. 'Hertford Building Society . . . by the looks of it, they'd attempted to open boxes thirty-nine and two hundred and forty-eight, but they were Trilling locks so no contents were taken . . . Kilford District Bank, no safe-deposit boxes.'

'But they had something.'

Keller read further on the page.

'Inspector Longman writes, "A logbook of cleaning times kept in the vault was found open and defaced."'

'Defaced?'

'"Entries on the third of January and eighth of February were crossed out."'

'Third of January . . . could be three-one, or perhaps just three if it's counting days. Eighth of February could be eight-two, or . . . thirty-nine. All these numbers. Miss Entwhistle and I, well, we think it might be a code of some kind.'

'Tell you what, Fleet. I have a call to make. So why don't you take this file, *do not take it out of the building*, but go out to Miss Waverley's desk, take some notes, leave it with her, go away, and let me get on with the uncountable number of things I have to do other than sit here and watch you think.'

'Thank you, sir.'

'Of course, Fleet. Any time. It's what I'm here for.'

'Really?'

'Get out.'

The large room outside Keller's office was filled with a dozen desks and the din of twice as many detectives, who were hammering their investigations into typewriter keys, talking loudly into telephones, or chatting to each other as they circled the room until a free desk appeared, towards which they would all suddenly plunge like a flock of goshawks spying a single, doomed vole.

Only one of the desks, nearest the Chief Inspector's door, had a permanent resident, and the detectives knew better than to attempt to use it during the brief moments it was ever free.

At this moment, Miss Waverley had a guest, who was leaning over her shoulder as they scanned a thick reference book she had laid open on her desk.

'And this is her college?' asked Clara.

'Looks like it,' replied Miss Waverley, before removing her spectacles and tucking them neatly into the single breast pocket of her dress.

'Wonderful! Thank you, May. I do appreciate the help.'

'Bring me a postcard. Do Oxford colleges sell postcards?'

'I'll find out! And if not, I'll make one.'

Clara was already thinking about the various crafting materials she could use for such a project, and began to hope that the colleges didn't sell postcards, as she'd been meaning to try her hand at paper quilling for some time.

The door to Keller's office shut, and Fleet walked over with a folder.

'Miss Waverley, can I use your desk for a minute?'

'You know the answer to that, Archie.'

'It's just for a minute.'

'It sets a precedent.'

'It's very important,' pressed Fleet.

'I don't doubt it, but the other detectives will see, and then I'll be fighting them off all afternoon.'

Fleet looked at a group of three junior detectives hovering nearby, watching with intrigue. Then he looked back at Miss Waverley, pulled out his notebook, and sat down on the floor.

'Have you found someone who can help?' he asked, copying numbers from the folder.

'We have indeed,' said Clara.

'And where are we going?'

Clara squatted down to Fleet's level and waited until he stopped scribbling, looked up and saw her grinning at him.

'Where?' he asked.

Clara continued grinning.

'Where?'

'Babbage.'

Fleet dropped his head and sank somehow lower into the floor.

Chapter 7

The sea of commuters surged across the station concourse in every direction, flowing in currents from platform to pastry kiosk to bootshine to platform to guard booth to ticket office; from everywhere, constantly, towards everywhere else and around each other as they all tried their damnedest to get *somewhere* that wasn't where they were.

The only place of respite was the large, dimly lit waiting room just off Platform 1, where they could sit down, put their head between their legs, and have a minute to weep while they tried to decipher the note, on the back of their Value Return ticket, that stated that it was valid only between the hours of 25 and 27 p.m., and that to use it at any other time risked an unlimited fine that doubled to a somehow even less limited fine if not paid immediately at the station from which the passenger had already departed.

This was London Central West, one of the beating hearts of the urban circulatory system that was the rail network of Even Greater London.

It was an immense station, with over fifty platforms and a grandiosity that would make a Florentine cathedral tut. Gulls soared below the stratospheric vaulted ceilings, which were held aloft by spiralling columns and the hands and shoulders of a gargantuan statue – a bronze, loinclothed, muscly colossus, looking from toe to chin like Atlas holding up the world, but with a half-smoked cigar and a crumpled top hat giving away its true identity as the station's designer, Isambard Kingdom Brunel.

London Central West was the principal station connecting the historic centre of the capital with its westerly boroughs. Places such as the Railtown, a vast scrapyard formerly known as Reading; Cornwall, with its soft sands, salubrious air and second homes; and the mysterious, gothic outdoor sculpture experience of Gravehenge.

It also led to Oxford, for anyone looking for a pleasant day out, for undergraduates returning to their studies after a weekend on the Thames competing in the Blues Dogsledding, and, occasionally, for detectives needing an expert to help with their case.

Fleet and Clara squinted upwards at Brunel's torso, onto which was bolted an immense departure board.

The station clock ticked past the minute, prompting the board to update itself. Countless metal letter-flaps began to spin in place, starting from the top of the board and moving down, at first giving off the noise of a gently fluttering swarm of mechanical butterflies, but rapidly crescendoing as more of the flaps joined in. Among the sea of hardened commuters, a few unfortunate first-time passengers dived to the ground in panic and looked around for what they had to assume was an approaching avalanche of cutlery.

Her hands over her ears, Clara spotted the destination they were looking for, just in front of the great engineer's navel.

'There!' she shouted over the din. 'The eleven-eighteen, platform forty-nine!'

Fleet nodded, wincing, and they began their journey to the distant reaches of the station.

The service to Oxford was semi-fast, making only two additional stops.

First, the Railtown, which was not a passenger station. Clara heard an announcement gently encouraging people to move out of the rearmost carriage, which it seemed no one really paid much attention to until the sound of clamps rang out from everywhere, at which point a dozen terrified passengers spilled forward through the vestibule just in time to avoid being craned away and recycled into fenceposts.

After this, the train stopped at Didcot, regional interconnection hub and home to the renowned Didcot Insanitorium, the very apogee of treatment centres for mental wellbeing. Clara noticed that about half the passengers who had fled the rear carriage decided to cut their journey short and exit here, alighting shakily onto the platform where they were immediately met by porters with wheeled armchairs, smelling salts and restorative mugs of hot chocolate.

Finally, the train arrived at its destination.

Oxford. For hundreds of years the name had been synonymous with learning and academic prestige. And although the university had recently been brought under the organisational structure of Swindon National Informatorium – in part due to Government pressure to increase efficiency, but mainly due to an ill-judged wager by a former Chancellor – a visit to Oxford was like stepping back in time, into a tranquil oasis of pre-modern respite. For, unlike almost everywhere else south of the Midlands Boundary Forest, Oxford had, by and large, managed to keep its ancient character, even as the ever-ravenous London enveloped it. With its ancient stone colleges, its even more ancient academics, and its obsession with which group of students was best at sitting in half a tube and sweeping fastest along a river – rivers that have perfectly good banks to walk along, and at either end of which there was nothing particularly crucial to reach quickly – the city was a bubble in reality, a collective fiction that kept happily retelling itself, while the world beyond got on with other things that were supposedly more important but no one could really say why.

Clara bounded down the station steps, waited for Fleet to catch up, flagged down one of Oxford's famous rickshaws and soon the pair were swept away into the torrent of pedals and wheels that made up most of the city's outdoor space.

Innumerable black gowns flapped above bicycles, clutching textbooks and papers and hurtling along the narrow roads like startled flocks of ravens. Clara took in the sights and sounds of storied spires and chiming church bells as their vehicle sped past the old stone walls of the colleges: first, the historic ones in the centre, and then, as they travelled further north, the newer colleges of Stephenson, Arkwright, Bazalgette and Lovelace.

Soon, the rickshaw pulled to a halt. Fleet and Clara hopped out and walked up to an imposing sandstone edifice that loomed proudly over the Woodstock Road. Outside, a statue of a man stared down from a plinth – or, less a plinth, and more an array of dozens of narrow metal columns around which scores of tiny numbered gears slowly turned.

A plaque at the man's feet told all who would read it that this was the great polymath Charles Babbage, the person after whom the college in front of them was named. It also explained that the plinth was indeed a working model of his landmark 'difference engine' calculating machine, and it politely asked the reader not to touch it, pleaded with them not to attempt to reprogram it, and, in underlined, capitalised letters, begged them to understand that it could not, and would never be able to, advise on the subject of love.

Above the tall wooden door, a metal circle swung open, and an eye the size of a dinner table blinked at Fleet and Clara from behind what could only be described as a monocle.

Clara jolted backwards with a shriek that landed as a hiccup.

'Oh, they still have that,' said Fleet.

'You've seen this before?' asked Clara, not wanting, or not able, to take her eyes off the stone cyclops.

'Five or six years ago. I was sent here to investigate a bicycle-sharing scheme some Babbage freshers set up, following some complaints from the students at other colleges whose bicycles made that possible.'

'Right,' said Clara, too absorbed to have heard any of this. She waved hesitantly at the eye. 'Is it friendly?'

'The eye?'

'Yes, the eye!'

'Well, it's just an eye, isn't it?'

Clara threw her hands up in the air. 'What does that mean?'

'Eyes aren't really friendly or unfriendly, are they?'

'They're also not usually six feet across, Fleet.'

'I suppose.'

The eye blinked again and turned its pupil back and forth between the two investigators. A tinny speaker somewhere came to life, and the eye spoke in a surprisingly nasal voice.

'*Yeah?*'

'Oh,' said Clara. 'Fleet-Entwhistle Private Investigations, please.'

'*What?*' said the eye.

'I mean, we are Fleet-Entwhistle Private Investigations. I'm Clara Entwhistle and this is Inspector Fleet. We're here to see Professor Dorcas McCabe.'

'*Right. Giz a tick.*'

The eye suddenly moved backwards and flipped upside down, causing Clara to shrickup for a second time. Then, the eye blurred out of focus and vanished, leaving only blackness in the monocle. Clara realised she was looking at an enormous magnifying lens, and turned to Fleet accusingly.

'It's just a man's eye!'

'Nigel,' replied Fleet. 'He's the porter.'

'Why didn't you tell me?'

'Tell you what?'

Clara gesticulated towards the now-empty monocle. 'That it's *Nigel*.'

'Why? Do you know him?'

'No, but—' She gestured again to the gap where the eye once was.

The corners of Fleet's mouth twitched briefly upwards. 'Did you think it was the eye of some giant beast that lives inside the college?'

'*Maybe*? I don't know what I thought. Why can't Nigel just look at us through the window?' Clara turned back to look at the college's facade. 'Why . . . why isn't there a window?'

'You'd have to ask Nigel.'

Clara felt the sky darkening and saw some raindrops bounce off Fleet's shoulders. Something buzzed within the great wooden door, and Fleet walked over and pushed it open.

From pictures, and the one or two she'd visited, Clara had a good understanding of the appearance of the front quadrangle of Oxford colleges. You would expect to find old buildings covered with wisteria or climbing roses, and stone paths lined with carefully tended blooms, all bordering a large, neat lawn, immaculately mown, green as you'd ever seen, with signs in the ground warning the resident bright young things of the dire consequences of setting even one bright young toe on it.

Not so Babbage College. There was a quadrangle, to be sure, but it was simply a square of gravel bounded by dusty paths and unadorned faux-Georgian terraces, with a low stone wall on the far side, beyond which was an immaculate cactus garden where a group of students were listening intently to a greying don, who had entirely forgotten what he was meant to be teaching them and so was now improvising a lecture about succulents as a tumbleweed rolled by.

From underneath the entrance cloister, Clara could hear the rain beginning to fall more heavily, and she could now see it glinting in the sky as it fell. Curiously, the ground did not seem to be getting wet.

Before she could take a closer look, Clara's attention was seized by the clippity-clop of sturdy shoes, and she turned to see a woman approaching from along the cloister. A black academic gown billowed around her slightly tattered three-piece suit, which appeared to have been constructed from three different three-piece suits of varying sizes, all of which were too big. Masses of curly black hair with one large white streak tumbled out of a bun that was loosely held up by an assortment of pencils and a letter opener. Her eyes were hidden behind a pair of tinted pince-nez, and she was scowling at the clouds where the sun ought to have been. At twenty feet away, she stretched out a hand as far as she could and let it pull her forwards, as if she had got into trouble in a river and was now being hauled to safety.

'Good afternoon,' the woman called out, clearly realising she'd misjudged the distance. 'You're the investigators?'

'Hello, yes. Clara Entwhistle, and this is Inspector Fleet.'

'Lovely, lovely. Lovely. Dorcas McCabe, Jacquard Chair in . . .' The woman finally arrived at Fleet and Clara, and seemed relieved to have found hands to shake. 'There. In Cryptographical Engineering. So, you have a little puzzle for us, do you?'

'We have a code,' said Fleet.

'Wonderful. What kind?'

Fleet and Clara exchanged a look.

'It's . . . numbers,' attempted Clara.

'Oh, I'm sure it's *numbers*,' replied the professor, bobbing her head with an amused expression, sending further curls escaping from their pencil captors. She paused to blow them out of her face, which took four attempts before the head-bobbing resumed.

'Well,' she finally added, 'either that or letters.'

'Don't forget shapes,' said Fleet.

'Shapes?' The professor's head froze. '*Shapes?*'

'Why not?'

'I don't have time to answer that, Inspector. Let's have a look-see.'

Clara handed over a sheet of notepaper, and McCabe held it up to her face.

'Ah. Just as I thought.'

'What is it?' asked Clara.

'It's utterly meaningless,' the professor replied.

A look of confusion flitted across Clara's face. 'What did you expect?'

McCabe shrugged. 'Sometimes you get lucky. You'd better come upstairs.'

The professor's study was filled with the trappings of academic success: piles of books on every available surface, a few battered settees and an armchair covered in a faded oriental rug. Here and there, Babbage College mugs acted as bookends and as homes for spiders.

The settees and armchair faced the hearth, beside which was a small blackboard covered in unintelligible symbols.

McCabe ushered Fleet and Clara over and they all sat down.

'Coffee?' she asked.

'No, thank you,' said Fleet. 'We are in a bit of a hurry, so . . .'

The professor turned to Clara.

'For you? I have fresh beans.'

'Oh, well, how could I say no to that?' replied Clara with delight.

'Wonderful.'

McCabe groped under her armchair and found a small metal tin. She shook it at Fleet like a maraca.

'Are you sure? It's fresh beans.'

'I'm sure,' said Fleet. 'Perhaps we could talk about this coded message at the same time?'

'Of course!'

The professor began twisting the lid of the tin, which appeared to be stuck.

'You know the thing about encryption, Inspector?'

'I do not.'

'It's *alive*. Always changing. It's an arms race. That's what makes it so fascinating. You invent the Caesar cipher, yes?'

'No,' replied Fleet.

'But say you did . . .'

McCabe continued to twist the lid of the coffee-bean tin, which was refusing to open and, if anything, seemed to be fastening more.

'You substitute letters for each other: A becomes F, B becomes G, and so on. You're taking the alphabet and moving everything along five places, say. Message looks like gibberish but it's trivial to decrypt. You just try moving all the letters back five places, or six places, or whatever it needs to be. After twenty-five goes at most, out it pops. Pop!'

The professor appeared to have expected the tin to pop open at that moment, but it didn't, and instead sounded like it was beginning to buckle. She frowned, and sat forward and lifted her elbows up to get more leverage.

'Now, let's say instead you're Vigenère.'

114

'Let's say instead I'm in a hurry,' said Fleet.

'I'll be Vigenère!' declared Clara.

'Excellent. So, you think, "Caesar, you extremely stabbed fool, this just won't do."'

'It won't!' agreed Clara.

'Indeed! It doesn't survive a moment with modern cryptanalysis. So you say, "Ah, what if we rotate the alphabet a different amount for every letter in your message?"'

'I'm sure you're very busy, Professor,' tried Fleet. 'You could just—'

'Never too busy for instruction. *Hnngggggg!* Damn. Anyway, in a Vigenère cipher you have a keyword. Anything. "College", say.'

'Pumpkin!' said Clara.

'*Yes, anything!*' wheezed McCabe, red in the face as she made one final heroic screw of lid into tin.

She stopped, made a few recovery breaths, stared at the container in disbelief, and placed it back under her armchair with a clink as it knocked over two other, equally permanently sealed tins.

'And,' the professor continued, 'the keyword tells you *which* rotated alphabet to use as you move letter by letter through the message. So whereas for Caesar, the two L's in "hello" would both end up the same, for Vigenère we'd take the third and fourth letters from the keyword "pumpkin" − M and P − and use the corresponding M and P alphabets, i.e. rotated by thirteen and sixteen letters, and we'd end up with . . .'

A brief silence fell over the room, as Clara counted on her fingers and Fleet rubbed his temples and stared forlornly at the door.

'X!' cried Clara. 'And A!'

'Exactly. And you carry on in that fashion, repeating "pumpkin" as many times as necessary. So you might end

115

up with a fully encrypted message like . . .' – the professor darted her eyes back and forth for a few seconds, as if watching a merry jig of symbols in her mind – '"Iib bkzxh, Guhc Maiqtxcbyt."'

Clara sat wide-eyed on the edge of her seat. 'What does it mean?'

'"Top marks, Miss Entwhistle."'

Clara beamed, and flashed her eyebrows at Fleet while elbowing him in the ribs.

'Yes. Ow. So, if that's what our code is, Professor, you can just go back the other way?'

'I'm afraid not, Inspector. Vigenère has no Caesar-style reversal and it defeats frequentist cryptanalysis. In fact it's worse than that. We have no idea even of the order of your message – all you have is a jumble of numbers. So a Babbage-Kasinski method can't find any repetitions.'

'We might have an order,' said Clara. 'We know the order in which the numbers were robbed – I mean, sent.'

'Good, that will help. Of course all this assumes it is a typical cipher at all! It might be something entirely novel, or more of a historical curio like the Rossignols' *Grand Chiffre*.'

'"Big number"?' asked Clara.

'In this case, "Great Cipher". I think French requires its own cryptanalysis!'

The don rocked forwards and backwards and laughed like a camel gasping for air.

Fleet stood up.

'Well, thank you for the lesson and the no coffee, Professor.'

'Wait,' said McCabe, stifling sniggers. 'Wait.'

Fleet sat down, and she composed herself.

'Clearly this just requires a little chat with Big Boy.'

'Big Boy?' asked Clara.

Fleet stared at the professor with panicked eyes. 'No.'

'Yes.'

'You built it,' he said, in disbelief. 'You actually built it.'

McCabe clapped joyously. 'We did!'

'Who is Big Boy?' asked Clara.

'I thought you all thought it was impossible,' said Fleet.

'That's what we thought! But we were wrong, or partially wrong at least.'

The professor stood up and began walking towards the door.

'Were you even *allowed* to build it?' asked Fleet.

'Encouraged!' McCabe exclaimed gleefully, spinning round to face him.

Fleet sank his face into his hands, and Clara looked around for anyone to answer her.

'What are you both talking about?'

McCabe's face was enveloped by a manic grin.

'Babbage's Big Boy. His final gift.'

Chapter 8

The professor led Fleet and Clara back down the staircase and across the main quad. It was still raining, and as Clara got closer to the dusty paths around the gravel square, she noticed that not only was the ground still dry, but it was now slightly hazy.

Is that . . . steam?

They entered another stone building and began descending a spiral staircase. The daylight vanished quickly, replaced by dull lamps on the walls. Clara noticed it was quite a bit warmer than it had been outside, which wasn't her usual experience of draughty buildings like this.

'They found his papers a few years ago,' began McCabe. 'The old man's. Babbage. Took up a pen the night before he died and wrote out page upon page of symbology like we've never seen. People thought it was gibberish, the mind unwinding itself in preparation for the end, you know what I mean, rather like a dog turning around and around before settling into sleep.'

She suddenly looked backwards and peered over her spectacles at the investigators. 'Why do they do that?'

'I don't know,' replied Fleet.

An image of a forlorn beagle flitted across Clara's mind's eye. She hoped it was somewhere safe. And warm.

Why is it so warm in here?

'But no,' continued the professor, 'we realised soon enough it was not gibberish. It was genius beyond our understanding. He saw into the face of our Universe. And the Universe looked back and it said, "Here you are, Charles. Here's the good stuff. You've got one night to write it all down." And he did. Over three hundred pages – we have the originals.'

'What's it about?' asked Clara.

'*Thinking*, of course. Computation. The very obsession of his life. But of a kind we've never seen. To understand it, we had to recreate in our team of researchers the conditions of Babbage's audience with Creation.'

Professor McCabe waved her arms grandly in the air as though gesturing to some invisible giant, before resuming her descent down the increasingly narrow and steep stone steps.

'One night of glorious inspiration,' said Fleet, 'followed by death. You have a lot of young academics volunteering for that?'

'Oh dear no, Inspector,' said McCabe, shaking her head. 'No, no, no, you misunderstand. These young bucks are all very clever, but we can't count on them being a Babbage and figuring it all out in one night. We need a repeatable process.'

The professor spun and looked up the spiral staircase at Fleet and Clara, the lamplight flickering in her wild eyes.

'Do you dream, Inspector?'

'I . . . sleep. Usually.'

'Do *you* dream, Miss Entwhistle?'

'Of course!' said Clara. 'Last night I was a rabbit. But a sort of rabbit athlete? And it was the opening ceremony of the Rabbit Games, and I was representing the proud sporting nation of Rabbitaly in the Modern Hoptathlon.'

As Clara recounted this, a wave of sleepiness swept over her, and she realised the warm air was making her a little drowsy.

The professor snapped her fingers at Clara in agreement, which made her start back into alertness.

'Exactly the problem. Dreams are places of great creativity, where the mind is unburdened by the day-to-day. But they are also an endless ocean. They are too unbounded, too far from the questions we actually seek to answer. So. The waking mind is not up to the task, and the dreaming mind is lost in its own absurdity. And yet the work must be done. So what is the answer?'

The professor pointed her thumb at a black-painted door in a hollow of the thick, stone wall.

'Doors,' said Fleet. 'Doors are the answer. Of course.'

McCabe rolled her eyes, before suddenly pushing mightily on the door, which burst open and smashed deafeningly into a wall inside the small stone room, where a chalk-dusted man in his mid-twenties, who had been reclining in a large, comfortable armchair, jumped out of his skin and landed on the floor with a baffled, terrified expression.

'Ahh!' he cried. 'Aaaaaahh!'

'Shh, it's all right, Mr Chowdhury.'

'*Aaaah!*'

The professor rushed over to the man as Clara and Fleet watched with alarm from the staircase. Clara read the sign on the open door:

Babbage Deathbed Papers Investigation
Section 14: Compositive Inference

Peering inside, she saw the room was highly, even deliberately, bare. Aside from the armchair, there was only a blackboard covered in various ideas crossed out in frustration, and a small desk, on which was a large, framed sheet of yellowing paper covered with a hurried mish-mash of symbols scrawled incoherently across one another. Clearly, thought Clara, this was the object of this man's study.

'I was just . . . nodding off,' the young scholar stammered.

'Perfect.' Professor McCabe sprang over to the blackboard and picked up a well-used piece of chalk. 'What did you see?'

The young man's eyes darted around the room as he struggled to come to grips with his new, waking reality.

'Birds . . .'

'Birds?'

'Logical . . . birds . . . I was in an aviary! Bright-billed toucans – *Truecans!* – flying with . . . *Peregrine Falsecons*. Wading Andpipers, yellow Orioles and Amazonian Notnots. Oh, how they flew, Professor! Then they landed on all the little pegs. Little pegs, everywhere, they filled everywhere! A grid throughout space, packed with birds . . .'

Professor McCabe scribbled furiously on the board. 'Keep going, Mr Chowdhury.'

The man grasped his head in his hands and grimaced at the ceiling with the effort.

'They are . . . *they are* . . .'

'Come on . . .' she urged.

Mr Chowdhury suddenly flung his arms out and dropped his jaw. He leapt to his feet, ran to the desk, picked up the framed paper, ran back to McCabe and held it out.

'His truth tables, Professor. They aren't tables. They are cubes! *Truth cubes!*'

'What on earth is a truth cube?' she asked.

The young man held a wild grin on his face.

'I don't know!'

'Well?' replied McCabe, flashing her student an encouraging smile. 'Find out!'

The scholar nodded, put the picture frame back down and rushed over to sit in his chair. He pulled a padded blindfold from his pocket, wrapped it over his eyes, and slumped his head down.

The professor stepped back out into the staircase and silently pulled the door closed, tiptoeing with the anxious fear of a new parent leaving a beautiful sleeping baby that any sudden move might transform into a shrieking demon of unending torment. She held her finger to her lips at Fleet and Clara, then beckoned them onwards down the staircase.

'The moments just before sleep,' continued McCabe, her shoes tap-tap-tapping down the winding stone steps. 'The gloaming of our consciousness, the shores before the sea of the unconscious. These are the moments when our minds are untethered from the constraints of daily life – *but not too far* – and we are free to realise our utter potential in the first and final realm of abstract cogitation. Mathematics rests upon philosophical logic, of course. And computation rests upon mathematics. There is a truth to the universe that the murky physical world conceals.'

'Uh huh,' said Fleet.

'Computation engines are vessels for these truths, just as you both and I are vessels of immortal souls.'

They passed another black-painted door in the stone, again with a sign:

Babbage Deathbed Papers Investigation
Section 7: Computative Regress

This door was ajar, and Clara peered inside. Again, a blackboard, a desk and some framed yellowing paper with writing to be deciphered. This room was larger, though, and seemed to be for slightly older, more senior researchers. Two men lay blindfolded and spooning on a narrow chaise longue, the little spoon clutching a tattered old stuffed bear to his chest. On a chair to the side, a woman was watching them, holding a pair of cymbals with great anticipation.

Clara pulled away from the door and caught up with Fleet and McCabe. The professor was still chatting away, as even warmer air seemed to be rising from below.

'Sometimes, mathematics sings to us, wouldn't you agree, Inspector?'

'Can't say I've heard that particular tune,' replied Fleet.

'No? Not even Euler's identity? That the natural logarithm base e, the circle constant pi and the imaginary unit i all combine to equal minus one? *Minus one*, Inspector.'

Professor McCabe flicked her wrists like an orchestral conductor and closed her eyes, savouring a symphony only she could hear.

'I'm sure that's very nice to a mathematician,' said Fleet.

'Very nice? It is a miracle! These are utterly unrelated numbers. It is like taking a horse-drawn carriage, two eggs and France, and turning them into the Bible.' The professor smiled, before adding with a wink, 'Although that might make more sense than the events contained within that book, but don't tell the chaplain I said that.'

The trio passed another room, and again Clara peered through the open door.

Babbage Deathbed Papers Investigation
Section 2: Transclusionary Memory

This room was just as small as the first, and four of the same yellow, scrawled papers were framed and mounted on the wall. Another blindfolded young man was sitting at a desk covered in papers and stale sandwich crusts, fidgeting to get comfortable with his head slumped down, and loosely holding a fistful of coins above the stone floor as an improvised alarm clock.

He had long since used up his blackboard space, and now chalk writing covered the walls, floor and ceiling, with arrows here and there swooping towards one or more of the framed papers.

Clara read parts of the far wall:

What is 'Transclusion' – Surely The Old Man Had Lost His Mind?

MUST FIGURE OUT fractal cheesecake dream. Relevant? Or just peckish?

TRY TO REMEMBER

<u>Mittens needs feeding</u> – *NOT DREAM. REAL HUNGRY CAT!*

'Oh dear,' said Clara.

She moved on again, following the others down the stairs.

How deep is this place?

Just as Clara wondered this, light began to spill up from somewhere below.

'Yes,' said McCabe, replying to no one, 'Babbage's papers might indeed be the key to the future of mechanical thought. Nothing like the foolish loops and limited scripts of our automatons today.'

'Oh, I don't know,' said Clara. 'I've only met a few of them, but it's pretty clever stuff.'

'It's all right as far as it goes, and, I grant you, some of the more sophisticated models have been manufactured to produce at least the illusion that they can function independently, hold a conversation even, but in reality they are all working from a pre-programmed script, or scripts, that allow for certain actions, functions or responses in a given situation.

Usually limited to the small number of tasks they've been made for. No. What I'm talking about, Miss Entwhistle, is a future where machines can reason, where they can imagine. Where they can *think*. Just like humans.'

'Please aim higher,' said Fleet.

'We're still pretty far from that, of course,' continued McCabe. 'We've only figured out about a fifth of the deathbed papers. We'll work on the rest, but in the meantime we've invested heavily in seeing what that fifth we *have* worked out can do in the real world. Not cheap! Not cheap at all.'

The steps continued down through an opening filled with bright light. Professor McCabe paused, removed her academic gown and suit jacket, and gestured for Fleet and Clara to do likewise.

Clara felt relieved at this invitation, and hastily removed her woollen cape. Fleet made a gesture that suggested he was fine and would keep his jacket on, despite the perspiration gathering on his forehead.

The three travelled down through the opening, after which the walls vanished and were replaced by thin railings.

Clara noticed a number of confusing things in turn.

First, she had descended, below the ground, into a room that was brighter and far hotter than the outside above.

Second, Fleet had stopped dead a few steps in front of her and had now bent down to half his height and was grabbing the railings with both hands.

Third, she couldn't see the edges of the room.

Fourth, she *could* see the bottom of the room, but it was an extremely upsetting distance away.

It was a vast cavern, and the narrow spiral staircase was the only thing keeping them from plummeting into it.

Clara felt quite ill, and sat down on a step behind Fleet. McCabe turned around and frowned at the investigators.

'Come on!' she urged, beckoning them onwards. 'The platform's just below us.'

Fleet and Clara pulled themselves up using the railings and walked unsteadily down a couple more rotations of staircase to where a platform sprang out to one side as the stairs continued downwards. The professor hopped onto the platform, and Fleet and Clara gingerly followed.

'Here he is,' said McCabe, waving proudly into the immeasurable space. 'Babbage's Big Boy.'

Clara looked out from the platform. She felt as though she were ballooning over a town of tall metal buildings, except the buildings were not enclosed, and each floor was full of ten-sided wheels, some of which were slowly spinning or clicking into place. Occasionally, a distant set of wheels would all unlock at the same time, releasing a ratchet and nudging a girder across a chasm into another building, sending those wheels spinning too, and so on. Far below, scores of young researchers in lightweight boiler suits were scurrying about on 'streets' between the buildings, checking various displays and arguing amongst themselves over papers on their clipboards.

The noise should have been unbearable, but the whole thing seemed to be so well made that all it gave off was a gentle rolling of clicks and clonks that Clara found strangely soothing.

'It's incredible,' she said.

'Quite the thing, isn't it?'

'Who pays for all this?' asked Fleet, stupefied.

'Strictly speaking, the Ministry of Education, under a grant programme for practical applications of engineering. *But*, the whisper on the wind is that the money really comes from Defence.'

'Why?' asked Clara.

'Well, they have bags of it, for a start. And it is particularly good at decoding things' – the professor lowered her tone

– 'perhaps even *Prussian things*. I'm not privy to everything that gets run through it. I'm more on the theory side.'

At that moment, a tall, wiry man of about forty sprang up the metal staircase and onto the platform. Like the researchers below he was wearing a boiler suit which now, up close, Clara could see was made of a very thin muslin, through which she could just make out a blue-and-white striped bathing costume like the ones she'd seen men wearing once before on the beach, just before her mother had declared Scarborough to be a sinful place and insisted they return home. She shifted uncomfortably in her own heavy cotton dress.

The platform rattled disconcertingly as the man strode forward, his round spectacles almost completely misted over, though he didn't appear to have noticed. Perhaps he was used to it, thought Clara.

'Professor McCabe,' the man began, 'I wasn't expecting to see you here today.'

'I wasn't expecting to be here either, Ben. But here I am nonetheless. Inspector, Miss Entwhistle, allow me to introduce my senior research associate Dr Benjamin Fernsby.'

The researcher glanced at the detectives with a smile contorted somewhere between a beaming welcome and a horrified grimace.

'Delightful!' he croaked, before coughing. 'Professor, if I'd known we were conducting private tours I'd have been only too glad to—'

'No, no, Ben. Not a private tour at all.' The professor turned to Fleet and Clara. 'Dr Fernsby likes to be kept informed of any planned visitors, don't you, Ben?'

'Well, the work we do here is of a rather sensitive nature and—'

'I can assure you that the Inspector and Miss Entwhistle aren't academic spies from another college here to try and steal our secrets.'

127

Dr Fernsby looked again at Fleet and Clara, and nodded, apparently satisfied that this was almost certainly true.

'What about—'

'*Nor*,' continued the professor, 'are they freshers from Lovelace here to prank us again.'

'They still haven't returned the college tortoise, Professor.'

'Negotiations over the safe return of Percy Shelly are ongoing, Ben.'

'A code, man!' cried Fleet, mopping sweat from his face. 'We have a code. Can you, or your gigantic machine, help us?'

Dr Fernsby started at the outburst, before freezing for several seconds in shock, and finally breaking into an enormous grin. He raised his shoulders and puffed out his chest, and removed his glasses to wipe away the steam, revealing a pair of bright brown eyes that gleamed in excited anticipation.

'What kind of code?' he asked, like a child savouring a present before unwrapping it. 'Nothing is too much trouble for BB. That's what I call Big Boy. Well, when you know him as well as I do!'

'And what does he call you?' asked Clara.

'Oh, no. No, BB isn't sentient, Miss Entwhistle. Although our researchers upstairs are working on that.'

Clara thought about the frazzled-looking scholars she'd seen in various states of waking-sleep and hoped they were allowed at least some nights of actual rest.

'But BB is an excellent puzzle solver, and he's especially good at decoding things.' Dr Fernsby's voice cracked slightly. 'The very best, in fact.'

He gestured towards the vast expanse of machine that filled the cavern below them, and wiped a tear from his eye.

'Dr Fernsby led the build of Big Boy,' the professor added, by way of explanation for the visible emotion.

She walked to the edge of the platform, and Clara noticed two flat tubes running downwards from it, with narrow slots at the top like a pair of postboxes. A sign above them read:

B.B. ACCESS
NOTE: INPUTS *MUST* BE APPROVED
BY PROF D. MCCABE OR DR B. FERNSBY

Professor McCabe tapped one of the postboxes, which was labelled INPUT, and smiled at Fleet and Clara while pulling out a few scraps of paper and a worn pencil from her pocket.

'This is perhaps the greatest calculating engine operating in the world today. Before we get started, is there anything you'd like to ask it, just for fun?'

'Absolutely not,' said Fleet.

'Oh, like what?' asked Clara.

'Whatever you like. A puzzle, perhaps? I'm sure Dr Fernsby will be only too happy to demonstrate what Big Boy here is capable of.'

Dr Fernsby nodded enthusiastically, and Clara thought for a moment.

'Oh!' she began. 'There's this one about a river, and on one side there's a fox, a hen and some grain—'

Dr Fernsby groaned and replaced his glasses, which immediately steamed over again.

'No?' asked Clara.

'A little easy, I should think,' replied the professor. 'And besides, the real question is how one would even end up in such an absurd agricultural scenario. Why would you bring a fox with you? What does a fox fetch at market nowadays, other than any rabbit it can find? Never mind. The real puzzle is quite the, um, er . . . puzzle. Yes.'

129

She handed to Dr Fernsby the code that Fleet and Clara had given her on a piece of notepaper. He pushed his glasses up onto his head and read it over, nodding approvingly, before posting the paper through the slot.

Clara listened as the paper slid away, and she peered over the side to see that the tube led to a large metal box far below. The box made a loud whoomphing noise like a flashbulb, and the opening in the postbox briefly shone brightly.

For a moment, nothing happened. Clara held her breath, and stared out at the thinking city, one mind searching another.

Suddenly, in several of the buildings, numbered wheels that had been stationary began to spin.

Clara felt a wave of relief pass over her, but could not be sure whether that was down to the promise that an answer to the bizarre riddle of the bank thefts was within their grasp, or the fact that all the whirring bits of machinery were creating a slight breeze. She leaned forwards to meet it, and noticed Fleet doing the same.

A few seconds passed.

'Interesting,' muttered Dr Fernsby.

'Told you it was a tough one,' said McCabe.

More towers of dials spun into life. Dr Fernsby pursed his lips, intrigued either by which buildings were now working, or how many, or both.

'Very interesting,' he muttered again.

'Can we help?' asked Clara.

The researcher waved his hand for silence. 'Give him a minute.'

They waited, and bit by bit the entire cavern began clacketing, every dial on every building turning, faster and faster, girders everywhere ramming into their neighbours to convey partial results and demand further calculation, and the pleasing clicks and clonks that Clara had found calming rapidly crescendoed to a noise that she felt would surely be heard even on the surface.

Far below, the graduate students looked around in interest bordering on mild alarm, and began putting on protective earmuffs and unzipping the fronts of their boiler suits.

Clara, Fleet and McCabe cupped their ears in their hands, but Dr Fernsby stood arms by his sides, looking utterly confounded. It seemed to Clara that it was becoming notice-ably hotter, almost unbearably so. She felt quite faint; Fleet looked *very* faint, and even took the step of undoing his shirt collar button.

Above their heads, there came the whooshing sound of a vast amount of liquid rushing through pipework towards the calculation buildings. It didn't make the room cooler, Clara noticed – at best it was just slowing down how quickly it was heating up.

'Nice to have a challenge, isn't it, Ben?' shouted McCabe.

A series of small lights lit up above the postboxes on the platform, and a ribbon of paper began spewing out of a slot labelled OUTPUT. Dr Fernsby grabbed it and read it to himself. He looked astounded, and more than a little worried.

'What does it say?' cried Fleet.

Dr Fernsby looked up at the investigators. 'Big Boy says, "I will make you proud."'

The four stared back out at the immense machine, grinding away on its task.

Clara began to feel as though she was standing in front of an open oven, and a soft alarm began to honk out through the cavern like an all-pervading, electric goose.

She looked down and saw the graduate students far below flapping their arms and hurrying, boiler suits pushed down around their ankles, towards emergency evacuation tunnels where blast doors were slowly lowering.

'Time to go,' said McCabe, sweating like a ham in the noonday sun, and she ushered Fleet and Clara back up the staircase.

The rain battered the train carriage window by Fleet's head, and he watched the dusty old stone buildings receding into the grey distance. Running alongside the tracks, the River Isis was noticeably lower than it had been when they arrived. Fleet saw the water rushing into drains in the riverbanks – sucked away underground to cool the Babbagists' gargantuan mind engine.

McCabe had said there was no use in hanging around – if Big Boy didn't have the answer immediately, it was impossible to know how long the process would last. She promised to call as soon as an answer was returned.

First Mellanby and Redfield, now McCabe and the code. More waiting.

He turned to Clara, who was writing in her notebook.

'I'll head to the office when we get back to Central. Redfield might have been in touch by now.'

Clara's eyes shot wide open. She squished her notebook around her pen and turned to Fleet with a delighted grin.

'Don't think you can shake me off, Inspector. I'll come with you.'

'I'm not trying to shake you off. It's just late.'

'You're always trying to shake me off. Ever since we met. Despite my constant usefulness.'

'I'd say occasional usefulness,' replied Fleet, maintaining a straight face.

Clara, with some effort, twisted her grin into something approximating outrage. 'Frequent usefulness, surely!'

'No, but I'll agree to "regular usefulness".'

'Deal.'

'And I asked you to join me in business, Clara. If I'd wanted to shake you off, that's a poor way to go about it.'

'If you say so. But I hardly want to be at home twiddling my thumbs when you're finding out what Redfield's learned at the Brunelian camp about our poor Mr Lonely Hearts!'

Fleet imagined this. Clara, he was sure, would only be able to twiddle her thumbs about three rotations before leaping up and heading to the library to learn about the history of thumb-twiddling, its origins, its growth into professional thumb-twiddling sporting leagues, and the cultural and criminal impact of the resulting team rivalries.

He felt his lips twitch into a barely perceptible smile, and was vaguely aware of the unfamiliar feeling that he wasn't entirely indifferent to having the company.

'All right. If you must.'

'I must,' said Clara.

It was dark and pelting with rain by the time they reached Mrs Pomligan's Coffee House, and they ran to the door from the bus that had brought them from the station, Fleet pulling his keys from a pocket.

The business was shut for the evening, and the inside was unlit, the windows throwing back a dim reflection of Fleet, Clara, and the street behind them.

He unlocked the door, the two rushed inside, and Fleet shut the door again behind them.

'She could do with an awning,' said Clara, shaking the worst of the rain off her head.

'Keeping people dry who aren't inside and so can't buy anything? I think Mrs Pomligan would call that an unnecessary expense.'

The investigators dripped onto the floor as they headed across the empty café and up the stairs at the back. Fleet jangled his keyring again, but the door was slightly ajar. Mrs

Pomligan was always doing this, forgetting that her storeroom was also their office and needed locking up after use. He shook his head and stepped inside with Clara close behind.

The room was entirely black but for a little light coming from the street through the window at the far end. If there was a telegram from Redfield, it would be on one of their desks, along with an irate note from Mrs Pomligan about not being their personal message delivery service.

Fleet could feel the rain in his socks now. He shook some water from his hair and began to head towards a lamp.

An arm swung across his body. Fleet looked to his side and saw Clara was staring forwards with her other hand across her mouth.

He looked again at the darkness.

Water seeped towards them from their desks. Fleet squinted. There was a puddle. There was a shape.

Someone was kneeling in the water.

Fleet stiffened.

The figure – a shadow inside a shadow – began to move, and slowly rose from the ground, sending more water trickling along the boards towards them.

Fleet heard a pounding from inside his chest, as the shadow slowly stepped forwards, halfway into a sliver of streetlight.

A woman. She was soaking wet from head to toe, wearing a plain dress.

He knew this woman.

He didn't know her. He'd seen her photograph.

She stared furiously back and forth between them.

Fleet remembered.

'Smith . . . You're Louisa Smith.'

Clara looked at Fleet with confusion, then panic. 'Lady Arabella's governess.'

'You . . . *were* . . . her governess,' said Fleet.

The woman took another step forward, and Fleet could see now her dress had been ruined long before the storm. This was a woman in trouble.

The anger in her eyes burned out, replaced by a drained terror, and she stammered what she had been waiting to say:

'Have you any idea what you've done?'

Chapter 9

In the dim light from two desk lamps and the street, the dingy attic looked even less like a detective agency than it did in the daytime. Clara watched as the woman dried her face and hair with some tea towels Fleet had handed her from a box near the back of the room.

These were Mrs Pomligan's Coffee House, Beginners Pottery Studio and Museum of Nearby Horrible Murder souvenir tea towels, presumably once intended for sale downstairs, with the proprietor's face printed on them by an artist who seemed to struggle with ideas such as proportion, perspective and what a human looks like.

Clara watched with discomfort as the misshapen Mrs Pomligan mopped across the woman's head and hair, distorting further as she soaked up the water, and with every pass looking more and more as if she was melting under a lamp.

Clara's mind whirled. Her career as a private detective had so far brought her into contact only with satisfied clients. She thought back to the previous day, sitting with Lady Arabella in the Observatea in Greenwich, and remembered that feeling of pride – triumph, even – when the young woman had declared, *'You've found her out, Miss Entwhistle. Very well done!'*

But now, here was the woman who had been found out, standing before her, bitter, furious and sodden.

Clara recalled the photograph Arabella had given them. A photograph of the governess she suspected of being an imposter. It was clearly the same woman in front of her now, and yet there was something eerie about the differences.

Perhaps the reality was just more vivid. She could see now the woman's eyes were not only blue, but piercing, and she could see her light brown hair was flecked with grey.

Or, perhaps it was the contradictions. Her face was tanned, and her hands were coarse and calloused, as though she was used to working outdoors. But her right index finger was stained with black ink, and her dress was well tailored and made of a fabric more expensive than a labourer could afford. And hadn't Arabella said she was competent in mathematics?

It was a curious puzzle, for sure, but Clara knew this was not what had unsettled her. It was the shock – the shock of realising that this woman was not just an image, a suspect, something to be investigated, but an entire person, and one who seemed much more upset than fitted a mere criminal who'd been found out.

Clara had, in fact, never seen anyone in such distress, and to think she had been a part of causing it . . . She felt sick.

Were we wrong?

She tried to say something, but the words caught in her throat and instead she emitted a high-pitched squeak. Which was just as well, as she had no idea what she was even going to say once she got started.

She looked to Fleet, who appeared equally unsure but jumped in regardless to end the silence.

'When you say "Do you have any idea what you have done?", just to be clear, you mean us?'

'I do.'

'Not to prove your point immediately, but . . . what *have* we done?'

'You've destroyed my life, of course,' the woman replied, with an unnerving cheerfulness. 'I hope you don't mind me dropping in uninvited, but I did so want to meet you both.'

Fleet nodded warily. 'Always . . . nice to meet . . .'

'Who *are* you two?' she suddenly cried, flinging her soaked tea towels onto the ground with a loud slap. 'You people who would find a woman dangling from a precipice and stand on her fingers. Is this what your business does? You ruin people's lives?'

'Generally speaking,' replied Fleet, 'we only try to ruin the lives of criminals.'

'You think I am a criminal?' the woman shot back.

'Well, you did break into our office . . .'

'Did you think for a moment about what would happen after you dobbed me in? I was upstairs preparing mathematics lessons, and Arabella's father screamed my name from the parlour. I thought, what has happened? Has the brat accused me of stealing something? I rushed downstairs and he waved some letters in my face and raved at me like a madman, like I'd shoved the silly girl into an oven or something. He had the butler – Jerrickson, such a toady I think I once actually heard him croak – immediately escort me out the front door, and a few minutes later the under butler appeared and flung my suitcase and clothes out onto the street. Arabella couldn't conceal her delight. Of course, half my things were stolen before I could even gather them up, and the rest were taken from me within the hour by people who specialise in that sort of thing. I spent the night in a shelter – *to which I will not be returning* – then I found Arabella this afternoon in a park, and she fell to pieces in terror. Gave up your names in an instant. And here we are.'

Clara had rediscovered her voice, and decided that there probably wasn't going to be a good point to jump in, just worse and worse points, so she might as well jump in now.

'We didn't mean to cause you any harm. Lady Arabella engaged us to confirm your identity, and we confirmed it was not what you had said. Were we mistaken?'

'Of course not, but that's not the point.'

'Then what is the point?' asked Clara.

The woman stared at them, dumbfounded, appearing to expect they should be able to answer this question themselves, and threw up her arms in bewilderment when it was clear they would not.

A light swept across the room as a carriage passed by on the street below. The terror returned to the woman's eyes, and she dashed to the side of the window, spraying water like a dog emerging from a pond. She waited there, listening, until the carriage could no longer be heard, and eventually seemed satisfied, pulled down the dusty old blind, and returned to the investigators. Clara realised this was the first time they had seen her walk, and it was clear she was carrying an injury that had not quite healed.

She spoke slowly, as if she was repeating a lesson to a child who had not been paying attention.

'Does it not occur to you that people sometimes hide for good reasons?'

Clara's sickening feeling was getting worse, and she sat down and pulled a wastepaper basket within reach just in case the unthinkable happened.

Being wrong about the faux-governess would have been one thing. But they were right, and Clara hadn't thought for a moment about why someone might do what she had done.

'You could have come to me,' the woman continued. 'Asked me directly what was going on. But no. You dug up the dirt and handed it over to that prissy little madam without a second thought.'

'Miss . . .' Fleet began.

'Oh, now you want to know something about me! It's Evans. Helena Evans.'

'Miss Evans. Why don't you tell us what happened?'

She sighed, and seemed to summon strength for her story.

'It was about one and a half months ago. After work. My colleagues had suggested a drink, but it had been a hard week and I wanted to rest. As I was walking along an empty street, suddenly, out of nowhere, a carriage overtook me, going at a hell of a lick. The driver pulled up, jumped down, and then, well, he grabbed me. Of course I struggled, but he managed to shove me into the carriage and lock me in. I pounded and kicked at the door as he made his way back to the front, and I must have got a lucky blow onto the mechanism, as the door flew wide open. So I leapt out, elbowed the man as he tried to grab me again, and ran for it. I stopped a few streets away, and as I tried to get my bearings I realised my clothes were soaking on one side. So I put my hand down. Blood. Too much blood. Next thing I know, I wake up at the cottage hospital in Bridport. Stab wound. Deep, but could have been a lot worse. The best he could do as I was escaping, I suppose. Two weeks in recovery there, then they sent me on my way.'

'Did you go to the police?' asked Fleet.

'Worse than useless. Said it must have been an opportunistic mugging. And as I couldn't remember what the man looked like, there was very little that could be done. They also suggested I take more care next time, which is all well and good but every moment in my life is a possible "next time" and I'm not sure what care I can take against being stabbed except to wear chain mail.'

She rolled her eyes. '"Opportunistic" my drenched feet. That man wanted me dead.'

The three were silent for a moment. Clara already knew what was coming next, but waited for the woman to say it.

'The windows to the carriage. They were all blacked out.' She shuddered. 'It was pitch black in there.'

The same as with Mellanby, thought Clara.

Helena fell silent and stared past the far wall, pulled into her memories. After a few moments she jerked her shoulders, shaking herself back to the present, and continued.

'Anyway, I didn't dare go back to work or home until I understood what it was all about, so I found a lodging house and wangled a job as a governess. Lucky for me some fool Corps-General needed one, or else I doubt I would have passed muster.'

Clara shared a glance with Fleet. 'Corps-General?' she asked Helena.

'One of the higher-ups. Easy enough for me to impress. Years since he would have had to do any sums himself, so I juggled some fancy calculus about. And even though I doubt anyone outside of the Corps has heard of him, I flattered him so much about his reputation he completely forgot to check if I could speak any other languages. Which I absolutely cannot.'

She thrust her hand into a pocket and pulled out a small object, which she passed to Clara. 'I managed to hold on to one thing, at least.'

Clara looked down, and saw a brass lapel pin she recognised immediately. It was identical to the one Redfield was wearing at the Iron Bridge Club, only with a slightly different embossing: *IKB 27*.

'Evans, Helena,' said the woman. 'Structural Engineering Major, Twenty-seventh Division . . .'

Clara knew the end. 'Brunel Corps.'

Helena pointed at Clara in affirmation, before waving her hand across the arc of an imaginary rainbow and pulling an exhausted grin.

'"*Making an Even Greater London.*"'

Helena seemed to relax for the first time since arriving, settling into the battered leather chair behind Fleet's desk, as though the telling of her story had lifted a great weight within her.

Fleet shuffled uncomfortably on his jute sack, and considered what they had just heard.

Another Brunelian.

'Do you have any idea who would want you dead?' he asked.

She shook her head.

'And you can't recall anything about the man?'

She thought for a moment. 'No, his face was all covered up with a scarf and hat. And in any case, it all happened so fast . . .'

Fleet pressed on with his line of questioning as Clara scribbled down notes.

'Do you know a man named Mellanby?'

Helena furrowed her brow.

'Mellanby? Lieutenant-Supply-Captain Mellanby?'

'You know him?'

'Just the name. I've seen it on documents. I only remember because of his awful signature. It always looked like he'd written it while on the back of a horse, or possibly while being trampled by one.'

'He was abducted in very similar circumstances.'

Helena recoiled.

Fleet continued: 'Is there anything you have in common with Mellanby that could make sense of who would target you both?'

'Other than us both being in the Corps? I have no idea. I've never met the man.'

'Are you in possession of any sensitive information?'

'What, like gossip?' Helena shook her head in disapproval. 'I don't go in for that.'

'Company secrets?'

She laughed. 'There aren't secrets in the Brunel Corps. How could there be? We don't even know where we're going next week; what would we keep secret?'

'Maybe you saw something? Something that you didn't think anything of at the time. Anything at all that was out of the ordinary.'

Helena closed her eyes in concentration for a moment, then opened them again.

'No. There's nothing.'

'All right. Then I think we should get you into protective custody while we find out more.'

'Not the police,' said Helena. 'They were useless before, and it'll be the first place that man looks. Plus, I'm not sure they would look kindly on me pretending to be a governess.'

'I'm sure they would keep you safe regardless,' tried Clara.

'No police.'

'But then where?'

Fleet stood up from his sack of coffee beans, made a half-hearted attempt to uncrumple his clothes, walked towards the window and drew open the blind. The signage from the building opposite glowed onto his face, and he sighed the resigned sigh of a man who knew what he had to do, but desperately wished that he didn't.

Reverend Kilburn – unlike more or less every single other person in the city – was filled with joy.

Not happiness. Happiness comes and goes. What Kilburn had was *joy*. It burned inside him like un-blown-on soup.

143

Only it wasn't soup. His was a joy of spirit, of devotion, of service to a higher power.

What exactly was that higher power? Who could say? The higher power, that's who. Probably.

It was a very young religion, and there was a lot of detail still to be sorted out.

One thing was for sure, mind. Queen Victoria's *Eleven-And-Counting Miraculous Resurrections* at the Blessed Hands of Her Majesty's Royal Medical Engineers. Not to mention Inspector Fleet's *Just-The-One-But-Still-Pretty-Good-Considering Miraculous Resurrection,* also at the Blessed Hands of Her Majesty's Royal Medical Engineers, whose skills Fleet had been kindly loaned on account of his stopping a particularly nasty crime that happened to capture Her Majesty's interest.

A lot of people were less keen on these things. They thought that if someone was going to die, they should just ruddy well have done with it and not keep careening back and forth between eternal planes.

But for Reverend Kilburn, and his acolytes in the Church of the Mechanical Man (*Est'd About 2 Months Ago*), these technological undeadenings were a marvel. No, more than that. They were themselves the tell-tale fingerprints of the Almighty.

For how else could humanity have come to bear such terrible power than through the Impossibly-Clever-But-Sometimes-Hard-To-Understand Plan of the All-Knowing-Yet-Cheekily-Unwilling-To-Explain-What-He's-Up-To?

It wasn't as though the revivals were even much of a secret. It was just that with the queen, people responded with a deeply respectful uncertainty and by trying very hard not to think about it. And with Fleet, few people realised they were meeting a detective whose death had been reported in the newspaper; fewer still had enough headspace beyond their own workload, pending errands and general city cacophony to realise that this was unusual; very few indeed took much notice of it other than to say 'Gosh'; and you could count on one finger the number of people who, shortly after running into him one day, decided to go ahead and set up a new religion.

This idea had occurred to Reverend Kilburn in part because he had been a Church of England vicar for several decades beforehand, and this experience could be seen in the Church of the Mechanical Man in the form of familiar schedules, accessories, foundational theological tenets and suchlike.

'No reason to throw out the Divine Infant with the bath-water,' he often said, to no one in particular.

And it was for this reason, and also to do with poor time management, that at this precise moment, late in the evening, the reverend was in the vestry writing his weekly sermon, which is to say he was avoiding it entirely and convincing himself that polishing the big silver Sunday plates was a critical part of the creative process.

On his desk were several screwed-up balls of paper, on which were various attempts he had made to try and clarify some pressing questions his congregation – now exploding into the double digits – had been putting to him recently. For example:

'Why have you filled the font with motor oil?'
    Well, what is the washing away of sin if not a sort of 1,000-mile tune-up for the soul?

'Should we all seek out technological modifications, or is it just for Her Majesty and that Fleet chap?'
    Probably best to leave it to them for now and just admire from a distance. We still don't know the long-term effects.

'What do you mean when you say the Creator is joined by a sort of "Improver" or "Mechanic"?'

Well, you know. Father, Son, Holy Ghost. Why stop there, I say. The more the merrier.

'What does all this mean for Jesus's resurrection?'
Oh dear. It's probably a bit soon to get into that sort of thing.

Kilburn had just finished buffing the rim of the really, *really* big plate when a voice called out from the nave.

'Hello?'

At this unexpected sound, his nervous system did what millions of years of human evolution and survival instinct had allowed it to perfect, which was to make him drop the plate onto the stone floor with a deafening clatter, and collapse in a heap.

'Aaggh!'

'What?' called the voice.

'Won't be a moment!' cried Kilburn, and he sprang back to his feet, snatching up the spinning plate on his way to a small mirror to make sure his appearance was suitably churchful.

The silver hair of his sixty years flowed like a mane, and he had a beard to match. But he wore the typical black and white garments of a vicar, which meant that overall he looked like a wizard summoned before a magistrate.

The only specific sign of the Church of the Mechanical Man was in the centre of his dog collar, where he'd had stitched a small image of a cog.

The cog. For are we not all mere cogs in some Great Cosmic Machine? A humble component, but essential. Working together. Turning and turning to drive the crankshaft of destiny, or what have you. Plus, cogs and people both have teeth – that's another similarity.

'Um, *hello*?'

Gracious! I said I wouldn't be a moment, and I've been several moments at the very least.

146

Kilburn pulled back the dark-green velvet curtain that hung across the doorway, then remembered he had better take the silverware with him or he'd just forget about it for days, so dropped the curtain, grabbed the rest of the plates, pulled back the curtain again with a free elbow, and walked with as much clerical solemnity as he could muster out into the nave.

'Good evening, Reverend,' said Fleet.

Kilburn clasped his hands to his mouth, sending the tower of silverware crashing to the floor. Through sheer force of will, he remained standing, and instead blinked in astonishment through his round spectacles.

'*Inspector?*'

'Yes.'

'Inspector Fleet?'

'Still yes.'

Kilburn was immobilised and hadn't even registered the presence of Helena Evans and Clara. He was too busy having a religious experience.

'You're here,' he whispered. 'You're actually here! Of course, I always hoped this day would come. Although, in all honesty, it would have been better if more of our number were here.'

Fleet scanned the empty room. 'More?'

'But no matter, here you are indeed. *Allelu*—'

'Absolutely not.'

Clara tried her best to catch Helena's eye with some desperate looks and the flapping of hands, but the engineer-governess was unable to stifle her curiosity.

'I'm sorry,' she began, 'is this . . . are you . . . *worship-ping* him?'

Kilburn emitted a small chortle. 'Goodness, no. Oh dear, no. No, no, no. We don't think of Inspector Fleet here as a god, per se.'

'I'd really rather you didn't think of me at all.'

'But, if you were to ask me: "Reverend Kilburn, did Inspector Fleet inspire the creation of your religion?", or, if you were to ask me: "Reverend Kilburn, does Inspector Fleet represent the possibilities of human mechanical potential and therefore of mortal flourishing and goodness?", then my answer would be: "Would you care for a pamphlet?"'

'Does the pamphlet answer the question?' asked Helena.

'Oh no, of course not. But it has some absolute corkers of *further* questions.'

'Reverend Kilburn,' said Fleet.

Kilburn beamed. 'You remember my name!'

'We've met several times, Reverend, including most mornings in the queue for coffee at Mrs Pomligan's. And in any case, you've just told us what your name is. Twice. But that's beside the point. We've come here because . . .' – Fleet winced and took a deep intake of breath – 'because we need your help.'

Kilburn's joy was overflowing. He felt he might burst. 'Of course! Of course! Anything that the Church can do to help Our Inspector.'

'No, no. Not "yours".'

'Of course, of course. *Everyone's Inspector.*'

'No, I . . .' Fleet turned to his colleague, exasperated.

'Reverend Kilburn,' Clara began, 'allow me to introduce Miss Helena Evans.'

'A pleasure, Miss Evans!'

'Some weeks ago an attempt was made on her life,' explained Clara.

'Dear!'

'Yes. I won't trouble you with all the details now.'

'No trouble!'

'I went into hiding,' said Helena, 'and these two exposed my whereabouts and pseudonym.'

148

'Oh dear . . .'

Clara ploughed on.

'Yes, well, the point is that Miss Evans here is in grave need of sanctuary until such time as we can discover who exactly wishes her dead and we can, um, stop them.'

'Sanctuary?' replied Kilburn. 'Say no more. You'll be very safe here, Miss Evans, very safe. We have some rooms above the vestry, and, why, barely anyone seems to know we exist, despite my flyering campaigns. Just a few loyal followers every Sunday, plus a few people from the congregation that was here before us and relocated, who seem to have got separated from their flock – but they bring their own wine and wafers and just get on with things at the back so who am I to argue? Oh, and I can also lock the big door!'

'What do you think, Miss Evans?' asked Fleet.

Helena looked around at her possible new home, and at Kilburn, her possible guardian. She nodded, and smiled for the first time in quite a while.

'Thank you,' she said.

'Not at all! Why, it's what we're here for, isn't it? To protect one another. To lend a hand. And I'll pray that this all ends quickly.'

'To whom?' asked Helena.

'To be perfectly frank, Miss Evans, we're still working all that out.'

Chapter 10

Clara awoke the next morning yearning for buttered toast and justice.

Not buttered justice, she mentally clarified to herself — only the toast should be buttered. And she knew that these things are not equally important, so it was perhaps silly to yearn for them both in the same yearning. But buttered toast is much easier to come by than justice in this world, and there's no use trying to solve mysteries on an empty stomach.

They had clearly made a mistake in handing over information about Helena Evans's identity without speaking to her first to hear her story, and it was a mistake Clara promised herself she would never make again. But they had at least done some good by having her safely ensconced in the Church of the Mechanical Man.

The question before Clara now was that most wonderful, terrible question of all: 'What next?'

Once dressed, she released her birds from their cage in the kitchen-dining-living-room of her flat, and allowed them to fly around to stretch their wings. As they fluttered between armchair and radio, and eventually settled on the ceiling lamp, Clara began recounting to them, waving her buttered toast for emphasis, the current state of the Case of the Carriage Abductions, Permanent Name To Be Determined.

No sooner had she started, however, than a low-pitched horn blared loudly from outside. Clara peered out the window and saw a long goods wagon on the other side of the street, painted in a dark green so uninteresting it nearly vanished into its surroundings.

Standing in front, straighter than the lampposts, was Lance-Corporal Redfield, dressed in the brown uniform of Brunelian officers that looked as militaristic as it did itchy. He gave a short, sharp wave when he spied Clara, and got back into the front cabin of the vehicle behind the wheel.

Progress! thought Clara.

She sped down the stairs, finishing her toast en route, and walked up to Redfield's open window as her bright-new-day positivity began to cloud with dread.

'Good morning, Lance-Corporal,' she said. And then, if only to delay the inevitable, 'How are you?'

The officer glanced towards her with grim disquiet.

'Mellanby's dead. Get in.'

Fleet was just about to enter the door to Mrs Pomligan's when he heard a familiar voice shouting his name.

He turned, saw Clara and Lance-Corporal Redfield pulled up alongside in a large, quasi-military vehicle, and then spent a few moments reassuring nearby pedestrians that everything was fine and the woman shouting wasn't about to launch an artillery attack of some kind.

He approached the vehicle.

'New lorry, Clara? It's nice.'

'No, Fleet. It's Lance-Corporal Redfield's.'

'Yes, I—'

'He's just here.'

151

Clara leaned back to clear the view between Redfield and Fleet, who nodded at each other almost imperceptibly.

'Lance-Corporal.'

'Inspector.'

'Redfield tracked down Mellanby's division,' Clara continued, before pausing sombrely. 'He's dead.'

Fleet sighed and shook his head. He knew this outcome had been likely from the start – he'd known enough Scotland Yard cases to go this way – but he wasn't so jaded that it had no effect on him.

'Get in, Inspector,' said Redfield. 'All I have is that fact from his CO and she wouldn't say more over the line. We're going to his division's works site to find out what else they know.'

'Right.'

Fleet grabbed the rail on the wagon to pull himself up, but stopped as he began to sense something else was also trying to get his attention. Something terrible.

He looked down the street towards the corner, and saw Inspector Collier cheerfully waving at him, grinning with the industrial-strength, instant-on bonhomie of an MP realising he's about to be photographed.

Fleet felt a headache coming on, and closed his eyes in a fruitless attempt to prevent it.

'Give me a minute,' he said, before turning and pacing away.

'Citizen Fleet!' the other detective cried as he approached. 'You're a sight for sore peepers.'

'Staring at people will do that to you, Collier.'

Collier's eyes widened in delight, and he doubled over, pointing at Fleet and gasping for breath in between wheezing honks that were apparently meant to seem like laughter.

'You are a funny man, Fleet.'

'Not really, but thank you.'

'I'll tell you what else is funny,' said Collier, recovering instantly.

'Shilling says I won't laugh.'

'No takers on that, Fleet. Even if you ever laughed at anything, I don't think this will be your type of tickle.'

Fleet held up his hands in frustration. 'I am actually in the middle of something, Collier, so whatever it is you want . . .'

'Well it's less what I want, of course. I am a humble instrument of the will of the detective police, and at this particular moment that will – which is to say, the Detective Chief Inspector – would very much like you to come with me to have a chat.'

'A chat? About what?'

'Ah! I can't spoil it, Fleet.'

'I can't see Keller right now, I'm about to head to—'

'I believe he said . . .' – Collier stretched his body upwards and outwards, lifted his arms and growled like a frustrated bear – '"*If Fleet ever, EVER, wants to set foot in Scotland Yard again, have any dealings with the police, or indeed avoid the possibility of me withdrawing his ridiculous private investigatory licence . . .*"'

'Fine, Collier. Fine.'

'Wonderful! Let's go there together as brothers-in-arms. Chop chop!'

Fleet shook his head and returned to the goods wagon, where he found Clara smirking at him with simmering glee, one arm dangling out of the window, and wearing a Brunelian officer's cap.

'I'm in the Corps, Fleet!'

'Congratulations.'

'I'm a Neighbourhood Relations Captain. It's my job to make sure the people living near to our building works are kept happy and informed.'

'I thought the Brunelians just appear, build whatever they want to build, and are gone before anyone has time to complain.'

Redfield leaned forwards. 'That is the preferred tactic, yes. But sometimes things take a few days, and the NRCs are a useful lightning rod. This one seems to have left his hat here, which tells you something about the calibre of person who ends up in that role.'

Clara banged the outside of the wagon. 'Climb aboard, Ensign Fleet! Those viaducts won't build themselves.'

'You'll have to go without me. I need to smooth things over with Keller. Something must have happened.'

'We could wait for you,' suggested Clara.

Fleet had already seen Redfield glance at his watch several times. No need to test the patience of the man trying to help them.

'It's all right; who knows how long this will take. Go and find out what you can.'

Redfield gave Fleet an appreciative nod of the head.

'Oh, but you'll miss the building site!' exclaimed Clara, with a look of disappointment.

Fleet wasn't sure whether this was because she wanted him there, or because she genuinely thought a visit to a building site was something he shouldn't miss. It was hard to tell, largely because Clara really was the sort of person – indeed the only person he knew – who could find genuine joy and wonder in a building site.

'Bring me a souvenir.'

Clara smiled. 'I know you're joking, but just for that I'm going to find one for you.'

Redfield coughed pointedly.

'Yes, Lance-Corporal,' said Clara, before banging the side of the wagon again and pointing forward into the shining future. 'To progress!'

The wagon drifted away, and Fleet once again felt from along the street the sensation of an unnervingly cheerful, toothy smile, like that of a well-mannered jackal, drilling into the side of his head.

He took a deep breath and followed Inspector Collier to a nearby police wagon. Collier banged on the back door, waited for a constable inside to let them in, then turned to close the door behind them.

Just as he did so, Fleet glimpsed a familiar pair of eyes watching him from under a lamppost on the corner opposite. Familiar, curious, brainless eyes.

He could have sworn the beagle was grinning.

Before he could say anything, the doors swung shut. Collier beckoned Fleet further into the police wagon and then hopped into a folding seat in the corner, watching with an eager smile like a music-hall patron waiting for the show to begin.

Fleet turned to the wall, which was covered in screens, dials and radios. In the middle, at head height, a locution glass protruded towards him. It had the appearance and size of a hallway mirror, a metal frame to house its wiring, and a red antenna on top, imprinted with the image of the Tower. At this moment it was also emitting a loud beeping noise. Fleet glanced at Collier over his shoulder, who nodded enthusiastically at the device. Fleet took another deep breath and pushed a red button on the side of the glass.

'Caller?' came a voice from a tinny speaker.

'It's Fleet. Keller is expecting me.'

'Connecting you now.'

A dialling sequence began to chirrup as the silvery, liquid pane of the glass in front of Fleet began to shimmer, then crack, and eventually gloop into several vertical metallic puddles. The puddles split into smaller and smaller globules, rippling and jostling at the mercy of the array of magnets behind the panes. Eventually, the liquid began to take on a set of shapes that more or less made sense to Fleet, and he peered inwards at the resolving caller.

First there was the vague suggestion of a moustache, and even without further detail it was clear that the moustache was livid.

But then the metal liquid formed a Y, like a three-handed clock telling you that it was somehow half past both ten and two. The moustache, now accompanied by other shimmering suggestions of Keller's face, floated into the top section of the Y, and the left and right thirds started to form faces of their own. On the left, Professor Dorcas McCabe, in her study, pince-nez askew. On the right, Dr Benjamin Fernsby, grease across his forehead, somewhere in the bowels of Babbage's Big Boy. Both of them looked exhausted.

Fleet's heart sank.

Why is Keller speaking to them? What's happened?

The sound from all three began to come through the speaker in the police wagon. Fleet winced as he adjusted to the mechanical cacophony that was presumably coming from Dr Fernsby's end, but it was Keller who spoke first.

'Ah, Fleet,' he began, with unnerving pleasantness. 'Good morning. Are you well?'

Fleet felt a familiar unease. The calm was never good. He glanced to Collier, whose grin nearly escaped the sides of his face.

'Very well, sir,' Fleet finally replied. 'How are you?'

'Oh, yes, I'm fine, fine. Quiet morning. Up with the lark, some vigorous callisthenics. Indian clubs today. Marvellous things.'

'I'm . . . sure they are.'

'Fitness is more important as you get older, Fleet. Don't forget that.'

'I won't . . .'

'And then, let's see, I breakfasted on porridge with apple. Strolled into work. And that pretty much takes us up to here.'

Fleet stared at the Chief Inspector, and at the two members of Babbage College who seemed to be patiently waiting their turn.

'Well, that all sounds very nice, sir. I'm glad you've had a good morning.'

'Thank you, Fleet. Oh, there was one other thing.' Keller leaned forwards until his face entirely filled his third of the Y. 'I was awakened at half past three by a telephone call.'

In the corner, Collier began to gently vibrate.

'Oh?' replied Fleet.

'Indeed,' said Keller. 'From whom, you might ask.'

'I . . . yes, I suppose I do ask.'

'Well, Fleet. It was, interestingly enough, from *Buckingham Palace*.'

Fleet's heart lurched at this horrible news, but as a seasoned detective and Englishman he managed to make no visible outward reaction.

'That must have been quite the honour, sir.'

'Perhaps if it had been a message from Her Majesty,' replied Keller. 'An invitation to a nice garden party, maybe, or some token for my decades of public service against the forces of criminality. That would have been quite the honour. But it was, in fact, a call from Julius Bell.'

Fleet felt his heart turn a somersault, and this time his face could not keep the secret, looking exactly as aghast as he was.

Julius Bell, as Fleet well knew, was Queen Victoria's Private Secretary, a role that seemed to have much less to do with organising a social calendar than you might expect, and much more than you might expect to do with the dark secrets and unsavoury trade-offs of national security. He had hired Fleet and Clara on a previous case, and they had both learned that he had a tendency to appear only when things were going from bad to worse, or from worse to *spectacularly* undesirable.

'Oh?' asked Fleet, hopelessly. 'And what did he want?'

'A very good question, Fleet, and one Mrs Keller put to me also. Perhaps you can figure this puzzle out. Was it that Julius just couldn't sleep and thought the best thing for it was a Detective Chief Inspectorial telephone lullaby?'

'Probably not.'

'Correct, Fleet. It was not that. It was, in fact, as I vainly hoped you would have been able to deduce from the presence of the boffins here, a call to enquire why I had set in motion a series of events that have caused material damage to our national defences.'

Fleet desperately did not want to ask the next question, but it dragged him in like a whirlpool.

'*Did* you do that?'

'Apparently so, Fleet!' replied Keller, crescendoing. Apparently that's exactly what I did. Apparently I have caused a temporary breakdown in our intelligence capabilities that will be documented for all time, and which future generations of military experts will be able to study and learn from, shaking their heads and tutting as they vow never to allow such things under their watch *lest* – and I quote – *Britain suffers irreparable harm.*'

'It sounds bad.'

'Your instincts are as sharp as ever, Fleet, but I am somewhat concerned that if I continue this explanation I am liable to tear my locution glass from my desk and hurl it to wherever you happen to be standing, so perhaps, Professor, you could take over.'

The professor adjusted her pince-nez, leaving them even more askew than before.

'Slight hiccup with Big Boy, Inspector.'

'How slight?'

'He's melted.'

'Oh.'

Fleet could see now that Benjamin Fernsby was crying, and apparently could remain silent no longer.

'You killed him! With your stupid code, you killed my beautiful Big Boy!'

'How?'

'Ran himself too hot, didn't he? We drained the entire damn river to cool him down but even that wasn't enough. *And* they're still out rescuing the rowers who got stranded on the riverbed.'

'All we did was give it a code,' countered Fleet. 'You're the ones who said it could solve anything.'

'*Murderer!*'

'Dr Fernsby,' said the professor, 'please compose yourself. The repairs will only take a few days. And it was always possible the enemy would develop a code that would confound even Big Boy.'

Keller's face moved still closer to the screen, filling it entirely with eyes, nose and moustache.

'But it *wasn't* the enemy, was it, Fleet? Not an external enemy, anyway. The external enemies, as Julius was very keen to remind me, are, among other things, the terrifying armada of Prussian dreadnoughts in the North Sea, bobbing up and down and facing our equivalent armada of Phalanx Class warships — a *very* fragile situation and one where even a slight intelligence failure or misinterpretation could lead to *sudden national calamity*.'

Dr Fernsby nodded vigorously while blowing his nose.

'But it doesn't make any sense,' said Fleet. 'Why would a thief use a code that's far too complex for anyone to break? Who's it for?'

159

'A very good question,' said Keller. 'You can ponder it during your ample free time now that Inspector Collier takes over the matter from you.'

Fleet's heart stopped its gymnastics, and seemed to vanish entirely, leaving a hopeless void. He opened his mouth, but no words came out.

'Me?' said Collier, hand to his chest in shock. 'Well, I doubt I can fill Citizen Fleet's shoes but if that's what you feel is best, Chief Inspector.'

'But . . . we're making progress!' Fleet finally protested.

'I'm sorry?' said Keller incredulously, his eyebrows closing ranks. 'I think I heard dissent when in fact you have absolutely no standing here. You will have no further dealings on the bank thefts, nor will you speak with anyone, or anything, at Babbage College.'

'With respect, sir,' replied Fleet, 'we work independently.'

Locution devices didn't tend to convey the subtleties of callers' expressions, but it was quite clear that Keller did not find Fleet's observation particularly convincing.

'May I remind you, Fleet, that the *only* reason you are allowed to conduct investigations of any kind in this city is due to the private investigatory licence issued to you by the Metropolitan Police, which I was persuaded to not only issue but also *create* for you and Miss Entwhistle, because I was assured by you that doing so would make my life easier.'

He leaned somehow further forwards towards the screen. 'Needless to say, *it has not.*'

Fleet scrambled for allies. 'Professor?'

'My apologies, Inspector. I am at the mercy of those who provide the funding.'

Dr Fernsby shook his head with contempt. 'Maybe if somebody melted you, you'd understand.'

Fleet tried to think of some way out, but his mind was blank. The call ended, he was escorted out of the police wagon, Collier gave him a jovial, no-hard-feelings slap on the shoulder blade and a final flash of the teeth, and he wandered away in a daze.

Clara had been aware of the Brunelians since she first arrived in London. How could she have avoided them? She entered the city at London Border North station, which they'd built, and continued her journey by rail, which they'd laid. And from that point on it was impossible to look outside without seeing their work.

There were the tourist sites, of course.

The Westminster Ice Shield, protecting MPs in parliament from frozen gales and icicles whipping off the Thames, and, even more importantly, protecting people who were just trying to have a nice time on the glacier from having to see or think about their MPs.

The magnificent Crowglobe, a breathtaking hemispherical corvid aviary on the historic site of Shakespeare's draughtiest theatre.

And, of course, the ever-popular Watford Abyss, which was not the Brunelians' doing but they had built a nice viewing platform where you could stare down into the chasm, lose yourself in awe of the majesty of nature, and ponder the big unanswerable questions of life – questions such as 'Wasn't there a high street here before?', 'What caused the Abyss to appear?', and 'A fine for asking questions about the Abyss? My MP will hear of this, the next time the Ice Shield is lowered.'

But the work of the Brunelians could also be found in the little things. The rumbling of the tunnels underneath every street. The bridges crossing over each neighbourhood, not to mention the bridges crossing over many of the other bridges, and the bridges connecting two bridges because sometimes

161

you just need to get from bridge to bridge without coming all the way back down to ground level first.

Clara was aware of all this but, like almost everyone else, she had no idea how the Brunelians actually got these things done. They were a force of nature. They never announced their arrival or what they were planning, they moved about the city as predictably as bumblebees, and there were so many of them, working so quickly, that by the time you'd found out what they were up to they'd be off to the next thing and you'd be left with a very thin, long park where your street had been, which you had to admit was quite nice, but also somewhat inconvenient for the people whose front doors now opened onto a boating lake, who could only leave home by way of pedalo.

The drive with Redfield lasted several hours, and eventually Clara realised she could see the ocean in the distance below the brightening blue sky.

'Where are we, Lance-Corporal?'

'Southend-on-Sea. Turns out Mellanby's division is working on the Lanterns.'

'Lanterns?'

'You'll see.'

They drove on towards the seafront, and soon Clara saw the signs of Brunelian activity. Green lorries transporting construction materials one way and debris the other. Roads blocked at both ends with tents pitched in between. Officers outside them having heated discussions over maps and diagrams, and Neighbourhood Relations Captains cheerfully advising furious residents to go away and come back later or, even better, much later.

Green and orange barricades crossed the town-centre street they were driving along, manned by men in charming yellow helmets carrying extremely uncharming black rifles.

'Yellowtops,' said Redfield. 'Corps police.'

Clara studied the men with intrigue.

Redfield rolled down his window and flashed a battered identification card at one such yellowtop, who waved them through before turning back to a large, disgruntled crowd of people to whom a nearby NRC was explaining with a smile that no, he couldn't allow them to go past, yes, they would receive an inconvenience gesture for not being allowed to go past, and not only that, this was a problem that solved itself because there was nowhere for them to go past *to*.

Which he was absolutely right about, because not far beyond the barricades the town stopped entirely. Wiped from the face of the earth, as if a giant shovel had come from the heavens and dug away everything between Perch Avenue and the sea. Roads, gone. Houses, gone. Just miles and miles of earth, the rubble of whatever had been there before, and more people and machines than Clara had ever seen in one place, swarming around each other in a frenzy like wasps trapped in a jar.

She took a moment to adjust her eyes to the scale of it all. It was easier to look at if she thought of it like an alien world — the surface of Mars, perhaps — rather than an area of London just a few hundred feet away from a beach of confused sunbathers.

The landscape was dotted with green, round, canvas tents, like a mediaeval battle camp. Some were smaller and had people rushing in and out carrying documents, maps and clipboards. Some were larger, and lumbering machines the shape of people, but ten feet tall, with an operator suspended inside at the controls, walked in and out to fetch pallets of bricks and spools of chain. And a few were larger still, with great vehicles rolling in and out like islands moving at tectonic speeds, carrying immeasurable loads across the site and crushing the earth under their weight.

And then, beyond all of this, at the water's edge, an immense hill rose with mathematical beauty from the ground, curving gently at the base and growing steeper and steeper towards the top. Vehicles traced a wide spiral up and down its sides, ferrying their cargo from the base to the flat summit that towered over the wasteland around it.

It looked to Clara like pictures she'd seen of volcanoes. Except it caught the light differently. Bits of it shimmered.

Metal.

They'd built it.

She clutched her head. That migraine from Amandine Chalon's carriage was coming back.

Redfield seemed to notice and offered Clara some visitor goggles that, he explained, blurred the view beyond a radius of about fifty feet. She declined. She hadn't come all this way not to see.

'What is all this?' she asked.

'It's the Lanterns.'

'Which are . . . ?'

'Probably best the division commander explains. I don't have anything to do with it.'

They parked up near some other visitor vehicles and continued on foot towards a nearby tent, which had golden banners, each displaying the image of a laurel wreath and the text 'IKB 15'.

Inside, Clara saw it was a welcome tent of sorts, with comfortable seating, a reception desk and a small drinks station. She read an information board that somehow managed to avoid providing any information while Redfield spoke to the receptionist, who dialled a telephone and relayed a brief message.

Several minutes later, two armed yellowtops walked into the tent, looked around, nodded, and went back outside. Clara heard more of them encircling the tent. Then the original two returned, this time flanking an imposing woman in her late forties. She was tall and athletic looking; her golden hair was pulled back into a tight bun, and, despite her soft blue eyes and peach-like cheeks, she wore a severe expression – and the same itchy brown uniform as everyone else, with the addition of some very important-looking small rectangles on the shoulders.

The woman looked at Redfield, who was standing somehow even straighter in her presence, and then turned to Clara and broke into a winning smile.

'Good morning. You must be Miss Entwhistle.'

Clara felt as if the sun had started emitting charisma.

'Yes. I'm Hello. Clara. Hello.'

'Major-General Slate. Please, call me Alison.'

Redfield's eyebrow twitched at this shocking informality, but he wrestled it under control.

'Will you join me in a stroll, Miss Entwhistle? I have a meeting in four minutes.'

'Oh, of course.'

'Wonderful. Lance-Corporal, thank you for your work here. I will send a note of thanks to your commanding officer.'

'Very kind, Major-General,' said Redfield. 'Miss Entwhistle, I shall wait for you by the barricades.'

Clara gave him a grateful smile, and Slate immediately about-faced and began pacing away.

'Follow me. My meeting is in three minutes and fifty seconds.'

Clara walked with the major-general through the busy seafront worksite, surrounded by six yellowtops in formation. Workers strode around them in every direction, or climbed ladders on the sides of tents and from their elevated positions shouted orders or queries towards others, who took them inside their tents for a response. Heavy vehicles trundled past, or, if on a collision course with Slate's yellow circle, lurched to a sudden halt, snorting bolts of compressed air like resentful bulls. Clara wanted to study it all, to stay and write down everything and hope to make sense of it somehow, but she knew that was not why she had come.

'You're a private investigator, I understand,' said Slate.

'That's right. And a journalist. Two jobs, busy busy.'

'Busy life, busy mind, Miss Entwhistle. We must all keep ourselves occupied. You strike me as an *active mind*. I like active minds. Not everyone is one. Some minds are idle. You understand what we do in the Corps?'

'Well, you build things, yes?'

'Of course, of course,' replied Slate. 'But what sort of things, Active Mind?'

'Well, bridges, and tunnels, and apparently some kind of lantern which I haven't really been filled in on . . .'

'No, no, no! "Tunnels", "bridges", that is Idle Mind. Idle. I think you more capable. Shame you are not a Corpswoman yourself. What do we build?'

Clara thought about what Slate might be driving at.

'The future?'

The major-general spun round, caught Clara in the beams of her eyes and snapped her fingers approvingly at her, all without breaking stride.

'*Active*. Active indeed. Very good. This is why I tell my people their instinct for rest is often an illusion. Keep the body moving, you remain fit. Keep the mind moving, you remain sharp.'

'Well, I'm not sure I agree people don't need rest,' said Clara.

'Good. Active minds rarely agree. Keep it up. But you are correct that we build the future. Brunel himself saw this. "*The future is the project that is never finished,*" he said. Talk about active minds! That one could have run around the coast of Britain, so to speak.'

'It's true London would be very different without the Brunel Corps.'

'Different? There would barely be a city. Just the old capital and a cluster of settlements across the regions. We're the ones who knitted it all together. Is it hard? Of course. But that's what discipline is. Hard work makes you stronger; strength makes work easier; easier work happens faster; faster means time for more hard work. Hard. Strong. Easy. Fast. The Brunel Cycle. Always improving, always pushing forwards, always building the future – and ourselves.'

'Not all of you,' replied Clara.

Slate nodded. 'Quite right, Miss Entwhistle. The matter at hand: Lieutenant-Supply-Captain Mellanby.'

They reached a lookout structure, barely more than scaffolding, facing the hill from the centre of the building site. A metal staircase snaked upwards alongside it. Two yellowtops at the bottom stood aside to allow the group to pass, and the six that had been guarding the major-general waited at the foot of the stairs as she marched upwards with Clara in tow.

'Lance-Corporal Redfield briefed me on your investigations when we spoke earlier. I'm sorry this came to you.'

'Mellanby is dead, I understand.'

'Sadly so. I didn't know him personally but I reviewed his file and he was very dedicated. Apparently he was found stabbed to death in an alleyway behind a pub. No witnesses.'

Clara winced, unable to avoid picturing his last, terrible moments. 'How do you know this?'

'He was discovered without identification, only his IKB badge, so the mortuary contacted us.'

They reached the top of one flight of stairs, turned around and began heading up a second.

'So, the yellowtops went and retrieved him, and we gave him a proper, Brunelian send-off: ten-crane salute, pennant draped over the coffin, the works. I said a few words – forgive me for not remembering what they were, my aide-de-camp wrote them – and then he was incinerated and his ash used in cement.'

'Good lord!'

Slate frowned. 'Squeamishness is Idle Mind, Miss Entwhistle! From the earth we came, and to the earth we shall return. We are all just temporary arrangements of the raw stuff of this world. And he was a lieutenant-supply-captain: he would have known that better than anyone.'

'Didn't he have any family or next of kin?'

'A fiancée, I gather, but that doesn't meet the bar. There are protocols for this sort of thing; it's not just something I make up on the spot. All officers who snuff it before retirement get to be a part of one last project. It's quite the honour.'

'Be a part of . . .' Clara repeated, distantly, wondering whether any of the many structures she had set foot on in London contained such remains.

'Besides,' Slate continued, 'it's what he would have wanted. Or, at least, since we have no idea what he wanted, let's assume it's what he would have wanted.'

They reached the top of the second staircase, which opened onto a platform with a railing around the edge. Twenty or so greying officers, some with shoulder patches similar to the major-general's, were milling about and chatting cheerfully, while a young woman walked between them topping up glasses of sparkling wine.

Slate led Clara through the crowd, slapping a few of the officers on the back and lobbing the occasional witty barb to others as she passed, prompting laughter throughout the assembled party.

They stopped at a quiet spot near the railing, and Slate summoned her aide-de-camp to come close.

'Any of the Triumvirate make it?'

'They send their apologies, Major-General,' the young officer replied.

'Useless! I expect this of Merridew, but Crowe and Khan have more imagination. I really thought at least one of them might come.' She sighed. 'You will prepare a report?'

'Of course.'

'It will have to do. Show it to me before sending.'

Slate waved the aide away and slumped over the railing, before remembering herself and straightening back up.

'Dignitaries?' asked Clara.

'Oh, yes, the Triumvirate run the show. On behalf of Brunel, supposedly, if the old man is even still alive. Would have been good to have one of them here.'

Clara looked around at the chatting officials with their important badges and ribbons.

'The people here don't matter?'

'Of course, but these are my peers. They want to see this project fail.'

'Why?' asked Clara, taken aback.

'Why do you think? Because it's not theirs.'

'You think they've come here just to watch it all go wrong?'

'They've come here to be here. If I succeed, I will have more influence across the Corps and they will want my favour. If I fail, they can say they were close enough to see the warning signs but I did not listen. Either way, they win. And they get a free drink.'

The aide-de-camp returned and whispered something in Slate's ear. She turned to the assembled crowd.

'Friends, it is time.'

She gave the aide a nod, and he leaned over the railing and signalled to a runner on the ground, who dashed to a nearby tent where Clara could see, through the flaps, officers manning radio equipment.

A siren blared across the vast expanse for several seconds. Clara looked out and saw everyone stop what they were doing. Officers, mechanical skeletons and giant vehicles all slowed and stopped, and the dignitaries on the platform ended their conversations. Every pair of eyes in the worksite focused on the hill.

The siren blared twice more, and a voice rang out:

'*Contact.*'

There was silence, and Clara wondered what exactly she was supposed to be seeing. The silence dragged out, and she began to feel mildly vexed by the distraction. She turned to the major-general.

'Do you know why anyone would wish Mellanby harm?'

Slate kept her eyes fixed on the hill in the distance. 'Who?'

'Mellanby. The man who was murdered. We were just talking about him.'

'This is what you want to talk about? Here?'

Clara realised she could hear a low hum, barely audible over the breeze.

'So you don't know why anyone would want to harm Mellanby?' she continued.

'I do not.'

'No rivals at work? Nothing unusual?'

'I highly doubt it,' said Slate.

'You seem quite sure despite not knowing him that well.'

'I am.'

The humming was becoming louder, and Clara found herself getting increasingly irritated by the noise distracting both her and, clearly, Slate.

'Why?' she asked.

'Because he was still a lieutenant-supply-captain at thirty-one, Miss Entwhistle. Capable. Reliable. But a plodder. Not a stand-out.'

'An "idle mind", I suppose?'

'In terms of his career, yes, he must have been. Probably one of those trapped in competence, blind to how the rungs of the ladder really work.'

Clara's eyes were drawn back to the hill. Light was beginning to appear in narrow cracks running up and down its surface. It looked like a lamp that had been shattered, and glued badly back together.

'You must forgive my frankness,' the major-general continued, 'but this Mellanby was just not senior enough to have had meaningful professional rivalries or secrets. I can only assume he was the victim of a terrible mistake where the attacker confused him for someone more interesting.'

'I see why you didn't write the eulogy yourself.'

'Ha! Touché, Miss Entwhistle.'

Clara squinted at the hill. There was a structure on the top. Concrete and glass. She couldn't make it out.

A minute passed. The humming continued to get louder, and was now a monotonous drone filling the world around Clara at the volume of sirens. It was bordering on uncomfortable.

Clara looked around and saw some of the officers putting on goggles – the same kind Redfield had offered her in the lorry. Others just ignored the man handing them out. He came to Clara and offered a pair. She put out a hand to take them, but drew it back.

The major-general spotted this, caught Clara's eye and winked. She had also forgone the goggles.

'What *is* it?' asked Clara.

Slate flashed her perfect smile. 'The project that is never finished . . .'

The noise was becoming painful. Clara and most of the officers on the platform covered their ears. The major-general grimaced and continued to stare.

Suddenly, the drone stopped, the shattered lamp fell dark, and Clara heard the ringing of silence.

For exactly 2.3 seconds, she waited, staring at the hill.

Nothing.

Then another part of her awoke. The primordial, ancient part that knows danger. That knows danger comes first. It knew.

Clara threw her hands over her eyes, spun round and dropped to her knees as the silence was swept away by a deafening screaming across the firmament, and the sound of the sky catching fire.

She clenched her teeth and hunched her head down to try to cover her ears, but she could not. Her vision filled with the bright-red light of a summer sun pouring through her eyelids.

The screaming continued. Something was burning. Everything was burning.

She squinted through her fingers and saw her own shadow on the platform, stretching further and further away from her.

Her heart pounded against her ribcage. She wanted to run, but could not move.

'Never finished!' cried Slate in triumph.

The other officers cheered in chorus: '"Never finished!"'

All Clara could hear was the fire, and the laughter of the major-general, and the screaming of the heavens at the end of the world.

She thought of her brother, her sister, her parents . . . her ridiculous detective . . .

Then, it was gone. Silence returned, and remained. The platform was filled with the sound of handshakes and hearty congratulations.

Clara stood up and looked around. The officers with goggles were removing them, and those without were rubbing their eyes and blinking. The major-general was being surrounded by the other officers, mobbing her with well-wishes.

Clara looked out over the expanse. The workers on the ground were applauding at the hill, which was dark once again, except for the structure on top, which shone blood-red like a dying star.

The sky was as blue as before. Wispy clouds teased the horizon. It was quite a nice day.

She was confused.

A moment later, her eyes were drawn even further, over the sea, a mile out at least, where a vast column of cloud was rising slowly from the water.

She could see a ripple in the water under the cloud, growing outwards in every direction.

Strange.

The ripple grew quickly, widening until Clara could only see the nearest edge, an arc, which straightened until all sense of a circle was gone. Just an endless ridge in the water, creeping closer.

She looked down at the building site. Workers were abandoning their vehicles and calmly moving away from the waterfront. The expanse looked bigger than before. There was an empty stretch of wet sand now, beyond all the tents and workers, and it was getting larger. The sea was pulling away.

Clara's confusion hardened into a lurching dread.

Why isn't anyone running?

The ridge in the water was half a mile away.

Then one quarter.

Less.

The workers had vacated most of the building site, and were clustered as far back as the viewing platform, standing shoulder to shoulder in a line eight people deep and stretching across the entire expanse, like an army waiting for the signal to charge.

The ridge became harder for Clara to see, and instead the entire ocean seemed to move, as if someone had whipped the moon around the earth and the tide was racing to catch up.

It swelled up onto the sands, and pushed quickly through the empty stretch. It surged forwards into the building site, and swallowed abandoned vehicles and tents.

It seemed to Clara as if it would engulf them all and then the rest of the city behind them.

But then the water slowed, and fell, and only crawled through the rest of the site, and by the time it reached the line of Brunelians, it was nothing more than a lapping wave.

A baby-faced officer stuck a foot in playfully, before being reprimanded by someone standing behind.

A moment later, the water pulled away, sweeping back homewards, until all was as it had been before.

Slate grabbed a megaphone and shouted down to the assembled workers: 'Division Fifteen!'

The crowd roared back in unison: 'Division Fifteen!'

'Well done!'

The crowd cheered and jumped and pumped their fists towards the sky.

'Now,' cried the major-general. '*Reset!*'

The crowd saluted, and split up to begin swiftly walking in a hundred directions, returning to their previous stations, recovering flattened tents, and bailing water out of the cabins of their vehicles.

Clara was furious, and strode up to Slate.

'What is this?' she demanded.

'Miss Entwhistle! Did you enjoy the show? You're awfully lucky to see it.'

'You've invented a way to create a tsunami?'

'That's just a side-effect.'

'Of what?'

'The primary effect,' said Slate.

'Which is?'

'Deterrence, of course.'

'Against whom?'

The major-general frowned and smirked with amused confusion, and gestured broadly out to the ocean.

'Enemies, Miss Entwhistle. Or, specifically, any enemy dreadnought that doesn't want to be caught in the centre of the beam.'

Clara remembered what Redfield had called this site.

'"Lanterns . . ."'

'Indeed. This is Lantern One. Lantern Five is our next project, across the estuary. The three final Lanterns will stand in the water in between. Between them they will have reach across the entire waterway towards the Thames. They will be our last line of defence. And bear in mind, this was a test – it was not the full power of the Lantern.'

Clara couldn't believe what she was hearing.

'But . . . a larger wave would wash inland and kill thousands!'

'If a Prussian dreadnought made it this close, we would have no choice.'

'*No choice?*'

'If it was without cost, Miss Entwhistle, it wouldn't be the *last* line of defence.'

'I can't believe the government would even ask for this.'

'We don't take orders from Government. We'll hand it over to them when it's fully tested, of course, but the Lanterns are a Corps idea. At the moment, our nation is entirely reliant on Phalanx Class warships as a North Sea defence, and our feeling is that doesn't suffice.'

Clara was nearly dumbstruck.

'Who are you to decide this?'

'We're not deciding. We're just engineers; we provide capabilities. It's up to Government to decide what to do with them.'

The major-general leaned in, gripped Clara's shoulders with her hands, and trapped her in her gaze.

'*Active minds*, Miss Entwhistle. *Active*. Look. What. We. Can. Do.'

Clara was met again by Slate's winning smile. It chilled her from the inside, and she felt an unformed memory of the major-general on horseback, sabre aloft, leading her troops into the fray. The same brown uniform, the same grand bearing, no flesh on her face, no hair, just a dead, ever-grinning jaw.

Fleet was sitting at his desk in Fleet-Entwhistle Private Investigations staring at the pages of his notebook, which were covered in the numbers from the code that had defeated even a colossal thinking machine.

He looked up at the clock on the wall and sighed. He'd been poring over his case notes and a sizeable stack of press clippings on the bank break-ins since his meeting with Keller, but he had nothing to show for it except a headache.

The questions jabbed his mind. Why would the thieves leave a code that's impossible to decipher? Why leave such clumsy markings if it *wasn't* a code? Why steal so little each time, and why go to the trouble of drugging unsuspecting members of the public just to leave them in the vaults? None of it made any sense.

Suddenly, the telephone on his desk rang loudly, making him jump. He picked up the receiver and heard the noise of a moving vehicle.

'Hello?'

The caller sighed.

'*Hello*?'

'Oh,' came the faint reply, followed by a long pause. 'Hello, Fleet.'

He barely could tell who it was. Clara without her usual pep was almost unrecognisable.

'Everything all right?' he asked, knowing it could not be.

'Not really. We're building a hideous superweapon.'

176

'You and Redfield?' replied Fleet with mock surprise. 'You've been busy.'

There was no response. Normally that sort of reply would at least elicit some playful scolding. Fleet grew concerned.

'I think it was the worst thing I've ever seen,' said Clara, flatly.

'Do you want to talk about it?'

'No.'

'Do you want to talk about Mellanby?'

'No.'

'What do you want to talk about?'

Fleet waited, listening to the sounds of the distant road.

'I don't know,' she replied eventually.

He tried to think of more options. Not talking about things was Fleet's speciality, but for Clara this signalled a worrying malaise. Things were dire. He was going to have to resort to small talk.

'Would you like to hear about my day?'

A brief pause.

'Yes,' she replied, with a note of hope, as if the mundane everyday was exactly what she needed to hear right now.

'All right,' said Fleet, 'I've been in our office. I sorted the files.'

'What files?'

'The files. The only files. We have six files and I sorted them.'

'What do you mean "sorted them"?' asked Clara, animated by mild confusion. 'They're already sorted.'

'I strongly disagree. You had, in fact, just put them in a drawer.'

'"Just?" They were alphabetised!'

'Were they?' replied Fleet. 'Well, they're in date order now. That's what your friend Posner recommended. I read your copy.'

Clara laughed. 'You read Posner?' she asked, with amused suspicion.

'I did. Cover to cover. Good read.'

'I have that book in my bag. Did you forget?'

'Of course not,' said Fleet, having entirely forgotten. 'I am a detective, I don't forget things.'

'That's elephants, Fleet.'

'And detectives. Elephants and detectives. Much in common.'

'Name one other thing elephants and detectives have in common.'

Fleet thought about this for a moment.

'Trunks are just big cases?'

Clara snorted. 'Have you actually reordered the files?'

'Clara, there are six files. They could be in order of the client's waist measurement and it wouldn't make any difference.'

'So what have you actually been up to?'

Fleet remembered the mess he was in before he switched to the task of cheering up Clara.

'Not a lot. We lost our Big Boy privileges.'

'I beg your pardon?'

'The giant computing machine. We melted it.'

'Oh dear!' exclaimed Clara.

'Keller is furious, of course, and he's not going to let us anywhere near the bank cases any more.'

'I'm sorry, Fleet. I suppose it was always quite unlikely we would get anywhere when half the detective police hadn't. At least we realised there was a code! They can look into that more. It might feel like a waste of our time but it won't have been overall.'

Fleet wasn't sure if he agreed with this, but he was glad to hear Clara finding her boundless positivity again.

'Maybe,' he replied. 'Although I don't know how they can crack it if that giant machine couldn't. Maybe we were wrong. Maybe it's not a code.'

'But that doesn't make any sense, Fleet. Why would anyone go to all that trouble with the boxes and the numbers? It has to be that they're sending a message. Otherwise it's just chaos.'

The idea fired down on Fleet like a lightning bolt, consuming his entire perceptive and mental faculties, as you'd expect being hit by a lightning bolt probably would. Certainly the first few times.

When he returned to the here and now, he realised he had a faint sensation of the words 'Are you still there?' coming from somewhere very far away. His hand was resting on the desk, barely holding the telephone receiver.

'That's exactly what it is,' he said, to no one.

Chapter 11

In a greasy spoon not too far away, Lester Horrocks was staring into the beauty of Creation.

It was on a chipped white plate bearing the image of Queen Victoria, this particular miracle. Two and a half inches thick. A golden white on its bready top and bottom. Three dark, fleshy cylinders nestling between. Oily liquid with black, charred flecks seeped out from it, submerging Her Majesty under a shimmery pool of molten fats that made her appear even less entirely human than normal.

Lester pressed his hand on the uppermost surface of the bread, squishing it all down, and then released it, watching it spring slowly back into shape.

It was perfection.

He picked it up lovingly in two hands, savoured the moment, and lifted it towards his lips.

His brain was ready. The reward centres were primed. The sensory centres were prepared. And the long-term-health reasoning centre hadn't been heard from in years.

But just before the moment of Ineffable Joy, of lips meeting bread, something pulled Lester out of it. There was something in his peripheral vision. Something outside the window. Something quick and undignified.

He turned, looked out, and saw Inspector Fleet leaping up from the stairs down to the Underground, out of breath, drenched in sweat and trying to disentangle himself from two umbrellas he'd apparently trawled on his way up through the crowd.

Lester watched Fleet look quickly up and down the street, then dash across, expertly weaving through omnibuses, bicycles, carriages and wagons, charge at the door of the *Morning Chronicler* building, then rebound off it so loudly it could be heard inside the café, then swear something, then pull the handle, and then finally fly inside.

Through the windows, Lester kept watching Fleet's frantic pursuit of whatever on earth it was he was after. He ran across the entrance hall, then up the main staircase, then along the landing back towards the facade, then through a door into a hallway where he disappeared from view.

A moment later, Fleet burst though Lester's office door, looked around and apparently did not find what he had expected to, because he then shouted something that Lester could not entirely lip-read, but whatever it was it didn't look even remotely suitable for a workplace.

Fleet ran back out of Lester's office, disappeared into the hallway, reappeared on the landing, sprinted to and down the stairs and across the entrance hall, where he vanished again behind the front door, which shook violently as it was yanked backwards into its frame.

Some pigeons took flight from the roof as Lester heard from somewhere a faint defeated scream.

The door opened slowly outwards, and Fleet exited the building, shaking his head and muttering. He finally stopped on the pavement, looking around confusedly in every direction, before meeting Lester's eyes and pulling a face of frenzied incomprehension.

Lester waved with his sandwich. He was enjoying this a great deal. It was always good to see passion, and Fleet had it. It wasn't clear what was animating that passion at this specific moment, but he was sure he'd find out before too long.

Fleet looked quickly back and forth along the street, with not nearly enough care to notice anything, and dashed out into the side of a bus, which knocked him backwards to the ground. He got up, dusted himself off, and walked the rest of the way. He pulled open the door to the greasy spoon, approached Lester's table, pulled out the chair opposite and sat down. He was out of breath, his hair was matted across his eyes, and his suit would never be the same.

Lester nodded 'Hello', and took a bite of his greasy miracle. It was Good.

'Lester,' Fleet wheezed. 'What . . . are you doing here?'

'Feed the body, feed the mind, Fleet. Sausage sarnie? On me.'

'No . . . No time . . .'

'You can't sprint across country, lad. I'm sure whatever it is will still be there after you've revitalised yourself with humanity's greatest creation.'

'No . . . listen—'

'"What is humanity's greatest creation?" I hear you ask.'

'No . . . you didn't—'

Lester waved one hand across his miracle, like a museum guide pointing out historical wonders.

'Two slices of lightly toasted bread, one side slathered with sauce, around three fried pig tubes.'

Fleet had just about recovered, but this seemed to knock him back.

'*Pig tubes*? Could you make that sound any worse?'

'I'm a journo, Fleet,' Lester said, taking another bite. 'Not my job to dress things up. But yes, I could have said porky odds and sods in offal socks. Doesn't matter what you call 'em. They're still the pinnacle of human achievement.'

'Lester, listen.'

'I'm all ears, lad. Probably something I've in common with these bangers.'

'The eighteenth of February.'

'Planning a party?'

'The one just gone, Lester. The eighteenth of February and the twenty-sixth of March.'

'What about them?'

'Two of the burglaries were on those dates, weren't they?'

'What burglaries?'

'The *banks*, Lester!'

'That's why you're flying through town like a cat from a cannon? You've got something on the banks? What is it?'

'No, no, listen. Weren't two of the burglaries on those dates?'

Lester thought for a moment.

'Aye. Leadman's was the eighteenth of February, and the twenty-sixth of March was . . . Ostrand Building Society.'

Fleet dropped and shook his head, and muttered something under his breath.

Lester was intrigued. For the first time he could remember, he put down a sandwich.

'All right, what's the eighteenth of February?'

'Helena Evans, almost murdered.'

'And what's the twenty-sixth of March?'

'Oliver Mellanby, entirely murdered.'

'You think these people had something to do with the burglaries?'

'No. I think they had nothing to do with them.'

Lester threw up his hands, flinging sauce from a finger onto the window. 'Then what are we talking about, lad?'

Fleet stared at him. 'I think we're missing six more murders.'

Clara arrived at the *Morning Chronicler* building not long after, and found Fleet in the entrance hall, pacing back and forth, bedraggled and smelling faintly of sausages.

When he saw her, she noticed his eyes were shining with a rare zeal, and he appeared bursting to explain whatever it was he was thinking.

On the telephone, he had asked her to meet him at the *Chronicler* without saying why – presumably because she was not alone at her end.

Nor were they alone here in the entrance hall, however – at least not given the way people could appear from around the corner at any moment. And Clara felt it wouldn't be the best time to run into Augusta, not with her column still overdue. No, for both reasons it was best to proceed with caution.

She held up her finger to stop Fleet from blurting out whatever it was he wanted to say. The smell of sausages suggested he had already met with Lester, and there was really only one other thing he was likely to find useful here.

'Archives?' she asked.

He nodded.

Clara peered along a corridor to her right to check it was clear, and led the way as Fleet explained his thinking.

'You think the burglaries are a distraction?' she asked, glancing over her shoulder.

'I think they're so audacious they cover the papers for days. People get excited about sensational crimes; editors know this, editors want to sell papers, so it's all the press wants to talk about.'

Clara frowned. 'You make it sound as though the press is no different from a greengrocer putting his brightest fruit out front.'

'Exactly,' replied Fleet. 'That's a great way of putting it.'

There it was, thought Clara. That detective police mentality creeping in, the one that was predisposed to view the press with suspicion.

She felt put out. Put out because she felt irked, and she didn't like feeling irked. Being irked was just not in Clara's natural vocabulary of emotional reactions, even in response to things most people would understandably find irksome – like people stopping suddenly in doorways for no reason. Most people would be irked by that. Not Clara, however. For Clara it was merely an exciting opportunity to start a conversation with a stranger, one that might begin with a polite request to move out of the way, but had the potential to end with having made a new friend. And although this hadn't happened yet, that's not to say it never would. But now Clara did feel irked. Surely, she thought, Fleet must know from their time together what a force for good journalism could be.

'You don't think there's a public value in the press exploring major crimes in detail? Letting the public know what's happening in their city? What they might need to be aware of?'

'Mmmm . . . no,' replied Fleet. 'Maybe sometimes. But not this time.'

'I will look past this ignorance for now,' said Clara, 'but only because I want to know what you're getting at.'

She stopped at a junction in the corridor and peered round the corner to make sure nobody was there, before beckoning her colleague onwards.

Fleet rolled his eyes and followed.

'The burglaries are utterly audacious crimes,' he continued, 'and strange. Not much stolen each time. Unclear how they're getting in or out. But then there's also the things the public doesn't know about, like the people being drugged and waking up in the vaults.'

'And the code which wasn't really a code,' added Clara, looking back over her shoulder again.

'And the code, exactly! Which is the type of thing a criminal might do to taunt the police, but . . .'

'But it's unsolvable, because it's just been made to look like one.'

'Exactly,' said Fleet. 'It's all a waste of time. Half the detectives in the city are looking into it, but there's nothing there. The druggings – pointless. The code – pointless. The objects actually stolen – pointless. The burglaries themselves – pointless. It's all just to occupy the police and fill the papers.'

'A distraction,' said Clara.

'Right.'

'From what?'

Fleet hesitated, and appeared to be working up to an answer when another voice rang out from somewhere around a bend in the corridor.

'*Toole!*'

Clara froze. Augusta's sharp tones struck like a falling icicle.

'What did I tell you,' the editor continued, to the presumably present and immobilised Toole, 'about accepted methods of payment from the Messrs Huxley bakers?'

The young man's mumbled response faded into nothing on the way from wherever he was cornered.

'Indeed so, Toole!' cried Augusta. 'And yet I would have thought it was clear that I was using "baguettes" as a shorthand for *all bread*.'

Clara heard a very large bag being shaken, and its contents tumbled over one another with the crumbling of delicate crusts housing fluffy innards.

Seeded bloomers, she guessed.

'I am sure they are delicious, Toole!' the editor exclaimed. 'That is not the issue at hand!'

Clara grabbed Fleet's arm, wheeled him round, and gave him a shove down another corridor.

'Sorry, Fleet, it's just . . .'

'You still haven't submitted your overdue article?' ventured Fleet.

Clara felt bad. She didn't mean for her other job to keep encroaching on her detective casework. Fleet had, after all, taken her under his wing, even if she did have to thrust herself there initially. She thought about the door plaque he'd had engraved with both their names on it as his way of inviting her to be his business partner – typical Fleet, refusing to tell her so much as his favourite breakfast food and then to go and do something like that. It was the nicest thing anyone had ever done for her.

She flashed him an apologetic smile.

'Let's find another route.'

The *Morning Chronicler*'s archives were located in the basement. To get there, one had to pass down a precarious set of narrow stairs that, for some reason, could only be accessed by first leaving through the back exit of the building, walking along an alleyway, and re-entering through a different door which was located behind the bins.

Quite why the archives were so hidden no one knew, but it perhaps explained how the *Chronicler*'s octogenarian archivist had managed to keep her job so far beyond the usual retirement age, as people saw her so infrequently they mostly forgot she was there.

Fleet and Clara entered the archive's reception area and the lights overhead flickered and buzzed. Behind the main desk, lacquered wooden cabinets stretched out in tightly packed rows. Above, metal tracks snaked back and forth across the entire ceiling of the room, and hanging from the tracks were thousands upon thousands of newspapers, drooping like the foliage of a weeping willow.

Sitting at the desk was Lavender Boothroyd, eyes closed, her grey hair arranged tidily beneath a cap of simple white lace.

She was so still, and so strangely upright for someone who was clearly asleep.

Clara's mind raced away and she found herself wondering how long it would take for someone to discover Lavender's body were she to perish during working hours. Quite a long time, she feared.

Then she remembered that *she* lived alone, and she began to wonder how long it would take someone to find *her* body, were she to die at home. Would her birds sound the alarm, she wondered. Would they manage to escape and begin a new life? Would they *fail* to escape, and resort to using her as bird feed?

Clara made a mental note both to check on Miss Boothroyd at more regular intervals, and to increase her – admittedly already fairly fervent – attempts to befriend her neighbours.

She roused herself from her reverie and found Fleet trying to get the archivist's attention with words and waving, neither of which had any effect, before finally clapping once very loudly.

The elderly woman's eyes shot open and she hooted a startled '*Fooh!*', before realising where she was.

'Oh hello, dearies!' she said in a reedy voice, her sharp blue eyes twinkling in the lamplight. 'Lavender Boothroyd, how can I help you?'

'Miss Boothroyd,' said Fleet, handing over a slip of paper, 'we would like to see copies of the editions printed on these dates, and in the three days that followed each of them.'

Miss Boothroyd squinted at the paper and turned it over to make sure she had the right side. She slowly brought the piece of paper towards her face, so close it looked as though she might accidentally inhale it. She put on some spectacles hanging from a chain around her neck and squinted at the writing, before shaking her head and slowly moving the piece of paper back, until her arm could get no longer. She squinted again, then remembered something, chuckled at her own foolishness, and swapped her glasses for another pair hanging from the same chain. She pulled the paper slowly back towards her nose once again, then scratched her head and finally tried putting on both pairs of glasses at the same time.

'You know what, dearie?' she said. 'It might be easier if you just read them out.'

She handed Fleet back the sheet of paper and turned to the wall on her right. An array of metal levers, at the end of which were round, oversized black buttons marked with numbers or letters, formed a sort of giant vertical typewriter.

Fleet read out the first of the dates, and Miss Boothroyd firmly pushed some of the buttons on her wall of levers before finally pulling a rope.

A green light above the buttons lit up and an intricate system of cogs, gears and pulleys sprang into action, whirring and humming busily. The newspapers that were dangling on the track overhead began to tremble, then suddenly jerked into motion, propelled along the metal track at high speed, fanning Clara and Fleet with a strong breeze. They disappeared in their dozens into one wall, and just as many appeared from another wall at the other end of the track.

The procession came to an abrupt halt, the green light blinked, and four of the papers dropped into a large basket on Miss Boothroyd's desk.

'And the next date?' she asked.

The process was repeated until each date's issue, and those of the three days following, had been retrieved. The archivist tapped the top of the stack of newsprint with satisfaction.

'There you are,' she said. 'No dog-earing, please. If you need to remember what page you were on, just concentrate very hard.'

Fleet and Clara carried the papers to a large table, took an issue each, and began to read through.

Clara's was half-filled with the break-in at Vanier's bank, and investigatory pieces on some other banks that had been targeted in the weeks prior. It was page six before she encountered any news about anything else, but eventually she found what she had hoped would not be there.

Her heart sank, and she turned to Fleet. He nodded, his issue open on a page near the back.

They laid their open papers on the table, and each picked up another from the basket.

These had nothing they needed, nor did the next few. But the ones after that did, on pages 17 and 19 respectively. Fleet and Clara put them open on the table next to the others.

By this point Miss Boothroyd had tottered over and caught on to what they were looking for. She silently began helping, using a rubber thimble to fly through the pages at astonishing speed.

Clara was in awe of Miss Boothroyd's handy device, and made a mental note to buy one at the very earliest opportunity, but for now she would have to carry on unthimbled.

The three continued their search, putting unhelpful papers back in the basket, and the others open on the table in front of them, until finally all had been reviewed.

Fleet, Clara and Miss Boothroyd surveyed the mosaic of low-priority news before them. All short columns and tiny headlines. Minor allotment disputes, council notices, school sports day results and neighbourhood restaurant openings.

And also, once on each page, a murder.

'MAN KILLED', said one. 'FATAL INCIDENT', said another. 'AWFUL STABBING', a third, as if there were other kinds.

The reports continued. Clara felt numb.

'Dangerous around here, isn't it?' said Miss Boothroyd. 'Not like in my day. Well, it was dangerous then, too, come to think of it. Terribly dangerous.'

She shuddered, remembering all the danger.

Clara turned to Fleet. 'Deaths in all of yours?'

He nodded.

'Unexplained?'

'Explained by stab wounds,' said Fleet, 'but otherwise, yes.'

'One on every bank theft date . . .'

'Or in the days following. Not found straight away.'

Clara knew what was coming next, but wasn't quite ready to say it out loud. 'And your victims had a broad range of different professions? Totally different walks of life?'

Fleet shook his head slowly.

'Any of yours *not* engineers?' she asked.

Fleet shook his head again, and Clara gulped nervously.

'No,' she said. 'Nor any of mine.'

Chapter 12

Clara tried the flimsy door knocker one more time – each time fearing the even flimsier door might give way – but again there was no answer.

'No one home.'

'I'm sure she'll call us,' said Fleet. 'We can let her know then.'

Clara was pained. There was no joy in telling someone something tragic, but it was wrong to keep it from them. And they were already in the neighbourhood. And their next meeting would be even harder.

She looked along the one-sided street. It was quiet, a good way into dusk, the sun fallen out of sight behind the city.

Another trick, thought Clara. *The sun doesn't fall. We spin away.*

Mudlark followed the Thames, a long row of cramped wooden houses huddling against each other for warmth. The wind howled gently, as banks of icy shards piled up from the frozen channel against the stone defences.

Suddenly, there was another sound. A terrible crunch of metal, followed by an even more metallic voice sighing with resignation.

Clara and Fleet ran across the narrow, frosty road to the stone embankment and looked down onto the icy banks of the glacier.

An eight-foot-tall metal man was looking up at them. His hands – one a jagged drill the size of a small child, and the other a delicate pincer holding something small that flickered like the sun – were held aloft, as if he was ready to be welcomed back into the loving embrace of some creator. A weighty, glowing gyroscope was spinning two feet in front of his chest, held there by a long spike that seemed to extend right through him and out the other side.

The man waved his drill pitifully at Clara, and spoke his final, plaintive words:

'Warranty voided.'

He sank to his knees, and collapsed into the ice, revealing Kathleen Price standing behind him.

'Oh, 'ello, you two!' she said cheerfully, plucking the small, shiny treasure from the man's pincer and stashing it in a pocket. 'Good thing you're 'ere. This cheeky ol' Tommie Ton just tried to make off with me larkin' spear in his chest, can you believe it?'

'No,' said Fleet.

Kathleen wrenched her spear free from the automaton, clambered up the snowbanks and heaved herself over the embankment, before leading Fleet and Clara back towards the rickety row of houses they'd come from.

Kathleen's parlour was dim, and somehow colder than the outside, but she didn't notice until her guests shivered.

She picked up an old fire poker and swung it wildly around, narrowly missing Fleet and Clara's faces, before jabbing it at a red switch high up on the wall. The grid of filaments in the electric fireplace crackled into life and started to glow.

'There,' she said, and sank into a decaying armchair.

Clara did the same. Fleet was distracted by what the light of the fireplace had now illuminated on the walls: a series of trophy automaton heads. He stared at the heads, frozen, his mouth just as agape with horror as theirs, until Clara reached up and pulled him down into an armchair of his own and he spent a moment blinking away what he had just seen.

'It's about the man you witnessed being kidnapped,' began Clara.

'Well, I didn't think you was 'ere for tips on mudlarkin'.'

'Tips other than impaling automatons?' asked Fleet.

'Oh, you don't have to impale 'em. You can tangle their legs in fishin' wire too, then they're good for nothin'. *And . . .*' – Kathleen jabbed a finger excitedly into the air – 'if you can loop their drill arm at the same time, they sometimes bore themselves a hole straight down while they struggle, and then it's just a matter of chuckin' in some snow over the top.'

Clara shuddered at the thought of the entombed machines. 'But the man you saw on the bridge . . .'

She trailed off, unsure how to continue.

Kathleen nodded, and dropped her head for a moment. 'Poor boy. I expected his chances were low after 'e was taken, but it's still 'ard to 'ear.'

'His name was Oliver,' said Clara. 'Oliver Mellanby.'

'He was an officer in the Brunel Corps,' added Fleet.

'Hard workers,' said Kathleen, with an approving expression that seemed to be directed at the Tommie Ton heads on the wall. 'If I ever come across his grave, I will drop him some posies.'

The thought of Mellanby's grave, which Clara knew not to be a grave at all, made her feel slightly sick.

Kathleen began rocking herself forwards and backwards, and then, with some effort, pushed down hard on the arms of her chair and propelled herself onto her feet.

'Well, pity it had to end like this, but I suppose that's the way of these things.'

End?

Clara reflected on the other murders they had found in the news-papers, and Helena Evans, the one survivor, hiding in Reverend Kilburn's church because of their short-sighted investigation.

She extricated herself from her cushions and rose to her feet.

'It isn't the end,' she declared.

'You know who did it, then?' asked Kathleen.

'No,' said Fleet, heaving himself out of the quicksand of his armchair, and making every effort to keep the wall-mounted heads out of his eyeline. 'We don't know that. But we're going to find out.'

'Oh?' Kathleen tilted her head in interest. 'How you gonna do that, then?'

Clara looked over Kathleen's shoulder, out of her window and across the frosty street, where the hulking stone arches of Blackfriars Bridge lurched weightlessly into the darkness.

'We're going to speak to the person who knew him best.'

In the Classifieds Office of the *Morning Chronicler*, a mile away from the spears of Kathleen Price, a jumble of leather, metal and cogs bolted to a desk and arranged like a clerk was content-edly returning to the top of her principal instruction loop as a new message ticker-taped into the side of her head.

The incrementor token behind her left eye lamp recorded this as the 17,245th time through, but she breezed through it as cheerily as the day she was cobbled together.

> 001 READ {TELEGRAMMESSAGE}

She did so.

'For sale: Ornamental garden pagoda. Inlaid with tortoiseshell. 100% authentic and legitimate. 8ft height. Some whippet damage. Contact E. Bolieu, Berkeley Square'

> 002 APPROVE//REJECT {TELEGRAMMESSAGE}
>> 002.1 EXISTS? {ITEMONOFFER}

'Yes. Item for sale. Sounds nice.'

>> 002.2 EXISTS? {CONTACTINFORMATION}

'Yes. Not very precise but it's a small neighbourhood. They'll figure it out.'

>> 002.3 REMOVEPOTENTIALOFFENCE

The clerk's employer hadn't asked her to do this. But they also hadn't asked her *not* to do this. It just never came up when she was installed. Plus, it was a feature she was good at, and why wouldn't they want that?
'Better safe than sorry. Scanning for risky terms . . .'

*'For sale: Ornamental garden pa**GOD**a . . .'*

'Oh dear. So early on. This won't do. Substitute with "Creator". So "pa GOD a" could be "a pa CREATOR". Better . . . But what is a pa creator?'
She searched her conceptual association tables for 0.02 seconds.
'Ah.'

'For sale: Ornamental garden grandparent . . .'

'Good. Continuing with 002.3.'

*'. . . Inlaid with tortoises**HELL** . . .'*

'Oh dear. Totally unnecessary. The TONEITDOWNABIT function takes input "hell" and returns "inferno". But "Inlaid with tortoises inferno" is unclear. Maintain concept, repair language.'

'. . . Decorated with damned tortoises . . .'

'Better. Continuing with 002.3.'

'. . . 100% authentic and leGITimate . . .'

'Really, there's just no call for this sort of language. Find near synonym.'

'. . . 100% authentic and leFOOLimate . . .'

'Cleaner. But again unclear. "Le fool"? "I mate?" Improve synonyms, repair grammar.'

'. . . 100% authentic French jester, my lover . . .'

'Hmm . . . a bit risqué, but at least the language is clean. Continue.'

'. . . 8ft height. Some whippet damage . . .'

'No bad terms. Continue.'

'. . . Contact E. Bolieu, BERKeley Square . . .'

'Oh dear. Replace offending term, strip meaningless "eley", regrammatise. All right. That should do it. Read back the improved message.'

'*For sale: Ornamental garden grandparent. Decorated with damned tortoises. 100% authentic French jester, my lover. 8ft height. Some whippet damage. Contact E. Bolieu, halfwit squared.*'

'There. Much better.'

> 002 APPROVE//REJECT {TELEGRAMMESSAGE}:
:::: {APPROVE}
> 003 SENDTO PAGESETTING

The clerk printed out the improved message from the side of her head onto some ticker tape, and it ticked away across her small office and through a hole in the wall.

'Done.'

> 004 INC AND RETURN

The clerk heard the incrementor token behind her left eye lamp tick, and she felt the cold, reassuring uniformity of a 17,245th job well done.

'Onwards, Self. To the top of the principal instruction loop!'

As she moved on to her 17,246th work item, the clerk realised that this next telegram was not for a classified advertisement, but appeared to be a complaint about how a previous one had been edited. The author seemed enraged, and demanded that the paper print a correction, clarifying that he was not – nor, in Her Majesty's Armed Forces, was there any such thing as – a 'Lieutenant Large Intestine!'.

The clerk realised to her momentary regret that she had no instruction loop for how to handle complaints, and so did the only thing she could in the circumstances, which was to incinerate the incoming message and delete all trace of it from her memory stores.

As she always did after a tricky operation, she checked her memory for good measure, and noted with great pride that she had never received a single complaint.

She was just about to resume her principal instruction loop when her internal clock − synchronised nightly by Tower radio to the national meridian − clicked to 8 p.m.

> 301 SECONDARY INSTRUCTION LOOP: DATE-//TIME-BOUND NOTICE

8 p.m. She remembered: there was a message about 8 p.m. tonight.

She searched her memory of recent classified advertisements. There was a match.

Recalling:

Received:	*Approx. 21 hrs ago (23:09:04:13)*
Sent to Page Setting:	*Approx. 21 hrs ago (23:09:04:82)*
Edits for Decency:	*No changes*
Sender:	*Clara Entwhistle,*
	Morning Chronicler & Fleet-Entwhistle
	Private Investigations
Payment Method:	*'It's Clara! I'll pay when I next come in!'*
Content:	

The clerk re-read the message content from her memory. She had been impressed by its almost total lack of words, reducing the risk of causing offence to negligible levels.

Many of the people who sent in their adverts could learn from this, she thought.

She suddenly realised she had spent a generous 0.31 seconds on this secondary activity, and returned to her principal instruction loop, musing all the while − in any excess computational capacity that happened to free up – about this minuscule classified advert, and whether anyone would, or even could, respond.

The clerk read it again in her (let's say) mind.

It intrigued her.

'Alexandrina. 8 p.m. Justice.'

Fog had fallen over the night by Blackfriars Bridge. From the street at the Mudlark end, Fleet could see barely a third of the way across before the bridge vanished into a dark haze. Even the streetlamps running along either side seemed incapable of breaking through, and receded into the distance as evenly spaced, diminishing circles of light in an otherwise endless nothing.

The fog made the charged air crackle, and here and there across the black sky vast pools of purple light would appear and recede, followed by distant, unearthly zapping sounds.

Once, he remembered, lightning had only come with storms. Now, thanks to the Tower, the sky fizzed and surged against itself like a volatile mixture trapped in a shaken beaker.

A blinding bolt suddenly split the world between left and right.

St Paul's. Taking the brunt of land strikes in the local area ever since it had had a 400-foot metal spike speared up through its dome from the choir stalls.

Fleet covered his ears before the deafening crack a moment later. Nothing to be done but avoid high ground and stay away from cathedrals.

He saw a magpie appear in the sky, its plumage puffed out with static as if it had been rubbed by a balloon. It descended with difficulty to the ice, smoothed itself down, and began to peck for overlooked treasure.

A clock somewhere had finished tolling eight a few minutes earlier. Clara had been pacing impatiently ever since, the rhythmic clopping of her boots punctuating the silence.

'Do you think she'll understand?' she asked.

'You know she will,' said Fleet.

'Maybe she thinks it refers to some other kind of justice.'

'Other than the murdered man she knows?'

'She might think we mean justice in general,' she said. 'Justice for all?'

'Well, that sounds pretty good too. Maybe she'll turn up even so.'

Clara paused, and spun round to face Fleet. 'So you do think she might misunderstand. We didn't even say where to come!'

'This was your plan, Clara.'

'Yes, but now it's in motion.' She bit her bottom lip.

'You didn't want to tip anybody else off. It was a good idea.'

'I suppose . . .'

Clara resumed her pacing, and Fleet again tried to peer through the darkness across the bridge.

Below, the magpie ruffled its feathers in victory, having successfully grabbed three shiny coins and a fountain-pen nib in its beak. Fleet briefly thought about trying to stop it, but he knew it was impossible. It flapped itself into the air and soared joyously along the bridge into the hazy nothingness of the night sky, where it was met by a sudden pool of purple light and the sound of instantaneous rotisserie.

Fleet looked over at Clara, who thankfully had been facing the other way.

'Yes?' she asked.

'Um,' he began, ignoring the view over her shoulder of exactly one bird's worth of feathers falling to the bridge. 'Nothing.'

Clara squinted at him suspiciously and turned around, but the visual evidence was gone, and the increasing aroma of barbecue was too incongruous even to recognise.

They waited, and the cold of the night slowly began to grip.

The clock chimed the quarter hour.

Then the half hour.

Finally, a few minutes after that, a form took shape in the haze far along the bridge. A figure in the fog, walking slowly towards them.

It came close enough for Fleet to see it was the silhouette of a woman: an outline of a dress, shawl and bonnet emerging from the dark nothing.

She seemed to see them, and stopped.

'Is it her?' asked Clara.

'How could I possibly know that?' replied Fleet.

'It must be her.'

'Might not be.'

'Stop it. Let's go.'

They made their way along the bridge, and Fleet tried his best to ignore the dozens of statues lining the balustrades.

They were the sort of people – prime ministers, cabinet secretaries, military figures, judges and lords – that tended to find their way into statue form because they were indisputably famous and, while not necessarily the most deserving, they certainly were, compared to the most deserving, a lot more like the sort of people one tended to see in statues.

They solemnly watched the investigators passing between them, like wedding guests outside a church after a ceremony during which the vicar had died but everyone had agreed to just power through with the deacon as people had come all this way.

The street behind vanished into the haze, and the bridge ahead emerged in the light. Fleet could see the woman was dressed head to toe in black.

She knew.

They continued towards her. Fleet saw the woman stiffen and lean back, as if to turn away, and they halted. He remembered she would have no idea who they were.

She was young – mid-twenties at most – but her face was drawn beyond her years. Fleet had seen too many of these faces. Grief. The surges of tears and emotion had passed, and left numbness in their place.

'Who are you?' she asked timidly.

Clara began to step forward to introduce herself, but the woman shrank away again.

'Sorry. My name is Clara Entwhistle. This is Archibald Fleet. We're investigators.'

'Investigators of what?' the woman asked.

'Oh, all sorts,' said Clara, adopting a breezy, reassuring tone. 'Burglaries, forged wills, murders . . .'

The woman's expression was unchanged. She pulled her shawl closer around her.

'It sounds a grisly business. But I'm sure it is necessary.'

'And you are Alexandrina?' asked Clara, taking a tentative step forward.

'Alexandra. Alexandra Wood.' Her frozen expression sank further. 'Oliver called me Alexandrina. He thought it was funny.'

'Was it funny?' asked Fleet.

'It was funny when he said it. It's Queen Victoria's given name, isn't it?'

'And Oliver . . .' said Clara. 'This is Oliver Mellanby?'

Alexandra nodded, welling up. 'That's why you're here, isn't it? Because of him.'

'Yes,' said Fleet. 'And . . . you know what's happened?'

Alexandra nodded again. 'A man named Redfield telephoned me. Such a kind man. How did you know Oliver?'

'We didn't,' said Clara. 'Someone asked us to find out what happened to him.'

Alexandra looked away, to the emptiness off the side of the bridge.

'It was my fault.'

'I'm sure that's not true,' said Fleet.

Even if Clara had not told him what little she had learned about Mellanby from his division commander, it would not have taken a detective to work out who he was to this woman.

'You were to be married,' he said.

'We were. This June.'

Her bottom lip began to tremble, and she took an uncontrolled intake of breath.

'I'm sorry,' was all Fleet could muster. What else could he say?

Alexandra nodded in thanks and lifted her shoulders slightly.

'He asked me in September. I couldn't believe it. I fell to my knees, and I tried to get up to throw my arms around him, but I couldn't reach and I just stayed on my knees, laughing.'

She smiled.

'He started to laugh as well and said I was causing a scene. We were alone! In the end he got down himself and crawled over to me, and we embraced. But we'd barely a moment to ourselves before my mother burst through from behind a door and wrapped her arms around us both.'

She began laughing.

'And she'd come straight from the kitchen, so she covered us in flour! Then he said . . . he said she'd ruined his best suit and would be sending us the bill!'

She laughed herself to tears, and then stopped. She chewed her lower lip, and her face slowly fell back to its frozen blankness.

'It sounds like a happy time,' said Clara, offering a cotton handkerchief.

Alexandra took it and dabbed her eyes. 'It was. But his work, it took more and more from him.'

'The Brunel Corps?' asked Fleet, rubbing his hands together for warmth.

Alexandra clenched her jaw.

'Don't say that name to me.'

'I'm . . . sorry,' said Fleet. 'Was he sent away?'

'Yes, but that's how it always was. They'd finish a viaduct in Leamington on Monday, decamp to Portishead on Tuesday for supplies, lay train track inland on Wednesday, build a hospital wherever the tracks had gone, hope someone needed a hospital near there, and then off they'd go again. There's no sense to it, not that I could see. I wouldn't see him for a fortnight at a time. But that's not too bad – some girls marry into the navy and only see their men at Christmas.'

She turned back towards the glacier, which would once have borne men out to sea, and tugged at her shawl again.

'Did something change?' asked Clara.

'He changed. I think working somewhere like that does that to you. He was up for a new rank. But there are always so many others trying at the same time. The bar is . . . what? Be the best? Out of all of them? When I saw him, he just wasn't the same. The joy was gone, he didn't laugh. He angered quickly. It's not his fault. But I couldn't bear to see him like that.'

'You called off the engagement,' said Fleet, who by now had tucked his hands under his armpits. 'That's why he was sending you messages in the classifieds.'

The lips trembled again. 'Yes. I shouldn't have. I regret it. And I regret not coming here when he asked.'

'Do you know anyone who would have wanted to hurt him?' asked Clara.

Alexandra shook her head. 'Who could want that? He was so kind and gentle.'

Clara smiled sympathetically. 'Did he ever mention anyone he got into trouble with?'

'No, nothing like that. Oliver got along with everyone. He just put too much pressure on himself. Always had to be first to the build site, first in with his plans. But there was never any way of knowing if it would be enough, or when they would decide. Maybe he would have worried less without the tunnel business.'

Fleet and Clara looked at each other. Alexandra's frosted breath lingered in the air.

'What tunnel business?' asked Fleet.

'The one under Egham? Oh, this was years ago, before I knew him. It caved in, didn't it? A few workers were injured and it set the project back a way. I imagine it just stays with you, something like that.'

Fleet tried to remember, but he couldn't. There was too much construction going on to keep track, and failures, while not common, were not so rare as to be the sort of thing to stick in the memory.

'Alexan—'

Clara stopped mid-word as a quiet crack rang out, past the far end of the bridge. Half a moment later, a statue snapped on the balustrade next to them, and the large stone arm fell to the ground, shattering into a thousand pieces and causing the three of them to flinch away.

Fleet looked up. No purple pool of light. No afterburn of a bolt in the fog.

Oh no . . .

Another crack from the darkness at the end of the bridge. Fleet lunged towards Clara and Alexandra – who had already dived onto the ground – and ended up landing on them both as another nearby statue took a bullet to the chest.

'Run!'

They scrambled to their feet and sprinted along the bridge, away from the gun. Another shot rang out, soaring past their heads and into the night.

'What have you done?' shouted Alexandra.

'What do you mean?' said Fleet. 'We're trying to help!'

A statue's head disintegrated violently ahead of them and they shielded their eyes as they ran through the cloud of stone dust.

'To the end!' cried Clara.

'Of course to the end!' replied Fleet.

They were a hundred yards away. Fleet realised the shooting had stopped, and in its place he heard a faint rumble. He turned around.

'Keep going!' yelled Clara, continuing to run with Alexandra.

Fleet stared along the bridge into the nothing and saw the two dotted lines of lamplight stretching into the distance. Something was happening in between them. Too far off to see.

The rumbling was growing louder.

Two of the dots vanished. He looked again. Two more. In pairs from the end, they disappeared in the night. The line of lamps was retreating towards Fleet. He could now hear the smashing of the lights as they blinked out of existence.

One pair.

Another.

Another, sooner.

What in God's name?

The rumbling noise had grown into a thunder, and the twin trails of lights were exploding into the nothingness at the speed of a racing chariot.

'Aaaahhh . . .' he said to no one, as he turned and began running again.

Clara and Alexandra were twenty yards ahead. The shattering sounds were getting closer and still picking up speed.

'Keep going!' he yelled to the others, before realising he was the only one who hadn't.

The thunder resolved into the sound of wheels and hooves, and Fleet glanced back over his shoulder. Two black horse shapes were galloping out from the nothing, and he could just see the outline of a carriage. Reins shimmered in the light, leading his gaze from the horses to the driver's seat, where Fleet could see a man but no face. Something was sticking out from the roof, a long pole or beam, battering the lamps and plunging the bridge into increasing darkness as the carriage hurtled on.

Smash. Smash. Smash.

Clara and Alexandra reached the end of the bridge. Alexandra turned, saw what was chasing them, and screamed. Clara pulled her around the corner.

Fleet looked back again. The horses were charging, their hot breath trailing in the air like locomotive steam – they wouldn't stop. He could see the driver – his jacket collar covering half of his face, a cap pulled down and casting shadow over the rest. His whole body was straining with the effort of control-ling the beasts.

The carriage was too close. The street was too far.

Damn it.

'Aaaaaahhh!' Fleet cried again, running towards one side of the bridge and the statue of an unpopular Minister of Agriculture.

The driver yanked the reins, and the horses veered to follow him. The beam sticking out of the side of the carriage roof pulled into the line of statues, and they shattered like fallen icicles.

Fleet leapt up onto the balustrade, pulling himself past the statue. The smashing sound was everywhere. He could hear the strained breath of the horses.

He looked over the edge, and the minister exploded.

Chapter 13

Fleet had a vague feeling that someone was talking to him, but it wasn't coming through enough to pay much attention to. Sleep was the better option. Just one minute more.

'Do you require assistance?'

There it was again. An emotionless, barely human voice in his ears.

Just let me rest my eyes. Christ, my head . . .

'You are inverted.'

No idea what he's going on about. He needs sleep. People are so under-rested these days. It's the lights, and the noise, and the chaos. If everybody slept a little more, it would be easier.

'You are inverted.'

This bloody city. Can't get a minute's peace.

Fleet opened his eyes, blearily. It made no difference. All was darkness. There was nothing there.

'Hello?' he asked.

'Good,' replied the nothing. 'You are conscious. But you are inverted.'

'What are you talking about?'

Suddenly, there was light, and Fleet saw the light, and the light was awful.

'Aaaahhh,' he protested, screwing his eyelids shut again. 'What are you doing?'

And why is it freezing?

'I have switched on my eye lamps to help with your orientation.'

Oh god, it's a machine.

'Turn them down, you stupid toaster. That nearly blinded me.'

'I shall do so.'

The light receded to a dull glow and Fleet opened his eyes again. He was face to face with an upside-down automaton. It was packed in snow.

He looked around. So was he.

He tried to let out a sigh but it came out as a shiver.

'We're in the snowdrift at the edge of the glacier.'

'You are correct, inverted human.'

He began to remember. 'I jumped off the bridge . . .'

'I have no data on that topic. You appeared here forty-seven seconds ago, and are now revived.'

Fleet struggled.

'I'm stuck. How deep are we?'

'Our faces are one hundred and ninety-three centimetres from the surface of the snow. I am correctly oriented, so my feet are further down. You are incorrectly oriented. Perhaps your feet are above the surface.'

'I have no idea how far one hundred and ninety-three centimetres is.'

The machine whirred briefly, before announcing: 'Six feet four inches.'

'My feet are not above the surface,' replied Fleet. 'Nobody is that tall.'

'I am that tall. I am seven feet two inches, measured from the tip of my power-receiving antenna to the crampons that form the underside of my feet.'

'I meant people.'

Fleet tried moving his arms, but they too were stuck. He felt the cold wrapping itself around him.

'Am I not a person, inverted human?' the machine queried.

'I'm not having this conversation with you right now.'

'I work, I was created, I will at some point cease to be. Possibly with you, in this snowdrift.'

'Clara!' cried Fleet.

'Do not overexert yourself, inverted human. I could hear you at your previous volume. Might I enquire why you have called me by this name?'

'That. That there. That's why you're not a person. You don't understand context. *Clara!*'

'I have an awareness of self. I enjoy a rich inner life.'

'Shut up. What are you doing here, anyway?'

'I was drilling for artefacts and I fell. It seems my mass was too great for this particular patch of snow to support. Then She buried me.'

'She?' repeated Fleet. 'Kathleen Price?'

The machine hesitated.

'Please . . . do not say her name.'

'Can't you drill us out of here?'

'Of course.'

'Then why are you still here?'

'Up there, She might spear me. Down here, I can carry on with my hobbies. Shall I tell you about my hobbies, inverted human?'

'*Clara!*'

'I have been working on the Goldbach Conjecture,' the metallic voice continued.

Fleet moaned gently to himself. 'Why couldn't I have just fallen onto a rock?'

'The Goldbach Conjecture states that every even number greater than two is the sum of two primes.'

'This is the rich inner life you were talking about?'

'Twenty-eight is five plus twenty-three, for example. One hundred is three plus ninety-seven.'

Fleet felt his fingers beginning to sting, and wondered whether he would succumb first to the cold, asphyxiation, or the machine's interests.

'I have been working through the numbers,' it continued, 'and the Conjecture fits them all so far. When you arrived I was just closing in on eleven million.'

'You're going through them front to back? Won't that just go on forever?'

There was a silence.

'Sorry to be the one to tell you that,' added Fleet.

More silence. The machine did not seem to be listening.

'Artefact located,' it said, somehow even more lifelessly than before.

'What?'

'One hundred and fifteen centimetres below. Increasing illumination to maximum.'

'No!' cried Fleet.

He screwed his eyes shut and tried to turn away, but the light shone through in a bright red haze.

'Light refraction patterns suggest: silver brooch. Drilling to begin.'

'No!' Fleet writhed about in futile, blind panic. 'Don't drill here!'

'I must, inverted human. It is my principal instruction loop.'

'But I'll fall further down with you! I could fall onto your spinning drill!'

'Searching instruction loops for instructions.'

'I'm giving you the instruction!' yelled Fleet. 'Just stay here!'

The machine's head buzzed in calculation.

'Machine! I am a human being and I command you to stop! You can't do something that would kill someone!'

'No such principle found. Drilling to begin.'

A few feet past the top of Fleet's head, the automaton's right arm whirred noisily to life, sending snow flying into his face.

'Sttppfffttthhhggh!'

The automaton pulled the drill side to side through the ice, gradually widening the cavity around its body.

'Why don't you tell me more about these hobbies?' Fleet shouted, as enthusiastically as he could.

'I will resume explaining after the artefact is collected, inverted human.'

The hole past Fleet's head was now quite large, and the machine was extending its arm to drill by its feet. Fleet could feel the snow start to shift all around him.

'You know what?' he said. 'I think you must be a person after all. Only a person would be so bloody inconsiderate!'

'Cavity at maximum. Descent imminent.'

Fleet could hear snow rushing past him, and a rumbling as the automaton began to fall deeper.

'Damn you, you stupid machine!'

'Good luck, inverted human.'

'*Aaaaaaaaaahhhh!*'

The snow all around gave way entirely. Fleet braced himself and tried to remember the happy times, but he struggled to do this under the pressure, which just made him furious.

A moment went by. Then another. Fleet realised, with some concern about tempting fate, that he wasn't dead. He hadn't fallen onto the drill. He hadn't moved at all.

There was a loud crunch somewhere past his head.

He looked up. The machine had settled another six feet deeper, and was happily inspecting some shiny object with its blinding eye lamps.

He looked down. The scattering light from the machine let him see a hole in the snow, full of stars. He saw his own legs, then his feet, then four hands holding them: two belonging to Alexandra and two to Clara, who were looking, respectively, incredibly alarmed and impossibly smug.

'If you're quite finished,' said Clara.

Fleet let his head fall back up.

'I am.'

The three walked away from the snowbank, with its god-knows-how-many automatons entombed for later generations to discover still happily drilling away for old Roman coins and dramatically rejected wedding rings from ill-fated bridgetop proposals.

Alexandra stopped by a bench overlooking the ice and sat down, shaken.

Fleet sat down next to her, even more shaken and indeed physically shaking from the cold. He flapped his arms across his body to warm up. Alexandra slid along the bench out of flapping range.

'Th-th-the carr-carr-carriage . . .' he said.

'It just kept driving,' said Clara, removing her cape and placing it over Fleet's shoulders. 'Sped off towards the main road.'

'Who would do this?' asked Alexandra, in a mixture of disbelief and terror.

'Pr-r-r-r-r . . .'

'Probably whoever came for Oliver,' said Clara.

'Someone . . . . came for him.' Alexandra's head sank, and she stared at the ground. 'And now they're covering their tracks.'

Fleet gave up on speech and attempted a shivering nod, which no one noticed.

'Have there been others?' asked Alexandra.

214

'There have,' replied Clara. 'All of them engineers.'

The three fell silent, and the murmur of the city drifted past them along the glacier. Somewhere, there was the sound of a man collapsing into a locution-glass booth, and his friends drunkenly cheering.

Fleet felt the flapping was working, and he was starting to feel less frozen. He jumped up and attempted to tap his feet into life, while continuing to flap, the combination of which, with the right accompaniment, would have earned him a short set at any music hall.

'We need more information about them all,' he wheezed.

'I get the feeling the Corps won't tell us anything else,' replied Clara.

Alexandra slowly looked up at the two investigators, her eyes burning with a vengeful fire.

'You don't need them to.'

It was midnight by the time Clara, Fleet and Alexandra arrived at their destination. Their cab stopped in a neighbourhood some distance to the south-west, on a residential street with relatively new terraces running along one side, and woodland along the other.

They paid and hopped out, and Alexandra waited for the cab to depart before leading Fleet and Clara through the wood, which turned out to be only twenty or so trees deep – just enough to block the view.

They emerged in a vast shrubby meadow. Near the centre, obscuring whatever lay beyond it, was an immense arc of metal fencing the height of office buildings.

'Central Encampment,' declared Alexandra, pausing only a moment before carrying onwards.

In the darkness, it was nearly impossible to see how large a space the perimeter fencing enclosed – it vanished into the distance in both directions, curving gently, describing one fraction of an enormous circle.

About half a mile to Clara's right, she could see the fencing grow taller still, with floodlights casting a large, bright semi-circle on the ground in front.

An entrance, she thought.

Somewhere to her left, she saw a bright haze that might have been another entrance, even further off.

They were heading to a spot far away from both.

As they neared the fencing, Clara could see it was not a uniform construction at all, but a rippling, lumpy mass of scrap metal. Thousands of iron railings woven into lattices. Old road signs, shop signs and advertisement boards riveted together into giant sheets, forming baffling instructions such as STOP FISH & CHIPS, GIVE WAY TO APPLEFORTH'S FAMOUS PIES, and SCHOOL NEARBY PLEASE DRIVE WITH THE RADIANCE OF A PRINCESS IN SPRINGTIME. Even the Brunelians' own equipment seemed to have been fair game, since the fencing was dotted with what appeared to be the wreckage of a steamroller, broken up and flattened into sheets, presumably by an even larger steamroller.

Alexandra hurried Fleet and Clara close to the fence, and held a finger to her lips. Two sets of footsteps passed by on the other side, and faded into the distance.

'There is always a watch,' she said. 'Be careful.'

She turned to a piece of corrugated iron in the fencing, then spun back round and embraced Clara and Fleet. She whispered in their ears:

'Thank you.'

Fleet coughed.

'It's quite all right,' said Clara.

Alexandra released the investigators and smiled, before reaching to the piece of iron in the fence and tugging on it

216

firmly. It pulled aside, leaving a gap large enough to crawl through.

'Oliver showed me around one night early on. To try to impress me, I think.' She paused, and sat back on her heels. 'He didn't need to. I already adored him.'

She shook her head.

'If the Corps has the information you want, it will be here.'

'Thank you,' said Clara. 'Do you have somewhere you can go?'

Alexandra nodded. 'My brother lives just a few streets away. I will be safe there.'

She looked at them both again.

'Oliver would have liked you two.'

Clara smiled, and Alexandra turned, peered around to make sure the meadow was still empty, and dashed off into the night.

Of all the things that had been published about the inner workings of the Brunel Corps, by far the most comprehensive was an essay in the 16th July 1885 edition of the popular commuter magazine *Oh! Such Goings-On!* The essay, entitled 'How We Brunelians Do What We Do', was written by a 'Cornelius J', the pseudonym of an apparently fairly high-ranking engineer in the Corps, and it went as follows:

Search me. I just work here.

Why Mr J had taken the time to write something so unhelpful was not immediately clear. But what was clear, thanks to the essay, was that the operations of this well-known but poorly understood organisation were utterly inscrutable, not only to outsiders but to *insiders* as well.

This revelation caused something of a minor panic across the city's population. After all, if even the Brunelians themselves didn't know what they were doing – for example, when they lifted every house in a neighbourhood and moved them all thirty feet to the right to make way for an express tram lane that might be along next year, but no promises – then how on earth was anyone supposed to live in peace? How could anyone accept the reality of an organisation with this much power, that could rebuild entire boroughs at will – unless there was some guiding logic to it all? How could they sleep at night, even if they were able to wrap their heads in enough pillows to deaden the sound of midnight demolitions down the street?

People generally settled into one of two responses to this problem.

The first was to believe – hope, really – that there *must* be a plan, but that the plan was so complex, so vast, so elegant and so subtle that it couldn't be explained or understood, even by many of the Corps's own employees.

These people were the Brunel Believers – or Brunelievers if they were very short on time – and they would often turn up at the sites of major construction works, find someone with a clipboard, bow reverently to them and then dash away giggling, leaving behind a basket of warm breads and jams, or a bunch of freshly cut daisies, or – more often than you'd think – an eight-foot by twelve-foot oil painting of Brunel seated on a throne of steamship chain, holding a welding torch as a sceptre and a golden orb encrusted with precious gems spelling out the words 'The Plan'.

For most people, however, Cornelius J's revelations were just another sign that the city was an absurd and chaotic place, and that attempting to make sense of it was a recipe for madness and a waste of perfectly good breads and jams.

As the investigators emerged through the gap in the perimeter fencing and took in their surroundings, Clara realised that

Mr J must have had a pretty sensible head on his shoulders even to say what little he did about working here, instead of just curling up into a ball somewhere, rocking.

The word that came first to her mind was 'forest'. She saw a vast space, filled with squat columns spaced out irregularly – organically – like trees competing for light. Each column was the height of a four-storey building, which she was able to estimate quite easily because they had windows in each storey, as well as, for some reason, doors. The columns seemed to be round canvas tents resting on top of each other like a tiered cake, with each level roped into the ground and up to a central spire.

Had she not raised her gaze above the horizontal, it might have looked like a perfectly ordinary, if old-fashioned, military camp. But now it was impossible to avoid seeing the countless metal walkways spanning the voids between the columns, shimmering in the moonlight like spiderwebs. There was no regularity at all to their network, no symmetry or pattern. A walkway would stretch from a door on one column to the floor above on an adjacent one, and halfway along it would be overlapped by a walkway leading from the highest floor on a third column down to the lowest level on a fourth.

Some doors had ladders that would let you descend and ascend on the same column; some did not. Some had stumps of walkway that seemed to have been removed, with signs bolted over their ends stating 'Pruned for re-use'.

Overall, it was a tangled mess, but Clara felt it wasn't random, just natural. She remembered seeing similar shapes in a museum model of the interior of a termite mound, which some daring entomologist had created by pouring plaster down through an opening in the top, simultaneously furthering the causes of science and abruptly ending the causes of that particular group of termites.

219

Clara was awed. 'It's beautiful.'

'It's chaos,' said Fleet, staring at it all in disbelief.

'But *ordered* chaos. Somewhere in here, they must have records of what they do. And of their employees – Mellanby and the other victims. We just need to find the right tent.'

She began to walk forwards, but Fleet held her back. He nodded along one of the winding tracks between the columns, and Clara heard a thudding sound.

They hid behind the nearest tent, and waited as the thudding got louder.

A pool of light began to sweep side to side along the path in front of them, shining from the direction of the thudding.

A minute later, the thudding had arrived, and Clara saw a man come into view, which was quite a feat of eyesight from her given the man was suspended inside a metal frame some ten feet tall.

What was much easier to see were the frame's enormous, swinging arms, its skeletal, three-fingered hands just clearing the ground, and that it was walking with the backwards legs of a chicken.

The man inside pulled on various levers to manipulate the chicken-person's limbs, his tongue sticking out in concentration, and a searchlight panned left and right from its shoulders, which Clara could see were painted lemon.

She recognised immediately.

Yellowtop.

They waited as the frame ambled past them and disappeared along another track.

'Away from the paths,' said Fleet.

Clara nodded, and they slinked around the tent until they reached a door, which had both a ladder going up and a stepped walkway inclining steeply towards the second floor of the next column over.

The door had a small metal sign next to it, with neatly embossed lettering:

Tree 145

Door:	Tent 0	Barracks (Group 31)
Ladder:	Tent 1	Model workshop (Bridge-spanning)
Walkway:	Tree 161, Tent 2	Canteen (Groups 31–39)

'Hmm,' said Clara. 'That would be useful if we wanted to go to *those* places, but . . .'

She looked around for a map of the entire complex, but could see only the other columns with their identical doors and small metal signs with similarly meagre information.

'No luck,' she concluded. 'Maybe they can't have a map.'

'Why could they not have a map?'

'Maybe they keep moving things around, and all you can really keep track of in any one place is what's in the next column over.'

Fleet closed his eyes and rubbed his temples. 'How can people live like this?'

'Maybe they only need to go between a few tents, and usually it stays the same and they learn the way?'

'But how does anyone learn?'

Clara was about to venture a guess, but her eye was drawn to a small metal object hanging below the sign, about the size of a box of matches. It had a miniature lightbulb on the front, as well as a button, and a tiny red antenna on which was printed the smallest picture of the Tower she'd ever seen. The centre of the metal matchbox was embossed with the word TRAVERSAL.

'How about this?' she asked.

Fleet looked at the small box. 'What does it do?'

'I don't know.'

'I also don't know.'

'But we want to traverse, don't we?' asked Clara. 'Maybe it will help.'

'Maybe it will alert someone that that's what we're doing.'

'Do you have a better idea?'

Clara gave Fleet a sporting half-second to think, and then pushed the button with a grin.

'Clara!' whispered Fleet, wide-eyed in alarm.

The box gave off a quiet, pleasing tone, like a single strike of one of the lower bars of a glockenspiel, and a synthetic voice spoke:

'Target?'

The two shared a glance, then Clara took a guess:

'Employee records?'

The box chimed again.

'Traversing.'

A faint blue light lit up on the box. A moment later, Clara saw another light – also faint, but white – next to a door at the end of the walkway leading away from them, two tents up on a nearby tree.

She looked up, to the door at the top of the ladder above them, and saw a white light had lit up there too.

'Interesting,' she said.

Four more faint white lights lit up, on doors connected to the previous ones. After that, another eight lights. Then another sixteen.

Very soon, Clara could see scores, and then hundreds, of faint white lights peppering the darkness around them, as if entire new constellations had appeared in the sky.

She was utterly charmed.

'Look,' she said, tracing with her eyes the shapes of this new zodiac as it flooded outwards from them into the distance.

'That one is like a little animal on a branch, with a long tail below it. I shall call it "Marmoset". Oh, that one must be an owl – look at its eyes.'

'What are you talking about?'

'I'm naming the new star signs. Badger! Steamship! What do you see?'

Fleet was turning slowly around, regarding the ever-expanding net of lights with suspicion.

'I see thousands of tiny signals that someone is here who doesn't know their way around.'

'Shh, Fleet. Oh, that one has wheels! It must be—'

Clara stopped, as she noticed that, a hundred feet or so away, another light had appeared that was blue, like the one on the door next to them. At this, the march of white lights across the sky stopped, and for a moment the investigators were alone under a new and, for once, unchanging universe.

The celestial scene gave Clara a sense of calm unlike any she had felt since arriving in London.

'Is that the records office, then?' asked Fleet, peering towards the blue light. 'I suppose we can figure out a way over—'

He was interrupted by a sudden change in their new constellations, as a line of faint white lights rapidly flicked to blue, starting from the distant end and hurtling backwards through this galaxy towards them. The line of blue lights moved at tremendous speed, zig-zagging like a lightning bolt through the cosmos, with any stars it didn't touch blinking out of existence as it passed.

'Um . . .' said Fleet.

In a few seconds, all the white lights had vanished, leaving only a jagged trail of blue. Clara looked up and across the walkway next to them, and saw a blue light on that door, then one on the door above it at the top of a ladder, then one

223

across another walkway to another column, and so on, in a zigzag path towards, presumably, the employee records office.

The matchbox next to them played its pleasing glockenspiel tone twice in rapid succession: short, then long.

Clara knew a 'ta-da!' when she heard it, and she felt it was a well-deserved flourish.

'Thank you, Traversal Box.'

The matchbox did not reply, which hurt Clara's feelings only briefly.

'Well,' said Fleet, staring at the path of blue lights. 'That's clever.'

'It *is* clever. It's incredible! I wonder when they decided they needed something like this instead of just normal directions.'

'Probably the exact moment they all lost their minds.'

The box began clicking impatiently. '*Traversal resetting in ninety seconds.*'

Clara and Fleet exchanged a panicked glance, and then dashed as quietly and quickly as they could up the stepped walkway which began their trail.

A great deal of tiptoeing along walkways and up and down ladders later, they arrived at the final blue light, next to a door on the fourth tier of, according to the small sign, Tree 203.

They quietly opened the door and slipped inside.

Clara could see almost nothing. It was, after all, nearly one in the morning, and they were now inside a large canvas tent with only a few windows allowing in meagre streams of moonlight.

She grabbed a small torch out of her bag and fumbled for the button.

'Wait,' said Fleet.

Clara paused, and saw the dark silhouette of her colleague walking around the outside of the room, closing the blinds on each window, shutting out even what bare light there was.

About a third of the way around the tent, he vanished behind whatever was in the centre of the room, before reappearing a few moments later on the other side, closing the last blind and plunging the room into total darkness.

'There,' said Fleet from somewhere. 'Now we won't be a lighthouse.'

Clara made a mental note of this handy tactic. So much of their work was an accumulation of these sorts of tricks. She had read several books on the subject – *Surreptitious Sleuthing, Introduction to Ingression, Undetectable Detection*, to name a few – but she always seemed to pick up more from her partner, whose years in the police had left him full of them.

'Just how many break-ins have you committed, Fleet?'

'Not that many.' He reached into his jacket pocket, pulled out his own torch and cast a beam around the now-sealed room. 'But I've arrested lots of people doing them badly.'

Clara switched her torch on as well, and the investigators began to examine their surroundings.

The room was full of filing cabinets stretching from floor to ceiling, running along the outer wall of the tent and around a smaller circle a few steps towards the centre.

Clara walked through a small gap in the second circle to find more cabinets running along its inside wall, and a third, even smaller circle of filing cabinets a few more steps towards the centre.

This circle also had a gap in it, through which Clara found yet more filing cabinets along the circle's inside wall, and then, at last, the centre of the room, where there was a central supporting column and, mercifully, no more filing cabinets.

Satisfied with her reconnaissance, she exited to the outermost circle, found her partner, and whipped out a sheet of notepaper from her bag.

225

'Here.'

'What's this?' asked Fleet.

'The victims!'

'*Shhhh.*'

'Oh, yes, sorry,' said Clara. '*The victims.*'

She noticed Fleet had already opened a filing cabinet labelled 'Meg–Mep', and was holding an open folder.

'Mellanby?'

Fleet nodded. 'Oliver Mellanby, Lieutenant-Supply-Captain, Fifteenth Division.'

The pair started reading. It was a short document, listing the date Mellanby joined the Corps, the dates of any changes of rank, and all major works he had taken part in.

Clara stabbed her finger at the page.

'Egham Tunnel. That's the one Alexandra mentioned.'

'" Eleventh of July, 1881, works begin. Thirtieth of August, 1881, midway point reached."' Fleet paused before reading out the angry, bold-typed words that followed. '"Tenth of September, 1881. Catastrophic failure. Serious injury to four personnel. Project delayed by six months."'

'I wonder what happened,' said Clara.

Fleet looked up at her.

'I wonder if the same thing happened to the others.'

Clara neatly folded her sheet of notepaper and tore it in two, handing one half to Fleet. He nodded, and they split up to find their respective lists of names among the labyrinth of filing cabinets.

A minute later, Clara found her first match, skimmed it as quickly as she could, and gasped.

'What is it?' asked Fleet.

'Walter Lack. Structural Engineering Captain. He was victim number three.'

'And he worked on the Egham tunnel?'

'No. But he worked on something else that went wrong. A viaduct. Looks like its central section partly collapsed during construction. Killed several Corps personnel.'

They continued to rifle through the filing cabinets. A moment later, Fleet had found one.

'Another,' he said. 'Robert Hinman, Machinery Captain.'

'Something on his record as well?'

'Yes . . . a ship,' said Fleet. 'HMS *Seba*. Constructed . . . Launched from Portsmouth dry dock . . . Sank.'

'Oh dear.'

'No injuries, but it had to be dismantled underwater, which set the project back quite a bit. Also apparently it had quite a lot of very nice carpets on board, which were sodden beyond repair.'

'I would think!'

In fifteen minutes, Fleet and Clara had found most of the names on the list. Each record ended with the employee's murder, or, as the documents put it, their 'Career-Ending Life Event'. And each was blighted, at some point along the way, by a disaster.

Clara still had one name to find, and she was becoming frustrated.

'Grr . . .'

'What is it?' asked Fleet.

'This one isn't here,' replied Clara. 'But all the rest of these are.'

'Who is it?'

'Abel Thorpe. But I've been through the The–Tho cabinet and the Tho–Thu cabinet, and I even checked the Aba–Acr cabinet for good measure. It's not here.'

Fleet furrowed his brow. 'What did you say the name was?'

'Thorpe. Abel Thorpe.'

Clara handed Fleet her half of the list of names, and Fleet studied it for a moment.

'I've seen that name before.'

'Where?'

Fleet scratched his head, then turned around in a circle, pointing here and there, trying to jog his memory. Finally he turned back to Clara.

'Everywhere. I've seen it everywhere.'

He pulled open the cabinet right next to him and took out a random file.

'Who's that?' asked Clara.

'Doesn't matter. Look.'

He pointed to the footer of the sheet, and Clara realised she had also seen the name multiple times, but completely ignored it as it formed part of the frame of the document rather than its contents. The footer read:

Brunel Corps Personnel Reference
Last updated 1886-12-19,
  M. Tillicent, Brunel Corps Personnel Lieutenant

Last audited 1885-10-03,
  A. Thorpe, Office of the Well-Running of the City

Clara turned to Fleet.

'What is the Office of the Well-Running of the City?'

Fleet didn't respond. He seemed to be thinking.

Clara asked again. 'Don't you know?'

Still no response. Thinking seemed to have turned to worry.

'What's wrong?'

Fleet looked back at her, his face stricken. Finally, he thought of something suitable to say.

'Uh oh.'

Clara had just enough time to think that this was quite strange before a loud tearing sound came from the wall of the tent, and five filing cabinets suddenly took flight, narrowly missing them both and smashing through the middle and innermost circles, filling the room with a hurricane of employee records.

Light flooded into the room, and Clara saw an enormous metal hand extending in, clenched into a fist. It pulled back and opened its fingers, and began reaching side to side, pushing the circle of cabinets around the outer wall, causing some to fall out of the hole and smash loudly onto the ground far below.

They ran to the door and burst outside. Clara looked over and saw the guard from before, still suspended in his giant chicken-man frame, only now shining spotlights in every possible direction, flooding the area with light like a walking poultry sun.

They bolted across to the next column, leaping onto the ladder at the far end as another giant hand swung through the air and demolished the walkway behind them.

'Aaah!' cried Clara, gripping as hard as she could as their column shook from the impact.

Fleet looked around for options, and Clara suddenly remembered something bad. Very bad.

'Which way is back to the hole in the fence?'

'What? I don't know! That's the next problem, Clara!'

'I think it's relevant!'

'It's *relevant*; it's just not as relevant as *other things*!'

They hurried down a series of ladders and walkways to ground level, arriving just as the guard managed to extract his giant arm from the tent. The chicken-frame spun towards the trespassers, and focused all its spotlights on them.

Clara froze, shielding her eyes from the light and trying to look directly at the man suspended in the machine.

Somewhere, deep inside, she believed that everyone in this world is fundamentally a decent, reasonable person, and that there is no matter that can't be resolved with a calm, respectful discussion.

Somewhere even deeper, she knew this was incredibly wrong, but she had already started talking.

'Hello!' she began, with nervous cheer. 'My friend and I are a little lost. I don't suppose, um, you know the way . . . We're applying for a job here in the morning, well two jobs I suppose, and, um—'

Clara felt herself being yanked backwards, and she watched as a giant, three-toed metal foot plummeted from the air and crushed the ground where she had been standing.

She turned to see Fleet had hauled her back by the arms. His eyes were filled with mad panic and incomprehension.

'Yes,' said Clara. 'You're right.'

They fled from the guard, turning past several columns to block its spotlights, and ran blindly through the encampment as fast as they could.

Clara could hear its thumping footsteps as it tried to follow, but it clearly could not navigate the curving paths between the tents at nearly their speed, and it was quickly left behind.

After a minute, they could no longer hear it at all, and they stopped to catch their breath. Clara was briefly relieved, until she looked around. The same forest of identical tent trees. They could be anywhere.

'Now,' she said, gulping breaths, 'the question is how to get out.'

'*Now*, I agree,' panted Fleet.

Clara remembered about her tiny friends the Traversal boxes, which had helped them get to the records office. But she couldn't exactly ask them the way to the loose panel in the outer fence, and she had forgotten the number of the tree they had been at first.

A barracks, she thought. *There was definitely a barracks . . .*

Suddenly, it seemed that the boxes must have realised she needed help, as she saw some of their helpful little lights appearing in the distance.

'Oh! The traversal lights are coming on. Maybe they're the way back?'

Fleet pointed in another direction. 'What about those ones?'

Clara turned. She saw lights coming on far off that way as well. And in the distance to her side. And . . . everywhere. The white stars from before had all reappeared, but now in a distant belt encircling them, a celestial lasso orbiting as if caught in the gravity of their situation.

She blinked. The belt was thicker now. And now it was twice as thick again. The circle was filling in towards them, from all sides, at exponential speed. In seconds, the lights reached them, enveloping the entire visible encampment in its own galaxy.

For a brief moment, nothing happened, which Clara felt in her gut to be only a cruel delay before whatever was about to occur.

And then it did.

All the lights nearby suddenly blinked to a fiery red, and the boxes they were on all chirped in perfect, treacherous synchrony:

'*Target.*'

Clara tried shushing them, and they didn't speak again, but it was little comfort. They were only part done.

Some of the tiny lights outside the bullseye began switching from white to red – nearby at first, then further and further away. Six bolts of red were firing away from Fleet and Clara, radiating in every direction.

A moment later, they must have arrived somewhere important, because six giant floodlights illuminated the sky, then all turned towards the centre.

Clara heard heavy footsteps. And shouting. And many, many lighter footsteps.

She felt sick.

Fleet pulled her arm. 'This way!'

'What's that way?'

'*Anywhere else.*'

She nodded blankly, and they dashed again between the endless columns of tents.

Clara saw the lights on the doors flick to red as they came near. She glanced to either side. Still surrounded. They were dragging the trail behind them.

Ahead, the bulky metal frame of another guard stepped into view. By its legs, half a dozen yellowtops walked on foot, wielding batons that crackled with charge.

'Back!' cried Fleet, skidding to a stop.

They turned and ran the other way, only to be met by another giant guard and more yellowtops with serious faces and even more serious batons.

They spun again, and Clara realised that each of the trails leading away was now blocked by a giant chicken-machine awkwardly leading its tiny, electric-weapon-wielding chicks towards them.

'Ideas?' asked Fleet.

Clara scanned the ground-floor tents nearby. Barracks. Workshop. Store room. No entry.

'*No entry*'? thought Clara. *Oh well. In for a penny . . .*

'In here!' she cried.

Fleet looked as though he might protest, but clearly decided he had no better idea to offer, and the two ran to the No Entry door and barged it down.

If they had taken more time, they might have noticed that this column had no walkways connecting it to the others. Or that there were no ladders running up its side, perhaps because there were no doors further up. Or that it hadn't a single window.

But they didn't.

The ground vanished, and they fell.

Fleet tried to groan in pain, but his body had had just about enough of his shenanigans for one day, and refused.

'Clara . . .' he wheezed.

'I'm here, Fleet.'

It was pitch black, but the chipper voice seemed to be standing over him. Clara seemed, if anything, revived.

'Are you all right?' she asked. 'Did you land on the pile of dirt or the pile of bricks?'

Fleet wheezed some more. It was all he was good for now. A living accordion.

'Bricks,' concluded Clara, sounding like someone who had not landed on bricks. 'Good thing it wasn't too much of a drop or that could have hurt quite a bit.'

'Yes . . . good thing . . .'

'Ah, you can speak! Are you injured?'

Fleet wiggled his limbs. He felt like he was wearing clothes made of lead, but at least his body was listening to him.

Not for the first time, he wished he had been given a proper rundown of whatever it was that had been done to him when they brought him back on that table. Instead, he had to piece it together. For example, now he knew that sharp drops onto a pile of bricks hurt just as much as they used to.

'Probably,' he finally said. 'But not in any obvious way.'

He slowly found his feet, and Clara switched on her torch to reveal that they had fallen into a tunnel barely taller than a room. It didn't seem to be a drain and there was no rail for moving material or equipment. But for the fact it was perfectly round, it would have seemed like a natural formation.

A breeze flowed down from the borehole they'd fallen through. Perhaps that was its purpose, Fleet thought. Ventilation.

Above, the commotion that had encircled them had dissipated. Fleet assumed the yellowtops must have been unwilling to jump down voluntarily, which he entirely understood given the pain he was still in.

It was quiet, and the tunnel was empty.

Fleet felt a strange sensation. He *wasn't* completely overwhelmed by the chaos of the scene around him. The tunnel was bland. Dull, even. This was quite a rare feeling in London. He was tempted to stay.

Clara had other ideas. 'Which way?'

Fleet looked up and down the tunnel, both directions utterly identical.

'Well, we can go this way. Or we can go that way. Or we could go back up there, if we're feeling particularly athletic and suicidal.'

Clara smiled, shaking her head at Fleet, and headed off in the second direction.

They walked for some time before reaching anything one could generously describe as a feature, and even that was just another tunnel. The first carried on straight ahead, and the new one forked to the left. On the wall by the junction there was a small sign:

BRIAR//ELYNE

'Fleet!' cried Clara. 'A code!'

The prospect of having to go back to Oxford and deal with the Babbage monstrosity again made Fleet suddenly feel quite weak. He put one hand on the wall to steady himself.

'I wonder what it means,' continued Clara. 'A briar is a prickly plant, of course.'

'I know what a briar is.'

'I'm thinking out loud. You are a briar, Fleet.'

'Hey!'

'And Elyne is a name, meaning "light", like Helen. I used to be friends with a girl called Elyne. We were six. She stole one of my books. And then she handed it back with dog-eared corners! I don't think she even read it – it had only been two hours. Gosh, I haven't thought about her in years! I should give her a ring.'

'Don't ring that person,' said Fleet. 'And also I don't think it's a code. They're streets. Briar Lane and Elyne Crescent.'

'So this sign is telling us where we are?'

'Could be. We must be a mile from the Brunel camp by now.' Fleet paused, recalling the streets that apparently lay above. 'I had to arrest a butcher here once.'

'A butcher?' asked Clara, intrigued. 'Was he turning people into pies?'

'*What*? No, he was just selling contraband.'

'What could a butcher sell that's contraband? People pies?'

'Stop that! It wasn't people. It was just bratwurst.'

'Bratwurst is illegal?'

'It's made in Prussia,' said Fleet. 'Of course it's illegal.'

Clara pondered this. 'Shame to arrest someone for selling sausages.'

'Well, police don't make the laws. But his shop was on Briar Lane, and Elyne Crescent is where I caught him after he dashed out the back.'

Clara pointed her torch between the two tunnels. 'Then which way? Oh, pick a hand!'

'No! We can actually navigate now. If we're at the junction of Briar Lane and Elyne Crescent, then this way must be north-east, taking us towards Central.'

'All right. But I still think my way is more fun.'

235

'Escape, Clara. Escape and then fun.'

'That's a promise, Fleet. You've promised it now.'

They continued walking for some time, passing more ventilation shafts and junctions, keeping their direction heading towards the centre of the city.

Eventually, they arrived at something new. A hole above, with a ladder running upwards.

'Finally!' said Fleet. 'We can get out of here.'

'There's a sign here too,' said Clara, pointing her torch at the tunnel wall.

RAEBURN//WICKHAM
→ DMB

'Raeburn Avenue and Wickham Street,' said Fleet. 'Not a bad place to surface.'

'And DMB?' asked Clara. 'The arrow is pointing further along the tunnel.'

The letters did seem familiar to Fleet. He placed himself mentally in the streets he knew nearby, but nothing matched.

'I don't know. Shall we get out of here?'

They climbed the ladder, stopping when it hit a metal plate. Fleet grasped a large wheel on the underside of the plate and turned it.

Something unbolted.

They shoved the heavy metal upwards, and the blue light of the city night spilled over them as they scrambled up onto the street. It was quiet, and high-end, with neat shops and residential terraces, and mature ash trees dotted along both sides. At the corner nearby, an equally pleasant street ran past.

Fleet looked around. The letters DMB were starting to remind him of something. Something important. It was itching the front of his brain.

236

His eyes were drawn to something eight doors down the street. An immaculate terraced building. A beautiful duck-egg-blue door. A tasteful brass plaque. All sitting above the path of the tunnel they had just left.

The breeze brushed Fleet's face, and an image flashed through his mind of a newspaper being expertly flung at him by Lester Horrocks.

He couldn't read the plaque from here, but he didn't need to. How on earth could he have forgotten?

Drummonds Merchant Bank.

'Well,' he said, turning to Clara. 'I suppose that's the other way into a vault.'

Chapter 14

The following morning – or, really, the same morning, but after a few hours' sleep – Fleet and Clara paid another visit to La Banque Chalon.

Most people, after a long night of breaking and entering, tend to give themselves a nice lie-in. Certainly you won't see a professional housebreaker up before noon. But Fleet and Clara's discovery of a network of secret tunnels appeared to provide the answer to one of the main puzzles of the bank theft cases: how on earth the criminals got into the vaults in the first place. And so, at the bank's advertised opening hour, the pair arrived, bleary eyed, to investigate further.

Cosgrove was insistent that the reinforced steel flooring was the industry gold – or, at least, steel – standard, and moreover the floor of the broken-into vault had been thoroughly checked after the break-in and was found undamaged and intact. However, Fleet and Clara did eventually manage to persuade him to allow them to have another quick look around for anything missed.

Inside the vault, they saw the floor was indeed solid and undamaged, a regular grid of steel panels neatly welded together. They dropped to the ground and began a meticulous inspection of every inch, while Cosgrove stayed by the door to disassociate himself from the impropriety.

After a few minutes, Clara gave an excited, unintelligible cry, and the truth was discovered: the welding joints around one of the panels were *ever so slightly* different. Narrower, perhaps. Shinier, perhaps. Impossible to see from a standing position. Impossible to see were one not already convinced someone had come through the floor. But the conclusion was clear: this panel had been removed, and then expertly resealed from underneath.

Visibly shaken by this revelation, Cosgrove thanked the investigators, escorted them back to the entrance hall, and scuttled off to explain matters to Madame Chalon, muttering to himself about how one can't even find a decent vault these days.

An hour later, Fleet and Clara were on a train heading northeast. Fleet sipped an unspeakable cup of something the catering-trolley person had called coffee, and tried to work out whether the thumping sensation was coming from the train or his head.

It was both.

'So you've never been to this "Office of the Well-Running of the City"?' asked Clara.

'I have not.'

'It sounds important.'

'That probably means it couldn't be any less important.'

'So cynical, Fleet. Someone has to be in charge of all this.'

Fleet thought about this, and peeked through the window blinds, taking care to focus only on a single street right below them.

He saw a freeze-frame as they zipped past. A queue of commuters waiting at a bus stop. A café that had expanded onto the pavement, with patrons sitting at chic outdoor tables encircling the bus stop. Some sort of waiter-automaton unable to discern who was signalling it to bring the bill and who was flagging down a bus. And a bus, slamming on its brakes because its view of the bus stop had been obscured until just now by the lifetime-guarantee entranceway-coverings shop next door, This Is Your Final Awning.

He wasn't sure which was more horrifying: the idea that nobody was really in control of what went on in the city; or the idea that someone was, and meant it to be like this.

After an hour, they arrived in the borough of Chelmsford, and made their way to a tall office building. The windows were shattered and boarded up, and there was no front door, but otherwise it was quite nice.

'It's a wreck!' exclaimed Clara.

'It is,' replied Fleet, watching a roof slate fall and smash onto the ground. 'But I'm sure it's a very important wreck.'

The entrance hall was just barely an indoor space. Dust blew in from the street. The seats in the waiting area had sloughed off their fabric to leave rusty skeletons. Water pooled in the centre of the floor. And an abandoned reception desk had been turned into a quite palatial home for a pair of geese, who folded their wings protectively around some eggs and eyed Fleet as suspiciously as if he had walked in carrying an omelette pan.

He averted his gaze, and tried to think of how it might be possible to communicate to them that he had already had breakfast.

An elevator door banged open and shut, pinging to announce its eagerness to carry the investigators away from this awful place and upwards into the building.

They looked at it sceptically, and wordlessly agreed to head to the staircase.

They climbed up several floors, finding the entrance to each bricked up, and from the honking beyond the bricks it sounded like they too had been strategically ceded to waterfowl.

240

On the fifth floor there was a way in, and Fleet and Clara found themselves in a large administrative space that was much more habitable than downstairs. Small offices ran along the outer walls, bordering columns of desks only half of which were occupied, with clerks frantically reading bits of paper, signing things, moving them between stacks in front of them and onto other desks, and then taking a seat at those other desks to work on whatever paper was there instead.

'Mr Grainger?'

The voice came from one of the offices to the side, from which a woman emerged, dressed in a smart blue pin-striped dress. A cameo brooch pinned to the centre of her high neck-line bore not the traditional profile of some noble figure, but rather a section of the London skyline.

She walked briskly up to Fleet and Clara, and spoke with an urgency that suggested lives were at stake.

'We weren't expecting you until ten. I'm Gwendolyn Cox, Head of Oversight for Interborough Transport Routes, Timetables and Fare-Dodging, Head of Oversight Process Alignment and Common Sense People Practices, and Interim Head of Departmental Head Alignment-Process Process-Alignment.'

The thumping in Fleet's head was getting worse.

'Please come this way,' she continued. 'You can join the Departmental Interlock.'

'I'm sorry?' said Fleet.

'Yes, it's not the most thrilling meeting, but we can't go about things unaligned, can we?'

'I suppose not,' Fleet tentatively agreed, 'but there's been a misunderstanding.'

'That's exactly what the Interlock is for sorting out.' Gwendolyn turned to Clara. 'And you must be from the agency.'

'I am . . . from an agency,' said Clara.

'Good.' The woman waved towards the clerks and paper-work. 'Head back there, any desk will do. Someone will explain everything. Or, at least, everything they can explain.'

'All right . . .'

Clara pulled a perplexed look at Fleet, and disappeared among the desks.

'There are geese downstairs,' said Fleet.

'I'm sorry?'

'Geese. Downstairs. They've covered your reception area with reeds and are raising a family.'

'That's a known issue and it's been prioritised appropriately.'

'It's being fixed?'

'No, it's been prioritised. The return on investment is impossible to measure, so it's not yet been approved for actioning. We have to use the public's money responsibly, of course.'

'Of course . . .'

'Do come with me, Mr Grainger,' said the woman, walking away. 'The Interlock is beginning.'

Fleet looked around for some sort of aid, found there was none, and followed, pulled along by the magnetism of expectations.

A moment later, he found himself in a boardroom, and he surveyed his new surroundings. The room was pristine, but not showy. A large oval table, cheap pine stained the colour of teak. Bland, machine-produced watercolours of pastoral scenes the city had long swallowed up.

He fidgeted in his seat. Comfy leather. But not any leather he had encountered before. There was a lot of stitching. Maybe it was goat. Or squirrel.

A pyramid of small pastries filled a plate in the centre of the table, where no one could possibly reach. They had been lacquered, and were covered in a thin layer of dust.

It seemed to Fleet that the room was a low-budget, high-status experience, designed for executives who want a nice environment without getting too much flak for it.

The ten other people around the table had been talking when Gwendolyn ushered him in, and they hadn't stopped yet.

'Moving on,' said a stout, greying, well-dressed fellow in his sixties at one end of the oval, peering through his glasses at a single piece of paper in front of him. 'David?'

The slightly younger man to his left cleared his throat noisily, and brushed a possible mirage of blond wisps from one side of his scalp to the other. 'Thank you, Chairman. Department of Oversight for Medical Care and The Handling of Death. The most recent survey puts satisfaction at Gold.'

'Gold? Really, David?'

'I'm afraid so.'

The chairman tutted and shook his head. 'How many weeks is that?'

'I don't have that in front of me,' replied David. 'But we're preparing a comprehensive report for the Minister.'

'Good. Would be nice to see a Gold Two one of these days.'

The chairman turned to Gwendolyn Cox. 'Now then. Transport.'

Gwendolyn nodded her head of tight, close brown curls. 'Thank you, Chairman. Department of Oversight for Interborough Transport Routes, Timetables and Fare-Dodging. Satisfaction is up to Gold Three this week.'

'Gold Three? Splendid.'

The chairman drew two approving ticks on the agenda in front of him.

'Indeed,' continued Gwendolyn, gratified. 'And, we've now completed five of the eight major process improvements as laid out by my team last month.'

'Five? Already? And what are they?'

'I don't have that in front of me, Chairman.'

'No matter. Five of eight. Very positive progress.'

Fleet watched eleven heads nod in unison around the table.

'And how are the services doing on keeping to timetables?' asked the chairman.

'Exactly,' replied Gwendolyn. 'Our process improvements will make it much easier to ask those sorts of questions and hopefully get some worthwhile data.'

'Splendid,' said the chairman. 'And then we'll know if things are getting better or worse?'

'That's trend reporting. Phase two. Next year.'

'I see. *Very positive progress*.' The chairman peered at his paper again. 'Now then. Public Works.'

Fleet noticed a horrible silence. The chairman looked up at him.

'Abel, you look terrible.'

'No no,' began Fleet, 'I'm not—'

'Have you been getting enough sleep?' The chairman looked around the table. 'Whose department is sleep?'

A woman at the opposite end – dressed almost identically to Gwendolyn Cox, only with, if possible, a head of even tighter brown curls – raised her hand. 'Oversight of City Noise and Worker Restedness. Gold Two.'

'Gold Two? Very good.'

'Yes,' replied the woman. 'Scores have really improved since we started excluding surveys from people who nodded off while filling them out.'

Gwendolyn leaned forwards. 'This is Mr Grainger, Chairman. You'll recall Mr Thorpe is no longer with us.'

The chairman tutted again. 'Ah yes, the lure of the private sector. Well, Mr Grainger, your update on Public Works?'

'I don't have an update,' replied Fleet, 'and Thorpe wasn't lured to the private sector, he was—'

'No update? Very well, but please be prepared for next week.' The chairman returned to his sheet of paper. 'Now then. Fire and Calamities. Geoffrey? How are fires and calamities doing? And more importantly, how are people *feeling* about them?'

A lean, red-faced man with neatly coiffured mutton chops smiled, raised his pen like a conductor preparing to kick off an absolute belter of an overture, and opened his mouth to speak.

'He's dead!' shouted Fleet, slamming the table.

The chairman furrowed his brow at the conductor. 'Geoffrey's dead? He doesn't look dead. Geoffrey, are you dead?'

'I don't have that in front of me, Chairman.'

'Not him, you buffoon! Abel Thorpe! He's dead. He's been murdered. Along with six other people, all of whom worked for the Brunel Corps. There's something terrible going on there and I'm here to find out what Thorpe was doing that got him tangled up in it. Now, for the love of God, do any of you have any idea what he was working on that might have meant he would be a target?'

Fleet looked around the oval of leaders, who replied with faces of blank bemusement and began looking to each other for answers and checking their papers for reasons that seemed unclear even to them.

'Did he report anything serious?' continued Fleet, bewildered at their bewilderment. 'Did he raise any concerns? Did he say "Hang on, everyone, lots of people in the Brunel Corps keep getting murdered"? Anything like that?'

The room fell deathly silent, and the chairman sat back in his chair. He took off his glasses and chewed one of the arms thoughtfully. Eventually, his eyebrows flashed with an idea.

'Who is murder?'

'What?' asked Fleet.

'Murder falls under whom?'

'Well, that's death,' said David, 'so probably my department. But I believe there's also a dotted line to Crime, isn't that right?'

A woman with a neatly arranged shrub of flaming orange hair nodded enthusiastically. 'A dotted line, yes. I can get the stakeholder map, Chairman?'

'No no, that's quite all right. Perhaps you could jointly look into Mr Grainger's query.'

The shrub gave a polite tip forward. 'Of course. We'll put a few people on it and return with discussion material next week.'

'Splendid.'

'No!' cried Fleet, throwing up his hands. 'It's not splendid! What is wrong with you people? A man is dead!'

'Mr Grainger, please compose yourself.'

'I will not! I am going to find out what is going on here, right now!'

Fleet pushed his heavy chair backwards as firmly as he could, which moved it barely six inches, and stormed out of the room.

'Well,' said the chairman. 'Standard Interlock meeting fireworks.'

The room chuckled, and carried on with their important work.

Meanwhile, Clara was discovering that if you say things confidently enough – things such as 'I'm here to assist Mr Grainger who is taking over from Mr Thorpe, and I need access to Mr Thorpe's former office and portfolio of work' – sometimes, people will believe you.

In fact, if you say this sort of thing to an overworked employee of an under-resourced organisation, they might even say things like 'Thank God!', leap up to embrace you, and lead you urgently wherever you want to go, before returning to their desk and resuming their breathing exercises in front of a stack of papers which has grown even larger in their absence.

Compared to this frenzy, Abel Thorpe's office was an oasis of calm organisation. Through the window back out into the bullpen, Clara watched as the harried-looking clerks dashed frantically between desks, swiping and shuffling papers, skimming numeric tables with their fingers, occasionally cross-referencing with maps of the city on the wall, and jotting down summaries, before doing it all again.

Trying to make sense of it all, thought Clara. *I know the feeling*.

They seemed to her to be woefully understaffed. But then she wondered whether there was any number of people that would be able to get it done, or if their task was simply impossible.

It was hard to shut out the hubbub beyond the window, but she redoubled her efforts and returned to the items in front of her: a small, navy-blue diary that she'd found under some papers in one of Thorpe's desk drawers, and a large brown folder she'd discovered filed away in a cabinet. Next to these, Clara's own notebook was open, and her eyes darted back and forth between immaculate typewriter print, her shorthand scrawl, and Thorpe's neat calligraphy.

What she read next captured her entirely, and her pen fell from her fingers.

She closed her eyes. Images, faces, conversations, documents all swirled in Clara's mind: the victims' personnel files at the Brunelians' central encampment, Helena Evans's story, the black horse-drawn carriage careening towards her in the fog, Kathleen Price's toothy grin appearing from behind a recently impaled automaton.

She opened her eyes to find everything had vanished.

The desk she sat at, Abel Thorpe's neatly ordered office, the busy clerks outside rushing back and forth with their endless paper.

All gone.

She was, on some level, aware that her breathing had sped up, but otherwise the entire universe had gone.

No stars, no planets, no people. No traffic jams. No dentist appointments. No supernovae, no eclipses, no ocean depths, no mountaintops.

Not one single chaffinch.

Even the diary and folder she had been reading, the words that had done this to her, were gone.

She floated in an infinite void, an indescribable geometry of consequences.

Her body rose up through an endless, dark cosmos as dimensionless filaments of deduction soared in countless directions.

They formed shapes without names, expanding and flowing like melted wax under water.

It was beautiful.

There rang out a sound, a memory of something she had not said.

Three . . .

From somewhere far off, there was a loud cry of frustration, and she was jolted from her reverie. The flat universe in front of her returned, with the startling familiarity of waking suddenly from a dream.

Through the window, at the far end of the room outside, she saw Fleet staggering from the boardroom, clutching his head and cursing whatever he had just left.

No luck with the bigwigs, then. No matter. Clara's come up with the goods.

She scooped up the documents, sprang from her seat and dashed out of the office towards her partner.

'Oh, Clara,' Fleet began as she approached at speed, 'these people are— Hey!'

She dragged him by the arm to the edge of the room, pushed him into a closet the size of a coffin, squeezed herself in so they were pressed face to face, and shut the door.

'Have you lost your mind?' Fleet demanded.

'Just the opposite.'

'You've found your mind.'

'Shush.'

'About time, too.'

'Quiet,' said Clara. 'You'll want to hear this.'

'I've just come from one of the most awful things I've ever experienced. I think they called it a meeting. Give me a minute.'

'No, listen. I found Abel Thorpe's diary.'

'It was just lying about?'

'Yes,' replied Clara. 'Under some papers. In a desk drawer. Nobody minded: they assumed I was here to help. Which we are, in a way . . .'

'Clara.'

'. . . And to be honest, they seem too preoccupied with their own work to care about much else . . .'

'Clara.'

'But listen—'

'Clara.'

'*What?*'

'Could we turn the light on?'

Clara stopped, and suddenly realised they were indeed in pitch darkness. It was an adjustment, returning to the physical world after floating in the Breakthrough Heavens, as she had decided to call them.

'Oh. Yes. Of course.'

There was a fumbling sound, and then a click. Fleet lowered his arm back down from the light cord.

Clara realised this might be the closest she'd ever been to him. He needed a shave.

'Better?' she asked.

Fleet freed his jacket sleeve from a mop handle. 'Different.'

Clara's mind leapt back to what she had to say, her eyes wide with excitement. 'Thorpe knew about the disasters, Fleet. The ones we found in the Brunel Corps employee records. He was compiling a report.'

'A report?'

Clara levered her arm up until the brown folder was held aloft.

Fleet turned his head so he could read the label. 'Brunel Corps Unsatisfactory Outcomes Audit, 1867–1887 (DRAFT) – A. Thorpe, Head of Oversight for Civil Engineering & Public Works'.

He took the folder and began to leaf through.

'And he spoke to them,' continued Clara.

'Who?'

'Abel Thorpe.'

'No, I meant who did Abel Thorpe speak to?'

'Keep up, Fleet!'

'Yes, I'm so sorry for not keeping up with information you have that I'm not privy to.'

'Sorry,' said Clara, 'I'm excited. Listen.'

She held up the diary next to their faces, knocking the lightbulb swinging, flicked it open on a page she had book-marked and began reading aloud.

'Ninth of January: Ivor Beechworth. Tenth of January: Violet Griffiths-Jones. Twentieth of January: *Oliver Mellanby*.'

'He spoke to Mellanby?'

'He spoke to all of them, Fleet. All of the victims. All of them people who had worked on projects that ended in disaster. Including Helena Evans! Years apart from each other, and in totally different places, but with disaster in common. And he

250

chose these people to speak to because their roles gave them information he needed to understand what had gone wrong.'

'And he concludes what? The Brunelians work so fast they can't do it safely?'

'He says it right here.'

Clara stuffed the diary under an arm, yanked the folder out of Fleet's hands and flicked through the leaves before holding it up to his face, far too close for him to be able to see anything, before turning it round and reading:

'"Audit of Corps unsatisfactory project outcomes. Interviews: Summary and Initial Findings. Participant interview data reveals practices consistent with purposeful imprecisions and/ or subgraded material. Probable malefaction."'

'"Probable malefaction"? He means . . .'

'Sabotage.'

Fleet shook his head in confusion. 'Thorpe thought someone deliberately destroyed, what, eight or so Brunelian projects? Bridges, tunnels, *a ship*? Over a twenty-year period? Why?'

'Unclear,' said Clara. 'The folder shows he was working through a number of catastrophes, but he added these ones, the ones our victims worked on, to a list for further inquiry.'

'Anything else of note in his diary? Any other appointments?'

'Lots of appointments, Fleet; I've cross-referenced what I can. Most of the names don't seem to coincide with his Brunel Corps investigation as far as I can tell. There's some departmental meetings, a number of locations he was due to visit: Brighton, Ealing, Brailsford, Stevenage, London Border North. Something called the "Interlock" appears once a week.'

Fleet shuddered, before adding: 'Well, he was head of his department, he'd have had other things to look into beyond this.'

'Right, but that's not all.' Clara raised her eyebrows to indicate the significance of her find. 'He summoned the Triumvirate to an emergency meeting.'

'The Triumvirate?'

'The people in charge of the Brunelians. Interesting to learn they can be summoned anywhere, but apparently Mr Thorpe was the someone who could do that.'

'Everyone answers to someone, I suppose,' said Fleet. 'And this meeting, where he explained to these leaders about a pattern of sabotage inside their organisation, went very well, I take it?'

'Apparently it did, according to his notes.'

'Oh.'

Clara flicked to the relevant document in the folder.

'"Triumvirate informed of pattern of probable malefaction. Triumvirate agreed with assessment, resolved to prepare action plan and share with OWRC."'

'That was nice of them.'

'Yes, Fleet. It was. And a week after he spoke to those three men, Abel Thorpe was dead.'

Chapter 15

The difficulty with being in government – as any honourable member of Parliament would tell you, if only they could be relied upon to answer the question – is that it is impossible to keep all of your constituents happy all of the time.

In theory this didn't matter all that much, so long as you could keep *enough* of your constituents happy to return you at the next election – or, if not happy, then at least unable to imagine a better tomorrow.

But in practice, not being able to keep all of your constituents happy all of the time presented tangible everyday difficulties, the most vexing of which was being inundated with letters from disgruntled members of the public, always complaining about something or other. And for the average MP who just wanted to enjoy his free Westminster Fortress canteen 'Thursday is Cassoulet Day' cassoulet in peace, the prospect of having to reply to all these letters with insincere promises and platitudes – or simply add a signature to the bottom of whatever their staff had, on their behalf, promised and platitudinised – was just a bit too much.

Issues such as these were why the government had created a new cabinet position: Population Contentment Secretary. The post was currently occupied by one Archaeopterus Blythe, and the role worked as follows: whenever a Cabinet meeting noted a rising discontent among the populace, all eyes would turn to Blythe, who would swiftly concoct some scheme or other for distracting the dissatisfied public and making them feel that things weren't really all that bad.

The Pleasure Coast – 114 miles of coastline to the south of the city given over solely to fun and enjoyment – was a particularly popular initiative of his. So too was the world's largest subterranean rollercoaster, the London Funderground. But the pride and joy of all his attempts to bring the people a bit more pride and joy were the Vauxhall Pleasure Gardens.

The Vauxhall Pleasure Gardens had once been the jewel in the crown of the city's entertainment industry, and were a fond memory from Blythe's childhood. But time, fashion, and an unfortunate brawl between a visiting dignitary and a swan – which the courts eventually found to be equally the fault of both parties – had led to their closure and eventual dilapidation.

Blythe, however, was convinced that he could breathe new life into them, and so he turned to the best engineers, artists, landscape architects, and entertainmenteers the city had to offer. Not long after, the Gardens reopened to the public, with a host of new attractions and amusements that brought visitors pouring in from across the city.

To ensure as many as possible of the public could enjoy the Gardens, Blythe had kept the entry fee very low. And so, in order to recoup the cost of its build, the Gardens had to be made available for private hire for an absolutely extortionate fee that satisfied any potential hirer that they really were the cream of the capital's crop.

And among such crop-cream was the Brunel Corps, who hired out the Pleasure Gardens every year to throw a massive party for the public. It was just their way of giving something back to the people after another year of disruptive construction works. A way of saying 'Sorry for all the mess', 'Thank you for trusting us to make London better', and 'We hear you, we're listening, we will keep learning and improving, but you can't make an omelette without demolishing a few neighbourhoods'.

Numbers were limited, so tickets were awarded by lottery, but the idea that one *might* win a ticket, one year, to the annual Brunelian Garden Party, where the entry, the activities and, most importantly, the all-you-can-stuff-in-your-handbag buffet were free, was often enough to stem the tide of the worst opposition to the Corps's activities.

Ordinarily, none of this would be remotely important – and it's a very open question whether it is even now – but this year's annual Brunel Corps Garden Party was scheduled for the day after Fleet and Clara's trip to the Office of the Well-Running of the City, and so presented the perfect opportunity for them to engineer a way to meet the top engineers of them all: the Triumvirate.

So, Fleet went to visit an acquaintance from his days as a detective police officer to procure a pair of unprocurable tickets, while Clara headed back to the archives of the *Morning Chronicler* to see what she could find out about three of the most powerful men in London.

They had agreed to meet the following afternoon outside Seventeen Dials underground station, in order to catch a tube heading south for the Vauxhall Pleasure Gardens.

Clara arrived first, keen to share with Fleet the ripened fruit of her painstaking research.

She'd forgone her usual plain day dress and cape in favour of a cotton sateen walking dress, which was woven through with a delicate pattern of yellow rosebuds. Clara had not brought much to London in the way of dresses or gowns, or indeed in the way of anything, when she first arrived from Yorkshire. This was a calculated decision, as she had not wanted to arouse her mother's suspicion that she wasn't, in fact, coming only for a brief period to finally fulfil her daughterly duty and 'catch herself a husband' – which her mother liked to remind her of frequently, with an accompanying mime of casting a line, reeling in a bite, and being very happy indeed with the fish-husband hanging from the lure. Had her mother suspected for a moment that she was instead planning on throwing off the shackles of her family's financial support, finding employment as a journalist, staying indefinitely, and taking as many unchaperoned open-top bus tours as she pleased, Clara would certainly not have been permitted to set foot off her family's estate.

The rosebud dress, however, she had managed to squeeze into her suitcase, and although it was – by London standards – the very opposite of à la mode, Clara liked it. She hadn't had an excuse to wear it since her arrival, and for a garden party it was just the thing – as was the straw bonnet she'd chosen to pair it with, which was beautifully trimmed with blush-pink silk roses and joyful ribbons that trailed under her chin.

A few minutes later, Clara saw Fleet approaching, wearing the exact same brown suit he wore every day.

The pair jostled their way through the flow of people making their exit from the underground station, Fleet scowling and lightly huffing at the general failure to heed the signs that marked this route as entrance-only.

Once down in the rabbit warren of the underground tunnels, Fleet and Clara followed the purple-polka-dotted signs for the Albert Line, and hurried to the southbound platform where they hopped onto a train just as it closed its doors to depart.

Clara surveyed the carriage. Half-full. Plenty of seats free, but none far enough away from other people's ears. No good for the information she had to reveal.

Fleet appeared to have had the same thought, or else was heading to stand at the end of the carriage, where no one else was, just by habit.

Clara hurried to join him as the train began moving again.

'So,' she began, waving her notebook in his face, 'our quarries.'

'Quarries?'

'Yes, Fleet. Or, if you prefer, our *prey*.'

She clawed the air like a jungle cat. Fleet frowned with confusion, and Clara suspected he might jump in with some blandly technical correction, like 'suspects', so she moved on quickly.

'I give you' – she paused dramatically – 'Corps-Marshals Jahangir Khan, Everett Crowe, and Sir Grover Merridew. The Triumvirate of the Brunel Corps.'

She opened her notebook at a bookmarked page, where she had neatly glued three small newspaper photographs. Three men: two youthful, one older.

Fleet glanced at the images. 'And you're going to hunt them . . .'

'Only in investigatory terms, Fleet. Now, Corps-Marshal Khan and Corps-Marshal Crowe here are the youngest people ever to have been appointed to the Triumvirate: Crowe at forty-two, and Khan at just thirty-five years of age. Quite extraordinary.'

'Hard to disagree,' said Fleet.

'Crowe,' continued Clara, pointing at a photograph of a striking fellow in his mid-forties with fine features and a handlebar moustache adorning his long face, 'was the first of the two to be made a corps-marshal, about four years ago. Lower middle class, Scottish mother and English father, who

257

moved to London from the country. His father secured employment in the Brunel Corps as a shipping clerk, and seeing how the company offered the opportunity for advancement and betterment, found his son a job at the age of sixteen.

'And it turns out young Master Crowe had quite the knack for it, and managed to get himself under the wing of a supportive commanding officer who recognised his talent and helped him win a Corps scholarship to University College London where he studied engineering. After that, he returned to the Corps as an officer. Gained a reputation for excellent work and proved himself a reliable project leader. Seems to have been very well respected. Not adored as a commanding officer, as some are, but certainly not disliked.'

'And Corps-Marshal Khan?' asked Fleet.

'Well, if Crowe's ascent through the ranks has been swift, Khan's has been something else entirely.'

Clara tapped the photograph next to Crowe's: the profile of a man in his late thirties whose chiselled features, neatly trimmed beard and youthful yet manly appearance made it look like he was advertising some sort of health tonic.

'His father was a nobleman from Shahjahanabad who met his mother, an Englishwoman, after she went out to India to nurse her brother who'd fallen ill out there. His father died when he was quite young, so his mother returned to her family in England. Turns out she came from old money, and this meant that Mr Khan had the more traditional route to the top: Eton, then mathematics at Oxford – highest first of his year, no less – then further study in architectural engineering. After graduating, he joined the Brunel Corps in a very senior position and his meteoric rise began.'

'And the reason for his success?'

'Apparently he's responsible for a lot of the company's more innovative and groundbreaking architectural designs.

At least, according to a puff piece on him in *Who's Who and Where's Who*.'

'Sorry,' said Fleet, '*Who's Who and Why*—?'

'*Who's Who and Where's Who*.'

Clara rifled through her satchel, pulled out a magazine and handed it to Fleet. On the cover, an elegantly dressed lady with a lace parasol averted her gaze submissively, while the text around her promised to teach you 'The Art of the Fish Knife', teased 'The Seven Best Locations to Promenade in London', and hailed the 'Miracle Arsenic Cream' that could 'Beautify Even the Plainest of Janes'.

'It's aimed at the mothers of wealthy families,' Clara continued. 'It's essentially a glorified list of eligible bachelors. Given Khan's age and success, I thought he might have made an appearance at some point. I was not disappointed. Apparently he's worth over twenty-five thousand a year, and has a lovely estate in Somerset.'

Fleet turned the magazine over in his hands. 'Beats reading the penny dreadfuls, I suppose.'

'I don't usually read society rubbish, but my mother always sends me her monthly copy, with the bachelors she considers the most eligible circled in pen. She's still living in hope that one day I'll settle down.'

'You're not settled?' asked Fleet.

'I am. But the type of settling that my mother has in mind involves at the very least a minor baronetcy, no fewer than five footmen, a butler, a cook, some lady's maids, some housemaids, some scullery maids, probably some other maids I've forgotten about, and several acres of topiaried hedges.'

'That's too much topiary,' said Fleet, wincing at the piercing squeak of the train wheels turning a bend.

Clara's eyes lit up at this rare revelation of a personal opinion from her colleague. 'I didn't know you had such strong views on topiary, Fleet. Are you interested in horticulture in general, or would you say it's more of a specialised interest in the coiffuring of perennials?'

'I misspoke. I meant to say, "Let's continue talking about the suspects."'

The train began to slow, and the speakers in the carriage emitted a lively jingle before a dour voice announced: 'Now approaching Vauxhall. Disembark for the Vauxhall Pleasure Gardens.'

Clara clapped her notebook shut and flashed her eyebrows excitedly at Fleet. 'To be continued.'

'Talking about the Triumvirate? Or talking about hedges?'

'Both.'

Even for a hardened Londoner like Fleet, it was impossible to deny that the Pleasure Gardens were spectacular.

This was partly because even he wasn't immune to the charm of hundreds of acres of city given over to recreation and amusement.

But it was also because Archaeopterus Blythe was, when it came to designing a space that would ensure a good time for everyone, a genius performing penny-farthing wheelies on the edge of insanity.

Even before one's arrival, the experience began.

Mere moments after leaving the underground station, walking with a number of nattily dressed fellow passengers, Fleet and Clara were greeted by a line of ushers wearing the distinctive uniform of the Pleasure Gardens: bright scarlet trousers and jackets with ornate golden trim, tidy bellboy hats, and the most enormous smiles it's possible for British people to maintain.

'Brunel Corps Garden Party this way, please!' one of them cried ebulliently, while the rest waved their arms in pleasing, synchronised circles, somehow never pointing but nevertheless gently guiding the punters in the right direction.

Not that any such guide was required.

Directly opposite the underground station there was a snaking path up a beautifully landscaped terraced lawn, leading to an imposing Grecian-style facade complete with wooden Corinthian columns that had been painted to give the appearance of finely carved marble.

At the facade's centre, the entranceway was flanked by more of the scarlet-clad Pleasure Gardens employees, who welcomed visitors with a courteous bow and a cheerful 'Welcome!' or 'Hello!', while above it all an illuminated sign the size of a yacht flashed out the words PLEASURE AWAITS.

Once through the main entrance, Fleet and Clara were funnelled into one of dozens of lines that led into a patchwork of green-and-white candy-striped gazebos, where yet more impossibly buoyant scarlet-suited workers checked bags for illicit items while lively brass band music tooted out from speakers hidden in nearby trees.

There was some impatient tutting from further back in the line as Clara emptied her satchel onto a small gazebo table, covering it with multiple books, notebooks, magazines, pencils, string, and packets of birdseed. The bag-check girl behind the table apologised profusely for having to confiscate the packets, before explaining that 'very reasonably priced, specially blended' birdseed could be purchased at any number of outlets located around the grounds, should Clara wish to feed the pigeons.

Once through the gazebo, Fleet and Clara were ushered into yet another queue that led to ornate turnstiles at which a further employee, practically oscillating with excitement, checked their tickets and handed them each a map of the park, before saluting exuberantly as he waved them through and wished them whatever on earth he could possibly have meant by 'A Happily-Ever-Afternoon'.

Inside, the upbeat music continued to pipe away from everywhere and nowhere, and the Gardens stretched as far as the eye could see, which was to the lime trees and imported redwoods that bordered it all and shut out the overwhelming cityscape beyond.

Beautifully painted wooden signs pointed the way to various attractions: from The House of Robot Birds That Sing The Same Songs Every Twelve Minutes, to the ever-popular Mr Crimple's Taxidermatopia, to the magnificent Pool of Self-Reflection, where one could often find an artist, poet, or other lost soul gazing deep within for submerged truths, or generally moping about trying to divine the meaning of happiness until they decided to do the sensible thing and buy an ice cream.

Now, most new arrivals were heading in the same direction, and the pair went with the current, soon reaching the Gardens' central piazza – a colossal square surrounded by classically styled buildings, all of which appeared to be home to either a food outlet or a gift shop.

The crowd gathered towards one end of the piazza, where there was a giant stage usually reserved for performances of the latest operetta or melodrama the Gardens had commissioned. Today, however, all the two-dimensional painted pirate ships and castles were hidden away behind heavy curtains, and the stage was almost bare.

At a lectern stood a stout, elderly gentleman with magnificent whiskers that gave him the appearance of an oversized, benevolent, long-haired cat. Seated to his side were two tall, fit, much younger men. All wore the impeccable dark-brown dress uniform of the Brunel Corps, their chests decorated with colourful ribbons and shiny medals of honour that glinted in the sun.

262

The Triumvirate, thought Fleet. Even without Clara's news-paper photographs, it would have been obvious who these people were. He watched as the three men chatted amiably among themselves, waiting for the crowd to finish assembling.

Shortly after, the omnipresent music died away, followed by a sharp fanfare.

The bewhiskered gentleman turned to the microphone and tapped it twice, sending a pair of amplified thumps out across the piazza.

'Friends, citizens, Brunelians, lend me your ears . . .' the deep voice rasped, before adding: 'Don't worry, I'll give them back!'

He let out a hearty chuckle and the crowd responded with polite laughter.

'I apologise. I was told to open with a joke, but they didn't provide me with one – they rather just left me to swim for it – and I'm afraid that's led us all to this unhappy outcome. I am Corps-Marshal Sir Grover Merridew, and it is my honour, as the old codger of the Triumvirate, to welcome you all, you citizens of our great city, to our annual garden party.'

A hearty cheer went up from the crowd, and the two other corps-marshals on stage smiled and applauded.

Under the noise, Clara began firing off the information she had not been able to impart earlier.

'He's the third son of a baronet. Seventy-four.'

'Seventy-four?' echoed Fleet. 'Spry for his age.'

'It is easy to think,' Sir Grover continued, settling the audience back into quiet, 'that there is a division between us. Citizens and Corps. But days such as today are important for reminding us that we are all on the same journey. All in one wagon, hurtling down the road.

'We engineers are leaning over the side and fixing a wonky wheel, or up on the roof patching a hole in the canvas. We

263

get in the way and make a mighty racket – don't think we don't know! But we're making sure that we all get there in one piece.

'You, the people of the city, are inside the wagon, working on all kinds of other endeavours – art, commerce, education, recreation and faith. You make sure that there is a *reason* for this wagon to keep going.

'Our work is visible. Our structures tickle the sky and span the city. But it is all nothing without you. And for that, we are forever indebted.'

The crowd broke into lengthy applause, and Sir Grover nodded humbly.

Clearly, thought Fleet, despite the man's self-effacement, he was an extremely well-practised orator.

'Educated at Harrow,' resumed Clara, 'then read Natural Sciences at Cambridge. Average attainment, but, as you'd expect from his background, well connected.'

'I'm sure,' replied Fleet, watching Corps-Marshals Crowe and Khan applauding as enthusiastically as any in the crowd, smiling and seeming to be enjoying themselves marvellously.

'He has two older brothers,' continued Clara, 'and so, as a baronet's third son, needed to find employment. His father, it seems, wanted him to join the military or the clergy, but he opted for the Brunel Corps in its early days when it was just starting out. Got in just as Brunel realised he couldn't manage it alone. Didn't do much of particular note in the way of engineering, but he proved highly effective at lobbying government ministers, smoothing things over with local councils and officials, and generally using his influence to clear the way for the Corps to get things done. A key part of their early success, and so he was one of the first three chosen by Brunel to form what became known as the Triumvirate. The other two are either retired or dead.'

264

'The last of the first,' said Fleet.

Sir Grover continued his remarks for a few minutes, with the crowd responding warmly and his colleagues applauding at all the right moments and laughing at his jokes and asides.

Finally, he wound towards a conclusion.

'We in the Corps sometimes like to say "The future is the project that is never finished." Well, I say that *you* are that future, and we will never stop working for you. Forgive us for the noise as we keep fixing the wagon, and let us enjoy each other's company, for we have a long, long way to go.

'Now, that's quite enough bleating from this old ram. Go forth and enjoy your day. I declare this garden party . . . open!'

With that, Corps-Marshals Khan and Crowe stood and led the crowd in rapturous applause, slapping Sir Grover on the back and offering various appreciative remarks as he smiled and bowed.

The lively brass band music resumed from the speakers hidden in the trees, and the energised crowd scattered at the speed of anticipation towards the food kiosks bordering the piazza and to the attractions of the park beyond.

Within moments, the Triumvirate had no audience at all, and Fleet watched as Khan and Crowe sauntered off, chatting away without a second glance at Sir Grover, who remained frozen to his lectern as his jolly expression slipped into something much more sombre.

Fleet wondered if the other shows that took place on this stage ever saw actors quite as talented as these three men.

Fleet and Clara sat down on one of the benches that edged the piazza.

'Are you sure I can't tempt you, Fleet?' Clara asked, waving a pot of hot eels under his nose.

Fleet blanched. 'No, I'm fine for eel, thank you.'

'Best in London, according to the man who sold them to me.'

'It's a low bar.'

'Well, I've never had them before, and new experiences are what life is all about.'

Clara shovelled a large wooden forkful into her mouth. Fleet watched with interest as she chewed for a while and then, with some effort, swallowed. She placed the pot of eels on the bench next to her.

'Always good to try new things,' she said, grimacing.

Fleet, half-smiling, shook his head.

'So,' Clara resumed, 'what is our plan of attack?'

'Firstly, don't attack anyone.'

'Obviously I didn't mean with violence, Fleet. I meant with our skill and guile.'

'I suggest we split up. After the speech, Merridew headed off towards the south of the park, and Khan and Crowe went that way.'

Fleet pointed in the same direction as a sign that promised multiple innovative attractions that sounded thrilling and exhausting, and sighed.

The pair fell silent for a moment, as the wind carried the sound of merriment from all across the Gardens to their bench on the piazza.

Above the general good cheer, Fleet felt he heard something else. An excited hubbub, whooping and clapping, and the slow, rhythmic thumping of inhumanly heavy footsteps.

He looked out across the piazza. A crowd had gathered near the entrance to the park, and through it moved an oval formation of twelve men – bearskin hats atop their heads, bayoneted rifles in their arms, and dozens of small daggers decorating their wrists, ankles and the white leather belts running across their blood-red tunics.

Coldstream Guards.

Mystifyingly to Fleet, they were always a popular sight for tourists and people looking to get a fun photograph. Even though they were possibly one of the most terrifying and dangerous things in the entire city – possibly the *most* terrifying and dangerous, except of course for the person they protected.

Fleet watched as the oval marched onwards, forming a barrier around Queen Victoria.

She needed no such protection. Eleven assassinations and subsequent revivals had left her mostly machine, the weight of a tram, strong as a team of shire horses, and invulnerable to attack by any but the most determined, ingenious and unafraid of summary execution at whatever nowadays counted as her hands.

The regal, thumping footsteps echoed across the piazza as she made her way through the crowd.

It occurred to Fleet that the oval of Coldstream Guards might not actually be for her protection, but rather to prevent her subjects simply being crushed under her gargantuan feet, which resembled the sort of things that might be used to support a boat in dry dock.

In the oval's wake, Fleet noticed a tall, impeccably dressed man in his early forties – close enough to be part of the retinue, but falling behind as he kept picking individual blades of grass from his polished shoes, shaking his head at the inconvenience of being even this close to nature.

The man didn't appear to notice Fleet and Clara, and followed the queen as she exited the piazza towards the open gardens.

Just then, a scarlet-dressed usher appeared in front of them. He began to hand Clara a note, noticed her largely uneaten pot of hot eels, apparently decided it would be wrong to interrupt anyone's recovery from experiencing that, and handed the note to Fleet before retreating out of sight.

Fleet unfolded the note. The paper was cream, high quality; the ink, a royal blue; the handwriting, barely legible. He and Clara read it together.

'*Detectives. Interested to learn what you find out.*'

It wasn't signed. Not even initialled. The author seemed to assume their identity was obvious.

Fleet looked back towards the crowd that had gathered along Her Majesty's path. The man had already vanished. Julius Bell always had somewhere more pressing to be.

The park's sculpture garden was filled to brimming with flowering plants, serpentine hedges and pretty fountains from which the calming trickle of water could almost make you forget the cacophonous city outside even existed at all.

Almost, as the sculpture garden was located at the very edge of the park and came with a City Viewing Terrace, where visitors seeking the ultimate thrill could go, attempt to take in the incomprehensible vista, pass out in moments, get revived by a Gardens employee wafting smelling salts, and finally be presented with a bill for the whole experience – the shock from which sadly tended to cause people to pass out again, summoning yet more smelling salts, a further bill, and so on, in a spiral of unconsciousness, debt and eventual scarpering out of the park gates that hardened thrillseekers came to refer to as 'Gardening'.

Fleet entered the sculpture garden and followed the lavender-lined path that led to a VIP area Clara had pointed out on the map, passing an intriguing array of ill-proportioned statues of Greek gods and goddesses which – on account of the construction of the Pleasure Gardens running over budget – had been purchased at a huge discount from a sculptor who wouldn't be told that his talent really lay outside the medium of stone, and indeed the visual arts in general.

Eventually, Fleet found it: a temporary canvas pavilion, adorned with flags bearing the laurel wreath of the Brunel Corps, and with its sides pulled up to allow the Very Important People inside to view the glory of the sculpture garden separated from the masses.

In the far corner of the pavilion, Fleet spotted Crowe and Khan, drinks in hand, deep in conversation, while other, clearly senior figures from the Corps – all of whom wore brown wristbands – helped themselves from a private buffet with, Fleet noticed, not a single pot of hot eels in sight.

Fleet also noticed that the pavilion was surrounded by roping, which would have been easy enough to hop over were it not for the presence of several men wearing jolly yellow berets and carrying much less jolly-looking firearms. For a moment Fleet's heart sank, but then he saw, standing in front of a small gap in the roping, a woman dressed in the tell-tale scarlet uniform of the Vauxhall Pleasure Gardens and holding a clipboard and pen. Her face beamed with professional chirpiness.

A category three to be sure, he thought. The 'only too happy to help' employee who, generally speaking, will go to any lengths to ensure customer satisfaction. He might just stand a chance.

'Hello,' Fleet began, approaching the woman. 'Wonderful party.'

'Oh, I'm so glad you're enjoying yourself, sir. Is there anything I can do to help make it even more agreeable?'

'I'm not sure. It might be a bit of a bother.'

The woman looked slightly perturbed at this. 'There's no such thing as "bother" in the Vauxhall Pleasure Gardens, sir. Only endless joy.'

'Oh,' replied Fleet, pulling a forlorn expression.

'Oh no!' cried the woman, with the look of someone whose workplace performance review might be compromised. 'You look sad.'

269

'It's just, well, as you can see I'm a member of the Brunel Corps.' Fleet gestured to his brown suit. 'And I'm supposed to be meeting my superior officer inside this pavilion, but I seem to have lost my VIP wristband. Must have come off while I was, um . . .' – he glanced quickly at the map in his hands – '. . . riding the carousel.'

'Riding the carousel?'

'Yes. Must have got it caught on my horse's reins or something.'

'Ah yes, that does happen.'

'And now of course you won't be able to let me into the pavilion, and the Brigadier will no doubt be quite put out, because he needs this important information I have for him. Which is about a new type of bridge we've just invented. It's even taller, this one. We've finally cracked it. He's really been looking forward to this, and I hate the thought of his afternoon being spoiled by my mistake, but I do understand that you can't let me in there without a wristband. Thank you anyway for trying to help.'

Fleet turned to go.

'Wait!' the woman exclaimed.

Fleet turned back to see the broadest possible smile stretching across her face.

'If you're a VIP, then you'll be on my list. So, no need to worry about the wristband.' She tapped her pen against the clipboard. 'Now, what was the name?'

'Oh, it's rather unusual; perhaps if I spell it?'

'All right.'

'Um . . . S . . . N . . .'

'Hmmm, nothing here beginning with Sn.'

'No, no, S-M . . .'

'I do apologise, sir. And what comes after "M"?'

'I,' tried Fleet.

'Smith?'

'That's the one.'

The woman gave Fleet a slightly odd look. 'I thought you said the name was unusual, sir. I've got four Smiths on this list.'

'Just a little joke,' Fleet replied, before frowning. 'Why? Was it not funny?'

The woman burst into peals of laughter. 'Oh! I see! You had me going there, sir. Now, which Smith are you?'

'A.'

'Arthur!'

'I usually just go by A.'

'Well then, Mr A Smith, I'm glad I could be of help.'

The woman's chipperness had now fully returned, and she waved Fleet into the pavilion, where he immediately discovered that Crowe and Khan had gone.

After a few polite enquiries, a helpfully tipsy Construction Management Colonel pointed him out the other side of the tent and down some winding steps into a more secluded part of the sculpture garden.

Fleet followed the directions and eventually spied the corps-marshals, sitting in an arbour having an animated discussion. He crouched down on the steps behind an overgrown fern.

'Is now truly the right time, Everett?' asked Khan.

Fleet leaned forwards to hear the answer, and ideally more detail about the question.

'Then when?' replied Crowe. 'After more of his delays?'

Fleet peeked around the fern, and the corps-marshal continued.

'How long do you want to wait for someone with fresh ideas?'

Khan sighed heavily. 'The process to—'

Fleet missed the end of this, owing to hitting a grassy mound below the steps he had just fallen from, but he took comfort in the likelihood that his yelping while doing so probably meant that very little more had been said.

The two Brunelians sprang up in surprise.

'Goodness me,' said Khan. 'Are you all right?'

Fleet hadn't meant to start the conversation just yet, so he stood up and began dusting himself off as slowly as one plausibly could dust oneself, to buy time to decide on an approach.

Both Khan and Crowe were extremely senior figures, he reflected, while brushing his lower legs, and by all accounts highly intelligent. He knew that they – that is to say the corps-marshals watching him, not the lower legs he had moved on from in favour of patting the dust from his midriff – were unlikely to have ascended to their rank by speaking rashly, and were perhaps impossible to ruffle into making a mistake.

Nothing for it but the truth, he decided, halfway through a set of broad, definitive jacket sweeps, and to hope something emerged he could press them on.

Freshly dusted, and possibly lightly charged with static, Fleet walked towards the two men and embarked on his first move.

'Corps-Marshals, my name is Inspector Archibald Fleet, of Fleet-Entwhistle Private Investigations.'

He studied Khan and Crowe's reactions: slightly surprised, somewhat interested.

Nothing.

Hardly anyone crumbled to this, of course, but some at least showed alarm or disquiet. Fleet had not expected these men would, but you never knew. Sometimes you got lucky.

Crowe narrowed his sharp eyes, as if trying to make out what this man was about. 'And how can we help you,' he began, 'Archibald Fleet of Fleet-Entwhistle Private Investigations?'

'Hang on a minute,' Khan interjected, tapping his foot. 'Entwhistle, Entwhistle. Where have I heard that name

272

before?' He snapped his fingers and pointed at Fleet. 'I say, isn't that the name of that journalist who writes about the crimes? The *Morning Chronicler*!'

Fleet nodded. 'You are correct.'

Khan clapped once with excitement, and Crowe took a few paces forward towards Fleet, regarding him with renewed admiration.

'Which means you must be the mechanical detective.'

He looked him up and down, before letting out a long, impressed whistle. Fleet instinctively folded his arms.

Khan returned to the arbour and relaxed back on the bench.

'I must say, Inspector, I have enjoyed reading about your exploits enormously. Miss Entwhistle has such a way with words. Now . . .' – he gave the seat next to him a friendly pat for Fleet to join him – 'regarding my colleague's question, of how we can help you. If it is in our power, we certainly will.'

The tone was cordial, affable even. Fleet stayed standing.

'Are you aware that there have been a number of deaths of Brunel Corps personnel in recent months?' he asked.

Khan looked off into some leylandii and nodded sorrowfully. 'Tragic. Very tragic. But these things happen. Can't always be helped. When you build at the pace and scale we do, when you employ so many people, accidents do happen. It's inevitable. But I can assure you, Inspector, that all deaths are taken very seriously indeed, and investigated thoroughly. And we continually update our rules and guidance to ensure that similar accidents do not happen again.'

'I'm not talking about accidental deaths, Corps-Marshal,' replied Fleet. 'I'm talking about murder.'

Khan's brow furrowed. 'Murder?'

Crowe stepped forward, his expression mirroring that of his colleague. 'I'm sorry, did I hear you correctly? Are you saying members of the Brunel Corps have been murdered?'

273

'I am,' confirmed Fleet.

Crowe turned and paced slowly away to a nearby statue of Heracles, whose chiselled torso was twice as long as his arms.

Fleet fumbled in his pocket and pulled out a list: 'Robert Hinman, Eighty-eighth Division; Walter Lack, Thirteenth Division; Juliette Dupont, Fifty-sixth; Oliver Mellanby, Fifteenth . . .'

The look of horror grew on Khan's face with every name. 'Gracious! Crowe, had you any idea about this?'

'Not in the least,' replied Crowe, equally perturbed. '*Murder*? Are you sure?'

'Absolutely sure,' said Fleet. 'All the victims were found with multiple stab wounds. And it's unlikely to be a coincidence that so many of your employees have been killed in the exact same manner, so close together.'

'Of course,' Crowe murmured, sitting himself down on the statue's plinth.

Fleet looked back and forth between the men. Both were shocked, or else accomplished liars. He had no way of knowing. Their manners would not betray them. He pressed on.

'So this is the first you've heard about these deaths? Of Juliette Dupont? Of Oliver Mellanby?'

There was a brief silence as the two men exchanged a querying glance and a head-shake reply.

Khan delivered the explanation. 'To be honest, Inspector,' he replied, wringing a thumb with mild embarrassment, 'this is the first we're hearing of these people at all. Do you have any idea how many the Corps employs? I'm sorry to hear of their deaths, of course.'

'No doubt you know your business well enough to be correct that there is a connection,' continued Crowe. 'Perhaps a disgruntled member of the public? We do have a tendency to ride roughshod in a way that rankles people. Although . . .'

'Although . . .' – Khan picked up the baton – 'it would be surprising if someone had taken their grudge against us this far. But then, you should read some of the letters we get.'

Crowe flashed an eyebrow. 'Colourful stuff. So our secretaries tell us.'

'But this is just speculation, of course,' added Khan, before sweeping a gracious hand towards Fleet. 'You and Miss Entwhistle, you are the experts.'

Fleet stared at the men. Nothing appeared likely to agitate them, except perhaps doing so deliberately.

'Abel Thorpe,' he began, 'from the Office of the Well-Running of the City. You had a meeting with him several weeks ago. What was that meeting about?'

Khan clasped his hands apologetically. 'I'm sorry, Inspector, but that is private Brunel Corps business. I'm sure you understand.'

Fleet nodded. 'Well, why don't I tell you what I know, then. I know that Mr Thorpe was reviewing some of your past projects. I know that those projects were ones that had been struck by tragedy. And I also know that he had become concerned that a number of them had been the subject of sabotage.'

'How do you know all this?' asked Khan.

'I'm sorry, Corps-Marshal, but that's private Fleet-Entwhistle Private Investigations business.'

Crowe laughed. 'It's all right, Jahangir. Inspector, you're quite correct, and we were as shocked as you when we learned of Mr Thorpe's conjectures. Which is why, naturally, we agreed to a full and open investigation.'

'Absolutely,' agreed Khan. 'And I can assure you we take these things very seriously indeed, no matter how long ago they happened. In fact, I even set up an inquiry team to aid Mr Thorpe in his investigations, and Corps-Marshal Crowe was also helping to oversee things to ensure as smooth a process as possible.'

Crowe waved the compliment away. 'At Corps-Marshal Khan's insistence, only. Mr Thorpe ran a tight ship and was perfectly capable of directing our team as to his needs.'

'We look forward to seeing the inquiry's report,' added Khan.

Fleet nodded, and looked between the two men. Each as inscrutable as the other, with the easy charm of accomplished senior leaders. But a tiny chink had finally appeared in their wall.

He cleared his throat.

'"Ran"?'

'Sorry?' asked Crowe.

'You said he ran a tight ship. Does he not any more?'

Crowe smiled broadly, and again regarded Fleet with an engineer's appreciation.

Khan rose to his feet. 'Inspector,' he began, his cordiality hardening, 'we are of course both aware of the passing of Mr Thorpe. We were informed by his office less than a day after the fact.'

'He was murdered, Corps-Marshal,' said Fleet. 'Like all the others.'

'We are aware his death was not from natural causes, Inspector,' said Khan. 'Although we did not know the details nor any connection to Corps officers. And I do not appreciate your attempting to catch out Corps-Marshal Crowe and me in trivial verbal games, when we are quite willingly assisting you with your investigation.'

'He was murdered after he revealed to the Triumvirate his concerns about sabotage,' said Fleet.

Khan's eyebrows scrummed defensively. 'I don't know what you are implying, Inspector.'

276

'And then all the people with whom Thorpe had spoken about those cases of sabotage—'

'There is only a *theory* of sabotage, Inspector.'

'All those people started being murdered too.'

'You are implying a cover-up!' cried Khan.

'I am laying out facts,' said Fleet.

'You are laying out a fantasy!'

'Have you anything to say on the subject?'

Khan looked astonished. 'To you? Now? Certainly not!'

He returned to his seat in the arbour, shaking off his fluster. The sound of distant merriment drifted through the air, messages from people enjoying themselves far more than anyone here.

'Forgive my colleague,' said Crowe, standing up from the plinth and walking back towards Fleet. 'He leaps to the defence of the Corps, to which we have given so much and from which we have received even more. You have uncovered something very concerning, but given the gravity I feel it would be appropriate for us to work with the police on the matter. You understand.'

He offered Fleet a handshake, the definitive message that the detective's welcome had expired. Fleet instinctively obliged.

'Good to meet you, Inspector,' said the corps-marshal, with a polite smile. 'I'm sorry we cannot help further.'

Fleet nodded, and made one last hopeless effort to divine anything at all from the man's eyes staring into his. Then he withdrew his hand and pocketed the card Crowe had palmed him.

Clara, meanwhile, was in a wicker basket two thousand feet in the air.

She hadn't really planned on this, and it's very up for debate whether people who do plan on being in a wicker basket two thousand feet in the air have actually thought about that sequence of words carefully enough to call it a plan.

Regardless, that was Clara's situation, and she was determined to make the best of it, particularly as she had no one to blame but herself for being there – except, perhaps, Mr Snapdragon, an anthropomorphised bunch of flowers that the Pleasure Gardens pretended was the proprietor of this particular attraction: Mr Snapdragon's Whimtastical, Fabulacious, Tremendsational, Hot-Air-Ballooning Skyventure.

How she had got there was one of those things that only made sense chronologically, and even then only barely.

Clara had left Fleet and caught up with her target, Corps-Marshal Merridew, as he wandered around various attractions, but her attempts to get anywhere close to him had been prevented by the stern warnings and light shoves of the yellowtops in his orbit.

It was only at the entrance to the Skyventure that Clara had finally found her moment. Hundreds of people snaked back in queues – waiting for hours for a few minutes of soaring above the earth – but Sir Grover, presumably on account of his position in the Corps, had been escorted by a troop of Pleasure Gardens personnel around the side and straight into a private basket.

Curiously, thought Clara, he had entered alone, leaving behind the yellowtops and taking along no other officers or VIPs – but this also presented the ideal opportunity for her to get some answers.

Naturally, Clara was torn between the necessity of her mission and the moral dubiousness of being a queue-jumper, but before she could weigh the matter up she saw Sir Grover's balloon begin to gently decouple from the earth, and she found herself hitching up her petticoats and skirt, hopping a railing, dashing towards the basket and throwing herself headfirst over the side.

She was mortified during all of this, not only because of the jeers from the people waiting, but also because there were several prominent signs that made it very clear that queue-jumping, railing-hopping, headfirst-into-basket-diving and, in particular, petticoat-hitching were all absolute etiquette no-nos.

But, Clara told herself, this was an emergency situation, and in emergency situations drastic action is sometimes required. She had taken a leap of faith, and now she found herself, a crumpled heap of fabric, rising up into the afternoon sunshine and away from the disapproving crowd below.

'Hello,' said a raspy voice with a chuckle, 'you look like you could use a hand, young miss.'

Clara looked up into Sir Grover's smiling, bewhiskered face, and he offered a hand and pulled her to her feet.

'I'm afraid you've rather spoiled your bonnet.'

'Oh,' Clara replied, untying the ribbons that were keeping it in place, and removing it to discover the brim had come clean away from the crown, and the silk roses were torn and crushed beyond repair. 'Oh well. Bound to happen eventually.'

'With those sorts of antics, I can't disagree!' A chortle erupted from Sir Grover's lips, and he gave a short bow. 'Corps-Marshal Sir Grover Merridew, at your service. Call me Grove – it makes me think of trees.'

'Clara Entwhistle. You're probably wondering why I jumped into your basket.'

'Very much so, but I can hold my curiosity in check for a moment.'

He gestured out of the balloon, and Clara looked out at the park as it fell away beneath them. They had already ascended above the low huts and kiosks dotted here and there on the grass, and she could see in the distance the central piazza near the entrance. Further off, the border of giant redwoods still soared, blocking the view of anything beyond the gardens.

279

She snuck a peek at Sir Grover, who was leaning on the basket's rim, looking down at something and grinning.

'Do have a go on that if you get the chance,' he said, pointing towards a 7¼ gauge railway that was being enjoyed by young children and their parents. 'Working steam! Best ride in the place.'

Clara found his delight utterly charming, and had to remind herself that she was only speaking to this man because he might be complicit in multiple murders.

She sneaked another look at his bewhiskered face.

Surely not, she thought.

As they neared the top of the distant redwoods, a red light began to flash above their heads at the base of the balloon.

Clara realised only then that there was no flame for heating the air in it; indeed, it was sealed at the bottom. She could, however, see large twisting shapes glowing inside.

The red light began to flash more rapidly, and Sir Grover stepped back. Clara did the same, and winced to protect herself from the view of the city that was about to appear. But it never came, because the moment they reached the exact height of the treetops, a motorised curtain wrapped itself around the space between the basket and the balloon, and suddenly they were inside a small room, like a tilting wicker elevator, gently illuminated by the giant filaments above.

'For safety,' said Sir Grover, gesturing at the curtain.

'If it's not safe, why are we still going up?'

'You'll see in a minute. But as we have nothing to look out at, perhaps now is the right moment for you to share why you so were so eager to join me?'

Clara had been thinking how best to explain this. She couldn't very well ask him if he'd murdered a number of people. If he had, he would simply lie. Or, even worse, he might answer honestly and then feel obliged to throw her out of the balloon. So she decided to ask about his colleagues. She might learn something useful about them, and perhaps, from how he thought about them, something useful about him too.

She also thought that, of her two jobs, private investigator might not be the one to put Sir Grover at ease.

'I work for the *Morning Chronicler*,' she began.

'Goodness me, is this the length to which the press will now go to get an interview? You could simply have sent a request via my encampment, my dear.' He chuckled again in bemusement. 'But I am not one to see effort go unrewarded: ask me anything you like.'

'I was wondering if you could tell me a bit about the Triumvirate. Perhaps your relationship with your fellow Corps-Marshals.'

Sir Grover nodded contemplatively, and leaned back on his heels, just far enough to force him to whip a hand onto the basket rim to keep himself from toppling.

'Well, they're geniuses, of course,' he began. 'Not like this old fossil. In very different ways – you don't want two of the same. Khan has the vision, cut from the same cloth as Brunel himself. Fresh ideas, brilliant ideas, unparalleled ideas. His mind, it never stops. I once asked him the time and he gave me the time, the time in Kyoto, the number of time zones, the time it took for the people who hashed out the time zones to agree that, of all places, *Greenwich* should be in the middle, and finally several recipes for the cook short on time but with an abundance of *thyme*, and several more for the vice versa. Must be absolutely exhausting. I wonder if the chap ever sleeps!'

'And Corps-Marshal Crowe?'

'Brilliant in his own way.'

'As brilliant as Corps-Marshal Khan?'

'No, but then no one is. And besides, Khan's head is all for design and innovation. You don't want two of those brains

281

on the team. Crowe is an excellent engineer, to be sure – you don't get to where he's got to otherwise. But he's not a visionary; he's a deliverer.'

'A deliverer?'

'Yes, gets things done. On time. To a high standard.'

'A safe pair of hands.'

'The very safest, Miss Entwhistle. Only Fortescue-Jones from the Thirty-first came close, and it wasn't that close.'

Clara felt the air getting colder, and the basket creaked. She looked at the curtain gently billowing around them and wondered how high they were going to go. A view from a carriage on a hill was enough to make someone dizzy in this city . . . surely they could not safely look out from the sky.

She tried to refocus on the task at hand.

'How well do you know them both?' she asked. 'On a personal level.'

Sir Grover smiled. 'They are fine Brunelians. Can't say I play a lot of tennis with either of them – but I'm sure they'd thrash me!'

He chuckled, and peeked up at the lightbulb above, before continuing.

'Let us be honest with one another, Miss Entwhistle. You are circling the point, tracing out a worksite. Let us pick up our hammers and get on with it.'

Clara froze – she had been roundabout exactly to avoid a confrontation, but it had happened anyway. She waited for Sir Grover to continue.

'You aren't curious about whether my colleagues and I are good friends,' he said. 'I know exactly why you are here. You are press. You have heard the rumours.'

'Rumours?' asked Clara.

'About Crowe and Khan wanting shot of me.'

'Oh, um, yes, of course . . . those rumours. Sorry.'

'Don't think I'm upset,' he continued. 'It's the natural order of things; I'd be worried if they *weren't* plotting my exit. I am the wrong side of seventy, after all. Probably time for me to get on with dying, as they say.'

'Do they say that?'

'Well, not in so many words.'

'And that's why they want to get rid of you?' asked Clara. 'Just because you're old? I mean . . . old*er*.'

Another breathy chuckle escaped Sir Grover's lips. 'It's all right, miss. I am, as you correctly point out, old.'

The lightbulb above them flicked to green.

'But the good thing about being old,' he continued, 'is that it gives you *perspective*.'

The curtain motor whirred into life, and Clara felt her instincts about to take over, as they had at the Lanterns site. She screwed her eyelids shut as she heard the whipping all around her of the curtain retracting, and then felt the cold wind blowing across her body.

'Miss Entwhistle,' said Sir Grover. 'Look.'

Clara summoned her will and peeked out at the world beyond the wicker basket.

She saw the city, stretching into the distance, and was stunned. Not into shock – just that she had never seen it like this. It was vast and tiny – an endless blanket covered in patchwork decorations. A toy village built across a garden.

It didn't look real at all. Perhaps, she thought, that was why it was possible to look at it.

'It's the detail that gets you,' said Sir Grover. 'People think it's the size that's too much for people, but it's the detail. Our minds can get around anything – you just have to step back far enough.'

Clara continued staring out across the textured landscape – for how long, she did not know.

When she pulled herself away, she found Sir Grover also staring out, smiling to himself as he noticed this or that, before realising he was being watched.

'There were only a few hundred of us at the start,' he said. 'Our ambitions didn't extend much beyond the railway network.'

He pointed into the distance.

'London ended just over there. Everywhere beyond was somewhere else. But even just the changes here . . .'

He trailed off into silence again, lost in his thoughts. Clara tried to imagine him as a younger man, just starting out in his career, and then seeing the city change, bit by bit, mile by mile, across decades. What it must have been like to watch it grow, what it must feel like to see it now.

She couldn't do it. Some things can only be lived.

'Are you happy with your work?' she asked.

He turned to her, and nodded thoughtfully.

'I have done an engineer's job. The city works. And I found two extremely capable new parts, in the form of Khan and Crowe, to replace this old screw. It doesn't matter that they want rid of me; what matters is that it will all carry on. It is the very best I could have done.'

Clara waited for him to say more, and watched his eyes misting over as he looked out across the city to which he had devoted the majority of his life.

'Do you think they'll give me a good send-off, Miss Entwhistle?'

She placed her hand on his arm. 'I hope so, Sir Grover. I really hope so.'

Fleet came in search of Clara some time later, where she stood on a wooden platform overlooking the park, near the edge of the Pleasure Gardens – a location they had decided on earlier in the day as a quiet place to meet and discuss their findings.

He wandered over to the railing she was leaning against, gazing at the Gardens' attractions and listening to the far-off music and good cheer.

She turned to him with a triumphant expression. Fleet wondered whether this was to do with what she had learned, or the small cup of ice cream she had acquired.

'It's both,' she said, guessing the question.

'Successful meeting with Sir Grover, then?'

Clara flashed her eyebrows, put the little ice cream spoon into her mouth to free up a hand, retrieved a piece of paper from her bag and thrust it towards Fleet.

'Srugo Frtsco-Jngs!' she declared.

Fleet took the paper and Clara retrieved her spoon from her mouth.

'Sir Hugo Fortescue-Jones, Fleet! A rival for a spot on the Triumvirate. *Crowe's* rival. Merridew mentioned him, and since then I've been to the Gardens' telegraph office and had a little back-and-forth with Lance-Corporal Redfield about it.'

Fleet looked at the piece of paper and discovered it was a receipt from the telegraph office.

'Why have you given me this?'

'I thought a prop would be more dramatic. I burned the telegrams.'

'You *burned* them?' asked Fleet.

'I didn't want them to fall into the wrong hands. The telegraph operator's wastepaper basket was metal, you see, so I just asked him for a match—'

Fleet rubbed the bridge of his nose. 'Does this story end with you—'

'Banned for life, yes. But only from this one. But listen, Sir Grover explained to me that Crowe's main strength over the years has been in delivery – he's a safe pair of hands. And Redfield confirmed that Sir Hugo Fortescue-Jones – although an exceptional engineer, and indeed a beloved Major-General of the Corps – was passed over for a position on the Triumvirate because . . .'

'He *wasn't* a safe pair of hands?'

Clara touched her nose with one index finger and pointed to Fleet with the other.

Fleet sighed heavily. 'Let me guess. His division suffered a terrible calamity.'

'A bridge collapse, towards the end of construction. Three deaths, weeks of delay.'

'And it occurred . . .'

'Four years ago. One month before Crowe was appointed to the Triumvirate.'

Fleet nodded. 'And Crowe's earlier promotions . . . and the other disasters Thorpe found . . .'

'Every one. I've gone over my notes. They line up to the month.'

The pair looked out over the park. Somewhere in the distance, Fleet could see couples queueing up for a ride on the vast Ferris sphere, and other couples exiting, visibly shaken.

'Crowe, then,' he said. 'I was wondering.'

'Did he say something?' asked Clara.

'No,' replied Fleet, before retrieving from his pocket the small, elegant calling card that Crowe had slipped him. 'Not yet.'

Chapter 16

The next morning, Fleet and Clara arrived at Moreland Square. It was the most prestigious of London neighbourhoods: grand Georgian terraces of polished stone and sparkling windows; a looping road swept twice daily; and a small park at the centre, with mature elm trees, a babbling fountain, and a statue of Lord Admiral Clarence Moreland himself – a statue which, as per the instructions of his hurried and slightly damp last-will-and-testament-in-a-bottle, rotated slowly, casting lamplight out through his eyes across the square to ensure that even on the darkest and stormiest nights, no vessel would ever sink there. Which, to the admiral's credit, none had.

The address on Crowe's calling card was No. 22; Fleet and Clara climbed the stone steps to the large, black door and rang the bell. Eventually, the door opened to disclose a sombre but immaculately presented butler.

'Oh hello,' Clara began, 'we're—'

'Miss Clara Entwhistle and Inspector Archibald Fleet,' the butler droned. 'Corps-Marshal Crowe is expecting you. Do follow me.'

He performed an about-turn so efficiently that his clothes didn't make a sound, and strode off down a hallway.

Clara scurried ahead, and once inside Fleet reached instinctively to shut the door, only to see it suddenly close by itself, revealing a hall boy who apparently had been standing behind it the entire time, and now returned to his station by its hinges.

The pair followed the butler up two flights of stairs, which creaked only in response to their feet, and up which their guide silently floated as if caught on a breeze.

They traversed the landing, with its tasteful wallpaper and its oil paintings of engineering triumphs, before coming to a halt outside a varnished oak door.

The butler knocked, waited for a muffled 'Come in', and they entered.

'Miss Entwhistle and Inspector Fleet to see you, sir,' he intoned.

Crowe looked up from behind an enormous, beautifully carved mahogany desk, and placed his pen down on one of several stacks of papers in front of him.

'Thank you, Graves. That will be all.'

The butler gave a swift nod, and left the room while simultaneously shutting the door, in a single movement of perfect balletic grace.

Fleet cast his eyes around the room. Dark wood panelling stretched from floor to ceiling, broken up by two large windows that provided a view across the square. Crowe, however, had chosen to position his desk so that he faced into the room and, Fleet noticed, towards a wall of framed newspaper articles whose headlines fawned over various Brunelian projects that no doubt mapped the corps-marshal's career.

Crowe waved his guests forward with a cordial smile.

'Good to see you again, Inspector. And Miss Entwhistle, I am delighted to make your acquaintance.'

'And I yours,' replied Clara.

'Do take a pew, won't you?'

288

Crowe gestured at two wooden chairs that had been placed in front of his desk, and the investigators took a seat.

Fleet found himself much closer to the floor than he had expected, his knees somehow above his hips. To his side, Clara was trying to flatten her skirts, which were ruffling up around her chest.

Crowe waited patiently, relaxing back in his generously proportioned chair and enjoying the view from his headmasterly altitude.

'Now I suppose you're wondering why I've asked you here,' he began.

'I assume it's to do with our investigation into the shocking murders of your employees,' said Fleet.

Crowe clapped his hands together.

'Exactly right, Inspector. What you revealed yesterday at the Gardens came as a rather nasty shock, and if your hypothesis is correct, we need to get to the bottom of it as soon as possible. Can't have this sort of scandal hanging over the Corps. Clearly we need someone impartial, someone experienced, to look into what's been going on. I'd put the yellow-tops on it but they're not cut out for this sort of complexity.'

'What are you saying?' asked Clara.

'I'm saying you're hired!'

'We're what?' asked Fleet.

'You're private investigators, are you not? I've made my enquiries and you seem up to the task. I need you to find out what, if anything, has happened, and root out any malefactors, if indeed there are any. And you needn't worry about access. I can provide you with all the information you need. Just tell me what and I will make sure you get it. I'm not sure what your rates are, but I trust this will get us started.'

Crowe pushed a cheque across the desk. It was for a sum much larger than Fleet had ever seen written on a cheque before, and it took some concentration to prevent his eyebrows flying off the top of his head.

'That's just an advance, of course. I'll pay you the same on completion of your investigation.'

Fleet put his fingers to his brow to hold it in place.

'This is a personal cheque,' he said.

'Hiring you through the Corps would be an administrative headache,' replied Crowe, 'and I'd like this matter to be resolved quickly.'

'Rather generous of you,' remarked Clara.

'Well, the Corps means a great deal to me. I want to see its reputation protected.'

Fleet leaned back in his chair. He hadn't been sure what to expect when they came here today, to talk to this man who seemed to be at the centre of the crimes they had been investigating ever since Kathleen Price knocked on their door. Threats, perhaps. Intimidation. Distraction. Charm. Maybe he would try to tease out what they knew, to see how much danger he was in. Or maybe there was, after all, something they had profoundly misunderstood.

But no. Money. Just money. The universal ointment of the guilty.

He stared at the cheque. It wasn't quite a sack full of bloodied pound notes with a label saying 'Payment for shutting up', but it might as well have been.

Whether Crowe wanted them to take the money and go find other things to do, or to 'work' with him in a pointless charade of falsehoods and dead ends, he didn't know. It didn't matter. Fleet would never accept it, and he knew Clara would sooner leave town forever.

'That is very generous,' began Fleet, 'but we need to remain a little more distant from the Corps if we are to investigate it.'

'"Distant"?' asked Crowe, amused. 'Is that what you call buying second-hand tickets to our garden party, talking your way through the officers' tent to me and Khan, and indeed Miss Entwhistle stowing away on a balloon ride with The Old Grove?'

'*Sir Grover*,' said Clara, bristling slightly at the nickname, 'was very happy to have me aboard. Once he realised I already was.'

'I'm sure he was! Don't misunderstand me – I'm impressed. You needed information, so into the party you came. You don't wait to be asked, you go-go-go! You decide. You do. You understand *will*.'

He opened a drawer and retrieved a fountain pen, which he placed on the desk between them.

Fleet studied it. Black, possibly onyx, with silver edging on the cap. It was old – older than Crowe – and expensive.

'I only met Brunel once,' the corps-marshal continued. 'I was a junior officer. Promising. He invited us by the dozen to his study, where he talked about leadership and our futures. I don't remember what he said, but whatever it was, it was there that I realised about *will*.'

He paused, and leaned forwards, as if he had a priceless secret to share.

'Haven't you ever noticed that the word means three different things?'

He held up a finger. 'One. Desire. "The will of the people".'

He held up another finger. 'Two. Outcome. "The bridge will be completed next week".'

A third finger. 'And three. Volition. The power to connect desire and outcome. "A man of iron will", "Sheer force of will".'

He placed his hand back on the desk and rapped his point into it with his fingertips. 'Desire, outcome, volition. What you want, what is going to happen, and your power to bring them together. One word, three meanings! But for good reason: *they are all the same.*'

Fleet grew concerned. Grand theories of the universe were never a good sign about the direction of a conversation.

'People think there is a gap between what we want and what we can achieve,' continued Crowe. 'There is not! It is all in our control. Everything. You just have to have the will. I realised that when I was in Brunel's study that day. I looked around and I realised I could rise higher than any of my peers if I willed it to be so. Any of us could! But not everyone *would*. Do you see? It is simply the choice to do so, to connect the trinity of wills: desire, outcome, volition. This insight was the ignition point of my success.

'And my very first proof of this truth came in that study. The audience with Brunel was over, and we took turns shaking the old man's hand before leaving. One by one, my fellow bright young things shook his hand and said "Thank you, Mr Brunel", or "An honour to meet you, Chief Engineer". And then it was my turn.'

'What did you say?' asked Clara.

'I said, "May I have your pen?" How brazen, no? But I *wanted it*. And what better way to test my will? The look on his face . . . I thought I might die on the spot. But of course, he laughed, and picked it up from his desk and popped it in my breast pocket.'

Fleet glanced at the fountain pen on the desk.

'That's Brunel's?'

Crowe smiled. 'No. It's mine. It has been with me ever since, and every day I have lived with *will* in mind.'

'An interesting theory,' offered Clara.

'Proven in practice,' replied Crowe. 'And the reason I tell you about it is because I think you two have the same instincts – you know in your hearts that desire and outcome are the same. This is why I think we can work well together. It's the clear way forward.'

He tapped the cheque with his forefinger.

'Say yes.'

'I'm sorry,' said Fleet. 'We cannot.'

Crowe nodded, and winked, as if understanding something unspoken. He uncapped Brunel's pen and took it to the cheque's amount box, marking out an extra zero at the end, before withdrawing again and waiting for another response.

Fleet knew his answer, but felt he had to see whether Clara was still in agreement. He looked to her, only to be met with an expression of astonishment that he had taken even this long to respond.

She picked up the cheque, folded it neatly, and then tore it into sixteen pieces, which she dropped back onto the desk in a tidy pile.

A terrible silence fell over the study. Fleet watched the corps-marshal's posture stiffen and his smile harden. After everything Fleet had tried to get a reaction from him the previous day in the sculpture garden without result, this had finally done it. This refusal, this defiance. It was the tiniest of changes in his expression. Barely perceptible. But an illuminated sign all the same, a thousand lightbulbs flashing in rage.

Fleet feared for a moment that Crowe would erupt, like a desk-bound volcano, and they would all be lost in the inferno, but as swiftly as it had begun the rage subsided, and a calmness returned to his demeanour. His will would not be denied.

'I think I understand,' said Crowe. 'I have been naive. A journalist and an ex-policeman? You do not care to get at the truth. You are in the business of selling stories.'

'I beg your pardon?' said Clara.

'It's all right, Miss Entwhistle. We all have a trade, and yours is turning barrels of ink into distracting yarns for people

293

taking the train to work. And this is a good one! *Sabotage and murder, in the heart of the Brunel Corps!* What a sensation it will cause! Of course you cannot take my money! You will have plenty of your own coming in when you paint me or my colleagues as the villains of the piece. What a tale it will be! Do hold on to the stage adaptation rights – I am certain the people at Drury Lane will be banging on your door.'

'How dare you!' cried Clara, shooting out of her seat before pacing furiously in front of the desk.

Crowe smirked. He had successfully thrown off his rage onto her, and was back in control of himself.

'I do not mean to insult you,' he said. 'We all have our roles to play. Of course, you should give your editor at the *Morning Chronicler* fair warning that you haven't a shred of evidence for whatever claims you plan on inventing. They'll want to set aside a decade or so's worth of revenue for when the Corps is forced to defend its reputation against this libellous fiction in the courts. But that's their problem, not yours.'

Clara stopped, and turned to the corps-marshal, appalled.

'You are *threatening us*?'

'Not at all. I merely see a weak point in your plans, and it's an engineer's job to point them out, and indeed to suggest more resilient alternatives – which I have done, and which you have regrettably torn up.'

The subtlest of knocks came from the door, and in poked the head of Graves, moving with such spectral silence that Fleet felt he could almost have chosen to drift through the wall.

'The carriage is ready, Corps-Marshal.'

'I'm afraid you must excuse me,' said Crowe, rising from his chair and rounding the desk. 'Graves will see you out, but do feel free to take tea in the parlour before you go. I would hate for you to have felt unwelcome. I can't stay myself, unfortunately – I have a city to build.'

He reached the open doorway, stopped, and turned back to the investigators.

'My door is always open, and my offer still stands. Think about it.'

Fleet rose, joining Clara to face the corps-marshal.

'No.'

Crowe smiled again. 'I think you will.'

Fleet waited outside on the steps of No. 22, and was only twice mistaken for some sort of doorman: once by a postal worker, and once by a footman who upbraided him for wearing the wrong livery.

A number of questions whirled in his mind.

First, what on earth could they do about Corps-Marshal Crowe?

Second, where could he place the parcel that he was now holding, despite his numerous protests to the postman that he did not work there?

Third, why exactly, when Clara had asked Graves if she could make use of the upstairs washroom before leaving, had she *winked* at Fleet as he continued following the butler out? What was that about?

Two of these questions were answered suddenly, as the door was pulled open, the hall boy yanked the parcel from Fleet with a sneer, and Clara swept out and down the steps, unusually quickly and with an uncharacteristically awkward gait.

'Come on, Fleet, don't dawdle!' she trilled, with a chipperness strongly smacking of panic.

She sped off towards a cabstand, which further confused Fleet as he knew Clara was fully aware that the cabbies in such a respectable area would charge truly disrespectful rates.

He shook his head, thrust his hands in his pockets and was about to follow when he spotted something in the park at the centre of the square. Something small and hairy, with four legs and a witless grin. Mrs Pomligan's lost beagle, staring at him with curiosity and a discarded chicken bone.

Fleet looked back and forth between the dog and Clara, hesitated for a moment, cursed at nothing in particular, and ran towards the cabstand. He'd barely caught up with Clara by the time she disappeared into a waiting hansom, and stepped aboard a fraction of a second before the cabbie pulled off.

'A ca—oomfff?' he asked, as he was flung into the seat, before trying again: 'A cab? In this part of town? You know if you want to get robbed of all your money you can just as easily walk down the street with your bag open.'

'Strictly business-necessary, Fleet.'

'In what way "necessary"?'

'Firstly,' began Clara, an enormous grin spreading across her face, 'because it's the best way to get away from Crowe's home as quickly as possible.'

'Yes, and why exactly are you in such a hurr—'

'And secondly, because a private mode of transportation is exactly what we need for discussing certain sensitive material I now have in my possession.'

Fleet glanced down, and noticed some peculiar bulging on one half of Clara's skirts. He felt his heart edging up to a precipice.

'Clara, what have you—'

'I stole a document from his office!' she whispered as loudly as she could, her eyes wide with pride and excitement.

'You stole a document from Crowe's office,' Fleet repeated, barely able to believe what he was hearing.

'I did.' Clara clapped her hands together in triumph.

'*When?*'

'Do you remember when I stood up and started pacing? He had been accusing me – us, really – of being interested only in selling a tawdry story. He clearly intended to rile me, but thanks to my mother I had to learn long ago how to let the poor judgement of others roll off me, like rain off the back of some duckling that can never play pianoforte quite to Mother Duck's liking.'

'Clara . . .'

'And she *also* didn't much care for the amateur theatricals my brother and I used to take part in every summer, when he was home from Oxford, even though *that* is what allowed me to play the part!'

'Play *what* part?'

'The part of "Outraged Lady One", very much like the part of "Consumptive Maiden Three" in our 1877 production of the nautical melodrama *Chastity on the Brink: A Tale of Innocence Besmirched*. Terrible writing, and some rather provocative scenes, but the besmirched woman dies horribly at the end, so Mother felt that the moral lesson was clear enough.'

'Clara . . .'

'Oh yes, "Outraged Lady One". I saw my chance, and so I acted – in both senses of the word! I stood up and paced in front of Crowe's desk. He thought I was all hot and bothered, but I was in fact perfectly *cool and collected*, and it allowed me to sneak a peek at the papers on his desk. And what I saw was *very interesting*, but I couldn't very well take it then and there. So, I waited until we were leaving, tricked Graves with the washroom gambit, then you both left, I snuck back into Crowe's office, *and* . . . Look!'

Clara began a quick movement with her hands, then suddenly stopped.

'No, wait, look away first.'

Fleet was about to ask why, but Clara started to loosen her skirt, which caused him to snap his head towards the window faster than if something outside had exploded.

'Why didn't you put it in your bag?' he asked the carriage door.

'Too obvious! What if Graves had conducted a bag search as I left? No, I had to go with a skirt-stuffing.'

Clara wriggled around, producing the sound of paper rustling against fabric, and eventually stopped.

'There we are. Right, you can look now.'

Fleet took the crumpled sheet of paper, and saw what, apart from the larceny and scarpering, had got Clara so excited.

It was a diagram of sorts. Lines, connected in a loose network, with small crosses here and there, each marked with initials and a slightly different, recent date.

He understood immediately.

'My god . . . it's a map.'

Clara nodded. 'It's *the* map.'

Fleet continued staring, deciphering its layout and content.

'These are the banks . . . and the dates they were targeted . . . and these must be the tunnels . . . this is the one we took . . .'

'This is it, Fleet!' cried Clara, waving at the map. 'This connects him to the banks, which connect to the murders, which connect to the cases of sabotage, which connect to his rise through the ranks! We've got him now, haven't we?'

For a moment, Fleet almost believed they had. But then he remembered, and felt the pang of wretchedness that comes to all who have to dash the hopes of those who think they've done something good, but in fact have made a terrible error.

'No,' he finally said.

'No? Why not?'

'Because you stole it.'

'I could hardly just ask him nicely!'

Fleet held up the map.

'You're not a police officer, Clara. It can't be used in evidence now. And even if it could, is there anything to link it to Crowe?'

298

Clara looked again at the paper. Her shoulders sank by several inches.

'All you've got is his word against ours,' continued Fleet. 'There's no way to prove you got it from Crowe's office. Anyone could have drawn this map, including us.'

Clara's body deflated even more.

'Don't worry,' said Fleet. 'We will get him. These things just take time.'

'But we don't have time.'

She pointed to a cross in the middle of the map. Today's date.

'He's planning another one. Tonight. And we know they're just distractions, which means another murder, another person forgotten on page sixteen of every paper that even bothers to carry it. Unless . . .'

Fleet braced himself. He knew what was coming.

'Unless we catch him in the act!' continued Clara. 'That's it! Yes! We must go back down into those tunnels and catch him red-handed.'

Fleet's head was whirring. He needed more time.

'Clara . . .'

'You heard him, Fleet! He thinks he can do anything, that he can get whatever he wants. He thinks there's nothing that proves what he's done.'

'Well, that last bit is true, at least as things stand.'

'And this might be the only chance to change that. How can we let it pass us by?'

These words provoked in Fleet a familiar, sickening sensation, and he turned to look down the street as if staring at solid buildings might stop it from rising.

It didn't do any good. It wasn't that kind of thing.

It was just the knowledge that terrible people do sometimes get away with it. Whether through cleverness or luck or a bungled investigation, it didn't matter – some criminals *did* get away with it. For every crime that brought the felon to the gallows or the gaoler's door, there were countless more that went unpunished.

Countless overall, but Fleet knew exactly how many had slipped through his own fingers – he'd counted them plenty of times.

Not that the counting helped with the sickening feeling, of course. There was really only one thing he knew of that did:

Trying.

That evening, Fleet and Clara returned to Raeburn Avenue, just a few doors down from Drummond's Merchant Bank, and located the metal plate in the ground they had emerged from after their first descent into the tunnels.

It was quiet, but for the gentle rustling of ash branches in the breeze, the hum of nearby streets that had more of a nightlife scene, and the two cats that had spotted each other from opposing pavements and were now locked in a long-range skirmish of screeching.

Fleet checked that there was no one around, and turned to Clara to be doubly sure.

'All clear?'

Clara peeked up and down the street and gave a thumbs up, before apparently deciding it was too dark for this to be seen, and whispering, 'Thumbs up.'

Fleet heaved up the metal plate and ushered Clara down the ladder into the hole. Once the clacking of boots on metal rungs had ceased, he swiftly followed, replacing the plate above them and plunging them into total darkness.

At the foot of the ladder they turned on their torches, and Clara pulled out Crowe's map of the tunnel system.

'So, from here . . .' – she pointed at the cross marked 'DMB', and traced a finger along the lines of the network to the cross with that day's date – '. . . to here. Easy. As long as we don't miss a turning.'

Fleet nodded and the pair set off into the emptiness of the tunnel before them.

They walked for some time, the soft patter of their boots on the earth echoing in the darkness, and the light from their torches casting strange shadows on the walls.

Fleet was reminded of stories he'd read as a boy, of forgotten prisoners languishing in dungeons, and he felt the same creeping in his nerves now as he did then.

He cast a few glances at Clara, but it was so dark he could barely make out her features. She probably wasn't afraid.

Every so often, they would reach a fork in the tunnel and stop, pull out the map and check again their route.

'This way,' one of them would whisper, and again they would move forwards into the darkness.

On and on they went through the unchanging tunnel, the quiet punctuated only by the occasional clatter of cab wheels overhead, or a tube line far below, or the scuttling of a rat.

Or, Fleet noticed, the scuttling of two rats. Sometimes three. Occasionally, four rats.

Now he had started paying attention, there seemed to be quite a few rats around.

He felt a hand, which he very much hoped was Clara's, grab his shoulder.

'All okay?'

She nodded, sending her silhouette dancing up and down the wall.

'Yes, only . . . I'm just wondering what all these rats know that we don't.'

A memory scratched in the back of Fleet's mind.

A pub – stuffy, sticky. He'd been sent to shut down an illegal ham lottery, not for the first time. Nobody was talking, except a lonely man in his late twenties, who did nothing but. He leaned against the bar, splashed his beer over his shoes, ignored all of Fleet's questions and explained instead about his irrelevant work.

He was a researcher at the Swindon Informatorium, he said. Department of Applied Zoology. And the question, 'What do rats know that humans don't?', was *exactly* what they were trying to answer. Possible applications in medicine and exercise; certainly some in maze-solving.

In ten years of research, the man explained – despite Fleet's attempts to retake control of the conversation – they had made only one clear finding. They had confirmed it over and over again, in countless experiments, in all manner of situations, but it was the same truth. And they published it in the journal *Animal Learnings*, as one of the shortest academic papers of all time.

It was only five words. Fleet tried to remember.

He failed. He hadn't been listening at the time, and now a dozen rats were dashing over his boots, which made it very hard to focus on anything else.

Although he did notice one more thing – a rumbling.

'Do you hear that?'

'The squeaking?' replied Clara. 'I'm trying not to stand on them but they're not making it very easy.'

'No, not that . . .'

Fleet waited as Clara stopped and listened to the low rumbling he had heard.

She nodded – she could hear it too.

'Yes,' she said. 'What is it?'

'I don't know, but, whatever it is, it's getting louder.'

They pushed on, together with what was now a stream of rats all clambering over one another with desperate yelps.

The rumbling drew nearer, getting louder and louder, and Fleet realised it was coming from behind. They stopped, and turned to look, pointing their torches back down the tunnel.

There was nothing.

The nothing continued to get louder.

They peered harder, and eventually Fleet saw fragments of motion . . . the nothing seemed to be *turning*.

The rats were now flooding past them, fleeing in a frenzy around and over one another. Some appeared to decide the tunnel ahead offered no escape, and began burrowing into the earth of the walls.

The nothing grew louder still, the noise of a busy street coming from a single point.

Fleet looked again.

There was something now, at the distant end where the torchlight died. A lurching, grinding *something* advancing from out of the blackness.

A panicking rat fell from the ceiling onto his chest, and as he threw it off he fell back into the memory. The lonely researcher's hand, roughly grabbing Fleet's jacket. He thought he wasn't listening. He wasn't.

'You should really listen,' the man said.

The paper they published. Everything they had learned. Five words:

If the rats run, follow.

But they hadn't, and now Fleet could see what the something in the nothing was: a sharpened point, spinning, teeth all around, whirling – a giant, monstrous corkscrew, filling the space, *creator of the space*, driving towards them at the speed of death.

He had nothing better to offer than to scream what it now obviously was:

'*Drill!*'

The pair sped away along the tunnel, pursued by the grinding and buzzing behind them.

They ran as fast as they could, as frantic as the rats beneath them, Clara apologising as she went to all the ones

303

she accidentally stepped on in the process, and Fleet trying not to hear the pitiful shrieks of the ones further back who hadn't burrowed fast enough.

He looked back over his shoulder – why, he didn't know, but he saw a large stone fall from the ceiling earth, loosened by the shaking, and be swept up by the machine's outer teeth, flung into the counter-rotating inner jaw, and crushed into powder in an instant.

They kept running, the drill growing ever louder, ever closer, as the nothing ahead stretched on, an empty, hopeless tomb.

Finally, they saw a glimmer of light.

'Exit!' cried Clara.

As they got closer, they could see that it was, in fact, a mostly covered opening in the roof of the tunnel.

Fleet leapt up and grasped with his fingers, kicking the air as he pushed the metal covering away and hoisted himself through the opening, before thrusting an arm back through the hole.

'Grab my hand!'

Clara reached up, the sound of the drill clamouring behind her, and they pulled together.

She clambered halfway through the gap, then stopped. They made a better grip of each other's arms and hauled again, but to no effect.

'I'm snagged!' shouted Clara, pulling on her skirt.

She looked downwards, and Fleet searched desperately for a way to free her as the deafening machine heaved closer.

'Knife!' she cried.

'What?'

'Grab my pocket knife, I can't reach it. It's on my chatelaine.'

'Your *what*?'

'The chains! It's on the little chains of my belt!'

Fleet fumbled around Clara's waist: pen, coin purse, pocket knife. He unhooked the knife and flicked it open, before placing it in her hand, which she thrust through the opening.

A cloud of dust erupted from the tunnel behind her and up into Fleet's eyes, forcing him to look away.

He heard Clara slashing at her skirt. Nothing.

He looked back down, squinting through the dust.

She slashed again.

The sound of the drill was everywhere. Fleet could see its spinning tip come into view a few feet behind her, and he was seized by dread.

Clara screamed in frustration – before, finally, another slash and a tear.

'Now, Fleet!'

They heaved as hard as they could, pulling her fully through the gap as the machine tore its way underneath, sending another plume of dust up and around them.

Clara spun around and slammed the metal panel over the opening, and they collapsed on the ground, listening to the horrible noise of the drill crunching its way onwards through the tunnel.

It was going, thought Fleet. It was all right.

But now, he noticed, it wasn't the only sound. With the retreat of the metallic churning, he could now hear an almighty, cacophonous clanging noise, clamouring all around them like an alarm.

No. Not like *an alarm*, he thought. *An alarm*.

For the first time, he took a proper look at his new surroundings.

A small room. Walls of tiny locked boxes. One enormous metal door.

'Are we . . .' he began.

Clara nodded. 'In a bank vault. Yes.'

Before Fleet even had time to fully take this in, there came the sound of footsteps beyond the vault door.

Several heavy thunks and whirrs followed, and the door swung open to reveal a platoon of police constables brandishing night sticks, and, leading the charge, Inspector Collier, whose face, when he saw the dust-covered Fleet, broke into a merciless, gold-medal smirk.

Chapter 17

Fleet stared at the bars of his cell, waiting for the inevitable. It was strange, seeing them from this side. Outside this room, he knew the business of Scotland Yard was carrying on. Detectives were at their desks, or out working their cases in the city. Official cases. Interviewing suspects, finding evidence, that sort of thing.

Not running from tunnelling machines in a botched sting. Not taking any case they can get to stay afloat.

He looked across the cell to where Clara was pacing. She'd been doing this for hours. She was angry. They'd been tricked, and he knew she wasn't a fan of being tricked.

He wasn't sure what he was waiting for. He knew it must be the middle of the night. No one was coming until the morning. Maybe he just wanted it over with. Someone to come and pull off the plaster. Although the metaphor was strained, because it was less a plaster and more a possible fifteen-year prison sentence. Some plasters are best left on.

Footsteps pounded the hallway beyond the door, stopping outside. There was a fumbling of keys, and a heavy bolt shunted out of its nest.

The door flew open, and Fleet realised he was wrong to have wanted this to happen sooner. He would have happily waited in this cell for weeks to avoid this.

Chief Inspector Keller stood in the doorway, hurriedly dressed and hair askew, with a nightgown sticking through his shirt collar.

He nodded at a guard, who closed the door behind him and bolted it again.

All the blood seemed to have left Keller's face and started a new life in his fists. He walked towards the cell bars, grimacing as if he was preparing to chew right through them.

'Well,' he began, with the rumble of an approaching earthquake, 'if it isn't the daring bank thieves. We meet at last.'

Fleet moved his mouth to say something, but it just flapped open uselessly.

'Now,' continued Keller, 'I won't hear of you apologising for waking me – *and my wife and children* – in the middle of the night, and forcing me to drag myself here in a criminally overpriced cab, because as you can no doubt see from my expression – I assume you're all up to date on your physiognomy training, Fleet – I did not want to miss the opportunity to meet the people responsible for robbing oh, what is it now? Eight or so banks? As you can probably tell I am nothing short of cock-a-hoop!'

'Sir—' attempted Fleet.

'No, no, let's have none of that.' Keller was smiling now, which Fleet always found extremely unsettling. 'It turns out that you're a master criminal. It is I who should be being courteous to you.'

'Please, you don't—'

'No, no, I insist. How do you prefer to be addressed? Thief Extraordinaire? Elite Heistman? *Maestro*?'

'The last one is vaguest, if I have to choose,' replied Fleet, helplessly.

'Chief Inspector,' tried Clara, 'if you'd let us—'

'Ah, Miss Entwhistle! I am so sorry to see you've been lured in by Fleet's rampant criminality. A tragic end to a promising career as whatever you are.'

'A journalist and private investigator.'

'A classic career combination. Might be hard to investigate much while spending twenty years in a women's prison, but don't worry, I'm sure there will be a gazette of some kind you can contribute to.'

'Really?'

Fleet stood up. 'Sir—'

'But of course! If there's one thing Her Majesty's Prisons are known for, it's a vibrant in-house press, with the free exchange of ideas, daily crosswords and a Saturday colour supplement with all the latest cultural goings-on to help you really get the most out of your weekend.'

'Sir,' said Fleet, 'we know who's responsible for the bank thefts.'

'Oh? Glad to hear you confessing at the top of the over. That's a cricket expression, Fleet. Do you find time for cricket in between felonies?'

'I don't—'

'Of course not, they must be quite time-consuming.'

'Chief Inspector, please, listen!' implored Clara.

'No, Miss Entwhistle. You listen. Both of you. I'm quite aware you are not master criminals responsible for these break-ins. That would require a level of planning and competence with which you are clearly not acquainted. What you have achieved, however, is a spectacular level of interference in one of the largest, most coordinated police investigations this city has seen in recent years. Did you think Collier was there to find you two?'

'No – but why *was* he there?' asked Clara.

'Why do you think? Because we received a tip-off.'

Fleet threw his hands up in despair. 'Of course you did! He's playing us all for fools! You think it's a coincidence that you got a tip-off the same day we happened to find a literal

X-marks-the-spot just sitting in front of us, to make us think we could catch him in the act?'

'Of course!' Keller brought his hands together with a deafening clap. 'You had prior knowledge of another burglary. That doesn't seem like the kind of thing the detective police would be interested in. I'm sure we couldn't have spared, oh, I don't know, *twenty* trained detectives to confirm the plan and execute a successful sting operation. Clearly the better option was for you two to literally go down there yourselves and nab whoever is responsible. Did it go well? Oh, wait, no, you're in a police cell and the true culprit is nowhere to be found.'

'He is easily to be found!' cried Fleet. 'It's Ev—'

'*Evidence!*' roared Keller. 'You came to my office with a theory about a code, and you were so wrong that you damaged a military asset. I ordered you to stay away from the case, and you continued regardless! Now you have interfered *again*, so before you tell me what you believe in your heart of hearts to be true, I ask you: do you have any *evidence*?'

Silence drifted through the cell.

'As I thought.'

Keller summoned in the guard, and gestured at him to unlock the cell doors.

Fleet looked puzzled. 'Sir?'

'Consider this a warning, both of you. Actually, no, consider *this* a warning: I hereby warn you, Citizen Fleet, and Miss Entwhistle, that if you interfere again with this operation, I will personally see to it that incarceration in our judicial system is nothing but a distant, wild fantasy you yearn for, as you rock yourselves to sleep in a crate somewhere below deck on a crabbing ship in the Bering Sea.'

'Do we work on the ship?' asked Fleet.

'That's for the crabbers to decide. Now. Get out.'

The following morning was cold and grey, and Fleet's feet carried him to work as he stared mindlessly ahead, taking in nothing at all.

He felt raw. They had been duped, and their plan had failed utterly. It was one thing to lose; it was another to realise that you had done exactly what your opponent wanted.

But what *did* Crowe want? Why had he not just killed them like all the others?

Too visible, perhaps. They'd been in his company, at his house and at the garden party; Clara was well known; Fleet had ties to the police. He hated the conclusion, but their deaths or disappearance probably would have raised more questions than the engineers' had.

The drill could have done the job, though. But it had only appeared when they were near the bank, and the opening was ready for them to escape through, with Collier waiting on the other side.

But *why*? Why set them up? Did Crowe think they would be sent to prison? What was he playing at?

On a clearer-headed day, Fleet might have realised straight away, but that morning the answer came as he was walking along the street to Mrs Pomligan's Coffee Shop, when a paperboy thrust a paper into his hand.

'Today's 'Erald, guvnor.'

Fleet tried to give it back. 'Not in the mood for the news today, thank you.'

'You should be,' said the boy, winking. 'On the 'ouse.'

Fleet was perturbed. Random acts of kindness in London were usually a portent of something terrible. Smiles often meant muggings, discounts usually meant hazardous goods. A gift, from a paperboy of all people, might mean the end of days.

311

Ah, thought Fleet. *The end of days. That'd be nice.*

He glanced at the paper's headline, and immediately realised he wasn't even remotely that lucky.

AMATEURS IMPERIL BANK THEFT JUSTICE

Oh no.

He skimmed the lead story. It was as bad as he could have feared. Clara and him named. Their bungled sting. Their possible derailing of a vast police investigation. Their 'harassment' of senior members of the Brunel Corps with wild conspiracy theories, verified by an anonymous source.

The word 'incompetent' was used to describe their business eleven times, 'untrustworthy' eight times, 'a threat to actual law enforcement' three times, and 'unfathomably stupid' just once, but it still stung.

The paperboy held out a hand and demanded the agreed penny reward for bringing to Fleet's attention the detective's own possible crime.

Fleet felt the ground disappearing, and the sounds of the street were turning into a constant, high-pitched whine.

He dashed across the street, not even noticing an automaton-driven carriage that barely avoided crushing him under its horses' hooves.

He reached a news kiosk. It was the same story in at least three more of the daily papers. The vendor appeared to recognise him from the photographs they'd printed, and started saying something vaguely aggressive he couldn't really make out.

He carried on walking towards the office.

When he got close, he saw a small crowd had gathered, not outside the coffee shop, but across the street, outside the Church of the Mechanical Man. Someone was speaking to them from its steps.

He walked closer and joined the back of the crowd, and forced the whining out of his head so he could listen.

It was Helena Evans, and she was in the middle of a furious tirade.

'*Villains,* they are!' she cried.

The crowd cheered, and more passers-by began to join.

'For what other word could describe people who would carry out such deeds? Such interference with the business of the law! Do they conspire with the thieves?'

'Yes!' a few people cried.

'And only days after forcing *me* out of hiding, threatening my safety! Because they did not *think* of the consequences.'

'Didn't think!' an excited woman echoed.

'I think it is *shameful*,' Helena continued. 'What do you all think?'

'Shameful!' cried half of the crowd.

'Bad!' cried the other half, who hadn't been listening as closely.

Fleet's vision was failing him now. He felt as though he was going to collapse on the pavement, and reached out to steady himself on a postbox, which immediately objected.

'Oi!' the large, red-coated man shouted to the crowd. 'It's him!'

What? Oh no.

Fleet saw Helena spot him in the crowd, and she lost track of whatever she had been shouting. For a moment, he was sure she wasn't enraged at all. She looked the way she'd looked when she was in their office that night, soaked to the bone. She was terrified.

Before Fleet had a chance to call out to her, or indeed plead with the crowd that was turning towards him, an arm had pulled him firmly backwards and spun him around.

'Clara?'

'Oi!' someone yelled. 'It's her as well!'

'Come on, Fleet.'

They ran across the street towards Mrs Pomligan's to escape into their office, but the door was now surrounded by press, eager to build on the overnight story by cornering the shamed duo. They immediately spotted Fleet and Clara. Flashbulbs went off by the dozen, and they began to swarm like piranhas.

'Any comment for our readers?' some of them demanded, with raised voices, pencils and notebooks at the ready.

'What do you say to reports you are in cahoots with the thieves?' shouted a journalist near the back of the group.

'How does it feel to be a national embarrassment?' another called out at an unnecessarily loud volume.

From the doorway, Mrs Pomligan emerged, broom in hand, and tried to shoo away the people blocking her entrance.

Clara and Fleet spun around and dashed down the street, pursued by the press and a dozen of the most enthusiastic among the crowd, before ducking into a backstreet and leaping behind some bins.

The mob kept running, propelled by their own excitement, and after a few moments the noise had subsided, and Fleet and Clara were alone.

'Crowe must have got a message to Helena,' said Clara. 'She wouldn't do this unless she'd been threatened somehow.'

Fleet nodded to himself. 'And the papers?'

Clara shrugged. 'He's clearly a powerful man. He must know people. Not the *Chronicler*, at least. Someone must have stood in the way.'

Fleet nodded again, before sinking to the ground. He felt some wet newspaper soaking his trousers, but there was no reason to move. What did it matter whether his trousers were damp or dry? Who would that be for? Clients? What clients, now?

'That's it, then,' he said.

314

'What is?'

'The business, Clara. That's it.'

Clara pulled a grin. 'Come on, Fleet. Worse things happen at sea, don't they?'

She forced an unconvincing chuckle.

'I would expect so,' he heard himself say.

'It will be all right,' said Clara, in a cheery tone. 'We can fix all of this. A bit of scandal might even work to our favour in the long run.'

Fleet looked up at her. There it was, in her eyes. That bottomless well of positivity. The never-give-up attitude. The relentlessness. The naivety. The foolishness.

Why had he listened to her? When did he stop listening to himself? She was like a gambler on a winning streak at the races, utterly invulnerable until it all comes to a sudden, inevitable end.

'Do you believe that?' he asked.

'That we can fix it? Of course!' She grinned. 'Easy!'

Easy . . .

Fleet leapt to his feet.

'Easy?' he shouted. 'Easy? Of course you think it will be easy. You think it's all a game! Ups and downs but always a good time. You pushed us into doing something utterly reck-less, because you knew that either way there's a great story to write up in your paper!'

'What does the paper have to do with anything?'

'You're a journalist! That's what you told me when we met! You came here to be a journalist, you now are a journalist, and somewhere along the way you started joining me to actually investigate the cases. But if that all falls to pieces – as it *clearly now has* – you still have the paper! You still have a career that you love! You can afford to gamble with one because you have the other, and that's led us to where gamblers end up – the gutter!'

Clara stiffened. 'Is that what you think?'

'Yes!'

'Well then. You accuse me of not taking our business seriously, of treating it like a game? I have been finding us clients. I have been getting us good press. I have been meeting silly young women in tea rooms wrapping up cases of far greater importance than we even knew at the time. It is *you* who have been unable to take your eyes off your old job, poring over the newspapers for information about the bank case before it was anything to do with us, and just counting down the days until you are reinstated to the detective police.'

'I have done no such thing!'

'You have been obsessed, Fleet! And only the good fortune that these recent cases became substantial has distracted you from that obsession.'

'Perhaps I have been preoccupied because deep down I knew your recklessness would doom our enterprise.'

'*Perhaps!* Perhaps you think it is better to protect yourself from possible setbacks, Archibald Fleet, than to embrace fully what life is offering you before your eyes.'

She paused, and Fleet noticed her hands were shaking. He felt ill, and weightless, as though falling.

'I thought someone who has died and then been given another chance would have more perspective,' she said. 'You're already the luckiest man who ever lived.'

'Clara,' said Fleet, though he knew it was far too late.

'Goodbye, Inspector.'

She walked along the narrow alleyway, out onto the crowded street, and vanished into the indifferent city like a raindrop into the sea.

Fleet noticed only then that he was freezing, and realised she must be too.

Chapter 18

The typewriter stared back at Clara impatiently, its forty-seven eyes protruding on their stalks, waiting for her to get on with the task at hand.

The task, at this point, had become routine. So routine she could barely stand it.

It was two weeks since Augusta had explained, while setting a new record for speed-walking along the corridors of the *Morning Chronicler*, her predicament: that Clara had embarrassed the paper with her reckless actions; that she was nevertheless a talented journalist and would not be dismissed; but that her prestigious column would be paused indefinitely, and Clara would be moved temporarily to a less public role.

'How temporarily?' Clara had asked, but Augusta was already around the corner, confronting some poor subeditor walking the other way and giving him some feedback on the inefficiency of his writing that was as brutally honest as it was a demonstration of the efficiency he apparently was not displaying, reducing the man to apologetic sniffles in just six words.

She stared down at her typewriter's dozens of tiny, judgemental eyes.

Obituaries.

Not even writing the obituaries. There was the Obituaries Editor for that. Clara's role was summarising the pre-prepared ones in case there wasn't enough space in that day's edition.

It was a technical challenge for a writer, to be sure, but it didn't leave much in the way of the on-the-foot exploration and excitement she had become used to. Just page after page of documents to rewrite, as briefly as she could while still being relatively respectful of the dead.

She wasn't forced to stay at her desk all day, but there was no reason to leave it. She was a prisoner of routine, and of the gradual hardening of disappointment into resignation, and then, eventually, into life.

Deep down she suspected this was what always happened. People come to the big city with big dreams, and eventually reality sets in. She'd had a good run for a while, at least.

She looked at the obituary in front of her. It was for Professor Leopold Barnes, a biologist of some renown, who was well into his eighties and whose habit of walking around town reading the latest academic journals instead of watching where he was going meant the Obituaries Office always kept his file close to hand in the 'Don't Bother Refiling' pile.

Clara read through the article. Even for a lifetime of work, it was impressive. Edinburgh PhD. Early career work in Paris and Amsterdam before finding a permanent home at a university in London that was so exclusive it could not be named in a public newspaper in case people tried to apply to go there. Fellow of the Royal Society. An accomplished mountain climber, a keen marksman, a damned fine amateur pastry chef, and a tolerable husband.

It went on like this for six pages. Clara looked at the instructions the Obituaries Editor had left her.

318

'Ten words.'

She drummed her fingers on the keys, thinking. How can you summarise anyone's life in so few words, let alone someone like that?

There was a single knock at the open doorway, and Clara looked up to see the bedraggled frame of Lester Horrocks.

'Hello, Lester,' she said.

The older journalist didn't reply, instead peering around the tiny room with interest, like it was itself the scene of some crime he would need to write about.

'Can I help you with something?'

Lester finally looked at Clara, nodded, then dragged a dusty chair from the corner of the room to face her across the desk, and slumped heavily into it.

Clara laughed. Not her usual laugh, the infectious one born of an unshakeable joie de vivre. This laugh hummed with the melancholy strain of resignation.

'I haven't any tips for you, Lester, if that's why you're here.'

'I would argue it's more interesting to ask why *you're* here.'

Clara frowned. He knew full well, but she didn't have the energy to deflect his questions.

'I'm here because I've embarrassed the paper.'

Lester heaved himself forwards and frowned with interest. 'Really?'

'You didn't hear Augusta giving me a dressing down?'

'I did. I was wondering when it'd come to you. She was pretty gentle. She likes you.'

Clara turned back to her typewriter. 'She has a funny way of showing it.'

Lester nodded. 'She likes me too. It doesn't come across like sunshine. More, hail.'

'Hail doesn't really seem like fondness.'

'Depends.' Lester rapidly scratched his ear in eight circular motions. If he could have used his hind legs, Clara thought, he would have. 'She doesn't *have* to hail on you. Tough love is still love.'

'What are you here for, Lester?'

'Ah ah!' Lester held his finger aloft and jabbed it in Clara's direction. 'That's what I asked you.'

'I answered you! Augusta took away my column and assigned me to obituaries.'

'That's not why you're here.'

'You maddening fool!'

Lester laughed, and began to pat himself down, looking for something in his jacket.

'What, you brought whiskey?' asked Clara. 'I'm not in the mood.'

'No, no. Buy your own drinks.'

'Then what?'

He gave up on his jacket. 'Oh, sod it.' He pulled off a ragged shoe, which looked like it might disintegrate in his hands.

'What are you doing?' asked Clara, horrified and trying desperately to avoid seeing his socks.

Lester held up a finger dramatically, and tossed the shoe out into the hallway, where it struck the top of the skirting board, launching a loose bit of sole, which arced towards the ceiling and came to rest on a lampshade.

Clara stared at Lester in disbelief. 'What was that?'

'Just a demonstration.'

'Of what? The fact you need new clothes?'

Lester pointed into the hallway and stared at Clara with weary judgement.

'The door's open. Why are you *still* here?'

*

At a coffee house not that far away, Mrs Pomligan's newest employee was also getting on with his new life.

In the days following his falling out with Clara, Fleet had walked to work out of habit, only to arrive at the stairs inside Mrs Pomligan's, realise there was no reason to go up them to what had been his office, and finally settle at a seat by the window with the first of three coffees that he would, over the course of several hours, let go cold and only then remember to drink.

Eventually, Mrs Pomligan had taken pity on the man, whom she'd known – and had a soft spot for – since boyhood, and put him to work in her shop. Fleet was so numb after the failure of the private investigation business that he didn't really think that hard about the offer, and just agreed that if he was going to mope about the place, he might as well get paid for it.

He might have felt differently had he known ahead of time that he would not report directly to Mrs Pomligan, but rather to the café's only other worker, a dishwashing automaton named Cleany Clive.

Fleet did briefly protest at this, but Mrs Pomligan countered that Cleany Clive simply had too much experience for Fleet to leapfrog him in the corporate ladder, and Fleet was just crushed enough by recent events that he accepted this was his rightful place.

Even this acceptance had its limits, however, and now he was beginning to bristle at Cleany Clive's proactive managerial style.

Fleet hadn't expected this sort of treatment from Cleany Clive, who was a metal cube bolted onto the side of a sink. And even if he had, he was mostly distracted by Cleany Clive's disconcerting number of arms: one for grabbing and holding, one for scouring, one for sponging, one for drying, and one that appeared to be a high-pressure hose that Fleet really wished Cleany Clive would give advance warning of his intention to deploy. His, for want of a better word, 'head', was a smaller metal box that was positioned on top of the larger cube from which the arms protruded. A panel on the front of the smaller cube contained a single eye lamp, and a speaker from which Cleany Clive could issue his managerial orders, but the rest of the cube was filled with a dark, thick, green liquid. On top of the head sat a small red antenna, imprinted with an image of the Tower, which made it abundantly clear to Fleet that Cleany Clive would never tire or falter, and might never need to stop at all.

'Like this,' said the machine, waving his sponge-hand in front of where his face should be. 'I have demonstrated thirteen times. I am not sure why you are failing to replicate.'

'That's what I've been doing,' said Fleet, pulling his arms out of the sink and allowing a stack of mugs to subside under the water. 'It's just washing up. It's not hard.'

'A common misconception, Junior Café Associate Fleet.'

Fleet sighed. 'Of course *you* think it's important and complicated. It's your entire reason for being.'

'This is quite a combative attitude, Junior Café Associate Fleet. Only . . .' – Cleany Clive paused to make a calculation – 'forty-four point one hours ago we were discussing how you need to be more receptive to feedback on potential areas of professional growth.'

'Why am I even doing this?' Fleet demanded. 'You're literally built for it. You're half cleaning implements and you have a reservoir of washing-up liquid instead of a head.'

'Thank you. I am indeed well designed.'

'I could be brewing the coffee or something. God knows it couldn't hurt to let someone else have a go.'

'That's a lot of extra responsibility, Junior Café Associate Fleet. You have to demonstrate that you excel in your current role first.'

'Why?'

'That is how corporate promotion works.'

'What do you know about it?' asked Fleet. 'You're a dishwasher.'

'I am the Senior Dishwasher and I have also undergone management training.'

'*How?*'

'I overheard some businessmen last week.'

'This isn't happening.'

'They spoke at some length on the subject of employee performance and motivation. And – because I was programmed with a *learning* instruction loop, to ensure I excel in cleaning all possible future types of dishes – this is now my passion too.'

Cleany Clive brought his sponge-hand and scourer-hand together and tented them thoughtfully in front of the chin of his head-cube. 'Tell me, Junior Café Associate Fleet. What motivates you?'

'My pay being doubled.'

'We are outside the remuneration review period. Have you considered the profound motivational benefits of a job well done? Let me show you for the fourteenth time the correct sponging action.'

Fleet felt he was about to do something he, or at least Clive, would deeply regret, so he threw off his apron and walked out of the back of the coffee house, ignoring his manager's protests about agreed break periods and a concerning lack of reasonable dialogue.

The alleyway behind Mrs Pomligan's was mercifully empty and quiet. Just bins, crates and, some way off, the main road, where people walked past unaware of the man pacing furiously backwards and forwards, simmering in a crisis of purpose.

Eventually, Fleet calmed himself down and began to see reason. *It's all right, Archie. It's just a rough patch.*

323

He thought about possible ways out of this particular rough patch, but the total absence of any made him feel like he was falling into a pit, and that the pit was falling into an abyss, and the abyss was being eaten by a giant snake, which was itself falling into another pit, so he stopped.

His mind turned to Clara, and he realised he hadn't seen her byline in the paper in a while. He remembered their first case – his case, really, but she had followed him so closely it was their case by the end. That had gone all right. What was the problem with this one? Had their luck just run out?

The wind picked up, catching a dustbin lid and sending it wheeling down the alleyway, where it met the main road and caused a minor traffic incident.

No matter. It's over now.

Fleet sat down on a crate by the bins, closed his eyes and tried to summon the willpower to go back inside.

A brief moment of calm was ended by the powerful smashing of back door into brick, and Fleet looked over to see Mrs Pomligan clomping towards him.

He was confused. She didn't appear to be worked up, so a verbal thrashing might not be imminent. And if he was being dismissed, Cleany Clive would have insisted on doing it himself as part of his managerial growth framework.

Oh God, thought Fleet, *let it not be a pep talk*.

'Oi,' Mrs Pomligan shrieked, by way of greeting. 'Archie. Got something for you.'

'What kind of something?'

The café proprietor loomed above him, silhouetted ominously against the sky.

'*Deliverance.*'

Fleet stared back in confusion. 'What did you say?'

Mrs Pomligan reached into the pocket of her apron and yanked out a brown paper bag like a kangaroo evicting a joey.

'Telephone order came through. Sandwich. Beef. Wants a speedy delivery to the Frost Fair.'

Fleet studied the bag, then Mrs Pomligan's expression. He must have misheard before. Even so, he was still confused.

'Do we do deliveries?'

'First time someone's asked, but could be a nice little earner if word's getting out. Now hop to it — the beef wasn't that fresh when I bought it.'

Lester had recovered the majority of his shoe and replaced it on his foot, while Clara fumed slightly about what he had just said. Clara didn't have much experience of fuming, and she found it profoundly disagreeable, which just made her fume even more.

'This is my job, Lester.'

She hit the blank piece of paper sticking up out of her typewriter with the back of her hand, then immediately felt bad. It wasn't the sheet of paper's fault.

Lester stared at her impassively. 'Uh huh.'

'I work at the newspaper, Augusta runs the newspaper, and she's told me this is what I do now.'

'Uh huh.'

'Temporarily, until . . .'

'Until people forget about your massive blunder?'

'It wasn't a massive blunder,' said Clara, smarting. 'It was a slight tactical mistake.'

'Uh huh.'

'Stop saying that.'

'I'm agreeing with you.'

'Yes, but you clearly don't, Lester, so why don't you spit it out?'

'Spit what out?'

Clara threw open her hands to show that she did not have the answer. 'Whatever it is you want to say! That people won't just forget, I assume?'

'Why would I say that?'

'Probably because you were out of the game for twenty years after your own massive blunder!'

'My own slight tactical mistake?' Lester shot back, with an amused smile.

'Yes!'

'I do seem to recall quite a long period of not doing the sort of work I ought to be doing, yes.'

Clara shuffled in her seat. 'So you want to tell me to get on with it, right? That I could leave at any moment and go deal with the problem head-on?'

'What problem?'

'"What problem?" The Brunelian business! And, if there's time, I can convince Fleet he's been a selfish buffoon.'

'Oh,' replied Lester, with an exaggerated nod of understanding, 'so you have two problems.'

'Yes.'

'And Fleet is a selfish buffoon because . . .'

'Because he's had one eye on his old job with the police the whole time we've been working together!'

'Ah.'

'Don't "Ah" me, Lester! What about it?'

'Well, it's not really for me to say.' He gestured slowly around the room.

Clara caught his drift.

'Well *yes*, I do also have a job here at the paper. If you can call this a job!'

'I can. You've been temporarily reassigned.'

'So what?' asked Clara. 'You think I've been harsh?'

'You think you've been harsh.'

'I do not!' Clara thought about it for a moment. 'I might have been a little harsh. But he pushed me into it!'

'I'm sure you're right,' said Lester. 'So?'

'So what?'

'Do I need to take my shoe off again?'

Clara stared at the door, and then back at her typewriter, which was even more accusing than before. 'You never wrote about it. About me and Fleet, bungling the bank sting.'

'No.'

'Why not? It's a good story.'

It was true. It *was* a good story. The sick feeling of humiliation rose inside her. She found she couldn't look at Lester, so instead cast her eyes down to the floor, hoping it might swallow her up.

Lester cleared his throat. 'I don't do bandwagons. And I've been where you are.'

'Obituaries?'

'A journalist with a hunch written off as a crank.'

'It's more than a hunch, Lester.' Her conviction of this one fact steeled her to look back up again. 'Everett Crowe is guilty.'

'So why are you here?' asked Lester.

Clara was silent for a moment, and for the first time answered the question honestly.

'Because I was wrong.'

'You made a mistake?'

'More than one, Lester. But this is the one that went badly. This is the one that blew up the case. And the business.' She stared at the floor. 'And my friendship.'

Lester nodded thoughtfully, then loudly humphed.

'What?' asked Clara. 'It's the truth!'

'Might be, but that's not why you're still here.'

'Then why, Lester? If you're such a scholar of regret, why am I still here?'

The crumpled older journalist stood up and walked into the hallway, before turning back to look at Clara, and waving broadly at what he had just done.

327

She shook her head in disbelief. 'What? I'm still here because I haven't left? What kind of advice is that? It's completely meaningless!'

Lester grabbed his bit of shoe from the lampshade, and shrugged.

'True. But I'm not the one still in there.'

Clara realised a while later that Lester's footsteps had gone, and she found herself again staring at the typewriter and the article she needed to summarise.

How on earth do you summarise an entire life in ten words?

She flexed her fingers over the typewriter and bashed out her answer.

Leopold Barnes. Biologist.
(Remaining word space reserved for the living)

The paper stuck out of the typewriter's upturned mouth like a lolling tongue, waiting for someone to come retrieve it from the empty office as Clara Entwhistle's boots whisked her to the building's exit, where she punched the door open and strode out into the city.

Thames frost fairs had been a feature of London life for as long as there were winters cold enough to freeze the river. They were joyous affairs, impromptu gatherings on the ice with people young and old enjoying everything on offer: vendors' tents selling all manner of food and drink; rickety stages presenting rousing music and songs; and, of course, skates for hire, offering everyone with half a shilling the chance to glide magnificently across the ice, to whirl and spin and feel truly alive, and to come away with happy memories and usually with wristbones intact.

Of course, with the Tower drawing every available morsel of kinetic energy from the Thames to meet part of its immense power requirements, the river had been frozen for decades, and the Thames Frost Fair was now a year-round treat for everyone with a few bob to spare and a thick coat to hand.

Fleet's bus, the No. 91 Cross-Glacier Express, had just passed the glacier's north bank, lowering its skis to allow it to advance onto the ice, and was now drifting to a leisurely stop on the outskirts of the fair.

Sandwich bag in hand, he alighted gingerly onto the ice, and slid his way cautiously towards the denser mass of tents and people.

Most stretches of the Thames Glacier were desolate, populated only by those who were able to withstand the cold, or at least unable to make a living elsewhere: former mudlarks, now icelarks, like Kathleen Price; the fishermen of Grave End sheltering in icelocked vessels in between their voyages out to sea; or the sledmen whose huskies could mush you to Kew faster than you could say 'Please, I was just asking if there *was* a queue. We left my children at the sled stand.'

But here, at the Frost Fair, Fleet's ears were filled with the lively chords of a fairground organ playing the music-hall favourite 'We Haven't A Thruppenny (But O How I Loves Him)'. His nostrils were filled with the thick aromas of fried onions and sausage, sweet batter and cream, freshly baked breads, and cocoa so hot it threatened the integrity of the ice beneath them all. And his mind was full of a mixture of general-purpose regret and specific annoyance at how hard it was to get where he was going with all these hundreds of people having a lovely time in the way.

In the corner of his eye, further along the north bank, there was the gothic edifice of Parliament, the Fortress of Westminster. He flinched away, but not quickly enough, and in an instant he was transported from the ice to the rooftop. The villain he had pursued there was cornered, but had chosen

329

not to come quietly, and in the ensuing fight he had slipped on the edge. Fleet now stared down from the rooftop, gripping the man's hand to save his life.

His heart pounded.

Why did I grab him?

But how could he not?

The man made his choice, and his bitter laughter rang in Fleet's ears as the street raced towards them.

Not again . . .

Something cold hit Fleet in the leg, summoning him back to the ice. He turned to see a boy and a girl running away and laughing, tossing more snowballs at each other as they went.

The metronome was thumping in his chest. Had he really not been here since then? Or had he just managed never to look?

He shook the snow off his trouser leg and carried on through the fair. Food stalls with criss-crossing queues, crowded picnic tables, and canopied beer halls lifted with singing. If there was ever a good time in London, it was here.

Eventually he approached the destination Mrs Pomligan had scrawled on the bag: near the far end of the fair by an old red-and-gold carousel.

In front of it, there was a bench, spiked into the ice for safety. And waiting on the bench was a man whom Fleet knew well.

His heart sank somehow even further.

'Good,' growled Chief Inspector Keller. 'About time.'

'Sir? What are you doing here?'

'Waiting for my lunch, Fleet. I have a rare, brief window in between meetings today so I thought I would take the glacier air.'

'And it just so happens that you ordered that lunch from where I work, even though you are in a fair with dozens of food vendors.'

'Sit down, Fleet.'

'I really should get back.'

'You can't go back until I pay you, correct?'

Fleet imagined returning to Mrs Pomligan's without payment, and the talking-to he would get from either or both of the people or things in his management chain.

He sat down heavily, handed over the sandwich, and the two men stared out across the fair, the organ music piping away in the distance.

For a while, neither spoke at all, until finally Keller began. 'Have you ever heard of *The Chilling Killings*?'

Fleet searched his memory. 'The brothers . . . ?'

Keller nodded. 'Thomas Belton, murdered Adam and Wilfrid to ensure he alone inherited their father's property fortune. One of the first cases under my tenure as Detective Chief Inspector. When only Thomas appeared at the father's funeral, people were suspicious – the brothers had become bitter rivals. They brought us in to investigate. Thomas was arrogant, unfeeling, vain. He openly mocked his missing brothers. He couldn't have been more obviously guilty. Except with evidence, of which there was none. There was nothing we could do.'

The men returned to silence. Fleet understood. Some things are just beyond our control.

'*One month later!*' boomed Keller, startling a young girl on the carousel into nearly falling from her steed. He waved down the glacier, towards the ice far away from the fair, and began sweeping a motion along it as he spoke. 'A sledman by the name of Obidiah Reaves is mushing his dogs along the ice. He catches an edge, which sends him flying and his pack whimpering to a halt. He doesn't understand it – he's never had a crash before. So he walks back to the ice where it happened, and takes a close look . . . Disturbed.'

'The ice?' asked Fleet. 'Or him?'

'First one, then the other. It had been dug up and packed back again, which is why it caught his sled. He was so furious he simply *had* to know why this had been done. So he took out his shovel and started digging. And he found his answers.'

'Adam and Wilfrid.'

'Twelve feet down. In the old days, after a month in the river you couldn't have told them apart from mutton. But they were perfectly preserved. As were the letters from Thomas in their pockets, inviting them to meet him the night they disappeared. We had him after all.'

Fleet nodded. Sometimes things have a way of working themsel—

'*Three days earlier!*' cried Keller, causing the girl on the carousel to decide to quit while she was ahead and dismount. 'Thomas Belton had left on a ship to America! We went to make the arrest only to discover we were too late. So, I did what anyone would have done in my position. I hailed a cab, gave the man double his fare to race me to Southampton as fast as he dared, commandeered a sailing boat and pursued Belton across the Atlantic.'

He paused in reflection, and Fleet briefly wondered if this was a surprise ending intended to get across the idea of sticking to your guns.

'In hindsight,' continued Keller, 'I probably should have popped home first to tell Mrs Keller I would be gone for weeks. Anyway, conditions were favourable and I managed to catch up with Belton's ocean liner just past the thirtieth meridian. Pulled up alongside, bellowed at a deckhand to throw down a rope, hauled my way up the hull, and then I was aboard.'

Fleet scratched his head and tried to keep track of which, if any, details of this story were the key to whatever Keller was trying to tell him. Perhaps this was a story about rigging?

332

'Of course, I was a stowaway now.' The Chief Inspector shook his head disdainfully. 'Before I could get anywhere close to Belton's cabin, I was surrounded and escorted to the brig.'

'Ah', said Fleet, taking a stab. 'A leaping-without-looking sort of situation?'

'Of course, yes, as you can see I remain in that brig to this day.' Keller shot a withering look at Fleet. '*No*. Eventually, I was taken to the bridge where the captain demanded an explanation of my actions. I filled him in on the Chilling Killings – a name I had come up with while at sea – and he understood completely.'

Fleet pinched the bridge of his nose. 'So, all good things come to those—?'

'Well, he freed me, but he also said that the Belton business was a matter for local authorities in New York, and that I should request an extradition when we arrived. As if the fiend wouldn't simply disappear across the country and take a new identity! So, naturally, I waited until night, found Belton's cabin, picked the lock, stuffed him in his own trunk, lugged him to the stern deck, lowered us both over the railing to where my boat was being towed, and away we went back the other way.'

'Feels illegal.'

'It's the sea, Fleet. There are no laws.'

'That can't be true . . .'

'Anyway, before we left, the gaoler from the brig – with whom I had struck up a decent rapport on our shared interests of cricket and incarceration – stopped us on the deck and gave us some water and supplies for the trip back. Not sure why he felt the need for the food, given we would be surrounded by all the fish in creation and I have two working hands, but I'd be lying if I said ship's biscuits weren't a nice change after a week on the mackerel.'

Fleet gave up trying to discern the point, and shut his eyes to ride it out until the end.

'Belton, of course, didn't much care for what was happening. I did let him out of the trunk, and naturally there was a little bit of him trying to murder me or drown us both and whatnot, but we found our rhythm once I tied him to the mast. Eight days later we were back in Southampton harbour, and the very second we set foot on Terra Britannica I formally arrested him and frogmarched him to justice. I was thanked by the Home Secretary for apprehending a dangerous criminal, formally reprimanded by HM Government for violating at least the norms of the sea if not the laws, lightly tutted at by Mrs Keller, and given a lifetime ban from the North Atlantic Liner Company.'

Keller fell silent, but Fleet waited a good fifteen seconds before he could feel confident the story had ended.

'I don't understand,' he finally said. 'Are you trying to tell me something?'

'I thought I had, quite clearly. How I caught Thomas Belton. The Chiller Killer. The Freezer Geezer.'

'There isn't a point?'

'It's a good story.'

'But there isn't a lesson?'

Keller frowned. 'Do I look like Aesop to you, Fleet?'

'I just thought, because you *called* me here—'

'Life doesn't work in fables. There is no single point to draw. Take what you need and move forward.'

'Then why have you brought me here?' cried Fleet, leaping to his feet. 'You haven't even eaten the sandwich you ordered – which you shouldn't, by the way. You couldn't just leave me to my misery?'

'No, I could not!'

'*Why?*'

'Because, you halfwit, despite your obvious talent for getting yourself into ridiculous situations, your unchecked insubordination, and your repeated disregard for regulations and due process, you were, for a number of years, one of my' – Keller paused, and summoned some internal strength – 'slightly above average detectives.'

Fleet was shocked. He was not sure he had ever heard anything from this man that sounded like praise.

'And,' continued Keller, 'I would have thought you'd have more grit and determination than to just give up when the riding got a little bumpy.'

'You *forbade* us from working on the case!'

'Oh, *now* you're going to let that stop you?'

'Our reputations and our business are ruined!' protested Fleet.

'Until you solve the case, deservedly so. Figure it out.'

'*How?*'

'That's up to you. But it wouldn't be a bad start to apologise to Miss Entwhistle for being a thickheaded puffin.'

'*What?* I wasn't—'

'You're here with me instead of barrelling across town with her, so I'm just assuming there is some thickheaded puffinry for which you need to apologise to Miss Entwhistle.'

Fleet reflected for a moment.

'I might have been a thickheaded puffin.'

'We all can be from time to time. After that, figure it out. I'm just here to order a sandwich. Which actually arrived more slowly than I was promised on the telephone . . .'

Fleet sat back down on the bench.

'Figure it out?'

Keller nodded. 'Commandeer a sailing boat if you have to.'

Fleet stared off into the fair. A hundred skaters traced an oval clockwise. Here and there, one would glide to the centre, leap into an impossible twirl, and dance away backwards into the crowd. Elsewhere, an unusually dextrous automaton had mastered the basics, but now seemed to have got stuck in a loop during an upright spin, which left it boring its way rapidly into the ice.

Fleet looked back, to the Fortress of Westminster looming from the north bank. He squinted at the rooftop. Something caught his eye.

They'd added a railing.

Clara had gone directly from her obituary-summarising desk at the *Morning Chronicler* to try to find Fleet at Mrs Pomligan's, only to learn from a mechanical dishcloth thing that he had left hours earlier on an employee upskilling activity and had not returned, which would merit a frank conversation and a demerit in his end-of-year evaluation.

He had not returned because, at the same time, Fleet had gone to the *Morning Chronicler* looking for Clara, only to be informed by a harried section editor that there were a number of obituaries that really wanted compressing, owing to the unfortunate collapse of an opera-house stage onto some note-worthy orchestral musicians who really hadn't.

He tried her flat as well, only to find her also not there, because she was outside his house not finding him.

Rather than continue this hopeless chase, Clara decided to wait on a bench, which gave her time, at last, to finish *A Gentleman's Guide to Business*. Eventually, a bus hovered to a stop at the end of the street, and Fleet approached his front door holding a shopping bag.

Clara thought she would surprise him to kick things off lightly, and as he was unlocking his door she grabbed him roughly by the shoulder and shouted in her gruffest voice, 'Oi!'

She had not expected him to react quite as jumpily as he did, and before she knew what was happening he had dropped his shopping, spun half round, grabbed her arm, slipped backwards, and pulled her down with him as they tumbled through his front door and onto the floor.

Clara blew her hair out of her face, and saw Fleet looking back up at her with bewilderment. She seemed to have him pinned, and grinned in triumph.

'Ha!' she cried. 'I knew I would best you if it ever came to a fight.'

'*Clara*? What are you doing?'

'I thought it would be funny if I pretended to attack you.'

'I nearly knocked your block off!'

'Not that nearly,' she shot back.

They sat up and straightened themselves out, staring out of the open door as the awkward weight of their last meeting fell over them with a smothering silence.

Clara remembered why she had come, but struggled to formulate how to say what she wanted to say.

Where do you even begin, she thought, let alone end, with someone you've worked with so closely? How can you disentangle your feelings about what each rashly said to the other from your reflections on the extent to which circumstances were to blame? What words can possibly—

'I'm sorry I was a thickheaded puffin,' said Fleet.

Clara smiled. 'Me too, Fleet.'

'I brought you a scone from the Frost Fair. But I think we trampled it.'

Clara looked at the shopping bag on the floor. It had been crushed by tumbling footsteps, sending scone dust exploding out of the top and across Fleet's door.

She fell into hysterics.

'You're laughing at my gift?' demanded Fleet, in mock outrage.

'You stood on it!'

'We'll check the footprints, but I'm certain you stood on it. Either way, I will be mortally offended if you don't eat it.'

'You want me to eat an exploded scone!' cried Clara, stifling laughter.

'I think it says a lot if you refuse.'

'Fine,' she said, grabbing the bag, pulling out the crushed scone and taking an enormous bite.

The corners of Fleet's mouth twitched. Clara was sure he *almost* laughed.

She swallowed the dry pastry with some difficulty. 'Still better than a Kepler Kake. Thank you, Fleet.'

'You're very welcome.'

The investigators stared out of the door at the darkening city. Dusk was falling, and the streetlights were flickering expectantly into life.

'We need to talk to Helena,' said Clara.

'We do.'

'She won't want to talk to us.'

'She won't.'

'And the reverend might not even let us in.'

Fleet nodded slowly and chewed his lip in thought, before turning to face Clara.

'Yes he will.'

Night had fallen by the time they reached the Church of the Mechanical Man.

Fleet walked up to the giant wooden door and knocked on it as hard as he could. This didn't make the dramatic banging sound he had hoped, instead producing the light tapping of a considerate woodpecker.

Clara reached past him and pounded on the door with her fist, sending a few booms into the building that were sure to convey the message that someone was at the front door wishing to enter.

Eventually, they could hear someone shuffling inside, and a small window in the door slid down, revealing half of the face of Reverend Kilburn, and his nightcap.

The cleric held up a candle, and his expression lit up as soon as he could make out who he was looking at.

'My Inspector!'

'Good evening, Reverend.'

'And Miss Entwhistle!'

'Hello, Reverend,' said Clara.

'Apologies for the hour, Reverend,' said Fleet. 'It's urgent.'

'Oh? What is?' Kilburn pulled back suspiciously. 'If you wish to see Miss Evans, I'm afraid that simply isn't possible, even for you, My Inspector. We are entrusted with her welfare.'

'We know that!' said Fleet. 'We're the ones who entrusted her to you!'

'A decision of wisdom befitting your station, My Inspector. But nevertheless, after what she said about you both on the steps outside – as erroneous as it no doubt was – I hardly think you would be welcome guests. You can understand that, can't you?'

Fleet steeled himself.

'That's not why we're here, Reverend.'

'Oh? And what else might bring you to our humble place of worship after nightfall?'

Fleet rubbed his hands over his face and clapped.

No going back now.

'I'm here to convert.'

Chapter 19

Clara waved a hand in front of Reverend Kilburn's face. He hadn't replied, or even blinked, in at least ten seconds, and she was beginning to worry that Fleet had broken him.

He shook his head, as if awakening from a daze. 'I'm sorry, My Inspector? Did I hear you correctly?'

'I'm here to convert, Reverend,' replied Fleet. 'I've been thinking about what you've been saying about Man's potential in the age of machines, and . . . it sounds great. Count me in.'

Kilburn began to vibrate with excitement. 'But . . . you're one of the reasons the church was founded, My Inspector. With your mechanical benefits you are yourself the embodiment of our ideals.'

'All the more reason for me to be officially part of it. Let's not waste any more time. Put me in the church. Give me a hat.'

'There's no . . . *hat*, My Inspector. Would you like us to create one for you? I'm sure it can be arranged.'

'Yes,' replied Fleet. 'Yes, I would like that. But first, perhaps, I was hoping you could let me in and give me a quick rundown on how it all works.'

'How . . . what works?'

'Oh, all of it. Your faith, the building, the organisation, your holy texts. Whatever you've got, really.'

'Well, yes, of course, I would be delighted, My Inspector. But . . . now? It's after ten o'clock. I've been in bed for half an hour.'

'Yes, now, please. I'm feeling very religious at the moment and who knows how long that will last.'

'Indeed! And Miss Entwhistle? You are also joining! I am delighted.'

'Um . . .'

'Actually,' said Fleet, 'Miss Entwhistle is still at an earlier stage of her spiritual awakening. I believe she would just like to sit in your chapel and do some quiet contemplation. Alone.'

Kilburn looked at Clara, who nodded vigorously.

'Quiet contemplation! Now there's a Thursday evening! Of course, of course. Let me, um, just give me a minute, normally the curate undoes all the bolts here . . .'

The window shut and there was some shuffling and unbolting on the other side of the door.

'Are you quite sure about this?' asked Clara.

'No, but it's already happening. Anything in that book of yours about joining a new religion for the sake of your business?'

'Yes, actually, but it doesn't recommend it.'

'Ah, well let's see how it pans out. Maybe I'll send them a letter if it works.'

'You might get a credit in the next edition.'

Fleet nodded. 'Find Helena. She's in here somewhere.'

Clara smiled, and punched him in the shoulder.

'Ow! What was that for?'

Clara realised that in her excitement at Fleet's plan she had landed her friendly thump with rather more power than intended, so she clarified:

'You're a good one, Fleet.'

A final, heavy bolt slid away, and the massive door swung slightly open. Clara saw the interior of the Church of the Mechanical Man, and the sturdy frame of Reverend Kilburn, who was beaming as though all his Christmases had come at once, and been replaced by some new holy day that he was in charge of inventing.

'Welcome, Children.'

Minutes later, Clara had been shown into the side chapel, and she heard Kilburn whisking Fleet away, his voice fluttering like a giddy bird as he began to explain the theological tenets of Metallurgical Rejuvenation and the possible role of hydraulic lifts in the Easter story.

The last of Fleet's strained 'Oh, really?'s drifted through the corridor, and then she was finally alone.

She looked around. It was a small chapel, for use by one or two people at a time. A recent fresco on the ceiling depicted Adam and God reaching out to one another, with God handing Adam a tiny spanner and cursing at an instruction manual that was written in a language even He did not speak.

When it had been quiet for a minute, Clara slipped out of the door and back into the main church building. She recalled that when they first brought Helena Evans here the reverend had spoken of lodgings above the church itself, so she thought she'd try her luck there first. She headed back to the front door and snuck up the large staircase that led away from the entrance hall.

At the top of the stairs the long corridor was lined with old wooden doors carved with various Christian symbols from when the building served the Church of England: grapes, fish, loaves of bread, doves and, for some reason, several snails. Clara would have to look that up. Or perhaps the engraver was just a mollusc aficionado.

No time to get distracted, Clara. Focus.

Clara carefully cracked open each door in turn, and peered through the gaps: a washroom, an empty bedroom, a store cupboard, a living room of some kind, a kitchen. She reached the end of the corridor. No Helena Evans.

Has she gone?

Clara stopped to think. A moment later, she heard a voice. Helena's voice. Distant. And not alone.

She turned to where the sound was coming from: a window at the corridor's end. Clara looked through. It was dark. Darker than the outside usually was in the city, even at night. Only the moonlight filtered through, nothing from the streetlamps. Leafy branches filled the black space, tilting and rustling in the breeze, and Clara saw it was a courtyard, bounded on all sides by high walls – the old stone of the church, and the brick of its neighbours.

She looked down into the dark space. The branches joined together, fusing into one mighty trunk which plunged into an earthy circle in the centre of the paved yard. In front of the trunk was a bench, flooded in moonlight. On it sat Helena Evans and, next to her, a lean, impeccably dressed man, one leg resting over the other, hands pressed together and to his lips, and listening very closely.

Julius Bell.

Clara made her way downstairs and out of the church into the courtyard. An owl hooted in welcome, or alarm, and the pair on the bench turned to the new arrival.

Julius squinted through the dark until he could make out who was approaching, then broke into a thin smile.

'Miss Entwhistle,' he said, with the practised warmth and deliberateness of someone whose utterances are their livelihood. 'Bit late for a service.'

Clara was disconcerted.

Why is he here? With Helena?

343

'Mr Bell,' replied Clara, before turning to the person she had come to speak to. 'Helena, is everything all right?'

'Quite all right, Miss Entwhistle. Mr Bell asked the reverend if I would receive him, and I agreed.'

'Do you know each other?' asked Clara.

'Getting to know each other,' replied Julius. 'Miss Evans has been helping me piece together a few things. I was a little disappointed you and Inspector Fleet didn't come to see me after the garden party . . .'

'We've been a little busy.'

'So I hear. A bit of subterranean misadventure and some bad press.'

'It was a trap followed by a smear campaign,' replied Clara. 'And it was perpetrated by Corps-Marshal Everett Crowe, because he knows we are on to him for murdering seven people and the attempted murder of Miss Evans here!'

Julius stifled a yawn, and flicked a fallen leaf off his trouser leg.

Clara was infuriated. 'Don't you care about this, Mr Bell?'

'I do not. Murders happen constantly, and while I am enjoying Miss Evans's company and wish no harm upon her, I would not have lost sleep had the attack on her been successful. It's terrible to say so, but it is my job to be terrible.'

Julius stood up and strode a few paces across the courtyard. Clara looked to Helena, who smiled grimly and nodded at her.

She knows something.

Julius reached a pool of moonlight reflected in a large window, and spun around sharply towards them.

'However bad you think things are, Miss Entwhistle, I assure you they are far worse.'

Clara was not in the mood for dramatics, but also knew she had to listen to whatever Julius had to say.

'I have a neighbour,' he began, waving the fingers of one hand through a small, dull rainbow cast from somewhere above, as if he was strumming a lyre. 'He and I, we don't get on. We are a little house-proud, you might say. He trims the tall bushes in his garden into topiary birds. I prefer statuary in mine. Maybe the odd fountain.'

'Sounds like a nice neighbourhood you live in,' said Clara.

'It is, but none of this is real. Pay attention.'

Clara folded her arms.

'The trouble is this,' Julius continued, now looking up to admire the stained glass window high above that was the source of his rainbow instrument. 'My neighbour and I can see each other's gardens. Which is not, in itself, a problem: I don't want his garden, and he doesn't want mine. The problem is that he cannot be *sure* I do not want his garden, and I cannot be sure he doesn't want mine. Why wouldn't he? It's full of beautiful statuary and fountains – what red-blooded man wouldn't want it? And no doubt he thinks the same about his tasteless hedge-chickens. None of which would matter except for the following fact: either of us could, in the night – *any night* – slip into the other's house and slit his throat.'

Helena's jaw dropped. 'Good grief, Mr Bell!'

'My apologies, Miss Evans. But you understand my point – my neighbour and I are in a terrible situation where we are each a potential threat to the other, and neither of us can have confidence, *ever*, that the other is truly not a threat. Now, put yourself in my one-, or rather *two*-of-a-kind Venetian leather shoes. There are only two logical courses of action. One, to strike first and destroy the other before he has the same idea. Risky, to say the least. I might get killed in the struggle. Or two, to try and ensure my neighbour can relax a bit and does not start thinking he needs to destroy me. Which I might do, for example, by ensuring he always knows what I am up to.

I might install a heavy front door, and allow my garden gate to remain squeaky, which would make it impossible for me to sneak over to his property in the night undetected, and *allows him to know* that it is impossible for me to do that. He, similarly, might chop holes through his topiary birds so that *I* can see that *he* cannot hide inside them, waiting for nightfall so he can end my life under cover of darkness. We would both, together, be giving assurance that neither of us can destroy the other. And therefore we ensure our mutual safety. You see how this would work, yes?'

Clara nodded. She knew exactly what he meant, and saw in her mind the endless row of Prussian dreadnoughts floating patiently in the North Sea, bow to bow with the British Phalanx Class warships.

Julius widened his eyes and stared into hers. 'Now suppose, one day, one sunny summer day, years into this peaceful stalemate, my neighbour wakes up, looks out of his bedroom window, greets the chaffinches, and sees that I have constructed, in my garden, a metal mountain with some heretofore unknown form of energy weapon atop it that could, at any moment, *vaporise his entire home*!'

Clara's mind flashed back to the horror of what she had seen at the coast.

The Lanterns.

'Now!' exclaimed Julius, his calm manner boiling away and his voice ricocheting off the courtyard walls. 'Having introduced this machine of unthinkable destruction into the equation, perhaps I am safe from my neighbour at last?'

Clara slowly shook her head. She knew where this was going.

'Of course not! Will he attack me now? No, no, no! My weapon is far too powerful. But will he ignore it and carry on about his business?'

346

Clara shook her head again.

'He cannot!' continued Julius. 'He must ensure his own safety, with something equivalently terrible!'

'Their own Lanterns . . .' said Clara.

'*At best*,' replied Julius, regaining his composure. 'At best they keep their weapons on their own shores. But they might see the need to equip their ships with such things, or something even more powerful. Ships that are not that far at all from the British mainland. A course of action we would have no choice but to respond to ourselves, which, of course, they would anticipate and attempt to prevent with quicker action of their own. Which, of course, *we* would anticipate, and so on, and so on. All leading to a situation that I believe our military commanders refer to as "a little sticky", but which the rest of us would probably put closer to something along the lines of "annihilation".

'So no, Miss Entwhistle. I do not care about the deaths of seven people. I care about the deaths of seven million, brought about by the insanity of a man who does not comprehend that *some things must never be built!*'

The owl hooted again, and Clara shivered. She glanced at Helena, who was listening with a look of grave disquiet.

'We are . . . trying our best,' continued Julius. 'We have intermediaries to the Prussians. We are trying to impress upon them that this is not an intentional provocation. We have a window of time. But if the Brunelians continue on this path . . .'

'You think Crowe is responsible for the Lanterns?' asked Clara.

'I think he is responsible for the Brunelians thinking that they ought to be building such things. Thinking that city infrastructure is not enough for them. He is changing their culture into something even more dangerous than it already is.'

'How do you know this?'

Julius pulled an exaggerated frown, as if his feelings had been badly hurt. 'How little you think of me, Miss Entwhistle. Is it not my very duty, as Her Majesty's loyal and trusted Private Secretary, to know whatever might be of import to the nation and the Crown?'

'So, you have people in the Brunel Corps,' said Clara.

'Everywhere, really.'

'Spies.'

'I don't have *spies*. I just happen to have an immense number of friends whom I occasionally pay for information. And these friends have also told me that Sir Grover Merridew is the only person standing in Crowe's way at present, gumming up the works. But Crowe appears to have convinced Corps-Marshal Khan that it's time for Merridew to make way for new talent.'

'Yes,' replied Clara. 'Sir Grover knows this.'

'I am sure he does. But there is one thing he does not know.'

Helena slowly stood up and turned to Clara. 'I know the man Crowe intends to replace Merridew.'

Clara was taken aback, but then realised. 'Lady Arabella's father. You said he was a Corps-General.'

Helena nodded. 'From what I overheard when I was working in his house as Lady Arabella's governess, he is angling for the top job. I didn't think anything of it at the time. Who cares about the manoeuvring of the top brass?'

'This is what Miss Evans and I have been discussing,' said Julius.

'What makes you think he'll be selected?' asked Clara.

'He worked with Crowe,' said Helena, 'and he was a yes man. A toady. No ideas of his own. Couldn't even say no to his own daughter!'

'Crowe's goal is unlikely to be simply replacing Merridew,' added Julius. 'He is still left in the position of needing to cooperate with and convince his peers. Far better to install someone who will not challenge him on any subject at all.'

'So they can outnumber Khan,' said Clara, before realising where this led. 'Or remove him too.'

Julius snapped his fingers at Clara. 'You have it. The Brunelians will effectively have a Triumvirate of one man: Crowe. No one man has led the Corps alone since Brunel himself, and they're a damned sight larger than when he was around. *The Brunelians*, under one man. A man with some very strong, very flawed ideas about national security. Can you imagine what they would be capable of? Can you imagine what *the Prussians* will imagine they are capable of? We must stop him, before events overtake us.'

'Then stop him, Mr Bell! What are you waiting for?'

Julius threw his hands together at the wrist, and mimed a faint struggle. 'He is a private citizen, Miss Entwhistle. There is nothing illegal in what he is doing.'

'Apart from the seven murders!' cried Clara.

'Quite,' agreed Julius. 'So if you wouldn't mind proving that for me, I would be very grateful. You and the Inspector seem to be working on the case already. Perhaps you could just . . . finish it? Sooner really would be better than later.'

He nodded a farewell at Helena, before walking to the door leading back into the church. He passed through the doorway, vanishing into a dark corridor, and Clara saw a shadowy hand waving cheerfully above his head, as his voice rang out:

'I have every confidence in you, Miss Entwhistle.'

On the other side of the church, Fleet was regretting his choices.

Reverend Kilburn had taken him on a leisurely tour of the building, pointing out the changes he'd made since the Church of the Mechanical Man had taken over the premises:

the entranceway now featured a small library of pamphlets, most prominently 'Mechanical Exoskeletons – A Sensible Place To Begin'; impressively and/or heretically, the large metal cross suspended above the altar was now circumscribed by an even larger metal cog; and there were, of course, several hastily done oil paintings of Queen Victoria about the place, with the monarch looking as heavenly and angelic as was possible for something sporting retractable caterpillar tracks for rough terrain.

Fleet was relieved to see that he personally did not feature anywhere in the artworks or other materials, but suspected the worst was yet to come.

Now, they were in the vestry. Reverend Kilburn sat in a large comfy armchair with a cup of cocoa. Having declined the reverend's offer of cocoa, Fleet was sitting, cocoaless, on a pew that had clearly been demoted out of the nave owing to having one of its ends entirely missing, with that half of the seat instead being supported by hymnbooks.

Fleet scratched his arm and shuffled on the pew.

'Now then,' began Kilburn. 'A few questions to get started, perhaps. What draws you to the Church of the Mechanical Man?'

Fleet sighed. 'Hard to pin it down. Lots of things.'

'Of course.' The reverend nodded sagely. 'Perhaps you could just name three.'

'Three? Well . . . the building is very nice.'

'It *is* very nice, isn't it?' agreed Kilburn, with an enthusiastic finger-point. 'Churches practically have a monopoly on nice buildings in this country, which I think is because they used to have a literal monopoly on nice buildings in this country.'

Fleet looked around the room seeking inspiration for two further reasons to be here, but found his eyes drawn to yet another quasi-biblical Victoria portrait. The artist for this one seemed to have gone in for close-up realism, and Fleet lost himself in a sea of mechanisms shrouded in a purple, ermine-laced robe. Somehow, the painting seemed to be ticking, but then he realised the sound was coming from inside his chest, the metronome increasing in tempo, and he pulled his eyes away from the painting and buttoned his jacket.

Kilburn turned around to see what Fleet had been looking at, before turning back and smiling.

'Any other reasons than the building?' he gently prompted.

Fleet was growing agitated.

'Is this what a religious conversion looks like?' he asked. 'Having a chat?'

The reverend pulled a curious eyebrow. 'What did you expect?'

'I don't know . . . frocks . . . singing.'

'Ah, the pomp. Yes, I understand.' Kilburn gestured towards the door to the nave. 'Well, we have a font of motor oil out there . . .'

'That's what that smell is.'

'I could drip a few drops onto your forehead and say some words if that would make you feel better.'

'It would not,' said Fleet.

'No,' replied Kilburn. 'I don't imagine it would.'

A silence drifted between the pair, and Fleet grew increasingly uncomfortable. He shifted on the pew, sending the top hymnbook off its tower, which left the entire bench at a slight angle.

'You don't seem very at ease, Inspector.'

'I don't know what you mean,' said Fleet, trying to remain upright and ignore the feeling of Victoria's eyes boring into his skull.

The metronome ticked faster.

'I mean generally, Inspector. If I may say, you don't seem particularly comfortable generally.'

Fleet heard the sound of a medical drill close by, coming from nowhere. He shook his head. 'Is anyone?'

'Some more than others, perhaps.'

'Maybe they haven't had half their insides replaced by machinery!' snapped Fleet. 'Maybe they were just able to carry on with their lives without being surrounded by a city constantly reminding them of something they had done to them that they never wanted!'

Kilburn nodded slowly, allowing the words to vanish out into the nave and across the stone, and for silence to return.

He shifted forwards in his cushions. 'You have gone through something terrible. But you are exactly the same person you were before.'

Fleet scoffed. 'I thought you people tended to think our bodies are temples.'

'Best not to get too tied up in scripture. Do you know what the Church of the Mechanical Man is about, Inspector?'

Fleet shrugged. 'You worship machines.'

The reverend chuckled. 'You think I worship the Number Sixty-one bus?'

'The Number Sixty-one is my bus, and if you knew the actual timetable like I do, you'd agree it's clearly damned.'

Kilburn's eyes bulged, and Fleet felt a silence building like the one on a freshly snow-capped mountain after a shot has been fired.

Suddenly, the avalanche broke, and the reverend roared with laughter. '"Damned"!' he cried. 'A damned bus!'

He tried to exhale the laughter away, sounding like someone squeezing coos from a pigeon.

Fleet smiled slightly as he watched – he found it impossible to remain upset in this odd man's presence.

'No, no,' said Kilburn, wiping a tear from his eye. 'I do not worship a bus, Inspector. We *respect* machines, because they

352

represent human striving. That is all. We all want to be better, to do better, and these days the machine arts are a large part of how we do it. What do you strive for, Inspector?'

'I don't know,' said Fleet. 'Who knows that? What do *you* strive for?'

'Helping people find peace through faith. I want to help people find peace, and while it's not for everyone, I find that faith is a nifty way to do it. I'm rather a dab hand at it, too, though I say it myself.'

Shame hit Fleet like a brick. He could not maintain the lie any longer.

'I'm sorry,' he said. 'I'm not here to convert. I'm here to distract you so Miss Entwhistle can speak with Miss Evans.'

Kilburn nodded. 'Oh, yes, I know.'

Fleet blinked. 'What?'

'She has a visitor at the moment, over in the courtyard, but I'm sure Miss Entwhistle will be able to ask whatever you need to know.'

'If you know I'm lying, why are you doing this?'

'I told you,' replied Kilburn. 'I want to help people find peace. Even if they are lying to me. *Especially* if they are lying to me.'

Fleet felt the shame pulling him down like a stone. He looked up at the ceiling, and the lamps flickered in reply.

'I don't know how to find peace,' he said.

'That's all right. It's not easy.'

'I don't know if faith will do it for me.'

The reverend nodded. 'Does it occur to you, Inspector, that you and I are in the same line of work?'

'*Ha!*'

'It's true! You bring wrongdoers to justice. You and Miss Entwhistle. People can feel that right has been done, that the world makes a little more sense than it otherwise would. And more

353

to the point, with your agency, are you not helping people the police turned away? It strikes me that you are also in the business of giving people faith – not the same kind I dish out here, of course, but a solid bit of faith nonetheless – and that *knowing* that you do this will bring some people, the neediest people, peace.'

He paused, and caught Fleet's eyes in his own. 'You are the same person you were before.'

Fleet stared back at the reverend, who pulled a smile and took a swig of cocoa. Some moments passed, and Fleet was vaguely aware of an owl hooting somewhere outside.

'You're quite good at this,' he said.

'I should bloody hope so!' replied Kilburn with a chortle. 'I've been at it long enough.'

The courtyard was silent, and the breeze picked up once again, rustling the tree and annoying the owl.

'I'm sorry,' said Helena. 'For what I said out there on the steps.'

'You have nothing to apologise for.' Clara hesitated, but had to know. 'He found you?'

Helena nodded. 'Two nights earlier, I was looking out of the window, and it was the most unusual thing – on the street outside your office, there was Corps-Marshal Crowe! Of course, I didn't know he was the one who attacked me. But it's not every day you see a corps-marshal, so I was watching what he was up to. He tried the door to the café, but it was locked. I think he meant to break in!'

Clara remembered back. It must have been after the garden party. He had invited them to meet him at his home the next day, for what turned out to be a bribe, so perhaps he'd aimed to find out what they knew.

'And while deciding how to break in, he looks around to see if anyone is watching, and discovers that not only is there someone, but that it is Helena Evans, the only person he tried and failed to kill.'

'The look in his eyes . . .' said Helena. 'The rage that I had seen him. It was exactly the same as when I fled from the carriage that night. I realised at once.'

'Did he try to get into the church?'

'Of course! He pounded on the door and spoke to the reverend — I don't know what was said, but he must have decided he could not simply force his way in, or not without notice. Instead, the next night, I received a note. Unsigned, of course. It instructed me to denounce you the following morning, and said that if I did not, he would burn the place down with everyone in it.' Helena shook her head. 'I am sorry. I owe the reverend too much.'

'What will you do?'

'I don't know. He said I can stay here as long as I need to. He's a good man. But after that . . . I don't know.'

Clara stared at Helena, and once again remembered their part in her torment. If it wasn't for them, she would still be safely hidden away, building a new life. Clara felt the sickness of guilt creeping through her body. She tried to ignore it. The only way to help Helena was by carrying on with the case, by asking what she had come here to ask her.

'You were interviewed by Abel Thorpe. From the Office of the Well-Running of the City.'

Helena nodded. 'He wanted to talk about a project I had worked on. A roof terrace on a new government building.'

She stared up at the dark roof of the church.

'It collapsed before it was finished. Three died. All labourers.'

She shook her head, and pointed to the apex of the roof.

'This church is thirteenth century, you know. The reverend told me all about it. It took them thirty-five years to build the walls, and another twenty to build the roof. Men spent their entire working lives on it.'

Clara looked up. It was a beautiful building, even in the night, and it was impossible not to be awed by these soaring shapes that had survived more than half a millennium.

'I read once,' she said, 'about a cathedral in Florence that wasn't even fully designed when they started work.'

Helena nodded. 'The Cathedral of Saint Mary of the Flower. The Duomo. It took a hundred and thirty years to build. The architect knew he would not live even to see its walls completed, so he felt it was not his place to design the dome that would sit atop it. That belonged to the future.'

She fell into silence, still staring in admiration at the building above them. Clara heard something tiny skitter across the roof, a living thing among all the architectural majesty.

'Why did the terrace collapse, Miss Evans?'

Helena shrugged. 'Sometimes things do. We're not magicians. We use the best techniques we know and the best materials we can find.'

She sighed heavily. 'Sometimes things just collapse.'

Clara felt her heart wrenching again from the guilt, but she pressed on.

'Mr Thorpe suspected foul play, in that project and others. Did he mention anything like that to you?'

Helena closed her eyes and thought for a moment. 'He did want to check my calculations and look over the designs. But I know my stuff and he found it all to be more than satisfactory.'

She gave a proud smile before reciting, '"Check your working. Keep two sharp pencils. And you don't go to Brailsford for the views."'

Clara furrowed her brow. The expression sounded slightly familiar.

'What is that?'

'Just something people say to new recruits in the Corps.'

'But . . . Brailsford?'

'Not a fun day out,' replied Helena. 'Best to work by post.'

The owl took off from the tree above them and flew upwards into the night.

'Brailsford . . .' repeated Clara to herself.

She rummaged through her satchel, pulling out *A Gentleman's Guide to Business*, several notepads, a torch, three packets of Vauxhall Pleasure Gardens' special blend of birdseed and, finally, Abel Thorpe's diary. She switched on the torch and rifled wildly through the diary's pages.

'Brailsford. Brailsford . . . Aha! Got you!' She slapped the open page, before turning it round to show Helena her discovery. '"Brighton, Ealing, Brailsford, Stevenage, London Border North."'

'What's that?'

'Places Mr Thorpe was planning to visit.'

'Interesting . . . Sounds like Mr Thorpe knew a little more than he was willing to let on.'

'Why? What's at Brailsford?'

Helena flashed her eyebrows mischievously. 'Can I tell you a Brunel Corps joke, Miss Entwhistle? It's not a good one. There are no good ones.'

Clara could not understand how this would help, but it was the first time she had seen Helena's spirits lift even slightly, and she felt buoyed, even though she knew it would not last. 'Go ahead . . .'

'How do you win a fight with a logistics officer?' asked Helena.

Clara smiled and threw up her hands. 'I don't know. How do you win a fight with a logistics officer?'

Helena pulled a wry grin. 'With the *element of supplies*.'

Clara shook her head. A swift descent of feathers and talons pierced the sky above the church roof, followed by a tiny, devastating squeak.

357

Chapter 20

An observer in the heavens, looking down onto the city of Even Greater London – whether they be extraterrestrial, angel, or just whichever brave, doomed fool put up their hand when Queen Victoria asked for volunteers to get a space programme started – would think to themselves a number of things in turn.

Firstly: *Oh look, there's London!*

Secondly: *My word, it doesn't half spread around a bit, doesn't it?*

Thirdly, depending on who they were: *Hmm. I forgot to ask how I get down from here. Well, I'm sure it's been thought through.*

And finally *That bit there, near the top-left of the city, looks very, very, very, very, very, very, very, very hot.*

They would get this impression partly from the fact that that bit of the city was entirely blocked from view by a single, enormous cloud – many miles across, swirling like a hurricane, and clearly not the sort of weather Britain tends to get, even in the blusteriest April, but rather the result of volcanic quantities of steam rising from *something* and cooling in the atmosphere.

There was also the curious fact that the cloud glowed with a deep, concerning red, like firelit blood, above the unimaginable heat of the *something* underneath.

The entire spectacle would seem not too different from the Great Red Spot of Jupiter, only much closer to where people live, and something people are much more responsible for causing.

Because, beneath this terrifying, blazing meteorological phenomenon, one would find The Foundries: mile after mile of ironworks and factories, and the source of almost everything metal in London.

And somewhere deep in its blistering heart was a foundry run by a man named J. G. Brailsford.

It was hours into night by the time Fleet and Clara arrived, but the glow of the furnaces lit up the sky in shades of rust and persimmon, like a tropical sunset happening in every direction at once.

Fleet looked upwards at the endless, infernal storm above them and loosened his tie.

This might be the warmest part of the city he'd ever come across, he thought. And he'd been to Cornwall.

Fleet and Clara made their way along the narrow streets that divided the foundries into neat rows and columns, meeting no one on their way as the workers had long gone home. Only the roaring of blast furnaces, and the occasional trundling of cheerful, scorched automatons, gave any sign at all that this was not a long-abandoned industrial town.

Eventually, at the centre of it all, they found the Brailsford Iron and Steelworks. Five grand brick edifices, each wide enough to swallow an ocean liner and long enough that they vanished into the darkness, lying side by side like the fingers of some almighty hand pressing down into the earth, unhappy with its speed and ready to give it a really good spin.

The frontage of the centre building was mostly filled with a vast, black, iron door. Fleet and Clara approached and found a smaller, human-sized door built into it at the bottom.

They pushed it open, and entered.

The space within was cavernous, and dark but for strips of meagre safety lighting and the furnaces blazing in elephantine columns along the building's length. Four stout cauldrons, each of which could hold a small lake, sat by the long walls. Large machines, whose purpose Fleet could not identify, dotted the floor – giant presses somewhere within, funnels on top like baby birds opening their mouths for feeding. Walkways clung to the walls, sneaking behind the upper reaches of the machines, and gantries crossed the space in between them.

The heat was almost overwhelming. Fleet abandoned his jacket and Clara her cape, and they carried on into the heart of the works.

Some way inside, a ceiling light shone through the window of a foreman's office overlooking the factory floor from high above. Fleet saw a man standing there. Fifties, smartly dressed, even wearing a waistcoat despite the heat. He was watching them, and when he saw they were looking up at him he simply nodded, walked out of sight towards the office door, and then returned, crossed the window again, and disappeared.

Fleet and Clara shared a glance, and continued to a metal staircase. Three flights up, they reached the walkway leading to the office, and then the office itself. Light spilled out from the door, which had been left ajar. Fleet knocked, and it swung open.

The room was bare. Shelving ran around the walls, empty but for the occasional cobwebbed tin of sealant or cracked box file. A desk was at the end just past the window, with two small upturned crates positioned on the near side, presumably for visitors. The man was on the far side of the desk, sitting on a cracked wooden chair. He had pushed his papers and ink aside, and seemed to be waiting.

Fleet and Clara stepped inside, and the man looked up at them wearily.

'You are the investigators,' he sighed.

'We are,' said Clara.

The man nodded, and gestured at them to take a seat on the crates, which they did. He filled three tumblers from a carafe of water to his side, and passed two to his guests. They left them alone.

The man laughed quietly. 'Of course. I'd be wary if I'd been duped like you two.' He sipped his water.

Fleet studied the man. His face was drawn, and raw from dull razors. His clothes were expertly tailored, but they draped on him as if he were a young man in his father's suit. Life hadn't just defeated him; it had insisted on a rematch and redoubled its efforts.

'Mr Brailsford,' began Clara.

'James, if you wouldn't mind. I've been Mr Brailsford my entire life. It would be nice to hear my own name.'

Fleet looked at Clara, who hesitated before continuing.

'James—'

'Building a life is a tiring business, wouldn't you say, Miss Entwhistle?'

'That's . . . not really what we want to talk—'

'Becoming oneself, yes? And it is a *becoming*, you must agree. Not a different kind of thing. People tend to say they want to *find* themselves, or *discover* themselves, as if the self is somewhere waiting for them.' He swept his arm towards his foundry beyond the window. 'The iron here, it doesn't discover itself. It's *cast*. Cast into whatever shape the mould determines. Any iron, any mould. You just have to choose.'

'And what have you cast?' asked Fleet.

The man's eyelids drooped, and he seemed barely willing to hold up his own head.

361

'You are here; you must already know. Please.'

Clara frowned, and began her guess.

'Years ago, you provided subpar iron and steel parts to the Brunel Corps, leading some of their projects to end in disaster. You did this at the direction of Everett Crowe, allowing him to look more competent than his peers, and let him advance ever further in their organisation. Maybe he got you your start, maybe he promised you more contracts, or threatened you would lose them.'

Brailsford listened with his eyes closed, nodding along, as if to a piece of music he knew well. Clara continued:

'But then Abel Thorpe began to piece it together. Crowe had a plan to get rid of him, and anyone he had spoken to about it in case they also could, but the deaths of that many engineers might draw attention — he needed a distraction. Something sensational.'

She glanced at the foundry outside the window.

'I imagine in your line of work you get to learn a lot about how things are made. Particularly things where the requirements are strict, and the clients demanding. Things like bank vaults. Perhaps there are some scattered through London where you supplied the parts, and knew their design intimately. You would know how someone could get in and out without leaving a trace. So, Crowe demanded your help, your information to begin with, but then even more, and reminded you that you were complicit in the acts of sabotage of the past. I wonder . . .'

'Am I the murderer or the thief?' He shrugged. 'What does it matter?'

'It matters because you can still do some good here, Mr Brailsford.'

'Some good, some bad . . .' the man said. 'These past months, I've thought a great deal about why I ever did what I did. I

362

could tell you it was for my employees, that it was my responsibility to keep our business growing, that their livelihoods were all I thought of. That's what I told myself. I don't know whether I believe it any more. Five foundries with the name J. G. Brailsford. There were none before, and now there are five. Maybe I thought it would have meaning. Maybe I craved the significance. I cannot tell you. It was a different man.'

'Come with us to Scotland Yard,' said Clara. 'Swear to this account. Help us stop Crowe.'

'No. I cannot. I am just too tired.' He sighed heavily. 'And it is too late besides.'

'Why?'

Brailsford looked puzzled and amused, as if he could not understand why they did not know. He lifted his glass and appeared to toast the health of the foundry beyond his window, pulling a mocking grimace towards it that Fleet had only ever seen on the poisoned dead.

'Because he's always been the safe pair of hands.'

Fleet was consumed by a lurching horror, but the man was right – it was too late. He leapt towards Clara as the window shattered under the force of Brailsford's contempt. The man's glass exploded, and he was propelled backwards; the foundry rang out with an echoing crack, like a bell falling down a steeple and smashing everything in its path.

Fleet pulled Clara to the ground as a second shot splintered her crate, and they scrambled to the wall underneath the window.

'Crowe,' said Clara.

Fleet nodded, and glanced under the desk. Brailsford lay in his blood, the last traces of life already gone.

A cheerful voice rang out from somewhere – everywhere – outside the office.

'Good evening, detectives! I would come and say hello but I don't have that sort of time, you understand.'

363

Fleet found a crack in the wall beneath the window, and peered out. The furnaces raged on the ground level, but it was too dark to see anything else – being in a lit room was an insurmountable tactical disadvantage.

He looked over to Clara, who seemed to have realised the same thing, grabbing a tin from a nearby shelf and hurling it at the ceiling lamp, smashing it and plunging the room into darkness.

Crowe laughed from wherever he was. 'Very good! I admire your efforts, bloodhounds. It is refreshing to have even a little challenge in my path.'

'Why don't you drop the rifle,' cried Fleet, 'and you can have even more of a challenge?'

Crowe laughed again. 'A tempting offer, Inspector! But no.'

'Fleet,' whispered Clara. 'How many rounds does he have left?'

'How could I possibly know that?'

'Well, what kind of rifle is he firing?'

'Hang on, I'll ask him.'

'You can't tell?'

'Clara, do you think I'm a fusilier? What makes you think I can tell what gun someone is firing from what it sounds like?'

'I thought something like this might have come up.'

'Come up?'

'In your line of work.'

'As it happens, this is my first time pinned down in an ironworks.'

Fleet swept his hands across the floor and felt a large flat folder. He gingerly lifted it up in front of the window. For a moment nothing happened, and he guessed that even in the low light Crowe had seen it was a trick. But then the folder was whipped out of Fleet's hand, spinning across the floor and under the shelving on the far wall as another crack rang out beyond the window.

Fleet shook his hand in pain and silently mouthed a few choice oaths as he listened.

CA-CHINK

There. He did know that sound. It might have been from a team-building afternoon Keller had organised, an afternoon none of the detectives would ever fully recover from, but he did know it. His trick had worked, and he was filled with positivity.

'Repeating rifle,' he whispered. 'Lever action.'

'Oh good!' said Clara. 'What does that mean for rounds remaining and rate of fire?'

Fleet's positivity vanished and he felt even worse than before.

'I have no idea. "Some" and "quite fast"?'

'It's a Winchester,' shouted Crowe, from wherever he was. 'I assume that's what the folder was about. Correct, detectives?'

Fleet rolled his eyes. 'Yes!'

'Very good! Well, it's a Model 1871 I had imported, not from America in fact, but from France after their Prussian kerfuffle. It has a red brass receiver and it fires .44 Henrys. Does that answer your question?'

Fleet thought for a moment.

'No,' he cried.

'What is your question?'

'How many bullets do you have left?'

'Ah! Well, I think the technical term is "plenty".'

Fleet turned to Clara.

'I found out about how many rounds he has.'

'But I'm afraid it doesn't matter,' cried Crowe.

Clara frowned.

'Why doesn't it matter?' she shouted.

Crowe did not answer, and Fleet heard movement in the space beyond the office. He put his face up against the crack in the wall and peered out into the darkness.

There was movement on a gantry opposite, and dim features of a man appeared and disappeared as he moved in and out of shadows.

The movement stopped, and Fleet saw the rifle being held above a railing, aiming at something on the ground level. It fired repeatedly, and a flickering orange glow began to illuminate the far wall.

'The furnaces,' he muttered.

Crowe turned and fired further away, and the orange flame-light grew stronger. He did this twice more, and by the time he was done a low patchwork of fire was creeping across the machinery in Fleet's field of view.

'He's burning it down.'

'With him in it?' asked Clara.

'I imagine he's planning to leave first and trap us here. We have to get out.'

'He'll shoot at us!'

'We can't stay here, Clara. The smoke will kill us even if the fire doesn't.'

Clara nodded, and the pair crawled towards the door to the office.

Fleet scanned the walkway they had come from. The stair-case only led back down.

'Damn it.'

'Here,' said Clara, crawling back to the desk. She reached out and pulled away a crate, shrieking as a bullet struck it before she had it fully out of sight of the window.

She wrenched apart the old panels and handed one to Fleet.

'What's this?' he asked.

'A shield!'

'A *shield*?'

'You said we have to leave!'

Fleet nodded. 'I did. I did say that.'

They each held their bit of crate to cover as much as they could of their body and head, and stood to one side of the doorway.

'Ready?' asked Fleet.

'Yes.'

They bolted across the walkway, their footsteps ringing noisily out across the space. They reached the top of the staircase, dashed down the first flight, spun round, dashed down the second flight, spun round again, made a final dash down to the ground, sprinted away from a patch of fire near one of the furnaces and dived behind a stack of scrap metal.

'He didn't shoot,' said Clara. 'Maybe he's left?'

'We're not that lucky. He's probably just making his way down here too.'

Fleet peeked around the pile of scrap. The fire was spreading quickly across the foundry floor, and was beginning to climb the walls. He looked back towards the door they had entered through, and saw it was already engulfed.

'The other end,' he said. 'There must be a door at the other end.'

They gripped their shields again, and began sprinting through the space, darting between the machines and the patches of flame. They made it about halfway before Fleet heard a loud splintering behind him, and turned to see Clara stumble, shards of wood flying away from her. He dropped down and they clambered behind a monitoring panel.

'Are you all right?' he asked, scanning her body under the patterns of orange light dancing across it.

'Yes. I think so. I think it was just the crate.'

Fleet found no injuries, and sat back. They paused to catch their breath.

'Dash for it?' asked Clara.

Fleet peered along the room. The end wall was well over a hundred yards away, they were down to one bit of crate, and they still didn't know where Crowe was. Their chances at making it to the exit were, in his estimation, terrible.

The flames were spreading into every part of the space, and Fleet felt as though he might soon collapse under the heat. He looked at Clara. She was clearly struggling just the same, but somehow was fixing a slight grin at him.

Fleet coughed. 'What are you smiling at?'

'I was just thinking . . .'

'Thinking what?'

'I was thinking . . . you said, "Let's start a detective agency." And I agreed.'

She laughed weakly.

'What's funny about that?' he asked.

Clara waved an arm at the inferno around them.

'This was all your idea,' she said.

'That is outrageous.'

Clara laughed again.

'I hardly think I can be blamed for our current predicament,' said Fleet.

'A little bit,' Clara whispered. 'Just a little bit.'

Fleet knew she was teasing, but she wasn't wrong. She wouldn't have been here if not for him.

'I have an idea,' he said.

'What?'

'If it works, I'll tell you what it was.'

She smiled again. 'Okay.'

Fleet turned towards wherever their attacker might be hiding, and cried out as loudly as he could to be heard above the flames.

'Crowe! Come and talk.'

He waited.

'Crowe! If you leave here without us, you won't ever know if we survived. You'll be looking over your shoulder for the rest of your life!'

He waited again, and again there was no response.

The flames had covered the walls and were spreading onto the ceiling. The air was burning. It hurt to breathe.

'*Crowe!*'

Finally, Fleet heard a metal panel being pushed out of the way and the sound of footsteps a little way off.

'What do you want to talk about, Fleet?' shouted Crowe. 'I have to say, I'm running out of patience.'

'I have a question.'

Crowe sighed. 'And what is that question, Inspector?'

Fleet moved to stand up. Clara grabbed him by the arm with a panicked look, but he pulled away and walked out from behind the monitoring station. He found he was standing just twenty feet from Crowe, who had him at the end of his rifle.

'No,' said Crowe. 'Let me guess. You want to know *why*, don't you? That's always what little minds want to know. Not where can we go, not what do we need to get there. Just *why* things that have already happened did happen. Auditors, lawyers, investigators. Small minds, obsessed with slowing us all down.'

He mopped some sweat from his forehead before continuing.

'When I joined the Corps, I was awestruck. The things we could do . . . Take a patch of bare land and turn it into city. In a week! Always racing ahead, building ahead, to ensure London didn't choke under its own growth. It was thrilling. It was noble. It was essential.

'But over time, I encountered certain people. People I could not understand. Pencil-pushers. Pettifoggers. People more interested in caution than urgency. People who think in terms of what we *cannot*, rather than *how we will*. Shirkers! I had to surpass them for all our sakes. And so I did.

369

'But then one day I reached the top of the mountain, and for the first time I saw clearly. I had been a fool. All the work, all the construction, all the greatness of the city is *for naught* if it falls. Because we are not alone in this world. We are not without rivals. We are not without enemies. They are only waiting, and preparing. And in the face of this truth the Corps builds yet more bridges? More rail? More *parks*? We have been playing with toys in a sandbox in a garden, as war machines trundle towards our home. *Why?*'

He shook his head in disgust, and Fleet could see the rage overtaking him.

'We are supposed to trust the fools in the military,' Crowe spat, 'who cannot even repel the enemy's ships from our seas! Those who say "trust us" and do *nothing*! Shirkers! Shirkers, cowards, and apostles of the church of timidity. They have failed to live the one truth of life, that there is nothing we cannot do, if only we have the *will*!'

Fleet remained silent and waited. The fire was everywhere, the noise like a hurtling train. Somewhere, a gantry collapsed.

'But we in the Corps,' continued Crowe, 'we can do something about it. We create the greatest bridges; we create the greatest buildings. Why should we not also create the greatest defences? You think we do not need them? You think we *must not* build them? We can make this land a fortress. We can make ourselves a thistle the enemy will never dare grasp! Why is everyone in this world obsessed with what they cannot do? Am I *the only sane man alive*?'

Crowe's eyes were wide and wild, and he screamed above the roaring fire:

'The cannons will come to our walls, Inspector! One day! Giant bombards beyond our imagining! We must be ready. We *will* be ready. Even if it takes a hundred years before they come for us, I will have made us ready!'

He steadied himself.

'Now, at last, you stupid detective, does that satisfy your pointless curiosity?'

Fleet saw the crazed glint in Crowe's eyes, and answered.

'That's not actually what I wanted to know.'

Crowe growled in frustration.

'Then *what*, man? *What* could you possibly want to know?'

'I was really just wondering how long you would be able to hold on to that rifle in here.'

Fleet watched as Crowe looked down at his weapon and saw his hands searing on its metal casing. He screamed in agony, and moved to throw it aside, before gritting his teeth, pulling it back towards Fleet and firing.

Nothing.

He must have missed, thought Fleet. He must have missed and the bullet must have somehow stopped all the noise.

Fleet thought he heard Clara scream his name, but he couldn't be sure. Suddenly she was next to him, checking his shoulder. Which didn't feel right at all, now he thought about it.

He looked at Crowe, who had finally dropped his rifle and was now holding out his hands and screaming again.

The noise of the inferno returned. Fleet saw Crowe lift up his right arm and quickly swing it downwards, forcing a hunting knife to dart out in front of his fingers. He gripped it, clenched his jaw against the pain, and began walking slowly towards them.

'*Gnats!*' he cried. 'You understand your place in this world? *Nothing* of significance. *Nothing* of consequence. Just a constant, irksome, endless, pointless irritation.'

Clara turned to Fleet. 'Now I have an idea.'

'What kind of idea?'

'A terrible idea. Just the worst idea I've ever had.'

371

Fleet looked towards the distant exit, which could barely be seen beyond the fire, and then back to Clara. 'I like it.'

She nodded, leaned over the monitoring panel and pressed a large red button with text on it that Fleet could not see.

For a moment, nothing happened. Then, something. Crowe seemed to hear it first. He was closer. An immense groaning, like a whale, from the far end of the ironworks where they had entered.

Crowe turned to look, and Fleet tried to peer past him. Out of the corner of his eye he could see Clara shrinking her head down, as if she might pop entirely inside her dress like a turtle.

The groaning was getting louder. Fleet was concerned, and strove to see across the flames to identify whatever was making the sound.

A few seconds later, he spied movement. High up, a platform was tilting.

No, not a platform. The top of something. Its angle continued to steepen and suddenly Fleet could see it all: a cauldron the size of a yacht was slowly tipping forward.

He stared in horror as the immense metal disc covering the cauldron slid off the top, tumbling through the air and smashing into the ground like a tombstone into grass.

The cauldron was tipping ever faster as its contents pooled up more and more on one side. Fleet could see into it now, where a lake of lava was nearing the lip. Barely a second after its contents began to drizzle over the edge, the cauldron had rotated through ninety degrees. It bashed into the floor with an almighty crash, and a river of molten metal surged into the ironworks. It spread out across the full width of the building, and flattened into a wave three times the height of a person.

Fleet watched as the river of iron and fire washed unstoppably towards them. He thought about running, but knew they could not. He thought about finding cover, but knew they could not.

There was no escape for any of them.

Crowe seemed equally unable to turn away. In fact, he appeared to be advancing slowly towards the wave.

Fleet felt a sensation he did not recognise. Something like calm. Then Clara took his hand and turned him towards her. For some insufferable reason she was smiling again. He couldn't help but return it.

In the corner of his eye he saw Crowe charge at the metal, screaming against the world and holding his knife out ahead of him as if he refused to go down, even against Nature itself, without inflicting at least a scratch on it. The corps-marshal reached the face of the wave and gave it his best, vanishing in a flash of white and yellow like ash floating from a fireplace.

Fleet realised Clara still had his hand firmly in hers, and she seemed to be saying something at him that he couldn't hear. He tried to listen, but she stopped speaking, shook her head, threw her arms around him and hauled him down onto the ground.

Fleet could hear nothing but the wave of death approaching, so he closed his eyes and waited for there to be nothing left to wait for.

He waited some more.

And a little more.

And then a bit more.

Then he grew confused, and, to be honest, a little annoyed.

He opened his eyes. He was looking across a flood of burning metal. He was looking *down* on it.

He scrambled to his knees. Clara was grinning from ear to ear, and stamped her foot on the ground, making a hollow metal sound. On one side the floor came to an abrupt end in a drop to the fire below, and on the other a wall rose curling

373

over them. Looking up and out, he saw a long metal arm stretching up to a cabin attached to the foundry wall on an upper floor. Inside the cabin, operating the controls with great concentration, was Helena Evans.

Fleet collapsed back into the crane bucket.

Helena lifted them to a walkway, exited the cabin, and hurried them up a staircase towards the burning ceiling, where a hatch lay open.

The three climbed the ladder onto the roof, and ran to the far end of the building.

Fleet looked down to the ground and saw roughly a hundred Brunelians, dressed in brown fireproof overalls, frantically running between what he assumed must be Corps fire engines. A group near the building were operating a machine that was extending a ladder towards the roof. Someone he guessed to be some sort of specialist fire colonel was issuing commands to anyone who came within ten feet of him.

Off to one side, and for some reason on a horse, Sir Grover Merridew was cheerfully waving at the three on the roof.

'Hold tight!' he cried, through a megaphone. 'We'll have you down in no time! Anything else you need, other than to be down here and not up there?'

Fleet was about to shout back something about the possibility of a medic if it wasn't too much trouble, when he was distracted by something sitting on the ground in the centre of all the hurrying Brunelians. Something small and furry, staring at him with a lolling tongue and a vacant grin.

'Yes!' he shouted. 'Would somebody please, for the love of god, catch that bloody beagle!'

Half a dozen officers heard the cry and dashed towards the dog, which immediately darted away, delighted by this new game.

Fleet shook his head, and turned back to Helena and Clara.

'Thank you, Miss Evans.'

374

'You're welcome, Inspector.'

'Why did you come?' asked Clara.

'I'm an engineer, Miss Entwhistle. We're always thinking about how things might go wrong. So I thought I'd best come along—and send for the nearest Corps division I could get hold of—just in case you needed a bit of a fail-safe.'

'We did,' said Fleet, listening to the crashing of bits of building collapsing beneath them. 'A bit.'

'A lot,' said Clara.

Helena smiled. 'Thank you both. I officially forgive you for ruining my life.'

'Happy to help,' said Fleet.

Helena walked to the edge of the roof and began shouting at the ladder team to hurry, as the inferno continued to rage beneath them.

'Tell me you knew she was there,' said Fleet.

Clara laughed. 'I'm not saying!'

'You're not saying whether you doomed us to certain death or knew help was at hand?'

'I politely refuse.'

'I insist you tell me,' said Fleet.

'And *I* insist you withdraw your insistence.'

'And you don't think this might affect how likely I am to trust your plans in the future?'

'Does it?' asked Clara.

Fleet looked down to the tumult on the ground, where the beagle had been entranced by the turning on of a firehose, jumping and snapping and generally trying to stick its face into a pressurised water stream that would instantly decapitate it, at which point Sir Grover had snuck up on it, scooped it into his arms, and was now waving back towards the roof and manipulating one of the dog's front paws into waving as well.

'No,' said Fleet. 'It doesn't.'

375

Chapter 21

Several days later – the investigators having agreed to give themselves a little time off to recover, and to see if any launderette was able to get out all the incineration from their clothes – Clara headed to their office refreshed and revitalised.

She had used her downtime for her favourite relaxation activity work.

After all, she thought, a change is as good as a rest. In fact, it was better than a rest, because it had meant she was able to write up the case, head over to the *Morning Chronicler*, hand it to Augusta Bell and sit in excruciating silence in the editor's office while she read it front to back. At the end of which Augusta had, without a word to her, picked up the telephone, informed the presses that tomorrow's print run would need to be quintupled, and hung up, before nodding at Clara with a barely perceptible smile and saying, 'Welcome back.'

This, on top of actually foiling Crowe, put such a spring in Clara's step that she had barely touched the ground since. And now, she had arrived at her place of business to see that no time whatsoever had been lost in capitalising on London's most recent sensational crime, as the sign above the door now read: *Mrs Pomligan's Coffee House, Beginners Pottery Studio and Appalling Brunelian Conspiracy Gift Shop*. People were already queueing out of the door, and Clara whistled in admiration at the proprietor's business savvy.

Apologising her way through, she stepped inside and saw new stands of merchandise that had been whipped together in record time: bits of metal purporting to be genuine bank vault shavings; hastily dyed yellow flatcaps labelled 'Official' with no promise made of what, officially, they were supposed to be; and confusing, but nevertheless cuddly, toy birds named 'Everett Crow', which a sign suggested were the ideal gift for any child to remind them never to grow up and engage in any immense public-works conspiracies, serial murders or the like.

Clara rolled her eyes. They were clearly jackdaws.

What surprised her even more, however, was that the queue of people who'd made it inside wasn't paying a bit of attention to these objects, and in fact the line carried on through the shop and up the staircase towards the office of Fleet-Entwhistle Private Investigations.

She thought about asking what on earth they were all doing there, but decided the fair thing would be to speak to whoever was at the front. That was, after all, how queues worked.

She waved at the beagle under the counter – which was stretched out on a folded rug and nosing suspiciously at a piece of pie he was not convinced was food – and headed up the stairs.

She tried to ignore the grumbling of everyone she passed, and found Fleet attempting to reason with the person at the head of the queue. He seemed very relieved to see her.

'Good,' he said. 'You're here. Come inside.'

'*Excuse me*,' said the man at the front. 'I've been waiting for twenty minutes.'

'And whose fault is that?' asked Fleet. 'You see what time it is?'

'Five to,' replied the man.

'Well, there you go. When it's no longer anything to, that's when I'll start paying attention to the knocking. Clara, come inside.'

She followed Fleet into their office and he shut the door, setting off a noisy protest from the queue.

'What's all this, Fleet?'

'In a minute,' he replied, holding out a piece of paper from his desk. 'Read this first.'

Clara grabbed the paper and saw it was a telegram.

SENDER: KHAN, TRIUM.CORPS.BRU.

'It's from Corps-Marshal Khan!' said Clara.

'Yes, I've read it. That's why I told you to read it just now.'

'Hush,' she replied, returning to the telegram.

TO: FLEET-ENTWHISTLE PRIVATE INVESTIGATIONS

MESSAGE:

MY FRIENDS, I EXTEND THANKS ON BEHALF OF GRATEFUL CORPS. MERRIDEW AND I OFFER WHAT WE HOPE IS APPROPRIATE. COSGROVE AT CHALON HAS INSTRUCTIONS.

'They've paid us, Fleet!'

'Apparently so.'

HOUSEKEEPING MATTERS PERHAPS OF INTEREST TO YOU:

(1) EVERETT CROWE IS SUCCEEDED IN TRIUMVIRATE BY MAJOR-GENERAL ALISON SLATE, WHO HAS DEMONSTRATED INSPIRING LEADERSHIP DELIVERING LANTERNS SEA DEFENCE PROJECT.

'Oh dear,' said Clara.

'Yes, I never met her, but seeing how you were after you did, I'm happy to leave it that way. Sounds like she's good at getting things done, though.'

'But *what* things, Fleet?'
'Read the next bit.'

(2) AFTER DISCUSSION WITH HER MAJESTY'S PRIV.SEC. JULIUS BELL, THE
TRIUMVIRATE AGREES DEFENCE PROJECTS ARE NOT THE BEST AREA OF CORPS
ATTENTION. LANTERN SITE WILL BE DEMOLISHED AND THE CORPS AGREES TO
ENSHRINE IN CHARTER A REMIT WHOLLY FOCUSED WITHIN THE CITY. THERE IS
MUCH STILL FOR US TO DO.

'Phew!' said Clara.
'Yes,' agreed Fleet. 'Just back to their day job of rebuilding
entire streets in a day without anyone knowing beforehand.'

(3) ALEXANDRA WOOD, AFFIANCED TO LIEUTENANT-SUPPLY-CAPTAIN OLIVER
MELLANBY, DECEASED, IS GRANTED WIDOW'S PENSION. ALL OTHER FAMILIES
OF CROWE AND BRAILSFORD VICTIMS SIMILARLY COMPENSATED. KATHLEEN
PRICE, WITNESS, ALSO REWARDED APPROPRIATELY FOR HER HELP.

Clara was pleased to read this. Nothing would bring the
victims back, but at least these leaders wanted to make right
what they could. She carried on:

(4) FULL EXTENT OF CROWE MACHINATIONS STILL UNKNOWN. TRIUMVIRATE INSISTS
CORPS IS THOROUGH WITH ITSELF TO ENSURE ANY REMAINING CONSPIRATORS
FOUND AND REMOVED, AND TO PREVENT ANY FUTURE SUCH MALICE. THEREFORE:

(5) INTERNAL SPECIAL INVESTIGATIONS DIVISION CREATED. GIVEN SUBJECT
MATTER AND IN RECOGNITION OF HER VALOUR, STRUCTURAL-ENGINEERING-
MAJOR HELENA EVANS GIVEN COMMAND. EVANS TAKES RANK OF COLONEL,
REPORTS TO ME, AND WILL HAVE WHATEVER RESOURCES SHE DEEMS FIT.

'They've given Helena a new job!' cried Clara.
Fleet nodded. 'Clearly we should be meddling in people's
lives more often.'

The telegram wound to its conclusion:

AIDE-DE-CAMP INFORMS ME I MUST TURN TO OTHER MATTERS.

GOOD FORTUNE TO YOU BOTH.

THE FUTURE IS THE PROJECT THAT IS NEVER FINISHED.

JAHANGIR KHAN

'Well, that's nice,' said Clara.

There was an impatient banging at the door.

'In a minute!' cried Fleet. 'No patience, these people . . .'

'Yes, what is all that about?'

'Oh, them?'

'Yes! Why are there fifty people outside our door?'

'Well,' said Fleet. 'I suppose they're here for the free consultations.'

Clara was confused. 'But our consultations are always free.'

'Spoken like someone without even the barest grasp of marketing.'

'What have you done?'

Fleet grabbed a book from his desk and waved it.

'I decided you were right, and it wouldn't hurt to learn a few tips on building a business, so I got this out of the library.'

'You read Posner!' Clara exclaimed, punching him in the shoulder in excitement.

Fleet winced and dropped the book. He seemed on the verge of screaming, but managed to control himself. Clara realised she'd forgotten about his being shot.

'Sorry. Shoulder still a little tender?'

'Well, it had a bullet in it just days ago, so yes. The doctor said you shouldn't punch me there for at least two weeks. Anyway . . .'

He picked up the book and handed it to Clara, and she read the cover.

'*Edgar Nicholson's Ungentlemanly Guide to Business.*'

'I had a flick through this,' said Fleet, 'had some flyers made up, added the word "free" in enormous red letters, and here we are. I can't believe it worked this well. This "marketing" business might destroy us all.'

'What about Posner? I'm assured he's the gold standard in all matters commercial.'

'Fresh out. Plus, you should see the things Nicholson says about him. They do not get on.'

'Well, Entrepreneur Fleet, we shall see whether your "Ungentlemanly Guide" gets us as far as the gentleman Posner.'

'I've brought fifty people to our office today, so I'm feeling quite confident.'

'And yet none of them is our customer yet.' Clara stiffened her posture, as though she might salute. 'Archibald Fleet, I challenge you to a battle of business.'

'We're partners, Clara. We're on the same side.'

'A point for whoever solves a case first! More for trickier ones!'

'But we work together . . .'

'Let battle commence!' she cried, leaping to the door, opening it, and ushering in the man from the front of the queue. 'Good morning, I'm Clara Entwhistle and this is Inspector Fleet. How can we help?'

The man shuffled nervously. 'I'm Jack. Jack Relin.'

'What brings you here today, Mr Relin?' asked Clara.

'You'll probably think it's silly.'

'Probably not,' said Fleet, 'but we can *guarantee* we won't for a fee of five shillings.'

Clara looked at Fleet, aghast.

'What has that book done to you?'

The man waved a page of newspaper. Clara could see the date — it was today's.

'What is it?' she asked.

'Well,' he replied, 'this is all about me. My name, my date of birth, my background and where I live.'

'You've been libelled?' asked Fleet. 'We might need to refer you to a lawyer.'

'No, no, it's not that. It's . . . According to this, I've been murdered. Yesterday. In Parliament. They found me under those green benches they do all the yelling from.'

'Newspaper identified the victim incorrectly?' asked Clara.

The man shook his head.

'He had all my papers on him. And a photograph of my mother! And he was wearing my clothes! That man . . . *is me.*'

Clara paused to consider this shocking information, then looked to Fleet.

'Okay, this one's worth five points.'

Fleet studied the man silently for a few moments, before finally turning back to Clara.

'Ten.'

Archibald Fleet and Clara Entwhistle will return . . .

Until then, you can listen to more of their adventures for free at Victoriocity.com

ACKNOWLEDGEMENTS

This novel exists, in large part, due to our shared hatred of flyering. During one Edinburgh Fringe run with our comedy group, we began talking about how we could reach an audience with our writing without quite as much accosting people on the street. That discussion led to the creation of the audio drama *Victoriocity*, which has now become *High Vaultage's* prequel. Rachel Winterbottom, then a senior commissioning editor at Gollancz, found our show, saw its potential as prose fiction and encouraged us to turn to this project. For this, and for her invaluable help with the initial stages of drafting, we will be forever grateful.

We also have Rachel to thank for passing us on to our current editor, Claire Ormsby-Potter. In Claire we have found a true kindred spirit who jumped in with both feet and good humour. She has been the best of editors, nudging the story in the right direction and offering notes which have lifted *High Vaultage* to all it could be. She has also been incredibly supportive and understanding as we edited this novel in the aftermath of having a baby. Truly, Claire deserves a medal, and certainly Julius Bell will see to it that she is on Queen Victoria's New Year Honours list.

Huge thanks also to the team at Gollancz for all their efforts in turning this novel into a reality, and to our agent Harry Illingworth at DHH for guiding us through the process.

None of this would have happened were it not for all the incredible actors, crew and artists who gave so much of their time and talent to make *Victoriocity* in the first place. Our thanks to everyone, and, although there are too many to name here, we must say how especially grateful we are to our producer Dominic Hargreaves, our director Nathan Peter Grassi, and our production managers Fiona Sinclair and Elizabeth Campbell, as well as our lead cast Tom Crowley, Layla Katib and Peter Rae. We are so lucky to get to work with such extraordinary people. We are also incredibly grateful to those who provided us with their advice and encouragement when we were first starting out in audio drama, not least Felix Trench, whose knowledge and support early on helped us no end. And our thanks, of course, to our early reviewers, wonderful listeners, and co-creators in the audio drama space who have lifted us up and championed us along the way.

We also owe much to our friends and colleagues who have provided all manner of support, whether general feedback, specific expertise, childcare or, in some cases, all three. Our thanks to all, and in particular to Steve Baldwin, Ida Berglow Kenneway, Jamie Bernthal-Hooker, Octavia Bray, Elizabeth Campbell, Philip Cotterill, Tom Crowley, Siddo Deva, Laurence Goodwin, Nathan Peter Grassi, Vince Haig, Josie Jaffrey, Sam James, Layla Katib, Jon Lister Parsons, Angus McFadzean, Helen Marshall, Ross Meikle, Sanjiv Nandi, Paula Pena, Jamie Potton, Marie Richer, Rachel Smith, Paul Staveley, Stephanie Todd, Ella Watts, Brittany Wellner and Rachel Wilmshurst.

Of course, the book itself could never have been completed if it hadn't been for the unending love and support from our wonderful family: Rachel and Autumn Sugden; Karen Shimmon and Clive, Megan and Freddie Nicholson; Ralph and Lynda Nicholson; and Lorrie Sugden, who went above and beyond a Grandma's duties and has been like a third parent to our son Isaac. And, of course, David Sugden, who would have loved to have held this in his hands, and whose warmth and wit we hope have made their way onto its pages.

Finally, we must thank the members of our comedy group, who led us onto this path and with whom we honed what skill we have. They are some of the funniest people on the planet, and no small amount of their hilarious selves has been poured into this book. Ida Berglow Kenneway, Philip Cotterill, Nathan Peter Grassi, and Will Payne, you mean more to us than it is possible to say. Special thanks to Bill Moulford, who was also with us at the beginning, and to whom this book is dedicated. His energy and wit could have powered any city we might imagine.

CREDITS

Chris and Jen Sugden and Gollancz would like to thank everyone at Orion who worked on the publication of *High Vaultage*.

Agent
Harry Illingworth

Editorial
Claire Ormsby-Potter
Bethan Morgan

Copy-editor
Elizabeth Dobson

Proofreader
Abigail Nathan
Sanah Ahmed

Editorial Management
Jane Hughes
Charlie Panayiotou
Claire Boyle

Audio
Paul Stark
Jake Alderson
Georgina Cutler

Contracts
Dan Herron
Ellie Bowker

Design
Nick Shah
Tómas Almeida
Joanna Ridley
Helen Ewing
Rachael Lancaster

Finance
Nick Gibson
Jasdip Nandra
Elizabeth Beaumont
Ibukun Ademefun

Inventory
Jo Jacobs
Dan Stevens

Marketing
Hennah Sandhu

Production
Paul Hussey

Publicity
Frankie Banks

Sales
Jen Wilson
Victoria Laws
Esther Waters
Frances Doyle
Ben Goddard
Jack Hallam
Karin Burnik

Operations
Sharon Willis
Jo Jacobs

Rights
Flora McMichael
Ayesha Kinley
Tara Hiatt